Just Good Friends

**The *Escape to New Zealand* series
by Rosalind James**

Just This Once: Hannah and Drew's story

Just Good Friends: Kate and Koti's story

Just for Now: Jenna and Finn's story

Just for Fun: Emma and Nic's story

Escape to New Zealand: Book Two

Just Good Friends

Rosalind James

The Blues and the All Blacks are actual rugby teams. However, this is a work of fiction. Names, characters, places, and incidents are products of the author's imagination or are used fictitiously and are not to be construed as real. Any resemblance to actual events or persons, living or dead, is entirely coincidental.

Copyright © 2012 by Rosalind James

Prologue

Please, please, don't let him get in. Don't make me have to do this. Please, somebody help me.

Kate Lamonica crouched under her kitchen table, the worn yellow linoleum cold under her bare feet, and prayed. She shifted her weight, lurched a bit to one side as her knee caught in the fabric of her fleece robe. That wasn't going to work. She had to be able to move. Forcing herself to move deliberately, not to panic, she set the big knife down carefully on the seat of the chair beside her. Pulled her right arm out of the robe. Shifted her silent cell phone to her right hand with a quick movement, held it to her ear again before she shrugged her left arm out and shoved the bulky robe aside. The brightly printed red poppies on the fabric gleamed at the edge of her vision, incongruously cheerful in the dim light. She transferred the phone back to her left hand, picked up her knife again with the right, feeling better once it was back in her hand. Ready to use.

She was shivering a little now, her pajamas no match for the chill of the early February morning. Still no sound from outside, or from the phone in her hand. She lifted it from her ear to check the display. Her call was still connected. And she was still on hold. How could 911 put somebody on hold?

Pick up, she prayed. But the phone remained silent. No competent voice offering protection. No help at all. Instead, the sounds she'd been dreading. The rattle of the kitchen door handle, and Paul's voice calling to her.

"I know you're in there, Kate. Don't make me have to come get you. That's only going to make it worse for you."

She visualized again what she would do if he broke in. She'd wait until he was close. Then burst out from under the table in one movement, launch herself at him, and strike. Nothing tentative. No hesitation. Because if he made it in here, she was in real trouble. She had to take her chance. If the police didn't come, she was going to have to save herself.

"I never wanted to hurt you. You know that. I loved you. But you've let me down so many times. You haven't given me any choice."

She knew how he'd look to the arriving officers. If they ever came. His pressed slacks and button-down shirt, every blond hair in place. His easy smile, his plausible explanations. His insistence that she was the one with the problem, the vendetta against him.

Silence, then a *clunk* as something heavy dropped on the concrete slab. She could feel her heart knocking against her chest wall as she heard a scrape, then the sound of metal on metal against the door frame. She stared out from under the table as if she could see around the corner, through the door. Her hand tightened around the knife as her mind went over and over the scenario. Leap. Rush. Slash.

"911. What is your emergency?" The phone in her hand came to life at last. She started at the sudden noise in her ear, banging her head painfully against the bottom of the table. Juggled the phone for desperate moments. Forced herself to answer calmly as her eyes remained trained on a kitchen door she couldn't see.

"I need the police. 2111 Fifth Street. Apartment B. I have an intruder. He's threatened me, and he's trying to break in now."

"Is he on the property now?" the dispatcher asked, maddeningly calm.

"*Yes*. I just told you. Her voice sounded unnaturally high in her ears. "He's trying to break in, through my kitchen door. It's the ground floor. Around the side."

Her breath was coming in gasps now. She fought to control it, but the fear was rising into panic now. "Are you sending them? Are they coming?"

"Don't worry, ma'am," the calm voice reassured. "I've dispatched a unit. Stay on the line with me. Don't hang up."

Finally, the blessed sound of a siren in the distance. And Paul's voice through the door again.

"You shouldn't have called them. You've only made it harder for yourself. Because I'll be coming back for you. You can try to run, but you know that I'll find you in the end. There's nowhere you can hide that I won't find you."

She remained in her painful crouch, kept her grip on her knife and her phone, unable to trust that he'd really left. She had to be ready. Just in case. When she finally heard the knock, a deep voice reassuringly unlike Paul's identifying himself, it was a struggle to pull herself out from under the table. Her limbs were so stiff with tension and fright that she could barely uncoil them, and she was shaking with the aftereffects of adrenaline.

By the time the sympathetic officers had walked her to her car, checked the back seat, and watched her lock her doors, she was shaking again, but with fury as well as fear now. She followed their car to the station, then parked in front of the building and tried to decide what to do. She couldn't afford the luxury of denial anymore. Paul would be back. He might even be at her apartment again by now, waiting for her. She'd been lucky this time. But he only had to get lucky once. And meanwhile, she'd be living every day in fear. Moving from friend to friend, sleeping on couches, looking over her shoulder.

Screw this, she thought fiercely. She was done. Whatever it took, however much it cost her, she was getting out of this. Running somewhere he couldn't find her. To some distant place where she could live her life normally again. In peace.

Chapter 1

The line for Passport Control snaked and twisted, tired passengers waiting obediently, shuffling forward one slow foot at a time. Kate felt disoriented and dizzy with fatigue. Maybe it was the overnight flight, or the speed of the decisions she'd made over the past week, but her mind seemed to be lagging several steps behind reality right now. It kept drifting off, forcing her to bring it back again. To remind herself where she was, what she was doing.

"You're going *where?*" her father had demanded a few days earlier, arriving home to find her packing.

"New Zealand," she repeated patiently. "I've bought my ticket, and I leave the day after tomorrow."

"Surely this can't be necessary," her mother objected. "Couldn't you find a new job and a new place to live, maybe in a different city? Or even stay here with us for a while. You know how happy we'd be to have you, to know you were safe."

"That's just it, though," Kate tried to explain. "I don't think I would be safe, or that you would be either. It's only a matter of time before Paul turns up here looking for me. I hate knowing I'm putting you at risk, even being here a few days. I wouldn't have come at all if I'd known where else to go."

"I hope he does turn up," her father said grimly. "I'd know how to deal with him."

"You can't sit on the porch with a shotgun on your lap twenty-four hours a day, Dad," Kate sighed. "I know you want to protect me, but it isn't possible. Not for more than a couple days. Which is all that I'm staying."

"Besides," she said, sitting down wearily on the familiar, narrow bed of her childhood and hugging an embroidered cushion to her for comfort, "I can't live like this anymore. Maybe you're right. Maybe I could move to a new state, or even someplace else in California, and this would be over. Maybe he wouldn't find me. Who knows, maybe he'd even give up. But I don't think so. Stalkers are obsessive. It's what they do. Everything he's said, everything I've learned tells me I'm in danger. And I can't live like this anymore," she said again, tears filling her eyes. "I just can't. It's too much."

Her mother sat down next to her and put an arm around her shoulders. "You need to do whatever it is that's going to keep you safe. And make you feel safe, too. You know we want what's best for you. And if that means moving to New Zealand, well, that's the way it is. We'll help any way we can."

"Thanks, Mom." Kate blinked the tears away and gave her mother a fierce hug. "You guys are the best. Love you so much."

"Who is this Hannah, though, in New Zealand?" her father persisted. "Is she somebody who can help you once you're there? She doesn't sound like she's been in the country all that long herself."

"Only a couple years," Kate agreed. "She was a work friend. Before she moved to New Zealand, of course. Even though it's been a while, she offered to help right away when I called. She seems pretty confident that she and her husband can help me find a job. He's a big deal over there, apparently. A rugby player."

"How's a rugby player going to help you find a job as an accountant?" her father objected.

"I'm not quite sure myself, to tell you the truth," Kate admitted. "But Hannah was positive. It seemed like my best bet, and I'm going to take it."

"And they'll put you up for a few days when you arrive?" her mother asked. "I don't like to think of you getting to a strange country and being on your own."

"They do speak English, you know, Mom. I'll be fine. Better off than I am here, that's for sure. Who knows, it might even be fun."

The brave words seemed foolish now, in the echoing, alien territory of the arrivals hall. Her international travel experience was limited to a single trip to Canada. What was she doing here? Reaching the front of the line at last, she handed her passport with its two lonely stamps to an immigration officer.

"Working holiday visa," he commented. "What are you planning to do while you're here?"

"Accounting, I hope," she told him.

He raised his eyebrows. "That's one I don't hear every day, have to say. Beats kiwifruit picking, I'm sure." He stamped her passport firmly and handed it back to her. "Best of luck to you. And welcome to New Zealand."

By the time she had collected the two suitcases that contained all she had brought with her from her old life and made her way through various stops to the arrivals area, Kate was overwhelmed. The huge space, the crowds, the instructions given in a clipped accent barely intelligible in her exhausted state had all taken their toll. When she pushed her luggage cart through the automatic doors and saw Hannah waiting, she couldn't help the tears that spilled over as her friend folded her into welcoming arms.

"Oh, sweetie. What a tough time you've had. I'm so glad you're here." Hannah pulled a Kleenex out of her purse and handed it to Kate as she continued to cry. "Come on," she urged. "We'll get you a coffee, and then we'll take you home. You're going to feel so much better after a shower, I promise."

Kate wiped her eyes. "Sorry. I'm better now. What a first impression." She reached out to shake hands with the big man standing beside her friend. "Hi. You must be Drew. It's so good of you to agree to help me like this. You don't even know me, and here I am intruding on your life. I can't tell you how much I appreciate it."

"No worries." He smiled down at her easily. "We invited you, didn't we. Tell you the truth, you're doing me a favor as well. I'm off to Safa tomorrow for a couple weeks. I'm glad you'll be here with Hannah. I wasn't happy about leaving her alone that long."

"South Africa," Hannah translated. "Road trip. Two games in a row. And don't worry, you'll figure out what they're saying eventually."

"I hope it won't be too much for you, having me," Kate said, eyeing Hannah with concern.

"I'm pregnant, not sick," Hannah countered. "And perfectly healthy, despite how fragile Drew appears to think I am." She looked at her husband with affection as he took Kate's trolley over her objections.

"Let him push it," she counseled Kate. "We both know you could do it. But it'll make him much happier."

Once they were on their way into the city, Hannah turned in her seat to smile at Kate again. "I can't wait to go look at flats with you. I've already started setting up visits for Saturday. There are so many great neighborhoods here. I'm sure we'll be able to find you something that suits you. You're going to love it."

"They say converts make the best missionaries," Drew put in. "Reckon Hannah's proof of that. Best cheerleader En Zed could have."

"I'm glad to hear it's a good place to live, though," Kate said. "Because I'm not sure how long I'll be here. I just hope I can get a job fairly quickly."

"I've already got the word out," Drew assured her. "She'll be right."

"And believe me, he's connected," Hannah said. "Between the two of us, we'll have you employed before you know it. You'll probably wish you had a longer break."

"I guess this would be all right." Kate eyed the dark little flat dubiously, the following Saturday.

"No way," Hannah told her firmly. "Too gloomy. We can do better than this."

"This is a good neighborhood, Mt. Eden," she told Kate as they settled back into the car. "But that was the wrong flat. And you'd have quite a bus ride—or drive, of course—to the beach. Which isn't ideal."

"I've always just hoped to live someplace that didn't actually have drive-bys," Kate said. "I don't think I'm in any position to turn something down because it isn't on the beach."

"Sure you are," Hannah countered. "Maybe you won't be able to walk there. But we can get you closer than this."

"That would be a big plus. Are all the beaches as nice as where we swam this morning?"

"Oh yeah. They each have their own character. Just wait. Soon you'll think your own beach is the best, and you won't want to come swim at mine."

By the end of the day, though, Kate was discouraged. "Maybe I should take that first place after all," she told Hannah over dinner. "It was the cheapest one we saw. I didn't realize a decent furnished apartment, even a small one, would cost so much. And I still need to buy a car."

"No, you don't," Hannah said. "Because I'm going to loan you the Yaris while you're here. I have a new car, and I don't need it. I've meant to sell it, just haven't got around to it yet. You'll be doing me a favor, getting it out of the way."

"Won't Drew mind, though?"

"Not at all. It's mine, anyway. You'll have to pay for the Warrant of Fitness and get insurance, so it won't be entirely free. But that should help a lot. I did this myself, remember. I know how expensive moving here can be."

"I'd really appreciate that. Driving on the wrong side, though," Kate said worriedly.

"We'll go out early tomorrow and practice," Hannah promised. "Then you'll be able to check out other places on your own during the week. And you're supposed to say "left" side, you know. Right and left. Not right and wrong."

"Still going to feel wrong to me," Kate told her. "But I'll try."

"This is it, don't you think?" Kate asked Hannah on Friday evening.

"I think so," Hannah said, looking out a window at the treetop view. "Even though it's tiny."

"Just a granny flat," the realtor escorting them agreed. "Well done up, though, not like some of these dodgy places you see."

"Plus it's not on the ground floor, which makes me feel more secure," Kate said.

"Takapuna's quite safe," the realtor told her. "You won't need to worry much about that."

"That's good to know. I'm extra cautious, that's all." Kate's mind went back to the night she had sat at her kitchen table and, feeling the hair rise at the back of her neck, turned slowly around. The galvanizing shock of seeing Paul's face, pale against the window. Smiling at her through the glass. She shivered now, remembering. No ground-floor apartments. This one seemed secure enough, though. The single door opened onto a tiny landing, and all the windows locked. She had checked.

"One down. Now all I need is a job," she told Hannah resolutely once they were in the car on the way back to St. Heliers. "But I'm afraid that's going to be tougher."

"That reminds me. I have some news about that too. I completely forgot. Drew called me today and told me the Blues office has an opening for an accountant, can you believe it? And he's already talked to them about you. Email your CV—your resume—to them tomorrow and you should get an interview, at least."

"The Blues? You mean the team?" Kate asked in surprise.

"Sure. It's a business, you know. A little different from apparel, but money's money, right? I figured it wouldn't matter for an accountant."

"I'm not sure I want to work around a bunch of rugby players, though," Kate said dubiously.

"They're pretty nice," Hannah argued. "You've met one of them already, after all. Drew didn't seem scary, did he?"

"Well, a bit. Sorry. I know he's a good guy. But big guys make me nervous. And he's so . . . I don't know. Commanding."

Hannah laughed. "Granted. On to my second point, then. You'd be working in the back office. The boys might come in from time to time, but you wouldn't be dealing with them much, I wouldn't think. Most of the people working there are women."

"I'll check it out," Kate said. "I can talk to them, anyway. If they do offer me the job, I'll decide then. I can't afford to turn anything down without looking into it."

Stocking her new kitchen cupboards the next week after a ruinous first trip to the grocery store for supplies, Kate was revising her grocery budget in her head and worrying about her rapidly shrinking savings when her phone rang.

"It's Bethany Edmonds, here at the Blues," she heard. "I'd like to offer you the position, if you're interested." She named a salary that had Kate doing some more rapid calculations. She wouldn't have much left over at the end of each month, but she'd be able to live. She'd liked Bethany, as well as the cheerful, professional atmosphere she'd sensed in the Blues office. Hannah had been right that most of the employees were women. And Bethany had told her that she'd have limited contact with the players. As if she'd be disappointed by that. Little did she know.

It might be interesting to work for a sports team. Something different, anyway, she told herself bracingly. And she needed a job. If it didn't work out, she'd look for something else.

"I'm happy to accept," she told the other woman. "I do want to say one thing, though. I know that Drew had a lot to do with my getting this job. But I'll do my very best to make sure you don't regret offering it to me."

"He had a fair bit to do with my looking at your CV," Bethany corrected her. "But after that, it was down to you. As highly as we think of our captain around here, I wouldn't have offered you the post if I didn't believe you were the best candidate. Start on Monday, and we'll see how we go."

Chapter 2

"I was meeting Drew for dinner anyway, so I decided to come over and check on you," Hannah said. "The first week is always tough, I know. How're you settling in?"

"Good, so far." Kate got up from her brand-new desk to give Hannah a hug. "Getting to know what's what. Everyone's pretty easygoing, which helps."

"Always," Hannah agreed. "But you're a hard worker, and you pick things up fast. I know you'll be up to speed soon."

A sudden hush in the big room, followed by a buzz of conversation, had both of them turning to see what the fuss was about. A tall, absurdly handsome young man in track pants and gray hoodie was sauntering across the open office with a loping grace, casting out a grin and a word to the clearly enthusiastic staff members he passed.

He brought the dazzle to a stop in front of Hannah. "I heard you were in, thought I'd pop by and say hello." He smiled, white teeth flashing and dimples creasing in his bronzed face, and gave her a quick kiss on the cheek. "You're looking as gorgeous as ever. Want to run away with me?"

Hannah laughed. "Flatterer." She turned to Kate. "I'd better introduce you. This is Koti James, centre and first-class flirt. So watch yourself. And Koti, this is my friend Kate Lamonica. She's just joined the staff here as an accountant, but we used to work together, back in California."

"What an intro," Koti complained. "Good thing you aren't in the matchmaking business, Hannah. You'd be sacked straight away."

"How ya goin', Kate." He turned his brilliant smile on her. Pretty, he thought, even though she looked a bit small. Nice

12

hair, beautiful skin. She had a good figure, too, what he could see of it. He reached across the desk to shake hands—and get a closer look—as Kate murmured a response.

"Welcome to the Blues. What brought you all the way down here, besides Hannah?" He might as well take the opportunity to chat her up before she met the rest of the boys. "Had you been before, on holiday? Or did you just hear that the scenery was beautiful and the men were good-looking?"

"No, I'd never visited, but I needed a change," Kate answered, dropping his hand quickly. "And Hannah and Drew were good enough to help me find a spot here."

"Because Kate's the best," Hannah assured Koti. "The team's lucky to have her."

"And we're always happy to have another pretty girl around the place, eh," Koti confirmed with another dazzling smile. He was surprised to see Kate draw herself up stiffly and take a step back.

"I think—" Hannah started to say.

"Sorry I'm late." Drew came up from behind them, slid an arm around Hannah, and bent down to kiss her cheek. "Been in a meeting that's dragging on a bit. I need to get back to it for a few minutes more, I'm afraid. But I wanted to come out to let you know."

"Good to see you, Kate," he told her. "Settling in all right?"

"Yes, fine. Thanks for all your help."

"No worries. That was mostly Hannah."

"And why are you here?" the captain asked Koti with a frown. "Need something?"

Koti put up a protesting hand. "Just saying hello. Can I help it if you married my dream girl?"

"Your dream girl's six months pregnant, is she?" Hannah asked. "You have interesting tastes."

"You're pushing it," Drew warned Koti. "And if you ever do find your own dream girl, you won't be holding onto her long if you don't pay more attention to what she needs. You'll

13

have to take better care of her than this. Can't you see Hannah needs to sit down?"

He reached over to lift a chair across from an empty desk and set it down next to his wife. "You've got your hand on your lower back again," he told her. "You haven't been resting enough, I can tell. Sit."

"Woof," Hannah laughed as she sank into the chair. "You're right, though. That is better."

"Are you all right for another twenty minutes or so?" Drew asked. "I'll wrap up as fast as I can."

"I'm fine," Hannah assured him. "Go on back and do what you need to do. It'll give me a chance to catch up with Kate."

Drew nodded and left, throwing one last warning look at Koti as he went.

Kate watched him go, then turned back to Hannah with a frown. "Doesn't it bother you when he tells you what to do?"

"What, that he tries to take care of her?" Koti asked before Hannah could answer. "What could possibly be wrong with that?"

"Sorry, by the way," he apologized to Hannah. "Should have seen that myself, got you a chair."

"Surely Hannah knows if she needs to sit down or not," Kate countered. "She doesn't need you to tell her. Or anyone else, for that matter."

"So a man can't even look after his wife, the way you see it," Koti retorted. "Pretty extreme. Is that the way it is in the States now? Glad I don't live there."

"I didn't say that." Kate flushed. "Just that it can be another form of domination, if you're not careful. A woman isn't a child who needs to be looked after."

"Reckon we should be more like women," Koti shot back. "Sit around and share our feelings instead. God forbid we try to protect the women we love. It'd probably be better if we got rid of all that shocking testosterone entirely. Because first it's fetching a chair and holding a door, eh. Next thing you know, she's in a burqa."

14

"Whoa." Hannah held up her hands. "Time out. Drew doesn't push me around, Kate. Far from it. And Koti, where's all that famous charm? If the two of you want to argue about this, how about doing it when I'm not around? Come to think of it, how about not discussing my marriage in front of me, too? Have a heart. Do it behind my back, like everybody else."

"Sorry." Koti looked shamefaced. "Out of line."

"That was so rude of me," Kate said, chagrined. "After everything you've both done, too. Sorry, Hannah. I got carried away."

Hannah nodded in acknowledgment. "Thanks for coming by to say hello, Koti," she told him. "It's always good to see you."

"Dismissed." Koti smiled ruefully. "No worries."

"Kind of a jerk, isn't he?" Kate asked after Koti had left the room, accompanied by longing looks from the female staff. "He sure thinks a lot of himself."

"He's just a flirt, that's all," Hannah said. "And he gets a lot of reinforcement for it. Believe me, most women flirt back. But underneath it all, he's really a sweetheart."

"If you say so. I can't say I got that. Just because he's nice to you, you like him."

"Well, of course I do. How else am I going to judge somebody, except by how I see them behave?"

"Everyone's nice to you, though. Even me. Because everyone knows you're an angel on earth, and you like everybody," Kate complained. "That's a lousy test. How about if you judge him by the way he behaved towards me? Which would make him, let's see now, a jerk."

"I'm not sure that was your most shining moment either, though," Hannah told her with a wry smile.

"You're right," Kate said penitently. "And I apologize again. But Hannah. You've always been my role model. You know that. You've always been so strong, so independent."

15

"Don't get me wrong," she hurried on. "I can see how much Drew cares about you. It's really all right with you, though, having him talk about looking after you?"

"It's really all right. I take care of him too. It works both ways. And you're wrong, you know," Hannah told her gently. "I understand why you said what you did, after the experience you've had. Being protective is part of a man's makeup, true. But it's not the same thing as being domineering or abusive."

"Who's abusive?" Drew came up behind her.

"Not you," Hannah assured him.

"I hope not," he said, startled. "Ready to go?"

"Sure. See you later, Kate. Thanks for entertaining me for a few minutes. You're still going to the game with me Friday, right?"

"I'm counting on it. Have a nice dinner, guys."

Kate sighed as she watched them leave. She wished she could think somebody would ever look at her like that. True, she could take care of herself. But it would be nice to have someone love her that much.

"Be careful there."

Kate turned at the words. "Sorry?"

Her neighbor Corinne, a pleasant woman in her early thirties, nodded at her. "Dead easy on the eyes, Koti. But he's a player. Always has an eye out for the new girls in the office. If you want a bit of a fling, he's your boy. It may only be for a night or two, though."

"It sounds like he's cut quite a swath around here," Kate said with surprise. "For you to know that much about him."

"There've been a fair few girls through here who could give you a review of his performance, let's just say. Always someone ready to put her hand up where he's concerned. And some hearts broken too. That's why there was a vacancy for your position, you know."

"What? How?"

"Bridget. Lovely to look at, and a kind girl as well. Too soft, though. She fancied him for ages. When he started taking her out, she was over the moon, hearing wedding bells.

Course it didn't last more than a month or so. It never does, with him. He moved on to someone else, and that was the end of Bridget. The same old sad, short story."

"He cheated on her?"

"Not cheated, exactly," Corinne admitted. "Gave her the push all the same, though. She stuck it out here for a bit after that. But it got to be too much for her, seeing him around the place, and she gave notice. So, from what I hear, if you want a bit of fun, you'll have it. But be warned, that's all it'll be. He's not a keeper."

"Thanks for the warning," Kate told her. "But I think I can safely promise you that I'll never be interested in dating Koti James."

The sound of her alarm had Kate starting awake the next morning with a familiar lurch of fear, followed by a quick sigh of relief as she remembered where she was. She was safe across the world, she reminded herself. She didn't have to watch for Paul or think about him anymore. And she was going swimming this morning.

Thirty minutes later, she was bracing herself against the predawn chill as she entered the water at deserted Takapuna Beach and gutted her way through the first five minutes, always the most difficult part of her swim. Another month, maybe, and it would be time to break out the full wetsuit. Thank goodness the water here never got truly cold. She'd never been a member of the Polar Bear Club, able to leap into the frigid winter waters of the San Francisco Bay without a wetsuit. Or even the summer waters, for that matter. Not enough body fat. That might make her look better in a swimsuit, but it was a major disadvantage in cold water.

Moving here had its upside, even though it had been forced upon her, she realized as she watched the dawn tinting the sky over Rangitoto, the huge volcanic island rising to seaward. Swimming in a pool couldn't compare to the intoxicating feeling of slicing through the gentle waves, being a part of the ocean. And being able to roll out of bed and get here in a few minutes—that was just icing on the cake.

Exhilarated and fully awake, she emerged from the sea and ran to the cold shower on the beach. Rinsing off under the spray, she struggled as always to pull her clinging neoprene vest over her shoulders.

"Need a hand?"

She whirled, heart pounding and arms still caught in the vest, at the sound of the voice. Koti stood a few feet away, looking down at her.

"No!" She wrestled the cumbersome vest over her head as quickly as she could, feeling better when her arms were free. "What are you doing here?" She tried to sound calm as she turned off the spray and looked for her towel, only to find him holding it out to her. She wrapped it around herself, grateful for its protection, acutely aware of being dressed only in her swimsuit. It was a modest, athletic one-piece, but she still felt much too naked in the chilly morning.

"Just out for a jog," he said mildly. "Thought I recognized you."

"Pulling my vest over my head, you recognized me," she said stiffly. "You have a good memory."

"For pretty girls, I do," he grinned.

"I've got to go. Enjoy your run." She grabbed the bag with her things and headed for her car without looking back.

Koti watched her leave, confused. What was that all about? Women didn't usually run away from him. It wasn't like he was some random git, coming up to her on the beach. Although he might have done that anyway, he had to admit. She'd looked good in those togs. Especially cold. That had been particularly choice. She was as small as he'd guessed the day before, but everything was proportioned just right, her small waist flaring out to very nice curves above and below. He would bet he could span that waist with his hands.

He'd have to get past that prickly barrier first, though. Probably not worth it. He shrugged and resumed his easy jog. Even though he was due at practice in a couple hours, he always enjoyed starting the day here, in the early morning quiet.

"Still dropping your lip about that talking-to you got back there from Mac, eh."

Koti looked up from where he sat on the bench, hands on knees, to see Hemi Ranapia gazing down at him.

"Nah. Just thinking."

"Cuz." The veteran halfback sat down next to him. "You aren't far off clicking. You need to give it more in the training, though. And pay attention to what's happening in the game, how you can contribute, use that strength of yours where it counts."

"I was the fastest in the running drills today, though," Koti objected. "Like I am most days. Don't see how you—and Mac too—can say I'm piking out."

Hemi frowned at him. "*Kaore te kumara e whaakii ana tana reka.* Need me to translate that for you?"

Koti flushed. "Nah. Got it. My Uncle Nepia used to say the same thing. 'The kumara doesn't say how sweet he is.'"

"Reckon there's a reason we're both telling you the same thing. We all have eyes, don't we. We know what we see and don't see. We know you're fast. You don't need to tell us. What about the tackling drills, though? How would you say you did there?"

Koti shrugged. "Not my best skill, I'll admit. We all have our strengths and weaknesses."

"But you aren't always going to be the fella carrying the ball," Hemi pointed out patiently. "There are times we need you to make the tackle as well. And when you need to fossick about in the dark places that'll never appear on film."

"I'm a back, not a forward," Koti objected. "That's not what I'm here for."

Hemi stared at him in disbelief. "It's what everyone's here for, if we want the win. And the win's what's important. Points don't matter, at the end of the day. Tries don't matter, if we lose. It's a team game, not an individual competition.

No trophies for the most flash performance. You need to harden up and do your best for the team, whether that's something you enjoy or not. If the team looks good, you'll look good too. And if it doesn't, if we don't win . . ." He shrugged. "Then you don't look so flash anymore, do you. No matter how fast you've run."

Koti was still thinking about the conversation two days later as he jogged slowly back along the beach, letting the quiet of the early morning fill him with its peace. On match days like this Friday, he needed this ritual even more, the spaciousness of sea and sky settling him down, helping him start his day with a clear head.

Looking out into the water, he saw a swimmer heading toward shore. It was hard to tell from this distance, but he thought it was Kate. He didn't often see anyone in the water this early.

"Good morning again," he said cheerfully as she emerged from the water. He handed her the towel he had seen with her things. "You do this most days, eh."

She pulled the towel hastily around herself and stared at him. "Why are you here at the same time I am? Are you following me?"

"What?" he asked in disbelief. "Of course I'm not following you. Just having a bit of a run, stretching my legs like I do every morning."

"Why on this beach?" she persisted. "This is my beach."

"I don't think so." He'd given her a pass the first couple times, but she was starting to annoy him now. "This is a public place, same as every other beach in New Zealand. And I live in Takapuna. I could ask why you're on *my* beach."

"Maybe I'd better change my schedule, then," she muttered. "I'm not comfortable with you showing up every time I come here."

"That's mad." He felt his temper slip further. "You're not even my type. Too small. Too dark. Reckon I just won't talk to you if I see you, from now on. I'll avert my eyes, too. Believe me, that won't be any sacrifice."

"Fine," she snapped. "Just do your run and leave me alone." She grabbed her bag and stalked off to take her shower, deliberately turning her back on him before risking a quick peek to make sure he had left. She whipped her head back around when she saw him continuing to look after her. *Go away,* she prayed, as she forced herself to behave naturally.

The next time she looked around, he was headed off again, and she breathed a sigh of relief even as her pulse continued to pound. When she'd come out of the water and seen him standing there, it had sent a real jolt of fear through her. This couldn't be happening again. That would be too much of a coincidence.

She would tell Hannah about it, she decided. Just in case.

Chapter 3

"What?" Hannah asked, startled, when Kate described the encounters over dinner in the City that evening. "I'm sure Koti wasn't stalking you. He's a good guy, Kate."

"How do you know?" Kate pressed. "Stalkers can seem like perfectly nice, normal guys. They're good at that. I should know. And these guys are violent anyway, aren't they? I mean, that's their job."

"Kate," Hannah frowned. "You're talking about my husband. You do realize that."

"I'm sorry," Kate hastened to say. "I just mean, aren't they more likely to have those issues? Playing such an aggressive sport?"

"Not that I've seen. I'd say the opposite, most of them. They get all their aggression out on the field, I guess. And they leave it there. In fact, you know, lots of times they're friends with the boys they're playing against. When you watch them out there bashing each other, you'd think they were the worst of enemies. But remember that some of them are going to be teammates on the All Blacks. Or have played together in the past. They'll be visiting each other in the locker room after the game and having a beer together."

"And actually," she went on thoughtfully, "you're probably safer with one of the players than you are with random guys you'd meet here. Because they're so visible. If any of them had that kind of problem, you'd have heard something about it. I would have, for sure. This country's too small to hide that kind of thing. And the rugby world is even smaller."

"Well, I wanted to let you know, anyway. Just in case you're wrong," Kate insisted.

"I can understand why you're wary. I do remember, though, that Koti lives in Takapuna. Quite a few of the players live on the North Shore, for the same reason you like it. It's a beautiful area, and it has some of the best beaches around. My friend Reka lives there, in fact, not far from you. We should see her tonight. She's Hemi Ranapia's wife. Have you met him?"

"Not yet. At least I don't think so. I've only met a few of the players."

"I think you'll like both of them. They're Maori, like Koti, and I know they're fond of him. They wouldn't be if there were anything wrong with him. And you know, Drew, and Hemi too—any of the senior players, in fact—would never ignore one of the players abusing a woman. Especially not my friend. Believe me, none of those boys is going to mess with you."

"And there's that protection thing again," Kate pointed out. "You're telling me not to be scared of one man hurting me, because another man will hurt *him*. How is that supposed to make me feel better, that I'm protected from the violence of one man by the violence of another man?"

"Well, you're protected by the law too, of course," Hannah told her with a smile. "But personally, I'd put my money on Drew. His reaction time is a lot quicker."

"I do understand how you feel," she went on seriously. "Of course it's hard for you to trust in men's good intentions. But you know, that predatory behavior is an aberration, way out past the edge of normal masculinity. Most men aren't like that. You hadn't met anyone like that before Paul, had you?"

"No. You're right, of course. It's just that now, I'm always looking for it."

"I'm sure that's normal for someone in your situation. But I do hope you'll meet enough good men here that your view can start shifting a little."

"It's not just that," Kate admitted. "That I think all men are potential stalkers. I know that isn't true. At least I know it logically. But I don't trust my own judgment any more either. I mean, let's face it, I went out with Paul. It's not like he was forced on me. I was attracted to him, in the beginning. And looking back, I didn't pick up on those signals—the possessiveness especially—nearly quickly enough. Not until he was flashing them loud and clear for everyone to see."

"How did he do that? When did you realize there was something wrong with him?" Hannah wondered. "If you don't mind my asking."

"I don't mind. I've been kicking myself for so long about it, it might be good to tell you, get your perspective. It was after we'd been dating for five or six months. Things hadn't been going that great, and I was starting to have second thoughts about the whole thing. I went out to dinner one night with two of my girlfriends. Just having a good time, you know. Till he showed up. And then it all went south, really fast."

She pulled her sweater more tightly around her as she began to tell Hannah the story, the shock and fear she'd felt that night coming back to her, chilling her.

"What's he doing here?" her friend Molly had asked with a frown as their meals were being delivered.

"Who?" Kate turned around to see the tall man approaching them, looking as cool and polished as always in a white dress shirt and dark slacks. "Oh, no."

"What's going on?" she asked as Paul stopped at their table. "Is something wrong?"

He shrugged, his eyes darting around the group. Laura and Molly stared back at him, unsmiling. "Nothing's wrong. I was out myself, thought I'd stop by and say hello."

Kate sighed. "I need to talk to you. Let's go outside for a minute."

Once in the parking lot, she turned to face him. "Look, Paul. I explained this. That I needed some time with my friends. I've hardly seen them since we started dating. This is my one night to be with them. I don't understand why you have a problem with that. Or why you're here."

"I don't think they're good for you," he told her, a scowl contorting his handsome features. "Laura especially. She doesn't like me, I can tell."

Kate took a deep breath. "She has some issues with you, you're right. She thinks you're too possessive. And a little controlling. Frankly, I'm starting to think so too. I don't like you coming here tonight to check up on me. Because that's what you're doing, isn't it? Checking that I'm really with my friends, not out with another guy. And I don't appreciate it."

He flushed and took a step closer, looming over her. "You're lucky I did find you with them. And you don't appreciate it? Well, I don't appreciate you turning down an invitation to dinner with me in order to spend the evening with a bitch like that. Who's probably been sitting in there telling you to leave me."

Kate stepped back in shock. "I won't let you talk about my friends that way. And I'm not sure she's wrong. Because having you get in the middle of my friendships, or checking up on me, isn't going to work for me. It's time we rethink this."

"No." He reached for her arm. "We don't need to rethink anything except your choice of friends. We're right together. We belong together. You know we do."

"Let go of me, please." She made her voice as level and calm as she could, although inside her, annoyance was turning to something else. There was too much intensity in his face. She was beginning to feel uneasy, alone with him in the dark lot. "I'm in the middle of my evening. I'm having dinner with my friends. We'll talk about this tomorrow."

"No. We'll talk about it now. You're coming home with me now." His hold on her arm tightened as he began to pull her towards his car.

"Stop it." She tried without success to pull her arm from his grip. "Let go of me, Paul. I'm not going anywhere with you."

His only response was to pull harder, dragging her along beside him. Truly angry now, and beginning to be frightened as well, Kate pulled her arm back again as she swung her purse around with the other hand and hit him with it. The movement overbalanced her, causing her to stumble over her heels, but had no effect on him. He tightened his grip and gave her arm a vicious yank, making her cry out at the sudden pain.

"Are you OK?" Paul turned angrily at Laura's voice as she and Molly approached. "Because your dinner's getting cold," Laura said prosaically, her eyes moving between the two of them. "And we're getting tired of waiting for you."

"Go on back," Paul told them abruptly. "Kate's going home with me. We're just leaving."

"No, we're not." Kate tried to pull away again. "I'm going back in and finishing my dinner. Let go of me, Paul. Right now."

"Sounds like she means it," Laura told him. She took a step closer. "I think you'd better leave."

"Why don't you mind your own business, bitch," he spat. "This is between us."

"All right. That's it," Laura decided. "Kate, you need to dump this asshole."

"You're right." Kate made her voice as firm and strong as she could manage, even though she was shaking inside. "Paul, you and I are done. And you need to leave now."

"What?" He stared down at her. "You can't break up with me."

"I just did. So let go of me right now, or Laura's going to call 911."

"I'm already doing it," Laura told her, pulling out her phone.

Paul shoved Kate from him, causing her to stumble over her heels again. She fell awkwardly, her bare knees hitting the rough asphalt with a bruising impact. As she scrambled to her feet, she saw him grabbing Laura's phone out of her hand, hurling it across the parking lot to land with a crash. He turned on Laura herself then, putting his hand into her face and giving her a hard shove that sent her sprawling in her turn.

Kate ran to Laura, pulled her up with Molly's help. A noisy group heading for their cars gave the women the opportunity they needed. Ducking behind the exiting customers, they ran for the safety of the tiny vestibule. With trembling hands, Kate pulled her own cell phone from her purse and dialed 911.

"Are you sure that's a good idea?" Molly asked nervously. "Won't it just make him madder?"

"I don't care if it does," Kate snapped as Laura brushed off the muddied knees of her slacks. "He hurt us out there. And I'm reporting it."

"So you see," Kate told Hannah as she finished her story, "I was an idiot to get involved with someone like that in the first place. He'd started to seem too needy, but I never had a clue he could be violent. And then once I'd dumped him, I thought it was over. That I'd made a mistake, but I could move on. Obviously, I couldn't have been more wrong. I had no idea how twisted he was. Something must be wrong with my antennae, don't you think, that I didn't see that coming?"

Hannah looked at her thoughtfully. "I'm not a psychologist, but I think some people are good at that, at covering up their true selves, at least at first. Surely you aren't the first woman to be taken in by a bad guy. Have you talked to anyone about this?"

"No," Kate admitted. "I was pretty much in lockdown. In survival mode at the time."

"How about doing it now?"

"You think I need help, huh? Maybe you're right. I thought once I moved away, it would stop. But I'm still having bad dreams, and I'm so edgy all the time. I can't seem to move past it."

"You've had a horrible experience. Anyone would need help after that. It might not be a bad idea to check it out. But we'd better finish up here and get to the stadium. So you can watch men being aggressive. Maybe not the best plan for tonight, now that I think about it. But the good news is, they all know the rules, and once the game's over, so is the aggression."

Chapter 4

"And this is us, the WAG section," Hannah announced an hour later as they found their seats near midfield in Eden Park, the Blues' large stadium in the center of Auckland.

"The what?"

"Wives and Girlfriends. And I know," she laughed as Kate made a face, "it sounds terrible. I still hate it. But here's Reka." Hannah got up to give the striking dark-haired woman approaching them a hug, then introduced her to Kate.

"How ya goin', Kate," Reka smiled, shaking hands. "Come to see what you've let yourself in for, eh, working for the Blues?"

"I figure I'd better learn something about the game," Kate agreed, trying to shake off her unsettled mood and focus on the evening ahead. "I heard this should be a good one tonight."

"Should be, against the Brumbies," Reka confirmed.

"From Australia, right?" Kate asked. "Five teams each from Australia, South Africa, and New Zealand. I've figured that much out. And they all play each other. That must be a lot of travel."

"Half the games at home, half away, in the Super 15," Reka said. "The games in En Zed and the Boomerang Coast, in Oz—they aren't so bad. But it's a long way to Perth, and a full day to fly to Safa. Can't be too dependent if you're married to a rugby player. Because you're spending a fair bit of the season alone."

"Here's what I really don't understand, though," Kate told her. "I keep hearing about the All Blacks. Where's that team?

Because some of the guys on the Blues are also All Blacks. How can that be?"

"Easy," Hannah said. "Think All-Star team. All the countries that play Rugby Union—as opposed to Rugby League, you understand—have a national team, made up of the best players from their top-tier rugby teams. And those teams play each other, in addition to the guys on them playing with their home teams during the regular season. It makes for a lot of games. And a short off-season," she added as Reka nodded agreement.

"Top-tier as opposed to their lower-tier rugby teams? And whatever Rugby League is?" Kate asked.

Reka laughed. "Right. Too much rugby, you reckon? No worries. Just remember that if someone says "rugby," they're talking about Union. The rest of it you can ignore for now."

"Except that the All Blacks are important," Kate pointed out.

Both women had a chuckle over that. "Yeh," Reka agreed. "Go the Mighty All Blacks. Probably good to remember that as well. Especially around Hannah and me."

"You don't wait for the guys?" Kate asked as Hannah and Reka got up to leave after the game.

"It'd be a long wait," Hannah answered. "Trust me, it'll be awhile, by the time they're changed and have their injuries seen to. But I wanted to tell you both while we're here that we're planning a barbecue at our place next Sunday afternoon. Can you make it?"

"Will *he* be there?" Kate asked cautiously, as they made their way through their gate and down the stadium's ramp.

"Afraid so," Hannah told her sympathetically.

"Koti," she explained at Reka's inquisitive look. "They didn't hit it off, I'm afraid."

"With *Koti?* You're in a minority of one, then. Appealing to women is his special gift."

"Huh," Kate shrugged. "I guess that was lost on me. He seems like kind of a jerk, I have to say."

"He can be a bit of a tall poppy," Reka agreed. "But a good boy all the same. Not that much to him, maybe, but no real harm either. Beauty's only skin-deep, they say. But what a skin, eh."

"A tall poppy?" Kate asked wonderingly.

"That one took me a while," Hannah told her. "The basic meaning's simple enough. The tall poppy gets cut down. If you stick your neck out too far, think too much of yourself, you'll be put in your place. Arrogance is the cardinal sin here. It's all about modesty. No matter how good you are at what you do, you're not supposed to stand out too much. And I must say, after watching the athletes posturing and bragging back home, it's nice to watch football without all that celebrating."

"A tall poppy," Kate smiled. "That sounds just about right. Because I think Koti James needs cutting down to size."

"Good luck with that," Reka laughed. "The Kiwi clobbering machine hasn't managed it yet, and there've been a fair few attempts. You'd have a job."

"You live near us, in Takapuna, don't you?" she went on. "Can we give you a lift, Sunday? We won't stay too late. Three kids. But if you don't mind that, it'll save you driving all that way, let you have a drink or two as well. I'll be the designated driver."

"Thanks," Kate agreed with surprise. "That's awfully nice of you."

"No worries," Reka assured her. "Sweet as. Give us a chance to chat."

Kate dressed with care for the barbecue the next Sunday. If the truth were known, her pride had been a little stung when Koti had told her she wasn't his type. She didn't want to attract him, and she wasn't looking anyway. She was taking a serious sabbatical where men were concerned. But she'd still make sure she looked good.

"Why are so many of the women wearing black?" she whispered to Hannah once she was inside the beautiful terraced house overlooking St. Heliers Bay and the sparkling waters of Waitemata Harbour beyond. "Did somebody die?"

Hannah laughed. "For some reason, they always wear a lot of black here. And not just to support the team. All Black, all the time. It is kind of mournful, isn't it? Especially in such a rainy country. You'd think they'd want to liven things up a bit more."

"It'd work for you. It's OK on blondes. But I'd look like an Italian grandmother. Short, dark, and dumpy."

"You look great as you are," Hannah assured her, admiring Kate's simple tomato-red sheath dress, worn with her usual high heels. "You'll stand out."

"Wonderful," Kate answered glumly. "I was going for just a bit sexy. Instead, I feel like I'm wearing leopard-print pants. I'm not going to quit wearing bright colors, though. I'll just have to resign myself to being a freak. Oh well. Time to circulate. Good thing I've met a few people by now."

A bit late, Koti thought guiltily as he pulled up to the house. Hopefully Hannah would forgive him. But he'd been chatting to a girl he'd met on the beach, and time had slipped away. He had her mobile number now, anyway. Maybe he'd ring her later tonight, see if she fancied a drink. Or him.

Or maybe not, he thought as he entered the lounge and saw a very nice little body in a red dress. She had her back turned, chatting with Reka and Hemi and a few of the other guests. Nobody's girlfriend, unless she was new. He'd check it out, anyway.

He sauntered over and greeted the group. His hopes plummeted when the brunette turned and he saw it was Kate. He should have recognized that shining fall of dark hair, not to mention the figure. No surprise, she was frowning at him.

"How ya goin', Kate. In a good mood as usual, I see. Ready to warn me off yet, or should I go away and come back?"

"Hannah says I should apologize. Again." Kate stepped away from the others. "Sorry for accusing you of following me. I guess I should explain why I did that."

"It'd be good to know. Unless you're this stroppy all the time."

"We do rub each other the wrong way," she conceded. "But that's not all it is. Someone was stalking me, back home. That's why I'm here. And it's why I'm jumpy, too. I realize now that I overreacted. Sorry I accused you. That wasn't really fair."

"No, it wasn't. But I thought that kind of thing only happened to celebrities."

"Unfortunately, no. You'd be surprised how much it happens. And how little you can do about it."

"So who was it?" Koti pressed. "Somebody who was overwhelmed by your fetching personality?"

"OK, forget this." Kate turned to leave.

"Sorry. Out of line again," he told her hastily. "I want to know. Tell me."

She turned reluctantly back to him, eyes still stormy. "It wasn't a joke. I'm trying to give you the benefit of the doubt here because Hannah and Reka swear you're a nice guy. But I have to tell you, from what I've seen, I'm having a hard time believing it. I keep hearing how much women love you. All I can say is, New Zealand women must not be that discriminating. Do you actually get a lot of dates with that charming attitude?"

"I don't know what it is," he apologized. "You bring out the worst in me. I usually do much better. Sorry."

"I guess I'd have to see your seductive mode again. Obviously, you don't know how to talk to women any other way."

"That's not fair," he objected. "You've seen me being nice to Hannah, haven't you? And I'm nice to Reka too, you'll see. Because they're friends. Trust me, I'm not being seductive there. Value my life too much, don't I."

"They're friends," Kate said flatly. "Right. I'd be willing to bet that you haven't had a woman friend in your life. And wives of your teammates don't count," she cut him off. "A real friend who's a woman. Name one."

"Well?" she pressed.

"I'm thinking," he protested. "Right, then. My cousins."

"Nope." She shook her head. "No relatives."

"That's the women I know, though. My whanau."

"Your what?"

"My family. Extended family. Those are the girls I grew up with, that I know."

"But you don't date any of them, do you? They're off-limits, I'll bet."

"Maybe. Some of them," he conceded. "But that doesn't mean I couldn't be friends with a woman, just because I haven't done it much."

"Yes, it does," she insisted. "You only know how to deal with women if they're attached to a man you know, or related to you, or if you're trying to go to bed with them. You obviously don't have a clue outside of that. You couldn't be friends with a woman for two weeks without making a move on her."

"Course I could. Easy as. I'd make a bet that I could."

"Right," she scoffed. "How would we judge that? Have one of your lady friends tell me you've been a great friend to her? That you always give her a ride home in the morning?"

"You really don't think much of me, do you?" His temper was flaring now too.

She shrugged. "I'm calling it as I see it. And as I hear it. You're not exactly discreet."

"Whatever that means. For somebody who doesn't like me, you're pretty interested in my life, aren't you? But I'm going to show you you're wrong. I'll make that bet with you. I'll be your friend for a month. No, for six weeks. That's as good a test as I can think of. If I can be friends with you, reckon I can do it with any woman. We'll spend some time together. And you can see for yourself."

"You're willing to bet you can do that, for six weeks. Without making any moves," Kate said dubiously.

"No worries. Make my living with my hands, don't I. Not going to risk getting them bitten off. No rabies in New Zealand, but you may just be the one to introduce it."

"Well, this is off to a great start," she observed. "But I'll take that bet. That you can't do six weeks of friendship. What are the stakes?"

"If I win, you give me a big kiss in the office, in front of all the staff. And tell me how wonderful I am."

"Right. That's happening. But since I know you won't win, I'm not worrying. And if I win, which I am counting on, by the way . . . Let me think."

"I know," she decided. "*When* I win, you wear a pink hoodie. All day, except when you're actually practicing."

He winced. "That'd be dead embarrassing. Reckon I'd better win."

"And I win if you stop spending friend time with me, too," she clarified. "Which I predict you'll want to do pretty soon. Because it'll be sooooo boring for you. And we have to do something together . . . at least once a week. That shouldn't be too hard, as close as we live."

"Deal," he confirmed, putting out his hand. "And shaking hands doesn't count. Has to be a real move. Which isn't happening, trust me."

His big, firm hand enveloped Kate's as he stood over her. She pulled herself to her full five-foot-almost-two and demanded, in an imperious tone he couldn't help finding funny, "All right. You're on. What's our first friend date?"

"Uh, I don't know," he cast about. "Swimming, I reckon."

"You like to swim?" she asked in surprise.

"I'm a Kiwi. Course I like to swim. Next Sunday morning at nine, at Takapuna, then. And we'll have a coffee afterwards, at the café on the beach there. That should give you heaps of time to tell me what you think of me. That suit you?"

"OK," she agreed. "I'll meet you at nine, on the main steps."

"I'm so glad to see you two talking," Hannah said as she came up beside them. "I know you got off to a rocky start, but I do hope you can be friends."

"No worries," Koti grinned. "We're working on that."

Chapter 5

Kate shifted her position on the steps. Looked around her again, then checked her watch. Nine-ten. It was starting to look like Koti was going to stand her up, the first time out of the chute. Well, this looked like the easiest bet she'd ever collected on. Five more minutes, she decided. That was all she was giving him.

At nine-fifteen, she gave it up and marched to the water's edge, annoyed with herself for waiting so long. The swim took the edge off her irritation. She'd only wasted fifteen minutes of her day. And she wouldn't have been this relaxed if he'd been with her. After she'd made the bet, she'd wondered what she had been thinking. Why would she want to spend time with him? He had got under her skin, that was all. Well, missing out on his company wasn't any sacrifice. She'd be her own date today. She'd take herself out for a coffee afterwards, too.

When she was settled at a table in the beachside café with her raspberry muffin and cappuccino, she was startled to hear her phone ring. She dug through her bag and found it at last. It was Hannah, of course. Only five people had this number, and two of them were her parents, she reminded herself.

"Hi, Kate. I just got a really strange phone call from Koti James," her friend told her. "I didn't realize you were going out with him."

"I'm not. I *was* supposed to be swimming with him this morning, but he didn't show. No loss."

"Well, he wants to talk to you. He called me to get your number. I didn't give it to him, of course, but I got his, if you want to call him back."

"No, thanks," Kate decided. "I'm really not interested. Let's just say I'm still less than impressed by him. Sorry you were disturbed on your Sunday, though."

She pressed the *End* button. Looked down at her phone. She had to stop jumping every time she heard it ring, the chime of a text.

Can't wait to watch you die.

She was here. She was safe. That was over. Deliberately, she put the phone away. Got a fashion magazine from the rack. Sat with her coffee and her muffin and looked at clothes she couldn't afford. She'd had a great swim, it was a beautiful day, and she was on her own. Nobody to look out for. No company at all. Frightening, annoying, or otherwise.

She put the incident out of her mind over the next few days. There was so much to learn in the new job, she didn't have time or energy to waste in obsessing about some prima donna with a deficient sense of time. Even her fears were receding as she became more and more engrossed in her work. She was at her desk on Tuesday afternoon, immersed in tracking a particularly knotty publicity expense trail, when she was annoyed to be interrupted by the sound of a male voice.

"Uh, Kate. Can I talk to you a second?"

She looked up with a frown. Set down the paperwork she had been studying and cast a disillusioned eye over Koti. His hoodie today was navy blue. He really did have a limited wardrobe.

"Oh. You," she said without enthusiasm. "I'm pretty busy here. If you came to tell me you lost the bet, I already figured that out."

"I tried to get in touch with you," he said with exasperation. "Sorry I was late. But I did try to ring. Didn't have your mobile number though, and Hannah wouldn't give it to me. Didn't she give you the message? I expected you to ring me back. To text me, at least."

"Oh, she gave me the message. But I wasn't interested. I'd already had my swim, and my coffee too. Let's just say you were surplus to requirements by the time I heard from her."

"You should have given me the chance to explain, though," he protested.

"OK. Explain now. Somehow, I'm guessing you weren't in a car accident, or held hostage by terrorists. But let's hear it."

"I was tied up," he began, a bit shamefaced. "Lost track of the time. Forgot, if you want to know the truth, until ten or so. But as soon as I remembered, I tried to get in touch."

"Tied up," she mused. "Let me guess. You were . . . busy. *Getting* busy. Which seemed, hmm, just a *bit* more inviting at the time than a swim date with some bitchy girl who doesn't even like you."

"Could be." He tried his best charming grin. "But now that I've seen you again, I'm wondering what I was thinking. Especially since it *was* a swim date. Sweet as, with you. What d'you reckon? Want to try again, this weekend?"

"Wow, that's enticing. Let me think about it. Mmm . . . no. You lose." She picked up her pencil, tapped it impatiently against the desk. "Tomorrow work for you, pink hoodie-wise?"

He flushed angrily. "Why are you being so snotty about this? I've apologized. What more do you want?"

"An apology doesn't make bad behavior go away. Didn't anybody ever explain that to you? How hard is that, to say you're sorry? You think you can flash that smile, give me a come-hither look out of those big bedroom eyes, and that's it? All's forgiven, and you get a free pass?"

Koti turned at the sound of Corinne's half-muffled laugh at the next desk. "Didn't realize this was public."

"Sorry," Corinne said with a grin. "But I'd say that's spot on. Does my heart good to hear it, too. Good on ya, Kate."

Koti set his jaw. "I'm not ready to chuck it in. Let's start over. We'll make it two months. Starting next weekend. And if I stuff up once more like this, you win, no arguments. That do you?"

"All right," Kate agreed reluctantly. "But only because I'm critically short of entertainment right now. And I like the idea of raking you over the coals again next time."

"Oh, for heaven's sake," Kate muttered the following Saturday afternoon as she descended the broad steps to Takapuna Beach. There was Koti at the foot of the stairs, his usual hoodie having failed to preserve his anonymity, having his picture taken with two young women.

"Should I go away and come back later?" she drawled as she approached the group, just as one of the excited women switched places with the photographer to allow yet another picture to be taken.

"Last one, girls," Koti told them with a smile. "Got to go."

Kate rolled her eyes as they walked across the broad beach toward the water's edge. "That's quite a fan club you've got there. Must be nice."

"You think so?"

"Don't tell me you don't enjoy that. You sure seem to."

"Comes with the territory," he shrugged. "That doesn't mean I always enjoy it."

"Good spot here?" he turned to ask her as they neared the high-tide mark. "Want to swim to the point there, and back?" At her nod, he kicked off his flip-flops and pulled his hoodie and shirt over his head, dropping them with his towel onto the beach.

"You're kidding," Kate said, staring at him.

"What? Bad spot?" he asked, confused. "I thought you said it was all right."

"No. I mean, you. That's just . . . that's just ridiculous. Plus the tattoo, the pendant, everything. You're like some kind of walking advertisement for New Zealand."

"My tattoo isn't ridiculous," he said, genuinely offended now. "My moko honors my ancestors. My pendant isn't ridiculous either. It's not for decoration. You're slagging off my mana now."

"I'm sorry," she said quickly. "I didn't mean to be offensive. I just meant, I'm getting it now. You always have that hoodie on, that's all. I never realized what you looked like. A little blinded here. I've never seen anyone as ripped as that in real life."

He sighed. "It's how I look. I'm not going to apologize for it. I've been training and playing rugby most of my life, you know. And I'm Maori. I can't help being big, or having some muscles. You're just going to have to get over it."

"Should have worn my sunglasses," she muttered.

"Were you planning on dropping your own gear anytime soon, so we can get in the water?" he complained. "Freezing my arse off here."

"No. I don't think so," she decided. "I'm seriously insecure, all of a sudden. Let's forget it and go for coffee instead."

"Piking out first time, eh," he mocked. "Not up to the challenge. Reckon I've won already."

Kate's chin shot up. "You're right. But don't watch me take off my clothes. Look at Rangitoto or something for a minute. Because I'm embarrassed now."

He turned his back with a sigh. "This is what's ridiculous," he told her over his shoulder. "I've seen you in your togs twice now, remember? I have a pretty good memory of what you look like, too."

"I remember." She adjusted her goggles and stepped out into the water. "I'm not your type. Too small and too dark. That's OK. One of us being that beautiful is more than enough."

She pushed off and started swimming before he could answer. Just as well, Koti decided as he followed. He wasn't sure there was any good answer to that one. If he told her what he really thought, she'd probably poison his coffee. Or drown him.

"That's better," Kate told him with a satisfied nod, meeting him outside the changing rooms forty-five minutes later.

"What now?" he asked, confused.

"I like you covered up, I've decided. The hoodie and sunglasses help reduce the glare."

"Then let's go for a coffee, warm up," he told her. "And you can criticize my personality some more."

"You didn't Google me, then," he mused, after they had given their orders at the beach café and sat down to await them. He had insisted on paying, to her annoyance. "Or you'd have seen the tattoo, and all."

"Of course I didn't Google you. Look at naked pictures of you online? That'd be creepy. You didn't Google me, did you?" she asked in sudden alarm.

"Not naked. The odd shirtless photo, maybe. And nah, didn't Google you either. It'd spoil the surprise if I found out too much in advance. I'd rather find out about your animal-tamer past from you, get the whole story about how you started with rattlesnakes and worked your way up. But you weren't always this stroppy, I'm guessing. Does it have to do with the stalking thing?"

"Probably. Not all of it, though. Part of it's just being so short, and small on top of it. Everyone thinks you're cute." She scowled at him.

"No worries. I'm under no illusions," he assured her. "Terrifying, in fact."

She couldn't help a smile. "Like a mean little dog. That's what I'm going for here. But you're right. I'm even meaner now, I suppose."

"It just made me so mad," she tried to explain. "That somebody could come in and take away my life like that, and there was nothing I could do."

"Was this a partner? An ex?"

"Yes. Not serious. At least not to me. I was wrong, obviously. Wrong all the way. Because now I'm here, on the other side of the world. With a bad attitude, as you can see."

"Anyway." She finished her coffee and set it aside. "Time to go. I have lots to do this weekend, and I'm sure you do too. But this wasn't as tough as I expected, I have to admit. What do you think?"

"Long as my immunizations are up to date. Same thing next Sunday?"

"If you think you can show up. I warn you, I'm only waiting ten minutes max. Any longer than that, and you lose."

"Fair enough. I'll be there."

"And I buy the coffee next time. That's what friends do," she insisted as he shook his head. "You clearly don't know the rules here, and I do. We're taking turns."

"Going to have to wear the hoodie again, then. Too embarrassing," he grumbled.

Chapter 6

She should have planned some kind of outing for herself, Kate realized the next morning. Instead, another long, quiet Sunday stretched ahead of her. She'd start it with a run, she decided. She could explore Takapuna a bit more, anyway. And think up something fun to do this afternoon.

After the now-familiar route to the beach, she began making her way through the upscale residential neighborhood nearby, admiring the modern homes and historic villas set in large gardens full of late-summer flowers. A couple kissing on the sidewalk ahead of her were putting on a pretty good display too. Maybe a good idea to get a room, guys, she thought with amusement and a touch of envy. That was some fairly intense action.

The couple separated, the woman climbing into a car with a toss of her blonde mane and a flash of long, tanned legs in a short skirt, the man bending down to give her a last kiss through the open window, then slapping his open palm on the roof in farewell as she pulled away. Kate recognized him with dismay as she approached. Too late to cross the street now. Well, this was awkward.

She was forced to revise her opinion as Koti hailed her with his usual easy smile. No embarrassment there.

"Kate. How ya goin'. Exercising again, eh."

She slowed to a stop. He looked as good as always, she thought resentfully, even though he'd clearly just rolled out of bed. Unshaven, his hair a little tousled. Broad shoulders straining a faded T-shirt, unbelted khaki shorts slipping a bit from narrow hips.

"Hi, Koti. Yeah. Starting my day."

"I was about to go for a bit of a run myself, clear the cobwebs," he told her. "Just have to put my trainers on. Want to wait for me?"

A comment about his cobwebs hovered on the tip of her tongue. She pulled it back just in time. None of her business. She didn't want him to think she cared what he did, anyway.

"I'm sure you don't want to run at my pace," she said cheerfully instead. "Have a good one, though. I'll see you next week." She gave him a brief smile and took off up the road.

He watched her go. He'd have been happy to run at her pace, actually. Because she really did have the most gorgeous bum. He'd have enjoyed watching it work in those spandex shorts for a few kilometers.

"Reckon this is meant to be our day."

Kate turned in the queue at the Sunday Market's empanada stall to find Koti behind her, freshly shaved this time, hoodie in place once again.

"Hang on a tick," he told her as she received her spinach-filled pastry from the Argentinian vendor. "Let me get mine and I'll join you."

"Three different kinds, huh? You're hungry," she observed as they maneuvered out of the path of the passing crowd.

"Heaps of exercise this morning," he grinned.

To her annoyance, she found herself blushing. What did she have to be embarrassed about? She'd had a perfectly blameless morning.

"Come on," he told her. "I'll buy you a coffee, and we'll find a spot to eat these."

"Don't have a choice, do we," he added as she hesitated. "If we don't get this over with now, we're going to be meeting again over the frozen peas in New World tonight."

She couldn't help smiling. "It does seem that way, doesn't it? I'll take a coffee. Thanks. Though I'm supposed to be buying."

"Next week," he reminded her. "That was the deal."

"I see you've fully embraced the glamorous Kiwi lifestyle," he remarked as they sat on a bench eating their impromptu lunch. "A run, then the Takapuna Market. Add a bit of birdwatching and you'll qualify for citizenship."

"There are lots of things to do here, I'm sure," she objected. "I'm looking forward to experiencing them, now that I'm settled into my place and my job."

He laughed. "As long as you like the outdoor life, I reckon."

"Trust me," she told him, "I'm not looking for too much excitement in my life right now. A bit of quiet is going to suit me fine."

He sobered. "Hannah did tell me you'd had a bad time. Sorry for joking about it. I didn't realize."

She nodded. "Thanks. I appreciate the apology. And I'd better be going. See you next Sunday." She took a final sip of her drink, then gathered her purchases and stood to toss her rubbish in the bin. "Thanks again for the coffee too."

And the view, she added silently a few minutes later, watching him jog across the road. He really was too good-looking for any woman's peace of mind.

"I'm restless today," she told him when she joined him at the beach the next week. "I need to wear myself out. Are you up for a longer swim?"

"How long were you thinking?"

She shrugged. "Forty-five minutes? I know that'll be a long way for you, since you swim about twice as fast as I do. You don't have to spend that long in the water if you don't want to. You can meet me at the café afterwards."

"I'll swim that long with you," he promised. "It felt good last week. Stretched me out after the game."

"You need a better wetsuit," he commented after they had showered and changed at the end of their swim. "You're still shivering."

"I know," she said ruefully. "Too much time in the water. I've been trying to build up some tolerance. But I don't have enough mass, I guess. I get cold really easily, always have. I need a hot drink, that's all. Then I'll feel better."

"You are tiny," he agreed as they walked toward the café. "Am I allowed to say that?"

"Just don't call me adorable," she warned. "Or I won't be responsible for what I do."

"That wasn't the *a*-word I was thinking of. Aggravating, maybe. Annoying. Aggressive. Abrasive. And some more that'll come to me later, no doubt. But definitely not adorable."

"Nice vocabulary," she told him with a grin. "Good work. Or have you been thinking those up?"

"Nah. I had a fair few words in mind at the time, but none of them started with an *a*."

She laughed. "I'll bet. You, on the other hand, definitely rated some *a*-words. *Arrogant* being the only one fit for a public beach."

He looked down at her. It was the first time he'd really seen her smile, he realized. Her entire face lit up when she did, changing her from an attractive woman to something much more. "You know, you should smile more often," he said. "Because you're gorgeous, when you do."

"And that's made it disappear straight away," he sighed. "Never mind."

"So tell me about this bloke," he said when they were settled with their coffees. "The one you're running away from. He was really stalking you? That actually happens?"

"If you're weird and you fixate on somebody. I should never have gone out with him more than once. If I'd cut it off sooner, I wouldn't have ended up in this mess. I did get these glimpses right away that something was off. But he was a good-looking, charming guy. Like you."

"I hope not," he said, startled.

"Me too. Anyway, he was talking about things we could do the next month on our first date. I wasn't sure, though. I thought maybe I was being too harsh. I can do that at times."

"You don't say."

"Yeah, well, in this case I should have gone ahead and been harsh, trusted my instincts. I suppose all the attention, all that interest was flattering at first. But then he started wanting me to spend all my time with him. Wanted to know everything I was doing, every day. I should have broken up with him the minute that started happening, too. But I didn't do that either."

"And that was another mistake," he prompted when she fell silent.

"It sure was. Although I don't know, now. I'm not sure there's anything I could have done once he got so fixated. I've kicked myself all this time for what I did, what I didn't do. But looking back, I'm starting to think that maybe it wasn't my fault after all."

"How could it have been your fault?" he objected.

She shrugged. "I don't know. But it's hard not to think so. You get people saying things like, 'There are no victims, only volunteers.' It makes you wonder if it was something you did, something about you that invited it. It sure hasn't happened to anyone else I know."

"Sounds to me like you were unlucky, that's all."

"Thanks. You get points for that. I'm going to concede here that you just might be the nice guy Hannah and Reka say you are."

"Cheers for that. What did happen, though? What did he do?"

She hesitated a minute before she answered, twisting her napkin between her fingers. "He got scary. Violent. I did break up with him then. I was at least that smart. But he didn't go away. He started calling and texting even more. And I mean twenty, thirty times a day. While I was at work. At home. Everywhere. And I couldn't get him to stop. He just . . . . . it escalated from there."

She stopped abruptly, looked down at the shredded napkin in her hands. "Yeah. Well." She blew out a breath and began collecting her things. "That's enough sharing for one day. I don't want to think about it anymore. I'm sure you don't want to hear it anyway. And I need to get home. Want to make a plan for next week?"

He began to reach a hand across the table to her, pulled it back. "Right, next week. We're off to Christchurch, and it's a Saturday game, which means we won't be back till Sunday morning. Maybe we could go for a walk Sunday afternoon."

"You'll be tired, though, I'm sure. I know we said once a week, but if you'd rather come for a swim with me Wednesday morning next week instead, that might be easier."

"I was thinking about something easy, actually. Maybe North Head, in Devonport. Have you been there?"

"No, what is it?"

"Originally a Maori pa. Then a defensive outpost, guarding the harbor. Fun to explore. Beautiful views too, and a quick drive from here. We can take a walk, go for a coffee at the Naval Museum afterwards. What do you think?"

"Sounds fun. I'd like that."

"Right, then. Give me your address, and I'll pick you up. Two o'clock Sunday suit you?"

"How about if I meet you here instead?"

"You don't want me to know where you live, is that it?" he asked, brows raised.

"I learned that the hard way. Nothing against you. I just try to follow a set of safety rules now."

"You're going to have to give me your mobile number, all the same," he said. "I'll give you mine as well. Just in case something comes up."

"You're holding all the cards here anyway," he pointed out as she reluctantly complied. "All you have to do, if you don't like anything I do, is tell Hannah. Has Drew wrapped around her finger, eh. I do value my career—and my good looks. Wouldn't want either one spoilt."

"That's what she said. Not in so many words," Kate hurried on when Koti looked surprised. "Just that the players were probably the safest men around, for that reason."

"Met somebody braver than me, have you? Tell me who it is first, and I'll let you know if he's OK. And whether he has another girlfriend. Hannah isn't necessarily going to know about that."

"No, of course not." She frowned back at him. "I'm not interested in dating right now, let alone getting involved with anyone. I'm not exactly ready, in case you haven't noticed. Let's stop talking about my non-love life and get back to the topic. How about if I meet you at your house? I don't know exactly which one it is, though."

"How do I know you won't stalk me?" he protested. "I don't tell people where I live either."

"That's ridiculous."

"No more ridiculous than my stalking you."

"Back to Plan A, then. I'll meet you here," she decided. "Outside the café. Two o'clock."

"Right," he said with a sigh. "Bring a torch. For the tunnels," he explained at her confused look.

"Oh. A flashlight. All right. See you then."

Chapter 7

Kate slid into Koti's car with a groan the next week. "Something wrong?" he asked as he waited for her to fasten her seatbelt. "Fight something that bit back?"

"Very funny," she grumbled. "No, I took surfing lessons yesterday. And they were hard. I'm so sore today, I can hardly move."

"How'd you go, though?" he asked with interest.

"Terribly." She shook her head with a rueful grin. "I couldn't manage to stand up on the board, no matter how hard I tried. I fell off every single time, and had to swim to shore towing that useless surfboard. Then paddle back out to fall off again. It was exhausting."

"It's not easy to learn if you don't grow up doing it," he commiserated.

"Don't tell me. You know how to surf too."

"Course I know how to surf. You may not have noticed, but there isn't a lot to do in En Zed, other than spend time outdoors. Why do you think we invented all those extreme sports? Not just because we're strong and brave."

"Not to mention shy and retiring, in your case. Don't forget that. But I do wish I knew the secret of standing up on that board. It was pretty humbling. Everybody else managed at least once. The instructor was so nice and patient. Although I'm sure he went home and laughed about me. He told me to come back next weekend and he'd teach me again, even offered me a big discount on a private lesson. Clearly I'm a hopeless case."

He laughed. "No, that would be because he fancied you."

"How do you know? You weren't there."

"No worries. I didn't have to be there to know that. You look good in your togs. He wanted another look, that was all. And maybe a bit more."

"You're obviously very knowledgeable about these things. I defer to your expertise."

"May as well put my long experience of chatting girls up to use," he agreed. "Give you some insight."

"And here we are already, at North Head," he announced, as they pulled through the open gates and wound around the circular drive to the top of the hill. "Time flies when you're talking about sex."

"We weren't talking about sex," she said crossly as she grabbed her bag and got out of the car.

"Course we were. You just didn't realize it."

"Whatever. I'd like to know how you're hopping out of the car so easily, when I can barely drag myself out," she complained. "You're the one who played a rugby game last night. Why aren't you lying on the couch today?"

"I am a bit knackered, it's true. Spent some time in the spa this morning, once I got home. But walking's the best thing for sore muscles. It'll be good for you too."

"I'm sorry you lost last night. You played hard, though. I was impressed. Congratulations on your try."

"Thanks. Pity we didn't win. You watched, eh."

"I have to admit, I've been watching all the games. It's a lot more interesting now that I know you guys, even though I don't always understand what's going on. It seems so rough, though, with no padding. Aren't you bruised, after all those tackles? You hit the ground so hard. Not to mention the other guys slamming into you."

"Heaps of bruises under here," he grinned, gesturing toward his track pants and the ever-present hoodie. "Want to see?"

"And this would be flirting. Which is not allowed," she reminded him.

"Nah. You never said anything about flirting. Making a move isn't allowed. But I do my best flirting without touching."

"I'm changing the subject now," she decided. "Which path do we go on here?"

"We'll do the tunnels first. That's everybody's favorite."

"I can't believe these are open like this," Kate exclaimed as they walked cautiously through the first labyrinth, using their flashlights to navigate. "Aren't they afraid of somebody getting lost or hurt, and suing?"

"You can't sue here. Not allowed. That's what we have the ACC for."

"What's that?"

"Accident compensation. If you trip getting off the plane from the States, sprain your ankle, you're covered. All the way through to major injuries."

"So even if somebody's negligent, you can't sue them? That doesn't seem right."

"They can be prosecuted, still. But you won't get a payout, other than having your medical and time off work compensated. You don't get the big money you would in the States. But the lawyers don't take half of it either. Just another way of doing it."

"Seems to me," he went on, as they stepped out into the sunlight again, "that it makes life easier, all in all. When I've been to the States, I've been gobsmacked by all the rules, the signs everywhere telling you what you can't do. And the waiver forms you have to sign before you do anything at all. Here, we assume people can assess the risks for themselves, or for their own kids. Mind you, some Kiwis still think we're becoming too much of a nanny state."

"Really? How so? If they let people into these tunnels, I can't see how anyone could think that."

"You have to realize that New Zealand was settled by people far from anywhere, relying on themselves and their neighbors to get things done. True for Maori, and for the European settlers as well. We're normally pretty orderly. But we don't take kindly to being told what to do. Or what not to do."

"You know, you're more thoughtful than I realized," she told him as he came to a stop next to a gun emplacement looking out over the harbor. "Kind of surprising."

"Because a good-looking man can't have a brain. All show, no go. That's what you mean. Prejudge people much?"

She flushed. "I deserved that, I guess. I'd be angry if a man said that about a beautiful woman. Here I am, having to apologize again. Very uncomfortable. Put me out of my misery, please. Tell me what I'm looking at here."

"It's a defensive outpost. Has been from the beginning, when it was a Maori pa."

"What exactly is a pa?"

"A fortified village. They lived up here. You can still see the kumara storage pits—for sweet potatoes—dug into the volcanic craters around Auckland. All these green hills you see," he pointed to the horizon, "they're all volcanoes, and they were all pa. Because you always want to hold the high ground."

"And since Maori were always fighting each other," he told her with a smile, "that's important. Like Scottish castles. Always on the edge of the sea, or on top of a hill. Or both, like here. So you could see your enemy coming. And have food and water stored to withstand a siege."

"All right. And what about the guns and tunnels?"

"See what a view we have here? Not just across Waitemata Harbour, but out through the Hauraki Gulf, towards the Pacific. Only way for warships to get into Auckland."

"Was it ever used? New Zealand's never been attacked, has it?"

"Too far away from everywhere. And too small," he smiled ruefully. "Not of strategic importance to anyone. Story of our lives. Since World War II, it's been a reserve. A park. And the guns are only fired when royalty visits."

"It's a beautiful place, though. Can we walk to the top now?"

"And around by the beach too. This is one of my favorite spots," he confided. "One of the best views of the City and the Gulf. You can see so far out in every direction."

"You were right," Kate told him when they were sitting at the Naval Museum's café at the base of the hill after their walk, having another coffee together. "I'm feeling a little better now. Less stiff and sore. How about you?"

"Always good to take my mind off it, anyway," he agreed. "That's the best painkiller. Do something else and forget about it."

"This is such a beautiful spot anyway, the view of the water. This whole city is, for that matter."

"It is. Being from Cambridge, I appreciate it."

"That's inland, right?"

"Just a couple hours south," he nodded.

"But you still grew up being on the water a lot? How could that be?"

"Not very far away, is why. Raglan, one of our best surf beaches, is only about an hour out. Not that big a place, En Zed."

"I can't imagine being able to really surf," she sighed. "I had these visions of getting good at it. I wasn't expecting it to be so hard."

"Want to go out with me next weekend, then? Since you won't have to fight me off and all. You won't have to pay me either, in cash or otherwise."

"I'm still not sure you're right about that. He was probably just looking for another client. But you don't want to spend your time teaching me, do you? I don't know how much fun that'll be, if you're a good surfer. Which I'll bet you are."

"We need to have some kind of friend date. It may as well be surfing," he shrugged. "And I have a challenge now. Have to see if I can get you standing up on your board better than that worthless instructor."

"Where would we go? I'm not good enough to do anything hard, I warn you. For that matter, I'm not good enough to do anything easy yet."

"We'll check the conditions, find someplace where the surfing is good, but not too rough for you. Heaps of places to choose from around Auckland. You have all the West Coast beaches. Those are the real surf beaches, the famous ones you'll have heard of. They tend to be too wild for a beginner, though, so we'll miss those out for now. But the East Coast beaches, the side we're on here, are milder. Better when you're starting off."

"I'd like another chance to try. I didn't realize this bet came with surfing lessons," she told him with real gratitude. "Maybe you're better at this friend thing than I gave you credit for. And can I ask you one other favor?"

"What's that?"

"Will you explain to me about your tattoo, next time? I'd ask you to show me now, but I don't want to cause any heart attacks from you exposing your flesh in public, not with all these people around. I'd like to know, though. About the meaning of it and all. I've felt really bad about what I said the other week."

"I was offended at the time," he admitted. "But I realized what you meant after you explained."

"Your devastating gorgeousness overwhelming me," she clarified.

"Which you realize you've mentioned a fair few times now," he pointed out. "I thought I was the one meant to be obsessed with my looks."

"There they are, though, staring me in the face all the time. I have to get used to it, that's all. Maybe I need to buy a poster of you so I can desensitize myself. I'll bet there is one, isn't there? More than one, maybe."

"This is a boring subject. Are you ready to go?"

"If I'm going to buy my poster today, I'd better get in there before the stores close," she agreed.

Kate wasn't laughing, though, when she talked to her parents later that day.

"I hate to worry you," Isabel Lamonica told her. The video feed on Kate's computer screen showed her mother's own concern all too clearly. "But I think you ought to know that Paul called us. At least we're quite sure it was him."

"Oh no." The familiar sick dread dragged her down again. "I hoped he'd given up. What happened?"

"He called using another name and pretended to be your supervisor. He said you hadn't come in to work and weren't answering your phone. That he didn't have your home address, because you must have moved. And could I please give it to him so he could check on you."

"Obviously, we knew it was a fake," her father put in. "He was hoping we'd answer automatically, that we'd be worried about you. The good news is, he obviously doesn't know you've left the country."

"You didn't tell anyone else where you are, did you?" her mother asked anxiously. "I know how hard it was to disappear like that. But I'm not sure you can count on other people's secrecy."

"Don't worry. I didn't tell anyone. I figured if they don't know, they can't accidentally let it slip."

"But Mom," Kate burst out, "this is so hard. I'm stuck over here, cut out of my own life. Every time I think about it, I'm furious. And I don't know what to do with that."

"It can't last forever, though, can it?" her mother asked. "Surely, without any reinforcement, any reaction from you, this obsession has to end."

"That's what I've been told. But if he's still calling you . . . how am I going to know when it's safe to come back?"

"You should plan to stay a full year, anyway," her father counseled. "I know it seems like a long time right now, sweetheart. But we want you to be safe. If you need more money to do that, we'll help. You know you can count on us."

57

"Oh, Dad," Kate said, swallowing hard to keep from crying. "I miss you guys so much. It gets so hard to be strong, by myself." A few stubborn tears made their way out before she took a deep breath and got a grip on herself. She saw the distress on her parents' faces and hated being the cause of it. Resented everything they'd had to go through, worrying about her.

"Don't worry," she went on bracingly. "I have enough money. I'll be all right. I'm trying to see it as my long-delayed junior year abroad. It's a great place to live, anyway. If I'd come here of my own free will, I would have loved it, I'm sure."

"Honey, your dad and I were thinking, what if we came down there to see you? Surely we could do that without Paul knowing. How would he know where we went on vacation?"

"Because the neighbors would find out where you were going," Kate sighed. "I know it sounds far-fetched. But he scares me so much. If you don't hear anything for a few months, though, we could try that. It'd be something to look forward to. A beach Christmas, maybe. That'd be fun."

"We aren't going to do anything that puts you at risk, however remote," her father said firmly. "Your safety matters more to us than anything else. And I think that SOB is capable of anything. I'm so damn angry that I haven't been able to protect you from him. I'd like to go over there right now and put a stop to this."

"Dad. Whoa. Watch your temper," Kate cautioned. "It's not going to do me any good to have you get arrested. I'll get through this."

"You're being careful now, though, right?" her father insisted. "With men you meet there?"

"Don't worry. I've learned my lesson. And I'm not exactly interested in dating. The only men I even see are the players, and Hannah says I don't need to worry about them. They're under too much scrutiny to take that kind of risk."

"I don't think I want you dating a rugby player," her father said in alarm.

"Dad. I just told you, I'm not interested in dating," Kate answered patiently. "And they're not that bad," she surprised herself by adding. "More civilized than you'd expect."

She sat for a minute after ending the call, trying to sort out her tangled emotions. She was furious at Paul. How was it that he was the offender, yet she was the one deprived of her freedom to live where and how she wanted, while he suffered no consequences at all?

She ached to see her parents, her friends. Even to be in her tiny, less-than-fabulous apartment in her scruffy neighborhood. It was home. And this, however pleasant, wasn't. At first, it had been such a relief to get away, to be safe, that she hadn't cared. But now that she'd been here for a while, she was aware of her loneliness, her isolation from everything familiar. She debated calling Hannah. No, this was Drew's day off, and they'd be spending it together. She wished she knew more people. Maybe she should join a gym, take some classes instead of swimming alone all the time.

She'd invite Gretchen from Public Relations to lunch next week, she decided. Would make more of an effort in general. If she wanted friends, she'd have to go out and find them.

With shock, she realized why she hadn't felt as lonely as she'd expected in the past weeks. Because of the bet with Koti, she'd had at least one outing to count on every weekend, and had already started looking forward to their surfing date. This wasn't good. She definitely needed to make some more friends.

Chapter 8

"I'm not on the traveling squad?" Koti stared dumbly at Peter King, head coach of the All Blacks, the following Wednesday. "Why not?"

"Two fellas ahead of you who can play at 13," the coach explained. "We'll call you up if we need you, no worries. You'll be fit anyway, just those few weeks off."

"I'm playing as well as I was last year, though," Koti argued. "And I was on the squad every series then. What's changed?"

"A couple of the other boys have come up since then," King said. "And you know the selectors had to choose the players with the best form against a team like Wales."

"What's wrong with my form? You know I came back from England last season for the chance to play with the ABs. If I'm going to stay past this year, I need you to tell me what I have to do to be selected."

King sighed. "You're a good centre, Koti. You could even be a great one. But your workrate isn't where it should be. We've got to see you putting your head down, being consistent, if you want to be on the squad every time. You don't tick all the boxes, either. I don't see you tackling enough, or doing the ruckwork."

"That's not my skill, though," Koti objected. "Nobody's better than me at the offload. You know that. Not many faster, either."

"True enough, you get it done with the ball in hand. But I don't see you putting in the hard yards away from the ball. If you want to play in this code, and to be selected for every ABs series, you need to work harder, simple as that. And to make sure you're more focused on the team than on your own highlights."

It was useless to protest any more, Koti realized. Whatever he thought of the decision, it had been made. He turned and headed blindly to the locker room. After the game on Saturday, he'd be looking at three long weeks when the All Blacks were playing Wales. And he wasn't going to be any part of it.

He couldn't even go overseas, have a bit of a holiday. Nurse his wounds, he admitted. He'd still be here, training with the Blues.

"Just heard, cuz," Hemi said sympathetically as Koti entered the locker room. "You can't help bad luck. I'll miss you, though," he added, slapping the younger player on the shoulder.

Koti shook his head. "Not luck. It's my form. And I know, it's what you've tried to tell me. I still don't agree, though."

"Have a shower, get out of here," Hemi suggested. "Take some time, think it through. You never know when you'll be called up, anyway. Could still be playing in this series, for all you know."

"Nah. Not going to wish someone injured. Hope I'm enough of a team player for that."

He threw himself into practice with extra intensity during the next two days, and played as disciplined a game as he ever had that Saturday, wanting to show that the rejection hadn't affected his commitment to the Blues. Even a win over the Chiefs, though, aided by a try of his own, didn't help him shake his bad mood when he woke up on Sunday. It was too much to see the players selected for the All Black squad, and to contemplate watching the games himself on television.

He thought about canceling the surfing lesson with Kate. He wasn't going to be very good company today, especially after a hard game on only a few hours' sleep. But he had to get out of the house and do something. No sense sitting at home packing a sad. He'd get out on the water, forget about the team for a while. One thing was certain, he could count on Kate to give him stick, take his mind off his troubles. He had to admit, he enjoyed sharpening his wits against hers.

"Morning," she greeted him as he opened the car door outside the cafe. "I can't believe you made me meet you at six-thirty."

"If you'd let me collect you at your flat, you could've had a bit more sleep," he responded half-heartedly. "The best surf is in the early morning. Fewer swimmers too. You don't have the skill yet to stay out of their way."

"And thank you for pointing that out," she said tartly. Then looked at him more closely. "Are you too tired from last night? It's awfully early to be doing this, after your game. You played so hard."

"Nah. I needed to get out. Where's your kit?"

"Still in my car, over here."

"I haven't seen this car before, the RAV4. Nice," she told him as they transferred her gear.

"Good to have a four-wheel drive for the metal roads, plus towing and that." He strapped the longboard to the roof rack with his own. "Ready to go?"

"Is something wrong?" she asked as they set off. "I mean, I'm ready to start abusing you, but even I draw the line at torturing wounded animals. We don't have to do this, you know."

He groaned. "Is it that obvious?"

"Well, yes. The sparkle's a little dull this morning. Come on, tell me. What's wrong?"

"Not selected for the All Blacks for this series. The tests against Wales." No point in trying to keep it secret. She'd know soon enough.

"Really? But you played so well last night. And you played all last year, didn't you? What happened?"

He shrugged. "Selection isn't automatic, even if you've been on the team in the past. It's down to the selectors."

"Who are the selectors? You mean the coach?"

"The head coach is one. But there are three of them. They choose the team they think is strongest against the sides the ABs will be playing. And that didn't include me."

"Wow. I can see that's a big deal," she commiserated. "I'm sorry to hear that."

"Could you go back to being snarky now? Think I prefer you that way. Can't handle all this sympathy," he said, trying to make a joke of it. "I'll live. A bit of a rough time just now, that's all."

"I do know what that's like," she agreed. "Want me to distract you by telling me about my lousy week?"

"Let's hear it. It's a bit of a drive to Long Bay anyway."

"All right. First, I had the charming news that Paul—the guy who's been stalking me—had contacted my parents, trying to get my address from them."

"What?" he frowned. "They didn't tell him, did they?"

"No fear of that. But it means he's still out there trying. I'd have thought he'd have given up by now. Since, as you keep reminding me, I'm not exactly Soulmate material."

"Never said that," he objected. "Just that you're snarky." He grinned across at her. "Reckon some men like that. Keeps them on their toes."

"Well, I'll have to keep my eyes open for that rare breed. But meanwhile, it means I'm still cut off from all my friends and family, other than my parents. Because I can't trust anybody else to keep my whereabouts a secret. Nobody would mean to tell him, I'm sure. But he's pretty clever, and very plausible. He'd get it out of somebody, if they knew."

"You mean you came here without telling anyone?" he asked in amazement. "Other than your parents? And you haven't talked to anyone from back home since?"

"Nope." She shook her head. "That's one reason I'm so nasty. Cabin fever. Or friend fever, whatever you get when you're too isolated."

"Is this fella really that dangerous? That you have to go this far to escape him?"

"Yes," she said soberly. "He really is. But I don't want to get into that now. I'm supposed to be entertaining you. And that isn't entertaining, trust me. OK, next item. So there I was, all depressed on Sunday night. No family, no friends."

"Except me," he pointed out.

"Of course. You. How could I forget. No friends without an agenda, I mean. So I thought, I need to make some new friends, right?"

"Right. And?"

"I invited one of the women in the office to have lunch with me, because I liked her. And I decided I needed to make more of an effort to get to know people. The only person I know is Hannah. And she's pretty busy with her own life, the baby coming so soon and everything. I can't count on her to be my social life."

"So you invited somebody to lunch. Where's the disaster here?" he prompted.

"Apparently, although she's a very nice woman, she's also a lesbian. And she thought I was looking to experiment."

"What?" she protested at his shout of laughter. "It was so embarrassing, trying to explain. I felt like a total fool. I guess I came on pretty strong, the way I invited her out, told her I wanted to get to know her better, and of course she thought it meant something different. I think New Zealanders move more slowly than Americans. Plus I have no Gaydar," she added with a sigh.

"Reckon you're stuck with me," he grinned as he pulled into a carpark in the immense Long Bay Regional Park.

"Great," she said gloomily. "My only friend."

"Who's also a bloody good surfing instructor," he reminded her, unstrapping their boards from the Toyota.

"Aren't we going into the water?" she asked, surprised, when she emerged from the changing room with her wetsuit on to find him waiting on the beach, their boards laid out before him.

"Going to practice your technique first."

"Ummm . . . how do I practice that on the sand?"

"By listening to me, first thing. I'm the instructor, remember?"

"Right. Sorry. So what do I do?"

"Show me how you lie on the board." He stretched out on his own board next to her. "You're paddling out. Show me how you do that."

"Alternate arms," he corrected her. "Get too tired, otherwise. And now you've paddled to where you see the wave about to break. You want to stand up on your board. What do you do?"

"It's your pop-up technique," he decided as he watched her. "There's your trouble. Let me show you."

Under his surprisingly patient tutelage, she practiced pushing up on her board, then moving her feet underneath her in one smooth move, crouching low and then standing, arms outstretched.

"This seems better," she admitted twenty minutes later. "Much less awkward. Isn't it?"

"You're doing awesome," he assured her. "Now we go out in the water, try it there."

She still fell off, the first five times she tried. Over and over, she paddled her board under his guidance to the point where the wave would break. Pushed up, used her arms and her core muscles to bring her feet underneath her. And fell off, landing in the surf with her board trailing behind her like a leashed dog.

"Am I ever going to get this?" she sighed after the fifth failed attempt, hauling herself with difficulty back onto the board to paddle out beyond the break once again.

"You are. You're doing better. Try again."

Once more, she paddled. Pushed up. Concentrated as hard as she could on pulling her feet up under her in one fluid motion. And found herself crouching on her board.

"I did it!" she shouted. And promptly fell off again.

She heard the sound of his laughter behind her as she climbed back on her board near shore.

"Good on ya," he encouraged her as he paddled up. "Next time, though, instead of telling me, try standing up a bit. Not all the way up. Stay low. Then you'll be surfing."

For the seventh time that morning, she paddled out, shoulders already aching, beyond the break. Pushed up. Jumped her feet forward. Crouched. Rose. And surfed.

It was just a tiny wave, and it didn't take long to reach the shore. But she felt as though she'd just surfed the Breakers in Hawaii. She dropped back down to her board in triumph and turned to face the ocean, and Koti paddling up to her with a grin. "I did it! I surfed! I can't believe it!"

"Not so tired now, are you?" he teased.

"No! I want to go do it again!" she laughed.

She practiced again and again until she was rising more often than she was falling. Finally, her shoulders announced that they were done for the day.

"I'm beat," she told Koti as she finished yet another run. "I'm going to go take a shower and change. Why don't you go ahead and do some surfing on your own? I know it's not too exciting for you here, but take your time."

"I'll do that. Make sure you get rugged up, though. Once you stop working so hard, and you're out there in the wind, you'll get chilled."

Back on the beach, she sat on a picnic table and hugged her arms around her drawn-up knees, pulled her jacket more closely around her, and enjoyed watching Koti surf. It was hard to begrudge him being so effortlessly good at it, so ridiculously coordinated, when he had been so gracious with his time in helping her learn.

And he was good at it. Watching that lean form, all that muscular grace crouching and weaving as he sliced through the water, was a pure pleasure. She might have to buy that poster after all. Or just spend more time watching him. Because whether he was running with the ball, surfing, or swimming, he looked so good.

He stepped out of the water at last, his surfboard under his arm, and came up the beach to her.

"Don't sit on the table," he said with a frown.

"What? Why not?" she asked, confused, stepping down and checking its surface. "Is it dirty?"

"Nah. But it's not done, in Maoritanga. Bums and food don't mix, for obvious reasons. And it's one of those customs that's crossed over. Bad form even to lean against a desk here."

"Sorry. I didn't know." She flushed. "I've never heard that. I hope I haven't done it too much."

"That's why I thought I should tell you, because you wouldn't know. I was shocked, first time I went overseas. I remember seeing a TV advert, a kid sitting on a kitchen bench. My roomie and I stared at each other, couldn't believe it. Sometimes we don't realize what a small country we are, how few people share our own customs."

"A bench, though? Why would that be bad? Are there special rules?"

"Bench. Where you prepare the food. The work surface," he explained.

"Oh. The light dawns. The kitchen counter. Yeah, I can see if you had a rule about that, sitting on the counter would really be out of line. Anything else like that I should know? You're making me paranoid here."

"Only one I can think of like that is, don't sit on a pillow. Because the head is tapu. Sacred. Same idea. Bums and heads."

"Thanks. I'll remember those."

"No worries. Let me take a shower and get changed, and we'll go have lunch. There's a good café here. It's my shout."

"You're not buying me my whole lunch. We're just taking turns on the coffee."

"Right, then. We'll decide it a different way. We'll do it proportionally, by income. And what d'you reckon, I'm still buying."

She had to laugh. "All right, big spender. My turn next time, though. I'm hungry enough not to want to spend time arguing about it."

"You eat pretty well for such a little person," he observed after they got their meals, watching her begin to put away a large sandwich.

"Hummingbird metabolism," she agreed. "And Italian tastes. Good combination."

"Long as you don't get fat later."

"Never happen. My mom looks just like me. And there's that deadly charm again, talking about my getting fat."

"I don't know what it is," he sighed. "It's dangerous for me to start being honest with a woman, maybe. Losing my touch. But that's your coloring, eh. Italian."

"That's it. That's the temper, too," she grinned. "Southern Italian. Less than half, but it seems to be enough."

"I'm not much more than half Maori myself," he said. "And I agree, that's enough."

"That's what the tattoo is, right? Maori. Which I know almost nothing about. Will you tell me? We're fairly sheltered here. I can block the glare of your beauty from your eager public."

He rolled his eyes, but pulled up his sleeve obligingly to reveal the intricate design that covered his skin like a sleeve from forearm to shoulder. "It's a bit like a family tree, you could say. It represents my whakapapa—my ancestors, genealogy, from the bottom to the top. Here are my parents, my sisters"—he pointed to his upper arm—"and my own journey, on the shoulder. Everything on a ta moko has a meaning. Luckily, though, it's all done with regular inked tattooing now. It used to be done with chisels, on the face, the buttocks, the thighs. And it was scarring, not just inking."

"Ouch," Kate winced. "I don't even want to think about that."

"Tell me about your pendant," she continued, when she could drag her eyes away from the sculpted muscles of his arm, the curving designs following their shape. "It has a meaning too, right?"

"It's greenstone—pounamu. New Zealand jade. There are different shapes with different meanings, but you'll see that most Maori wear them. Mine's a Hei Toki—an adze blade. A symbol of strength and control. My uncle gave it to me when I went away to University, to remind me how to behave, I suppose."

"Why's it all so important? I don't quite understand that."

"Because Maori was an oral language. Nothing written down, in the beginning. Which means our culture's been carried on by songs and legends over the years. Symbols, too. That's why you'll see the same symbols used everywhere. Maori moko all have the curving shapes, for example, that you see on mine. That's the koru—the fiddlehead of the fern. Look around, and you'll see that all over. It symbolizes new life, new beginnings, the changes in life. But all the symbols represent our connection to Maoritanga and our ancestors. Which means if you disrespect them, you're disrespecting our mana—our spiritual power. And it matters. You need to be careful."

"Wow. I'm lucky you're still talking to me, I guess, after I said what I did. This is me apologizing again now. I really didn't mean any disrespect. It's just that you're like some kind of walking fantasy."

"Getting into deep waters again," he smiled. "Can't keep you out of trouble for a minute."

"Thanks for today," he told her as he drove them back to Takapuna. "It helped."

"Me too. Like I said, a pretty lousy week, though not as bad as yours. What's the plan next week?"

"Since I won't be playing," he said with a grimace, "I have more free time. Want to try surfing again on Saturday morning?"

"My shoulders might have recovered by then. They're awfully sore right now."

"Want a massage?" he grinned.

"No, thanks, Mr. Irresistible. I'll settle for a bath."

"Can I watch?"

"No!" she laughed. "You really are terrible. Besides, I'm not your type, remember?"

"I may be changing my mind," he mused.

"Oh, please," she scoffed. "Hannah's your dream girl. I haven't forgotten that. In case you haven't noticed, I'm nothing like her. In looks or personality. Not to mention that I'm more than a foot shorter than you are, which would be impossible."

"Impossible? How? Interesting, maybe. Because there are ways around that," he said, with another sideways grin. "I'll give it some thought. Maybe you should, too."

Kate resolutely put aside the image that conjured up. "We are not having this discussion," she told him firmly. "Unless you want to wear that pink hoodie. Let's make a plan for Saturday."

"Unless you have a date with your new girlfriend."

"Don't remind me," she groaned. "You're more likely to have a date with yours, anyway."

"Don't have one. I'm not dating anyone just now."

"Excuse me? What about that woman a few weeks ago? When I was running," she clarified as he looked blank.

"Oh." He shrugged. "Not a girlfriend. Just a . . . an acquaintance."

"Right," she said dryly. "Gotcha. Not dating anyone, just . . . acquainting yourself. If anyone's extra-cute, that is."

"It happens," he agreed cheerfully. "When I don't have a girlfriend. But not just anyone. I've been a footballer a fair few years now. Got that out of my system a while ago."

"And that's a tasteful image too." She shook her head. "I'm changing the subject once again. I seem to do that a lot. How many years have you been playing?"

"Professionally? This is my fifth. For the Chiefs in Hamilton, the first year. Then I went to England for two years. For the money, mostly. I missed New Zealand, though. My family, my mates, the sea. The land, for that matter. Everything, really. And I wanted to be an All Black. Wanted that most of all. So I came back. This is my second season with the Blues."

"And next time," he told her, pulling into the carpark again and helping her shift her gear to her own car, "we're talking about you. Don't know why I always end up giving you an earbashing."

"Because you're not so focused on doing other things, is why. I'll bet you don't normally sit around talking to women."

"I could do both," he argued. "I can multitask."

"I don't think so. I've seen where your mind goes, the minute I give it a chance. See you next week, then."

He was grinning again as he drove away, the image of her smile staying with him. He found himself trying to make her laugh these days, just to see her face light up like that. She made him laugh too, though. He didn't know why she amused him so much. That outsized feistiness, maybe, and the fierce resolve she had shown today during their surfing lesson, packed into that tiny body. Packed in so well, too. Even in a wetsuit, he liked looking at her. Everything might be small, but she was so curvy. That tiny waist got him, every time. He was beginning to be obsessed with putting his hands around it.

What would it feel like to be inside all that fizzing life force? One way or another, he decided, he was going to find out. She might pretend she wasn't interested, but he hadn't missed how her gaze had lingered on his arm when he was showing her his tattoo. He had to admit, he was enjoying being her friend more than he'd thought possible. But he had a feeling he was going to enjoy being her lover even more.

Chapter 9

Kate looked out the office window and swore to herself. No question, winter had arrived, now that they were into June. She'd been told that the city received a lot of rain, but she hadn't fully grasped what that meant. The sun still shone fairly often, but rain appeared for at least part of most days as well. And it wasn't just rain. This part of the country was so narrow, only a few kilometers wide, that it sometimes felt more like being on a ship at sea than living on dry land. Especially at times like this, when they were being battered by a gale sweeping up from Antarctica. The walk to the bus stop wasn't looking a bit attractive right now.

By the time she had left the building and run a block towards her stop, her hair was soaked, the cold rain dribbling down her neck. What a day to have forgotten her umbrella. She swore again as a car drove through a puddle next to the curb, splashing her boots with water. The car pulled in ahead of her, taillights glowing in the evening dusk. She belatedly recognized the sporty model even as she saw Koti stepping out of the driver's side.

"Get in. I'll give you a lift," he called.

Gratefully, she climbed in out of the driving rain. Ah, heated leather seats. That was better.

"Pissing down out there," he commiserated. "Better bring your umbrella tomorrow."

"Thank you for the tip, Captain Obvious. I'm planning on it."

He laughed. "You could say, thanks for the lift. On your way home?"

"I was contemplating taking in a gallery opening, seeing as I'm looking so lovely. Maybe the ballet later."

"You are a mess," he agreed. "How about going down to Quay Street with me first, though? We could have a beer."

"I don't know," she hesitated. "I'm pretty wet, and it's been a long day."

"All the more reason," he told her firmly. "You could have another go at me. You'd enjoy that, I know. To tell the truth, I could use the company myself tonight. You're always a good distraction."

"Well, if it's charity work," she conceded, "I suppose I could let you buy me a beer."

The drive on the motorway into Auckland's central business district was slow and congested in the driving rain, and Kate was thankful not to be shivering on the bus. Finally, though, Koti pulled into a carpark across from a historic building on the waterfront.

"This is a pretty good brewpub," he explained as he held the huge entry door open for her. "Comfortable on a rainy night. We could have tea as well. I'm hungry. And since I've seen you eat, I'll bet you are too."

"Nice to know my reputation as a delicate flower is safe with you," she told him when he came back from the bar with two beers in hand, their orders for cheeseburgers and chips placed. "I suppose I should have ordered a salad."

"No, why? I hate it when I take a girl out and she won't eat. Like I'll appreciate how feminine she is, with her tiny appetite. More likely to think she's anorexic, aren't I."

"It might be different if you dated normal women. And all right," she conceded as he looked at her with an inquiring grin, "maybe I have Googled you by now. A bunch of tall, skinny, interchangeable blondes, from what I saw."

"In a bit of a rut, you think? You may be right about that. Time for me to broaden my horizons, eh."

"Yeah, I can see that happening. But if I'm not going to ruin your reputation completely, I'm going to have to make myself look a little more presentable." She felt her damp hair, which she could tell was clinging unattractively to her scalp. "Be right back."

Coming out of the stall in the ladies' room, Kate was forced to detour around a stunning woman with the tall, lean proportions of a model. Leaning against the counter, her endless legs in tight dark jeans and high heels stretched out in front of her, she was taking up far too much space in the cramped quarters. The top of her spectacular cleavage escaped a purple chiffon top, while long, curling red hair framed strong cheekbones and a pair of green eyes that were looking at Kate with barely concealed hostility.

"Hello." Kate nodded and washed her hands. She turned for a paper towel and found her way blocked once again. What was this woman's problem? "Excuse me, please," she said, trying to contain her exasperation.

"Who are you?" the redhead challenged. "And what are you doing out with Koti?"

"Having dinner," Kate answered shortly. She didn't feel like getting involved in a confrontation, but she wasn't about to back down from some Amazon with an attitude problem either.

"Did he tell you he already has a girlfriend? Forgot to mention me, did he?"

Kate sighed. "We're just friends. Nothing for you to worry about."

The redhead swept Kate with a contemptuous gaze from head to toe. With anger and jealousy twisting her face, she didn't look quite so lovely. "Yeh, right. Don't have much to offer anyway, do you? Can't imagine you'll last more than a night."

Kate's hackles rose. She hadn't done anything wrong, and she wasn't going to cower in the face of hostility she didn't deserve, even if this woman had a good eight inches on her. "If he's really attached to you, his being friends with me can't be anything for you to worry about. And if he isn't, that doesn't have anything to do with me, I assure you. I'm afraid

I'll have to let you two work that out. Now if you'll excuse me, I need to get back to my dinner."

Kate could see the wheels turning as the redhead tried to puzzle out what she had said. And the moment when she finally gave it up and focused on her mission, announcing, "I think you should leave. Now."

Kate stared at her. "Are you crazy? I just told you, I'm having dinner with a friend. What are you going to do, scratch my eyes out? Are we going to have a fight in the bathroom over a guy? Are we in the eighth grade here?"

"He can make a choice, then," the redhead decided. "Right now."

"Oh, for heaven's sake," Kate sighed. "This is ridiculous. I'm not interested in being part of your little story, whatever it is. Look. I'll hang out here for five minutes. You go right ahead. Go on out there and have your say, if that's what you want. Take him home and make wild love to him, make sure he never goes anywhere without you again. If he's gone when I come out, I'll take the bus home."

"Go on," she urged as the woman hesitated. "Go for it. No skin off my nose."

Precisely five minutes later, she made her way back to the table. Koti was standing with the redhead at his side, her hand on his arm. Kate's heart sank. He was leaving with her. She'd have given him credit for better taste, anyway. Surely that was why she felt so dismayed at the prospect.

"Kate." Koti looked relieved. "I was ready to send in the search dogs. Dena says you've met."

"Yes, I've had the pleasure of Dena's acquaintance, though I didn't catch her name."

Koti turned back to Dena with a barely polite smile. "Thanks for stopping by to say hello. See you, then."

Dena scowled. Opened her mouth to say something, thought better of it, shut it again. She glared at Koti in mute fury, then stalked away on her high heels, male heads turning to watch her exit. Even angry, she was a magnificent sight, Kate had to admit.

"Where were you?" Koti demanded. "How could you leave me defenseless like that?"

"What?" Kate stared at him. "That woman practically accused me of being a homewrecker. I thought I was breaking up the romance of the century, coming between the two of you."

"In her dreams," Koti said shortly.

"Oh, boy. Now I have entertainment." Kate sat down and looked at him expectantly, picking up her cheeseburger from the plate that had arrived in her absence. It was a bit cold, but she found she didn't care. "And there I was, waiting in the ladies' room all this time for her to have her big love scene," she complained. "What did I miss?"

"You didn't miss anything," he grumbled, sitting down across from her at last and picking up his own burger. He watched as she took an enthusiastic bite. "Except her trying to make out I'd promised her something, and having a hissy fit."

"Who is she?" Kate pressed when she'd finished chewing. "If she isn't your girlfriend, she's delusional. And I find that hard to believe."

He shrugged. "I've taken her out from time to time. Which means her photo's turned up in the paper. Reckon that's what she doesn't want to lose. She's a model. The publicity's been good for her career."

"Clearly she thought there was something more to it than that. She wasn't happy at all about my being here. In fact, she was ready to fight me for you. I half expected her to jump me."

He started to laugh. "A catfight in the ladies' toilet. Sweet as. Wish I could've seen that. I'd have put my money on you, every time."

"Yeah, well, you know what they say. It's not the size of the dog in the fight, it's the size of the fight in the dog. She might have a few inches on me, but I'm tougher."

"I know you are," he grinned. "Soon as she broke a nail, that'd be the end of it. While you'd be hanging on like a pit bull till the bitter end, teeth stuck in her arm."

"Huh. Sorry to disappoint you, but I'm not ready to do battle over you yet. I told her to come on out here and give it her best shot, if she was so sure you two were an item. I half expected you to have left with her."

"No worries. Not happening. And that's quite an opinion you have of me, that I'd leave you stranded here to go off with another woman."

She frowned. "I'm not sure you understand this, Koti. But you and I are not dating. Those rules don't apply."

"You're not some mate that I can leave because I pulled in the pub. Still a woman, aren't you. I wouldn't do that."

"That's not necessary, but I appreciate the concern. I have to tell you, though, I don't think she's going to be available next time you call. That is one seriously pissed-off model."

"That's good, because I'm not going to be calling," he said firmly. "It's over."

It was true, he thought with some surprise. He'd enjoyed going out with Dena, had appreciated the picture they made together, her striking looks setting off his own. The sex hadn't been bad either, though it hadn't been anything earthshaking. But he'd never wanted to take it any further than that. Not that she'd ever evidenced much desire to get to know him better either. It was no loss to see the back of her, beautiful as she was. And the scene she'd made had been truly embarrassing. He'd never been so glad to see Kate. Although he still wished he could have seen the fight. He had a feeling it would have been spectacular.

Chapter 10

The amusement Kate had provided, though, was short-lived. By the next day, Koti had worked himself into a thoroughly bad mood again. Going to practice felt pointless with the next Blues game almost three weeks away. He had the uncomfortable feeling that he was training with the second string, with the All Blacks on the squad practicing at other facilities.

He needed some diversion, he decided. He'd go talk to Kate. With any luck, she'd get into a slanging match with him again, take his mind off things. He wasn't pleased, entering the back office, to see Kevin McNicholl standing by her desk. Practice was over. The young wing should have been out of the building by now, not here wasting Kate's time.

"How ya goin', Kate." Koti stopped in front of her desk. "Kevvie," he nodded. "What are you doing here?"

"Having a chat," the other man told him, his open, good-humored face hardening in unmistakable challenge.

"Can I do something for you, Koti?" Kate asked him.

Koti scowled at both of them. "I was just going to talk to you about Saturday."

"Koti's giving me surfing lessons," Kate explained to Kevin. "I'll meet you at the café, same as last time, OK?" she told Koti. "What time did you want to start?"

"Uh . . ." He stopped, at a loss. Looked at the two of them. Kevin folded his arms across his chest and stared back. He clearly wasn't going anywhere.

"I'll text you, let you know," Koti finally managed.

"All right," Kate answered cheerfully. "See you later, then."

As Koti turned and left, Kate couldn't help laughing a little to herself. Who would have thought she'd have two rugby players vying for her company? Koti was so obviously disgruntled and put out. It was good for him not to be the center of attention all the time, she decided as she turned back to Kevin. She was sure it was a novel experience for him.

But when Koti started in on the subject almost as soon as she'd hopped into his car on Saturday morning, she quickly found herself becoming less amused by his attitude.

"Why was Kevvie there, Thursday?" he asked her abruptly as he pulled out of the carpark onto the main road, in the middle of her question about surfing in today's windy conditions.

"Why do you think? He was asking me out. Apparently not every man in Auckland thinks I'm carrying hoof and mouth disease. I suppose I'd better take you up on that offer." She couldn't resist needling him a little. "To give me the lowdown on the players. Anything I should know about? Does he have any bombshell girlfriends who are going to confront me in the ladies' room? Should I watch out for a surprise attack from his wife and three children?"

"You shouldn't go out with him at all," he said with a scowl. "He's not right for you."

"Got a bad temper, huh," she mused. "Hmmm, maybe he'll insult me. That *would* hurt my feelings. But you know, I think I'll risk it. He seemed pretty nice."

"Damn it, Kate. I don't think you should be dating any of those boys. You don't know what they're like."

"I'll know better if I date them, won't I?" she answered reasonably. "Face it, Koti. You're just a dog in the manger. You don't want me for yourself, but the idea of my being seen with somebody else hurts your male pride. Let me remind you once again. I'm not your girlfriend. You don't have any say over who I date."

"Who said I didn't want you?" he objected.

"And, um, that would be . . . you," she reminded him. "Too nasty, too small, too dark, too aggressive . . ." she counted off on her fingers. "What did I miss?"

"I pointed a few things out, eh. A few personality flaws. That doesn't mean I don't like you. So are you seeing him, or not?" he demanded.

Suddenly, she was done with this. It had been funny at first, but he was starting to annoy her. "I'm not your property, Koti, and I don't owe you any explanations. Drop it, OK?"

"I told you about Dena. I explained that situation. Friends tell each other things."

"Not this. Not if you're going to be such a jerk about it."

"I need to know, though. To . . . to make sure you're safe."

"I've had enough male possessiveness for two lifetimes. We don't have a relationship, and your jealousy is totally out of line. Drop it."

"That's a bit harsh," he protested. "I'm not jealous. Concerned for you, that's all."

"Well, you can stop being concerned. We're done with this discussion. In fact, I'm done, period," she decided. "Take me back to my car, please."

"What? We're going surfing."

"No, we're not." She saw the bus stop coming up in the next block and realized she wanted to be out of this, right now. "Pull over."

"What? You're getting out of the car? Why? You're mad as a meat axe," he spluttered. "You want to go back so badly, no worries, I'll take you. You're not my favorite person just now either, you know."

"Pull. Over," she told him with absolute conviction, in a fierce tone he'd never heard from her before. Startled, he obeyed, to find her grabbing her bag and opening the door to get out of the car.

"You can take my gear back to the shop. Serve you right," she told him, slamming the door behind her with a resounding *thunk*.

Koti sat, stunned. Heard the blast of the bus's horn as the driver saw him parked in the bus stop, and pulled reflexively out into the street again, out of the way. What was he supposed to do now? This was rubbish. She'd completely overreacted to his perfectly reasonable concern for her safety. Right, then. He'd go surfing by himself. It'd be better anyway, without having to worry about looking after her.

He only lasted an hour, though. Somehow, it wasn't as satisfying as he'd expected. He'd been looking forward to seeing how she went on the board today after the previous week's lesson. He was starting to feel less comfortable with the way he had behaved as well. Now that he'd cooled off, he could see that he'd been a bit out of line. He still didn't like the idea of her going out with Kevin. But he probably shouldn't have told her so.

The next morning, he swallowed his pride and rang her. He'd thought about taking the coward's way out and texting, but he had the feeling that wasn't going to do the trick.

"Hello, Mr. Personality," he heard on the other end when she picked up. "You'd better be calling to apologize."

"Reckon I should be glad you're still taking my calls," he sighed. "How much do I have to grovel here? Can we admit I was a drongo and move on?"

"Maybe. If I look that up and it sounds sufficiently bad."

"I rang to ask if you'd forgive me, maybe wanted to try surfing again. I missed you yesterday. Want to watch you fall off some more."

"Oh, good try. You're really making points. Didn't you take my stuff back, though?"

"Nah. And before you start laying into me, I'll take it back later today, pay for the extra day's hire too. My fault. I know that. So you'll come out with me?"

"I will. But the only reason I'm willing to give you another chance is that I figured out why you were in such a bad mood yesterday. I'll bet it didn't improve last night, did it?"

"It was pretty dire, watching the game," he admitted. "You're right, I need distraction from my troubles. Can I pop round in an hour, give you a lift from your place?"

"You're crazy if you think I'm telling you where I live after that display," she told him firmly. "I'll meet you at the café, same as always."

After they had surfed themselves into chilled, happy fatigue and were sitting in a café over yet another coffee, Kate broached the subject she knew was uppermost in his mind.

"So I watched the game last night. I don't have much commentary, though, since I'm the least-knowledgeable rugby spectator in New Zealand. Other than too bad the All Blacks lost."

Koti smiled a bit painfully. "Should have had you over to watch with me. Maybe I'd have got some amusement value out of it, anyway."

"Yeah, I could have provided that. But hey, at least they do the best part at the beginning, get things off to a good start before I get lost. The haka," she explained at his questioning look. "I'd heard of it. But actually seeing it gave me chills. That's some fierce stuff."

"I hate to be sexist, but I think that's every woman's favorite bit of a test match. Something about all that rampant testosterone. The challenge, intimidating your opponent. Reckon women are genetically programmed to enjoy that."

"Really? I thought it was because so many of the players are good-looking, and those shorts you guys wear are so . . . short. All those thighs."

"What? I couldn't help but notice," she protested at his grin. "But here's what I was wondering. Doesn't it bother you to have all those non-Maori players performing that kind of traditional ritual?"

"Nah. The haka's been done by the All Blacks since the beginning. More than a hundred years now. And there've always been Maori boys on the team."

"No segregated teams in your past?"

He shook his head. "As well as the Maori and Pakeha, the Europeans, you have all the Islander boys. Samoan, Tongan. Because they're big and strong, like me," he said with a smile at her predictable eye-roll. "But the haka's one of the things that pulls us together, identifies us as New Zealanders, whether we're Maori or not, and no matter how long ago our families came here," he went on more seriously. "The All Blacks, that's the same thing. It's more than just a rugby team."

"I noticed. That's hard to miss."

"Our national religion. That's what they say," he acknowledged. "Not to say everyone in the country loves rugby. But that's what the kids grow up playing. And the All Blacks . . . that's the ultimate rugby, isn't it. Most successful national rugby team in the world, down the years. About the only thing we're world-famous in. We don't get much time on the world stage, so we appreciate it. If you're a Kiwi and you don't support the All Blacks—well, I wouldn't bring it up in the pub. And ask almost any boy in En Zed what he'd like to be when he grows up. He'll tell you, an All Black."

He shifted in his seat, and Kate felt a rush of compassion for him. "Hard to watch last night, I'll bet."

He nodded. "I could see where my opportunities would have been. I could've made that try in the twentieth minute. I was wild, not being there."

"What exactly did they say? Why weren't you selected?"

She listened to his reluctant account, then nodded. "So you need to improve those skills. Tackling and ruckwork. I barely know what that is, but it's basically going after the ball, right? Sort of getting down and dirty? Sounds like they're saying you need to do the less glamorous parts, be more of a team player. Like you're coming across as a glory hog."

He winced, but had to agree. "Yeh. That I need to pay attention to other things besides carrying the ball and offloading. Passing," he clarified. "Fair enough. Those are my skills, though. And I'm pretty flash at them. That's what I don't understand."

"But it seems like they're saying you need more than that to be the complete package. What are you going to do about it?"

"Dunno," he said glumly. "I could just go back to where I'm appreciated. Not sure it makes sense to try to change now, especially if I don't know whether I'll succeed. Could bust a gut for nothing. That doesn't make sense."

"Is there anyone you can ask for advice? Anyone you trust?"

"I could talk to Hemi," he admitted reluctantly. "Reckon he'd be willing."

"Which you don't want to do," she guessed, "because you'd have to admit that you need help. That you're not as perfect as your fan club thinks you are."

He scowled. "I don't think as much of myself as all that. Don't believe everything I read about myself either. But it's not easy to ask. Because Hemi's told me before that I need to work on my form. And I'd be saying he was right."

"He already knows that, though. He knows you haven't been selected, and why. Why would he think less of you if you asked him for advice now? It seems to me he'd think more of you for showing that kind of humility. And you could do it. You did it today, after all. That was a fairly good apology. And I'm a hard judge."

"I knew if I didn't, you'd be well and truly gone. I could see I only had one chance to get it right."

"You teach people how to treat you. Somebody told me that once, and it stuck," she explained. "It's been working pretty well for me, with one glaring exception."

"And you apologized so well, and refrained so beautifully from questioning me today, that I'm going to give you a big present and tell you something that will make you happy," she added, deciding he needed a laugh.

"What's that?" he asked, perking up noticeably.

"I did go out with Kevin last night, and it was pretty much a disaster. Because he's too nice for me. Isn't that a terrible thing to have to admit?" Kate started to laugh in spite of herself. "I thought he'd be the perfect person for me to ease back into dating with. I mean, nobody could call him dangerous, right? Clearly one of the world's good guys. Too good for me, I guess. Because I was censoring myself all evening, trying not to shock him. Clearly he'd bought into the whole cute, little, sweet thing. I could tell it was never going to work. I'd chew him up and spit him out."

"Bet you told him so, too," he said, starting to grin.

"I did," she smiled back. "I told him thanks very much, he was a great guy, but I thought I had too many sharp edges for him. I could tell he was relieved, though he was much too nice to say so."

"And here's the truly terrible thing," she confessed. "The whole time we were together, I was thinking about what you'd say. How you'd laugh if you could have seen us."

"I'm laughing just thinking about it," he agreed. "Never mind. When you pack that much explosive power into a small package, it takes a specialist to handle it. Kevvie's a good bloke, but he was out of his depth with you, I reckon."

"Oh, because you're so good at it," she shot back.

"Still standing, aren't I," he challenged. "Despite your many attempts to cut me down to size."

"I'll have to try harder, I guess."

"Oh no," he groaned. "Forget I said that. Not sure I can handle you trying any harder."

Chapter 11

Kate wasn't surprised to find Koti waiting for her when she arrived at the beach on Wednesday morning. He knew her swim days now, and had taken to joining her once or twice a week. She had to admit that it gave her a lift when he appeared. She sensed that he needed the company too, the distraction from his own thoughts. Swimming through the waves in the frequently cold, windy conditions was a challenge that required focus. She always felt better when she finished, even if she hadn't particularly enjoyed the swim, and she thought he did too.

Rinsing off afterwards was never very pleasant, though. Struggling out of a clammy wetsuit in the early-morning chill wasn't much fun at the best of times. And today her suit seemed to be fighting back. She worked to pull down the stubborn zipper, twisting her arm to increase her leverage. "Stupid thing," she muttered.

"Here." She felt the tug as his hand closed on the tapes and began to pull down, his other hand against her shoulder. She stiffened, then slapped his arm away and twisted out of his grip.

"Not a good idea. I think we've established that I need to set some boundaries here. This belongs to me. Hands off."

"Sure about that? Seems to me, if it's bothering you so much, you're beginning to wonder. I know I am."

"Koti." She turned around to face him. "Get this straight. We are not dating. We're friends, that's all."

"Oh, we're dating," he assured her. "Not having sex, maybe. But what do you call all this time we're spending together? And you're thinking about it as much as I am, I can tell. You jump every time I touch you. I've seen you checking me out, too."

"Yeah, but that's practically my civic duty, isn't it? Every woman in New Zealand has checked you out. Doesn't mean a thing. Anyway, you can't pretend you're really all that interested in me, no matter how much you like to tease me about it. I'm not your type, remember?"

She returned with a show of unconcern to working her way out of her wetsuit. Took her time pulling her towel around herself, unwilling to show him that she was affected by his scrutiny or the nearness of his half-naked body, looking much too good with his own wetsuit peeled down to his waist, acres of brown skin and sculpted muscle on display.

He groaned. "When are you going to forget I said that? And yeh, I'm interested. I'm bloody interested. Think about it all the time, don't I. I'm losing sleep here, thinking about it."

"Well, you can just stop thinking about it," she snapped, gathering up her wet things. "Because it's not going to happen."

Even as she said it, she realized that it was past time to address this directly. All this flirting was getting out of hand. Every time he made one of his suggestive comments, touched her hand, she felt her own pulse jump, felt the urge to move closer. To stroke his arm, his shoulder, just to see what his skin felt like under her hands. Started wondering what it would feel like to have that arm go around her waist, to be held against him. To kiss him, and have him kiss her back. She needed to set things straight right now, for both their sakes.

She took a deep breath and began. "Here's the way it is. Believe me, nobody's more surprised by this than I am, but I enjoy spending time with you. You're actually good company. And yes, you're a treat to look at too. I like you, and I'm attracted to you. But I'm not interested in being one in a long line of women you've slept with, or in having our friendship get awkward. And you know it would. When I do get into a relationship again, I want it to mean more than that."

"Why would it be awkward? Why wouldn't it be better?" he protested. "I know it'd be fun, anyway."

"See? That's it. That's why," she tried to explain. "I'm not interested in recreational sex, or some kind of friends-with-benefits thing, and that's all you do. Well, maybe I'm interested in it, technically, but I'm not doing it. I know myself, and I know it wouldn't work. So I'm not going there with you. And if that means you don't want to spend time with me anymore once sex is off the table, well, that's what the bet was about, wasn't it? I guess you lose."

"I don't give a toss about the bloody bet," he said in exasperation. "Be glad to say I lost. I'm ready to lose here and now. Just say the word. And how do you know what I do or don't do? I'm not interested in recreational sex with you either, if that means we have a quick root from time to time. I want more than that from you. I'm not seeing anyone else just now, if that's what you're worried about. And I like you too. Should have my head examined, but I do."

"This is hard," she said, shivering in the cold. "I'm wondering why it seemed like a good idea to have this conversation. But I don't think it'd work. We'd have at least two strikes against us already. I'm not really ready for any relationship yet. And I'm sure not ready to take on somebody with as much baggage as you have."

"What baggage? And you're freezing. Let's walk up so you can get changed. Can't hear what you're saying if your teeth are chattering, can I."

"Your checkered romantic history," she explained as they moved toward the changing rooms. "I know something about risk analysis, and you're a lousy risk. Not to mention trying to have a relationship with a pinup, some kind of female fantasy. Like all those poor guys who married Marilyn Monroe. I'd say that would make me the poster child for Women Who Choose Badly. As if I weren't already."

"I'm not a pinup, or a fantasy either," he objected. "Just a man. What do you want me to do, get ugly so you feel more comfortable?"

She sighed. "I don't want you to do anything, Koti. You're fine. Great, in fact. Just be my friend, OK? Go find another model to date. Call me gutless, but I'm not secure enough to go out with you. And you're right, I'm freezing, and I have to get to work. See you later."

She ducked into the changing room. Running away, she thought guiltily. She hoped she had cleared the air, though. Selfishly, she didn't want to stop seeing him. All right, maybe her hands longed to touch the spectacular body he uncovered every time he pulled off his wetsuit. Maybe she had impure thoughts about him at night, even the occasional dream she tried not to think about later. Not too much, anyway. But that didn't mean she had to act on her feelings. She'd had enough complications in her life for one year. She didn't need to add to them. She'd just put those thoughts out of her mind, that was all. She could be rational about this. Surely she could.

Koti stalked back to his car in frustrated impotence. Pulled off his wetsuit with jerky motions and threw it into the boot with unnecessary violence. Wrapped his towel around himself, started the car, and turned the heater up. Then sat and stared into space, not going anywhere.

Damn, she frustrated him. Her curvy, athletic little body, her golden skin, her shining dark hair all seemed to have been made just for him, inviting him to slide his hands over her. And all that prickly honesty, her quick mind, her fierce independence only added to the fascination. He'd been fantasizing for weeks about having her in bed. Or out of it. When he watched her pull off her wetsuit, he wanted to keep going, to pull her togs off her too, hold her against him to warm her, feel her wrap those small, lithe arms and legs around him.

Most of all, he wanted to be inside her, feel the heat of her energy surrounding him. It would be so easy, he thought, to slip inside. She was so small, he could hold her there, move her over him. He'd thought about it so much, it was as if he'd already done it. Only he hadn't. And it looked like he'd never get the chance.

He groaned and rested his head on the steering wheel. He was in trouble. He hadn't felt this randy for a woman he couldn't have since he was fourteen. Since he'd been passionately in love with Miss Johnston, his maths teacher. He'd walked around for months in a state of perpetual arousal, unable to concentrate on anything else. And this wasn't any better. Worse, because he had a fair idea now what it would feel like, with Kate.

Get a grip, boy, he told himself. He should call somebody else. He could do it, he knew. Even Dena. Despite what Kate believed, Koti was fairly certain that he could get Dena back if he wanted her. The problem was, he didn't want her, or anyone else. He wanted Kate.

He put the car into gear at last and pulled out of the carpark. She still wanted to be friends, anyway. He'd take advantage of that. He knew she was bloody interested too. He had too much experience not to know when a woman was aware of him, attracted to him. He'd have to keep trying, that was all. She hadn't told him to go away, after all. That had to be a good sign.

"Right, then," he told her the next day on the phone. "How about doing something with other people, reduce the chances of our jumping each other?"

"Sounds like a good idea," she agreed cautiously. "What did you have in mind?"

"Want to go blackwater rafting with me, down at Waitomo?"

"Blackwater rafting? How is that different from whitewater rafting? Is this some kind of only-in-New-Zealand thing again?"

"Yeh. Exactly. Cave exploration as an adrenaline sport. Sweet as. A bit scary maybe, but you'll be well looked after. All guided. The full tiki tour."

"I've made a rule now, not to back down from anything. And I'm not claustrophobic, so cave exploration sounds fun. What does it involve?"

"We'll drive a couple hours south, spend a few hours jumping around in a cave. All you need is your togs and a towel. Saturday suit you?"

"No, sorry," she said reluctantly. "I have plans."

"What . . ." he started. "Right. Not asking. How about Sunday?"

"Good job not asking," she said approvingly. He didn't need to know that her plans involved her work colleagues. Let him think it was a date. "Sunday's fine. What time?"

"The tour's about five hours. I could pick you up about seven-thirty. That way we could get something to eat on the way, still get there well before eleven. Won't be back till evening, though. You may want to rethink your principles, let me pick you up at home this time. I promise to forget your address straight away."

"All right," she conceded. "It's starting to feel a little silly. Whatever I might say, I know you're safe." Despite that, dictating her address felt like a big step.

"Brilliant. Safe," he said gloomily. "See you at seven-thirty Sunday, anyway. Good as gold."

Chapter 12

"I've never done karaoke," Kate told her three coworkers nervously as they entered the lively Japanese restaurant on Saturday night. "I don't have a great voice, either. Do I have to sing?"

"Not unless you want to," Corinne grinned. "But somehow, after a few drinks, I always want to. The boys look hotter and my voice sounds better when I've got beer goggles on."

"On that note," Heather suggested, "first bottle of wine is my shout. It'll be easier after that."

How she had missed this, Kate thought as she sipped from her glass of Sauvignon Blanc and listened to the women's lively chat. She'd almost forgotten what it was like to go out with a group of women, to be silly and laugh until she cried.

The karaoke portion of the evening was kicked off by a young man in skin-tight jeans and a bright yellow Dinosaur Comics T-shirt with the slogan, "Feelings are boring. Kissing is awesome." His blond hair tumbling over his forehead, he performed an over-the-top rendition of 'Billie Jean' that had the whole crowd laughing and clapping along.

"That was awesome. Come on, then. Who else wants to have a go? Don't be shy," the DJ urged.

"What the hell." Brenda finished her wine and hopped up on stage. To Kate's envy, she had a brassy, confident delivery that made up for whatever her voice lacked, as she belted out "Stand By Your Man" to an enthusiastic audience. Several others followed her example. The DJ was quick to turn down the volume when it was kinder, but the crowd good-naturedly applauded even the feebler attempts.

"Should I try?" Kate asked after another glass of wine.

"Definitely." Corinne encouraged. "It's just us. We won't remember anything tomorrow anyway."

"Just don't do 'I Will Survive,'" Heather counseled. "Most overdone karaoke song ever."

"Whoops. Thanks for the tip. Because that was my choice. OK, I'll try 'Mamma Mia.' Loud and fast. That's the ticket. Wish me luck."

A few bars in, though, and she was losing her confidence. What was she doing up here? She couldn't sing. The DJ began turning down the volume as she floundered, and Kate looked around in wild panic. The young man who'd sung first, seeing her distress, jumped back on stage, put his arm around her, and began to sing along. Kate laughed aloud and joined in with relief. Soon, caught up in the moment, she was dancing with him as well. If Pierce Brosnan could risk his dignity by singing the way he had in that movie, so could she, especially with help like this.

After their big finish, she threw her arms around her new friend and gave him a hug that he enthusiastically returned, adding a smacking kiss that had her grinning as she left the stage to whoops from the audience.

"I don't know who that was," Kate told the group as she came back to the table, flushed and laughing, "but he saved my life."

"Have another glass of wine," Brenda told her as she poured. "You earned it. And now that we have you well and truly on your way, you can tell us what the story is with you and Koti. Come on. Spill."

"You're bad, Brenda," Corinne chided. "The rest of us have been too polite to ask. But now that Brenda's come out with it, we're all dying to know."

"Gosh. Maybe I should make something up, then. Something exciting for you. Just friends, though. Sorry."

"How did *that* happen, though?" Corinne asked. "Somehow I can't picture him walking up to a woman and saying, "Oi. Wanna be my friend tonight?"

Kate laughed along with the others. "Nope. Probably not. We both live in Takapuna, though, so we'd see each other at the beach. And we both like to swim, so . . ." She shrugged. She'd never told anyone about their bet, and she wasn't going to start now.

"You *swim* with him?" Brenda asked, fanning herself with her hand. "Oh, my God. So hot. Mental picture here. You've seen him in his togs, and you haven't jumped him? How can you resist that? Don't you just want to lick him all over?"

All four of them dissolved in laughter. "Great image," Kate told her. "Thanks. That's super helpful. You bet, he looks hot in a swimsuit. I can't say I don't enjoy that part. But I'm an accountant. We're cautious types. We have to weigh all our options first, make a careful decision."

"Well, I'm a publicist. I'd weigh my options, then make a careful decision to lick him all over," Brenda announced, making everyone laugh again.

"I don't know," Corinne commented. "Setting aside what a bad risk he is, not sure I'd want to date anyone prettier than me, or who spent more time grooming than I do."

"Not actually true." Kate found herself coming to Koti's defense. "I mean, yeah, of course he knows he's good-looking. It'd be hard for him not to, wouldn't it? But he isn't really stuck on himself. It's not like he's looking in the mirror fixing his hair all the time."

"Right, then," Heather said. "One objection accounted for. So why *haven't* you jumped his bones?"

"Well, for one thing, I've never liked the idea of dating someone I worked with, or even worked close to. Because then there they are, aren't they? All big and awkward, if it doesn't work out. As we all know."

"Hmm. Big maybe. Not so awkward," Heather objected. "I'd take that risk, for that bit of fun. Except I have a partner," she sighed regretfully. "He wouldn't be too keen. But theoretically."

"And you're not here forever, right?" Corinne asked. "This is just until that boofhead who was stalking you gives up, then you're going back home, eh. Which makes it a bit of an OE for you."

"An OE?"

"Overseas Experience," Heather clarified. "Didn't you do that, after Uni? Kiwis like to go abroad for a year or two when they're young, see the world before they settle down."

"And everyone knows," Brenda went on, "that you get to have all those experiences—those *special* experiences—on your OE. What happens in Vegas stays in Vegas."

"Hmm." Kate took another sip of wine, "I never had one of those. Something to keep in mind."

"We'd have to hate you, though," Brenda pointed out. "Nah. Doesn't matter," she decided. "You should go for it anyway."

"We'd have to hate her more, though," Heather reminded Brenda. "Because she's American. It's one thing to see a Kiwi girl date a player. Even if she's someone in the office. Which does happen." The other women nodded in agreement. "But I'll tell you, your friend Hannah wasn't very popular, snaffling up Drew like that."

"We'd all like to hate her," Brenda said. "Except she's so bloody nice, you can't. How did she catch him, do you know? I've never heard the story."

"I don't know much either. Sorry again," Kate told them. "I'm not a very good source of gossip, am I? But from what little I've heard, if there was any catching going on, it was the other way around. Was that actually a big deal?"

The other women traded glances and laughed again. "You could say that," Corinne answered. "The women of New Zealand had a pity party for weeks over it. And if you pinch Koti from us too . . ." She shook her head. "Reckon there'll be some changes to the visa program."

"Well, don't worry," Kate assured them. "He's a surprisingly nice guy. But I'm not planning on sleeping with him, so it's not going to be an issue. The tall blonde models of the world can go for it."

"There was a redhead, too, right?" Heather asked. "Are they still an item?"

Kate laughed. "Nope. Looks like that one's over. And she wasn't too happy about it," she went on mischievously, the wine loosening her tongue. "I was there."

"Tell," Corinne demanded. As Kate recounted the story, the women hooted.

"It's terrible of me to think it's funny," Kate finished, wiping her eyes. "But she was such a bitch, I couldn't help it. Not to mention, I could have taken her," she added confidently. "Except the last thing Koti needs is to watch women fighting over him. I don't think he really has as big an ego as people think. But he doesn't need to grow it any more, let's put it that way."

"Rightyo, then," Brenda decided. "If he's available, next time he comes into the office, I'm having a chat. If you don't mind, that is."

Kate found herself brought up short. She didn't like the idea at all, actually. But if she and Koti were just friends, their love lives were their own business. She hadn't liked it when he'd puffed up at the thought of Kevin taking her out. And she couldn't have it both ways.

"Of course, if you want to," she said finally.

"Hmm," Brenda looked at her thoughtfully. "That took a bit. Sure about that?"

Kate groaned and put her head in her hands. "I hope it's just too much wine. I don't seem to be thinking straight. But I'm not going out with the guy. If you want to, you should go ahead. Don't mind me."

Seven-thirty came much too early the next morning. "You're not looking too flash," Koti observed when a bleary-eyed Kate answered the door at his ring. "Out on the razzle last night? Or maybe just out late with the coven. A bit enthusiastic with the broomsticks, eh."

"You think you're funny, but you're not," Kate scowled as she eased herself gingerly into his car. "You're right, though. I did have a late night. And a drink or two too many. Why does that always seem like such a good idea at the time?"

He grinned. "A question for the ages."

"Why do you look so cheerful, anyway?" she grumbled. "You're supposed to be the hard-living rugby player. How come you're always so annoyingly bright-eyed in the early morning?"

"Because I don't drink too much," he said piously. "What?" he protested at her derisive snort. "I'm in training. I don't give up completely like a few of the boys, but I don't have more than a beer or two at a time during the season. Whatever you think, I do take my career seriously."

"I'm too tired even to argue with you properly," she sighed. "I hate to fall behind on points here, but you're going to have to give me a pass till next time."

"Fair enough. Why don't you go to sleep? We'll stop for brekkie on the way. I'll wake you up, no worries."

By the time they arrived outside the tiny town of Waitomo and entered the rafting company's headquarters, Kate was feeling better. Even though she'd protested that she wasn't hungry, the eggs, toast, and coffee Koti had insisted she order at their earlier stop had helped settle her stomach and wake her up.

"What a surprise. The tour office is also a café. Is there anything you can do in New Zealand that doesn't involve a stop for coffee?" Kate wondered. "How can everyone be so laid-back, when you're all running on espresso fumes?"

"Because we only drink one at a time, and they're small. When I've been in the States, they keep coming around and refilling your cup. First time, reckon I'd drunk five cups before I realized. I don't think I shut my eyes that night."

"You might have something there," she admitted. "And now that my head's a little clearer, tell me what I owe you for this tour we're doing."

"My shout," he told her firmly. "I invited you, didn't I. Invite me next time, and I'll avert my eyes while you pay, I promise."

"Too late," he said cheerfully when she began to protest. "They're calling us. Time to go."

Chapter 13

As the group got themselves into wetsuits and gumboots, the ubiquitous footwear of muddy New Zealand, Kate was disheartened to notice some elbowing and whispering going on. Although their two guides obviously knew who Koti was, they weren't making a fuss. And the Canadians and Japanese in the group were happily oblivious. But the three young Australians weren't so restrained, and it soon became apparent that they weren't content to let the occasion go unremarked.

"Mind giving us your autograph, mate?" one of the young men asked as they climbed into the van that would take them to the cave. "My sister's dead keen on you."

The woman with him added, "How about a photo with me too? My mates will all be jealous when I tell them you were on our tour. I'm Liz, by the way." She turned from her seat in the row ahead and smiled at Koti invitingly.

"We don't want to hold up the tour. Maybe Koti will have time to sign for you afterwards," Kate told the young Aussie, deliberately avoiding looking at his girlfriend. "But personally, I want to get started."

"Got my watchdog here," Koti explained with a grin. "I have to do what she says, eh. She bites."

Once the van reached the caves, to Kate's relief, the guides were good-humoredly efficient in getting the group outfitted with harnesses and explaining their gear, and the subject was dropped.

"Want to start us off with the abseil, Koti?" Jessica, one of their two guides, had stayed at the top to launch them, while Ben had descended into the cave to await them below.

"Thirty-five meters to the bottom. Scream if you get scared, and we'll rescue you."

He stepped willingly into the dark hole leading down into the cave, letting out the rope to descend into the abyss. There wasn't any screaming, but Kate did hear a few choice words.

"Pretty narrow for those shoulders in a spot or two," Jessica explained. "He'll be giving himself a bit of a shove through."

She didn't seem concerned. "Doesn't anyone ever get stuck?" Kate asked. "You must get some clients who are a little . . . rotund."

Jessica laughed. "Too right. The Americans tend to be surprised that it's not easier. Reckon they expect Disneyland."

Kate was exhilarated to find herself descending at last in her turn into the dark. She, at least, had no problem getting through the narrow spots. But when Jessica selected her to be the first to whiz across a deep expanse of cave on a Flying Fox, she couldn't help a flash of alarm. "Doesn't somebody else want to be first?" she asked nervously.

"Piking out again?" Koti murmured in her ear.

"No." She glared in his direction in the dark and screwed up her courage. "OK, I'm ready," she told Jessica resolutely. But when she grabbed the handles, she had second thoughts.

"Wait," she started to say. But it was too late. Suddenly, she was flying on the long zip line, through the darkness and across the gaping space beneath. A scream escaped her as she flew and landed with a *whump* against the tires at the other end.

Koti was across next, putting his legs out to bounce off the tires with ease. "Think you screamed loud enough? Reckon they heard you in the next cave." The light from her headlamp illuminated his annoying grin as he joined her to wait for the others.

"Shut up," she muttered. "I went, didn't I?"

When she found herself jumping, inner tube held to her backside, ten feet down into an underground river, Kate was determined not to scream again. A loud squeak made its way out despite her best efforts as she hit the frigid water and fought to settle herself into her tube and grab the ropes lining the cavern to keep herself from floating downstream.

"Mice in this cave," came the voice from behind her.

"Your new girlfriend's braver than I am," she told him crossly. "She likes you better, too. Why don't you paddle on down and bother her instead?"

She heard his snort of laughter and decided her best bet was a dignified silence. She soon forgot about him, though, as they lined up at the direction of their guides, each person's feet on the tube of the caver in front of him. Then turned off their headlamps to see at first a few, then whole constellations of bright lights appearing on the cave ceiling overhead.

"These points of light you're seeing are glowworms. Actually, the larvae of a fly, only found in New Zealand," Ben's voice came echoing back to her. "They shine a light out their backsides to attract insects. And they're the reason so many thousands of tourists visit the Waitomo Caves every year."

Kate had to agree. If she hadn't known, she would have thought she was looking at an expanse of clear night sky, full of stars. The sensation was disorienting, her sense of space confused by the resemblance.

"And what we do down here," Ben went on, "since the acoustics are so choice, is have a bit of a sing. As it's a Maori cave, we sing a Maori song. And as we have a Maori with us today, we'll ask him to sing it."

Kate cringed. Did they really have to put Koti on the spot like that? Surely he couldn't want to sing, not in front of everybody.

To her surprise, Koti spoke up readily. "I could do *Homai o Ringa,* if you like."

The hair rose on the back of Kate's neck as he began to sing. The haunting melody filled the space around them, rose to the rocky ceiling above, merged with the sound of the rushing water. Even the chatty Australians were quiet for a moment as the last slow note died out, until the entire group burst into spontaneous applause.

"Sweet as," Jessica said approvingly from behind them. "Thanks."

"That was so beautiful," Kate told him quietly. "So moving too, even though I didn't understand it. What was it about?"

"It's a lament. A love song as well. Asking for comfort when you're sad."

"What do the words say, though? Can you translate?"

"Something like this. Extend your hands to hold my beating heart. Whisper words of love to lift up my grieving spirit. Give me peace, love me, embrace me. Give me a tranquil place to shelter on my . . . my difficult journey."

She shivered. "No wonder, then, that it affected me like that. The words are beautiful. But the melody was so sad. I had no idea you could sing like that. Or that you'd be willing to. You surprised me."

"It's what we do. We sing for everything. Weddings. Gatherings. Tangi—funerals, especially. And everything in between."

"Never met a Maori yet who couldn't sing," Ben's voice came back cheerfully. "Or who wasn't willing to, at the drop of a hat."

"I can't imagine asking some random person in the U.S. to sing in front of a group of strangers," Kate said. "Not without a whole lot of alcohol, anyway."

"To be fair, though," Koti told her, "most Pakeha—kids, anyway—can sing some of the Maori songs as well. Bet you can, Jessica, if you're singing down here every day."

"A few," Jessica agreed. "The standard ones. Not like that. We usually don't venture much beyond *Pokarekare Ana*. You gave us something special today."

"What's Poke . . . what she said?" Kate asked Koti as they leaned back to look at the glowworm stars shining brightly overhead.

"Another love song. You're bound to hear it soon enough, the first time you go to a Maori concert. It's lovely, just a bit overexposed by now."

"Maybe you'll sing it for me sometime," she suggested, still feeling overwhelmed by the beauty of his voice singing of grief and love, the sight of the constellations of lights against the blackness, the sound of the river. "Because I really, really liked that."

She was relieved when they came to a landing spot and shed their tubes, shaking her out of her softened mood. The adrenaline-infused aspect of their day returned with a scramble through the darkness down the now-shallow river, followed by a final climb up a waterfall that had her heart pumping with fear as well as exertion. When they finally emerged into the light again, hours after they had descended, she was shivering with cold and fatigue even in the thick wetsuit.

"Get in back. Less conversation," Koti murmured in her ear as they climbed into the van for the short return trip. Kate sank gratefully into the back corner of the large vehicle. She didn't even have the energy to tease Koti, much less take on aggressive Australians.

"You're freezing," he frowned as he saw her shaking. "Don't get stroppy, but I need to warm you up a bit."

She couldn't help pressing closer as he put both arms around her and pulled her against him, rubbing his hands vigorously over her back and arms to get her blood circulating again. She was so cold, she was past caring whether this was a good idea. His comforting solidity warmed her even through their wetsuits. And being held against him, she admitted to herself, felt as good as she'd always thought it would. The envious look she intercepted from Liz, the Australian blonde, didn't hurt either. The young woman had been doing her best to chat Koti up all day, her unfortunate boyfriend clearly relegated to second place.

Kate knew it wasn't very nice of her, but she couldn't suppress a flash of triumph. Eat your heart out, Blondie, she thought as Koti's hands moved over her and she pressed into him. Hope you enjoyed your tour, because that's the only one you're getting today. No close-up of the famous tattoo for you.

"Got you a cup of tea," Koti told her when she joined the group at a table back in the café, where bowls of soup were set out as well to warm them after their long spell underground.

Kate sipped the hot drink gratefully. "That was a wonderful experience. But it sure was chilly. I probably used up their entire hot water supply, I stood under the shower so long. The heat felt so good. How about you? Weren't you cold?"

Koti looked at her for a long moment. "Nah," he smiled down at her at last. "Not as tiny as you, am I."

"Mate. Can I get that autograph now?" one of the Australians was asking. Kate gave herself a mental shake. This was getting way too cozy. Jessica came to sit beside her as Koti was drawn into more autograph signing and picture-taking with the rest of their group. The Canadian and Japanese tourists, Kate was amused to see, were getting in on the action too.

"Would you mind taking a photo of me with him as well?" the guide asked, following the direction of Kate's gaze. "That'll be one for my Facebook page. It's gone down a treat with the group, having him along."

"Even the ones who didn't know who he was," Kate said wryly.

"Reckon he's worth having a look at anyway," Jessica agreed cheerfully.

Kate had to laugh. It was true, after all. And Jessica's honest appreciation was easier to take than the aggressive attentions of the buxom Liz, who was currently draping herself over Koti for a photo.

Jessica correctly interpreted Kate's frown. "Bit rough for you, dating someone that popular with the girls," she commiserated.

"Oh, no," Kate hastened to explain as Koti finally disengaged himself and came back to join them. "We're just friends."

"*Good* friends," he corrected, sliding into a seat opposite her and offering his brilliant smile. But somehow, the patented dazzle seemed different now. Felt personal, meant for her alone. Seeing it, something in her began to soften in response. She felt a smile of her own growing as she looked into his brown eyes, saw the warmth and appreciation in them.

Jessica cleared her throat. "Yeh, right. I can see that."

Kate brought her attention back with a start. "Koti, Jessica wants her picture taken with you too. Can you manage one more?"

"Long as we can have a real feed afterwards. Can't risk you chewing on my arm on the trip home."

When their substantial dinner had been followed by a dash through the pelting rain an hour later, Kate was glad to be inside the car again.

"Put the seat warmer on," Koti urged as he started the engine. "You're still cold, I can tell."

"I got too chilled on the tour," she admitted. "I haven't been able to warm up all the way, no matter what I've done."

"Here, put on my jumper," he offered, pulling it over his head. "That should help."

The wool was still warm from his body. Still carried his smell too, she realized, clean and just a little musky. She breathed in the scent and snuggled into the soft merino more deeply.

"Warm enough now?" he asked a few minutes later. At her murmured assent, he couldn't resist adding, "You might not have got so cold if you hadn't wasted all that energy screaming like a girl."

"Oh, well," she answered lazily, relaxed and drowsy now in the warmth of the car, the smell of him around her, the hypnotic slap of the windshield wipers. "I *am* a girl."

He laughed. "I've noticed. I've been impressed, though, at everything you're willing to try. Don't back down easily even when you're scared, do you?"

"I made a promise to myself that I wouldn't anymore. I've had my fill of giving in to fear. I need to go ahead and do the things that frighten me." It was easier to be honest, here in the dark intimacy of the car. "I know I need to get stronger. So I've started seeing somebody. A therapist. Talking to her about what happened. And that's one of the things that's come out of it. If I don't want to be scared all the time anymore, I have to accept the challenges. Beat the fear. Just like strength training for my body, I suppose. Working against resistance."

He nodded. "I can see that. Good on ya. What else would you try? Skydiving? Bungy jumping?"

"Very scary," she admitted with a sigh. "I'd have to work up to those. But I won't rule them out."

"Still turning down some challenges, though," he pointed out. "Still turning me down, eh."

"I'm willing to take reasonable risks. But not stupid ones. I won't go skydiving without a parachute, either."

"Could feel a bit like that, I'm starting to think. Freefalling," he said softly.

The words hung in the air between them. Kate found herself grateful again for the darkness. She struggled to come up with a sharp response, but for once, nothing came to mind. Wrapped in the warm cocoon of the oversized sweater, looking across at his profile, the strong bones and sensuous mouth visible in the glow of the dashboard lights, she had an overwhelming urge to move closer, feel his solidity and warmth beneath her hands again, the way she had in the van. It had felt so good, being wrapped in his arms. Whatever she tried to tell herself, she wanted to feel that way again.

As if responding to the charged atmosphere, the music playing in the car changed, a soft, slow reggae beat filling the air. Kate shook her head, tried to shake off the sudden intimacy that had sent a rush of heat through her.

"We need to change this song," she said unsteadily. "This isn't helping."

Koti shot a look at her in the darkness. "That's Bob Marley. A classic. You don't like it?"

"I don't need to hear him singing about giving me some good loving," she admitted. "This was too good a day for me. And you're being too nice. The singing, too. All that must have lowered my defenses. I need to remind myself of your less admirable qualities. Could you please tease me again?"

"I'd be glad to tease you. Be willing to do it all night. It's all I've been thinking about. All I want to do. Just say the word."

Kate found herself shifting in her seat as the heat, the thrill shot through her again. She had to get hold of herself. This was too dangerous. The rain, the music, his words. He was just flirting, she knew. But she was much too susceptible right now. She picked up his iPod and deliberately advanced the music. *Go away, Bob Marley,* she thought crossly. *Go titillate somebody else.*

"That's better," she sighed as an upbeat number began playing.

Koti cleared his throat. "How much longer do you think we can avoid this? It's getting hard for me."

"I don't know," she said. "The friends thing isn't working very well, is it? But could we not talk about it anymore right now? I'm confused."

"Makes two of us," he muttered. "Confused. Bothered. Randy as hell."

She laughed a little in rueful agreement, but didn't answer. They sat in silence, the music soft and slow again now as the wipers continued their rhythmic slap. The warmth and the darkness gradually lulled her into sleepiness, her late night and adventurous day beginning to catch up with her.

The third time she jerked awake, Koti told her with a sigh, "Go on and go to sleep. You don't need to keep your wits about you any more tonight, I promise. I'll wake you when we get close."

"Would you sing me that song?" she asked drowsily. "The one you were talking about. I really want to hear it. Please?"

"*Pokarekare Ana?* I don't mind." He turned off the music system. Settled back in his seat. Kate turned to watch him as he began to sing, his voice soft but true. She sighed as she listened to the sweet, simple melody, snuggling into the leather seatback and pulling the warm sweater more closely around her. She was safe here, she realized as she drifted off to the sound of his voice. Safe and warm. It was all right.

"Kate." She pulled herself up, out of layers of sleep, at the sound of his familiar voice. "We're here," he told her, reaching behind him to pull her bag from the back seat.

"You didn't forget my address, then," she mumbled as he came around to help her out of the car. Still clumsy with sleep, she was grateful for his arm around her. At least the rain had stopped.

"Good thing." He smiled down at her. "Thought I was going to have to carry you in. You were pretty far down."

She retrieved her keys from her bag, shivering again as they ascended the stairs to her first-floor flat. "Thanks." She turned at her door. "For letting me sleep. And for the day. It was wonderful."

"And it's ending even better, because I get to ask you to undress now. My jumper," he pointed out. "Unless you want me to get it from you at the office this week."

"Oh." She fumbled with the sweater in embarrassment. "Right. 'Here are your clothes back.' That'd get the grapevine going." She wrestled the oversized garment off at last and handed it back to him. "Thanks again."

"Bonus. Smells like you now," he commented as he pulled it over his own head. She flushed to realize she'd had the same thought.

"Go inside before you freeze." He leaned forward and kissed her gently. "See you for a swim Wednesday. Unless it's raining too hard."

Her hand on the open door, Kate turned and watched him walk back to his car. She could still feel the tingling warmth of his mouth against hers. He'd rushed away so fast. Yet earlier, in the car, he'd sounded serious. Which was it? Was he playing a game, or was he really as attracted to her as she was to him?

She shrugged at last in frustrated confusion and closed the door. She didn't know what was going on in his mind, and it didn't matter anyway. Because no matter how attracted she was, she wasn't prepared for a relationship with him. When it was time, she intended to start small. And Koti James, it was blindingly clear, played in the major leagues.

Chapter 14

"You look so tired," Kate told Hannah a few days later. "When are you planning to stop working?"

When Hannah had called to suggest lunch, Kate had jumped at the chance to catch up. Seeing her friend for the first time in several weeks, though, she couldn't help being concerned. Other than her belly, its contours clearly visible in a slim-cut tunic and leggings, Hannah didn't seem any heavier than she'd been when Kate had first known her. More fragile, if anything. And though she'd made an effort, makeup couldn't disguise the shadows beneath her eyes.

"You sound like Drew," Hannah said now, sighing and easing herself into a more comfortable position. "I'm fine. Just a little tired. And before you ask, yes, the baby's growing, and the midwife says I'm all right. I'm not one of those women who gain a lot of weight when they're pregnant, I guess. Eating and sleeping are a little tough right now, that's all."

"So why are you still working?" Kate pressed.

"I'm only doing half days now. That's why I could give myself a treat and meet you. I'll be stopping altogether after tomorrow. And then I'm not going back for a year, can you believe that?"

"You get that much maternity leave?" Kate asked with shock.

Hannah nodded. "Isn't it amazing? Only about three months is paid. But it'll be wonderful to be able to spend almost the entire first year with the baby, not have to worry about going back while he's little."

"I'm surprised you've worked this long, then. Wouldn't you be better off resting at home?"

"Thanks, Mom. Don't start. I've felt better working, half days anyway, than sitting at home waiting. But I already lost this argument. Did I tell you Drew's mum is coming up to stay next week? Just in case the baby starts arriving when he's not around. And, I suspect, to 'take care' of me." Hannah made air quotes with her hands and grimaced.

"Hope you like her. That's a lot of closeness. I'll admit, though, I'm glad to hear you won't be alone. Drew's in Christchurch, isn't he? I heard the All Blacks left this morning. I'm surprised he left you, the way you look."

Hannah groaned. "Don't tell him that. He'd agree with you. But he'll be back on Sunday. He'll only be gone three days, and I'm not due for weeks. It would have been ridiculous for him to stay home."

"Let me know if you need me for anything," Kate pressed. "Even if it's just company, or distraction. You know I'll be there for you. You've done so much for me."

"Thanks. I will. But Kate, I wanted to have lunch with you for another reason as well. Other than being nagged. Because I don't get nearly enough of that at home."

"I have some news that might be upsetting," Hannah continued more seriously, putting a hand on her friend's arm. "Not too bad, though, I hope."

Kate set down her fork, the familiar icy fingers of dread curling through her. "Paul," she said flatly.

"I'm afraid so," Hannah told her sympathetically. "I was talking to Beth back in the California office yesterday, and she told me he'd been in there asking about you. And that he heard something."

"What could he hear? I didn't think anyone knew anything."

"That you might have gone out of the country. Because you'd talked about the possibility, before it got so serious. Still, nobody there knows where you are, so they couldn't tell him. I haven't let on that you've even been in touch with me, much less that I've seen you. But Beth told me that Paul came into the office, posing as a private investigator. He showed your picture around, said he'd been hired to track you down for fraud."

"I'm sorry, Kate," she went on as her friend looked increasingly upset. "But I thought you should know. So you can keep being careful."

"You're right. I need to know," Kate said grimly. "Don't worry about me. Go on."

"Beth only found out about it later. Otherwise, you know she'd have made sure he was escorted out of the building. But apparently he talked to some of the people in Customer Service who didn't know about him, and they told him what they'd heard. They know not to talk now, anyway," Hannah said comfortingly at Kate's made a sound of distress. "Beth made sure of that. And it's not much to go on. 'Out of the country' covers a lot of territory. He's not going to be able to find you from that."

"But he's still looking," Kate countered. "When I heard from my parents a few weeks ago, I hoped that was a last gasp. But now he actually knows something. Thank God I didn't talk more to anyone. You're sure you haven't let on even to Beth that I'm here?"

"I'm sure. I just asked if anyone had heard from you. Because I still thought about you and was concerned. Even if Beth knew, she'd never say anything. You know that."

"What people don't know, they can't be tricked into telling," Kate reminded her. "All I can do is keep this low profile. Sooner or later, he'll give up. Find somebody new to obsess about, heaven help her."

Despite the brave words, though, the chill of the news stayed with her all day. She kept herself busy, commanded herself not to think about it. She'd done everything she could. There was no point in worrying any more.

She delayed leaving the office, though, unwilling to go out into the dark. She wished it were summer, that the night didn't close in so fast. Sure enough, when she was finally walking home from the bus stop in the rainy dark, she found herself jumpy and distracted, continually looking behind her. The sight of a man hurrying along under his own umbrella had her ducking into a shop until he passed. Of course it wasn't Paul. Would never have been Paul. He didn't know where she was, she reminded herself for the thousandth time. Still, she breathed a sigh of relief when she was in her apartment at last, pushing the deadbolt home.

A romantic comedy helped push the fear to the back of her mind during the evening. She read for another hour after the movie ended, unwilling to go to bed until she was too tired to stay awake another minute. Even so, she found herself unable to fall asleep. She would drift off for a few minutes, then jerk awake again, heart pounding at any sudden noise. There were plenty of those with the wind gusting outside, rattling windowpanes and sending branches scratching against walls.

Her exhausted mind and body finally succumbed, and she fell into a fitful sleep. And found herself in the ocean. For some reason, she was swimming at night, and it was raining, the waves high around her. And there he was, a dark form next to her, grabbing hold, pulling her under as she struggled. He was over her now, his hand on her head, fingers gripping her hair as he held her under the dark water. She pushed and flailed, trying desperately to get free, not to take the breath of water that would drown her. Her lungs burned as she fought him. And still the hand held her. Held her down under the cold, dark water.

Then she was running. Through the same wind and rain, lungs still bursting, this time with the effort of flight. She could feel his dark presence behind her. Hear his footsteps coming closer. He was going to catch her, and when he did, she knew, he would kill her. Instead of speeding up with the effort, she felt herself slowing down, her legs unable to power her. It was as if she were moving through clay, barely making progress. Closer and closer he came, closing the gap. Calling to her. His hands outstretched, grabbing for her.

Kate woke with a gasp, her own hands clutching the sheets. Her entire body was soaked in sweat and trembling with fear. A dream, she realized. It was only a bad dream. But the knowledge did nothing to calm her, or to slow her racing heart. She sat up, still shaking. Turned on the light, but found herself terrified to leave the bed, to venture into the darkness beyond. The silent space of the apartment outside her bedroom door seemed full of shadows and menace.

Paul wasn't here, and he never would be, she told herself again. But her heart continued to pound, her breath coming fast. It had felt too real. She was so frightened, she felt paralyzed. She grabbed for her cell phone, needing to reach out, to hear a friendly voice. Then hesitated. She couldn't call Hannah. Poor thing, she needed her sleep. And Kate hated to distress her more.

She selected another number, but stopped herself again. She really had nobody else to call, though, she realized. Her parents? No, she needed the security of somebody close. Somebody who could get to her if she did need help. She made up her mind at last, pressed the *Call* button.

And felt like a fool when Koti answered, his voice thick with sleep. It was 2:45, she saw with a belated look at the clock. He'd think she was ridiculous, waking him up just because she'd had a bad dream. He might even have someone with him, she realized with horror. She hadn't thought of that.

"Hello?" she heard again.

"Don't hang up," she begged. "It's me, Kate."

"Kate." His voice was sharper, fully awake now. "What's wrong? Are you all right?"

"I'm sorry. I know it's late. But . . . I'm so scared," she told him, voice trembling. "I have such a bad feeling. It was just a dream, but I still feel like he's here."

"I'm coming over. Don't open the door till I get there."

"You don't have to," she decided. "It's stupid. I'm sorry. He's not here, I know. I just needed to hear your voice."

"Be there in five minutes. Don't open the door," he said again.

When he stepped into the flat exactly six minutes later, Koti took one look at her white, strained face and pulled her into his arms. She rested her cheek against his chest and finally felt the tension easing, the warmth returning to her still-chilled limbs. She shouldn't feel so safe with him, she thought with confusion. But right now, she needed the reassurance of his strength, his very physical presence. She took a few deep breaths, fighting the tears that threatened to fall in the aftermath of her terror, and breathed in the warmth and scent of him as if it were oxygen.

She pulled away at last, feeling steadier, and took her first real look at him. And had to smile. He looked gorgeously rumpled in sweats that he had obviously pulled on in haste, and his shoes were untied. He really had run out the door to get to her.

"Thanks for coming over so fast," she said in a voice that still wasn't quite steady. "I'm so glad to see you. Come sit down."

He slipped his shoes off and left them by the door before following her.

"You don't have to do that," she told him. "Shoes are OK."

"You really haven't got out much," he said with a smile. "It's always a good idea to take your shoes off when you go into someone's home here. At least to ask."

"Another of those Maori things," she guessed.

"Afraid so."

"Thanks for telling me." She felt steadier already. It was a relief to have him here, to be talking about something else. She dropped into a corner of the couch and pulled one knee under her, patting the space next to her. "Come sit with me."

"Now tell me what happened," he commanded, moving to join her.

"It was just a stupid dream. But I was so scared when I woke up. It seemed so real. And I couldn't think of anyone else to call."

"It's all right," he assured her. "I'm glad you called me. What's got you so stirred up, though?"

Kate told him what Hannah had revealed. "I know it isn't reasonable to think he could find me here," she finished. "But when I heard that, it just . . . the fear came right back. All of it. The way it was before. I was sure he could get to me again somehow." She shivered, drawing both legs up now, wrapping her arms around them.

"Time for you to tell me more about this," Koti decided. "I need to know now. So I can help you, just in case. What did he do?"

"You know the first part. Phone calls. Texts. Emails. Only not . . . normal. If obsessively calling and texting somebody who's broken up with you is ever normal."

"Some people have a hard time giving up," he agreed. "But this went beyond that, eh."

"It sure did. I told him again and again that it was over, but it didn't get through. He sent flowers, too, almost every day. At first I talked to him. Told him not to send them any more. Then I told the front desk to refuse them. I changed my phone number and my email address. I couldn't change my office number, of course, but I stopped answering when I could tell it was him, and I hung up if he called from another number. I kept thinking it would end. But it just got worse."

"I've seen how you focus when you work. I can see that would be distracting. Infuriating."

"He kept coming by too, wanting to talk to me. Even after I asked them to turn him away at work, I'd leave the building, and he'd be there. Waiting. Or I'd drive to the grocery store on the weekend, and I'd see his car following me. Because he'd been watching my house. That's when I really started getting jumpy. I started having someone walk me to my car after work. Staying at friends' houses on the weekends instead of going home."

"Did you call the police?" he asked. "Isn't that harassment?"

She nodded jerkily. "Once he started following me, I finally realized what was happening. That he was a stalker. That he was disturbed, and maybe dangerous. I thought the police could tell him not to do it, and he'd stop," she said with disgust. "That's how ignorant I was. They told me to get a restraining order, so they could arrest him for violating it."

"Didn't that work?"

"Do you know how many women are killed every year with restraining orders in place? No, it didn't work. They can't do that much, not until the guy actually hurts you. And it made him mad. He had this idea in his mind. That I was his, and we were meant to be together. When I filed the restraining order, and he felt he was losing me, as he saw it . . . that's when the threats started."

"He threatened to hurt you?" Koti asked with a frown.

"No. He threatened to kill me. And he started leaving things for me. Dead things. First it was dead flowers. I'd leave to go to work, and there'd be a "bouquet" on my doorstep. But they were dead. All wrapped up in bright paper, with ribbons. And inside . . . dead and slimy. Then birds." She shuddered with remembered horror. "Anything dead he could find."

She put her face in her hands, took deep breaths, trying to calm herself. Felt Koti move closer, his arms going around her again.

"It's all right," he soothed her. "It's over."

She let him hold her, felt his calming strength and was grateful for the security he provided. "I thought it might be too. But now I don't think so. And I haven't got to the bad part yet."

"There's a worse part, eh. Tell me."

"The reason I'm here. The reason I ran away. After a while, my friend Ron started coming by in the morning to pick me up for work, and then driving me home again. Because I was scared to leave the house alone by then. But

Paul thought we were dating. And he told me that if he couldn't have me, he'd make sure nobody else could either."

"One morning," she said, taking a deep breath, "I got one of those messages. A bad one. But not in an email this time. On my new cell phone. Which was supposed to be secure. It said . . . " She swallowed. "It said, *'Can't wait to watch you die.'*"

"Shit," he breathed.

"And when I opened the door for the paper, there was a cat there."

"Dead?"

She nodded, forced herself to go on. "But not like the others. Not roadkill. It was the neighbor's. Paul had killed it. Strangled it. It still had the noose around its neck, Koti. That poor little black cat. And a note. On a piece of paper he'd shoved under its poor face. Just one word. *YOU.*"

"I looked at it, and I wanted to run, but I couldn't look away. I was just standing there, staring at it. Mesmerized." She stared into space now, remembering the horror of it. "Then I realized," she went on slowly, "he's watching this. He's enjoying it. He wants to make sure I'm scared enough, that I suffer enough first before I die. That's when I knew he really was going to kill me. I saw him coming for me. And I knew that this was it."

Koti saw in her face what reliving the event was doing to her. Kept an arm around her, her hand in his. "Tell me."

"I called the police, and they put me on hold. He was trying to get to me, trying to kill me, and I was on hold. For minutes. All the time listening to him trying to break in, talking to me. And all I could think was, when he got in, I had to stab him. I had to kill him. Because it was him or me."

She had her hands over her face again, crying now despite his arms around her. He pulled her into his chest, held her. He hated not knowing what to say, how to help.

"But he didn't get in, did he?" he asked once she was calmer again.

She shook her head, reached for the box of tissues on the coffee table and blew her nose. "The police came, finally. Of course, once he heard them, he ran away. But I knew he'd crossed the line. And that I couldn't stay with friends anymore, or go to work again. I was afraid of getting someone else hurt too. What if he'd killed Ron? He was just a nice guy who was trying to help me. So in the end, I drove out of town, to a motel. Driving in circles first, on and off the freeway, trying to make sure he couldn't follow me. I hid there. Used a pay phone to call my parents. After a couple days, I couldn't think what else to do, so I went to them. But I couldn't stay there either. I knew I had to run again. I had to hide, but I didn't know where to go. So I did the only thing I could think of, by then. I called Hannah. She was the farthest-away person I knew. I hoped she could help me find a job here. So I could disappear, and be safe again."

"And she did," she told him resolutely. "You know she did. I never went back to work again. Never saw or talked to anybody but my parents again. Never went back to my apartment again, either. My dad and uncle went and moved me out. My dad had a gun. He didn't want me to know, but I did. I think he was sorry Paul didn't show up. He wanted to kill him."

"Course he did," Koti agreed. "Any dad would've."

"Thank God he didn't. But Paul wouldn't have risked that anyway," Kate said with contempt. "He's a coward. He liked me in the first place because I was little. Made him feel like a big man. He'd never have taken on two grown men, especially men who were just looking for an excuse to kill him."

"So now you know." She sat up straight, turned to face him. "That's what I did. I ran away. As fast and as far as I could go. Brave, huh?"

"Yeh," he told her, squeezing her hand. "Yeh, I do think it was brave. I think it was amazing. You were in that kind of danger, and you thought about keeping the people you loved safe. I'm sure your parents wanted you to stay with them, that they would've done anything to protect you. Instead, you protected them. And to make a plan like you did, under that kind of stress, and then to come here alone and start over. All that took courage. More courage than most people will ever have."

"Thanks," she told him soberly. "I need to hear that. Because it didn't feel brave. It just felt like running away. Letting him win. And I didn't know I'd have to do it for so long. I thought once I was gone, he'd give up. Instead, here I am, still hiding. I can't talk to any of my friends. I can't even have a Facebook page like a normal person. I do things like that cave trip with you, and I want to tell somebody how great that was. But I can't. And I don't know when I'll ever be able to again."

"You can tell me," he said, trying to ease her fear, make her smile again. "I'll listen, any time you want to tell me how great I am." He put an arm around her, gave her his best cocky smile.

She laughed. It was a little shaky still, but at least it was a laugh. "It's good to know I can count on you."

"You can," he said, serious now. "I'm here now, aren't I? And it was raining," he pointed out. "Didn't even take the time to dress properly, or to comb my hair. That's dedication."

"I noticed. Thank goodness you were willing to come over. I was so scared. I would have survived, I know. But it didn't feel like that."

"Glad you called me," he assured her. "Glad I could be here for you. But how about if I make us a cuppa now? Because it's the bloody middle of the night, you know."

"I'll come with you. I don't really want to be by myself right now," she admitted. "Even in the other room."

"Must have made you ropeable, all that," Koti commented when they were settled back on the couch again with their tea. "Knowing the way you are. Bet you were furious."

Kate nodded, took a sip of the comforting beverage. "I truly believe it's only because of my temper that I'm alive now. I never felt sorry for Paul. Never agreed to meet him again, or wanted to listen to what he had to say. Believe it or not, that's a mistake lots of women make. And they wind up dead. I didn't discount my own instincts, either, in the end. The first time he hurt me was the last. And when he had me cowering in my apartment, I was terrified, but I was mad too. I decided that I was going to get my life back. I wasn't going to let him take it away. Either by killing me, or by not letting me live normally. I'm still furious about what he did, that I have to hide over here. But at least I'm alive, and I'm not looking over my shoulder all the time. Other than tonight, that is."

"Glad you told me. It makes me understand you better. Why you're the way you are. And why you did your block like that when I asked you about Kevvie."

"You don't think I'm just, what was it? Mad as a meat axe?"

"I may still think that. But I know why, now. I'll be able to duck, next time you go off."

"Mmmm," she agreed. It had been hard to talk about it, to relive the experience. But somehow, it had released the tension she'd held inside all day. She felt safe at last with Koti so reassuringly close, and found herself with an overwhelming desire to curl up and go to sleep.

"Can you stay a little bit?" she asked him. "Just till I fall asleep?"

"Why don't you go back to bed?" he suggested. "I'll sleep out here. Unless you want to share, of course."

"No, stay with me here. Just for a few minutes. Then you should go home and go to bed yourself. But I don't want to be alone right now."

He sighed. "OK. Wouldn't want to miss out on seeing you in those pajamas anyway. Not to mention the fuzzy socks. Why did I have a bad feeling you didn't sleep in a nightie?"

She smiled, then gave in to temptation and lay down, her head resting near him where he sat on the couch, taking comfort from his presence. "Sorry," she murmured with a yawn.

"Maybe if they didn't have sheep on them too," he complained, resting a hand on her shoulder and giving one of the woolly creatures a little rub with his thumb.

"I like my sheep. And we're in New Zealand. New Sheepland. You should like them too."

"Second to none in my admiration of sheep. Don't want to go to bed with them, that's all."

"I'm supposed to tell a joke here," she sighed, soothed by his warm hand, the feeling of him next to her. "But I'm too tired."

The next thing she knew, the alarm was buzzing. She came up from sleep slowly, disoriented. Why was she on the couch? As she stumbled into the bedroom to turn off the nagging buzz, the events of the night came back to her.

Had she really asked Koti to stay with her? In the early morning, the night's terrors receding, she could hardly believe it. He must have covered her up after she'd fallen asleep, too, she realized. She had awoken under her duvet. Going back out to the lounge to retrieve it, she stopped short at the sight of him, still in his sweats, coming in from the kitchen.

"Morning," he told her.

Kate's hands flew to her hair. "Why are you still here? Sorry," she amended at his frown, still smoothing her hair, but trying to be less obvious about it. She must be a mess. And she was wearing rumpled blue flannel pajamas with sheep and clouds on them. "I mean, thanks," she offered belatedly. "But you didn't have to stay. I'm sorry I interrupted your night like that."

"Didn't like to leave you. And stop fussing with your hair. You look fine. I saw you crying last night. And blowing your nose," he grinned. "It's safe to say all my illusions are shattered."

Kate sighed and sat down on the couch with a thump, pulling the duvet over her. "This is the problem with you being so good-looking. You look just like always. Even better unshaven, I hate to admit."

"Never mind," he comforted her. "Come have a cup of tea with me before I go home."

"Universal remedy," she said gloomily. "For late nights and awkward mornings."

"Not awkward for me. Come on, Kate. Where's that fighting spirit?"

"You're right," she decided. "But I'm brushing my hair *and* my teeth first. Restore a little dignity here."

"Where did you sleep?" she asked, coming into the kitchen a few minutes later and sitting down with him. She took a grateful sip of the hot, milky tea.

"On the carpet," he admitted. "Found a blanket. No worries," he added, seeing her distress. "Only a couple hours. Not too bad. I didn't like to leave you, in case you had another dream. Didn't want to make that trip again, eh."

"You're making a joke of it. But it was really nice of you. To come over in the first place, and then to stay. I don't know what I would have done without you. I would have had an uncomfortable night, that's for sure. I've never had a dream that scared me that much."

He reached across the table to take her hand. "You had a good reason to be scared. Seems to me, your mind was telling you that you still need to be careful. And I reckon that's true. Keep your eyes open, keep your door locked. Consider having a strong man move in."

"Yeah, that's happening. But I'm afraid you're right. It always takes me by surprise, how astute you are."

"I should be offended. But I won't bother. Because I've got a favor to ask too. I'd better slip it in here while you're softened up."

"I am not sleeping with you in exchange," she warned him.

"Never say never. Besides, you already have, haven't you? Nah, I wanted to ask you if you'd come over to my place, watch the ABs play tomorrow night."

"Do you think that's a good idea?" she asked carefully.

He sighed. "Nothing's going to happen that you don't want. You should know that by now."

"I do," she admitted. "That's the problem."

"And that makes this sound even better," he said cheerfully. "Game starts at seven-thirty. Come over early, and we'll have a bite to eat first. It'll be a takeaway, I'm afraid. I'm not much of a cook."

"All right. I owe you one for last night, that's for sure."

She walked him to the door when he rose to go. "Thanks again. Sorry for the rough night."

"No worries. Ring me any time you want me to visit you in the night. And I'll be here straight away." He reached for her and kissed her on the cheek. Looked at her in her ridiculous sheep pajamas, gave in and bent down to give her a proper kiss.

Kate felt a shock of recognition at the touch of his lips. As his firm mouth moved over hers, a bolt of heat arrowed straight through her. Without realizing what she was doing, she moved into him, ran her hands up his arms to his broad shoulders. She pulled him more closely to her as she kissed him back, and reveled in the feeling of his mouth, his body against hers. His arms tightened around her in response, pulling her even closer, kissing her harder, the heat building fast.

He lifted his head at last, a little stunned, and ran a hand down her back, still holding her close. "Whoa. Something happened there."

She stepped back, ran her hands through her hair self-consciously. "Yeah. Well."

"Time to move this along, you think? We could try it again tomorrow, see how we go."

Kate struggled to come up with a retort, but she was too disconcerted. She'd known it would feel good to kiss him, but she hadn't expected her body to respond quite so enthusiastically. She could still feel the tingling warmth where his mouth had touched hers, the feel of his shoulders under her hands, the press of his body against hers.

"I don't know," she finally said in confusion. "I'll think about it, OK?"

"Reckon we'll both be thinking about it. See you tomorrow night. Wear something pretty." He brushed his lips over hers once more, then headed down the stairs to his car.

Kate watched him go, gorgeous as always from behind even in his sweats, then shut the door and leaned against it for a moment. Well, on the plus side, she wasn't shivering with fear anymore. On the other hand, she was having a hard time remembering why this would be a bad idea. If only he hadn't been so kind, so caring, last night.

She had to get ready for work. No time to think about touching him again, or how firm and warm his lips had felt on hers. She shivered. Tomorrow night. Maybe he wouldn't look so good to her then. Maybe she'd have more willpower on a full night's sleep. But she doubted it.

Chapter 15

Kate studied her reflection. Gave a tug to the slim-fitting mango sweater she'd pulled over a short, kicky cocoa brown polka-dotted skirt and brown leggings. Too colorful? No, she decided. Bright colors had always given her courage, and she needed that right now. The underwear she'd chosen would do the job too. She'd look good tonight, no matter what she was wearing. Or not wearing.

"Time to go," she told the woman in the mirror. She wanted to see Koti anyway. Maybe he was feeling a bit uncomfortable himself right now, she thought hopefully. Then sighed. Probably not.

Koti's modern house, though less grand than Drew and Hannah's, threw her back into another moment of self-doubt as she compared it with her own tiny flat.

"I didn't realize you were this close to the beach," she told Koti nervously when he answered the door to her ring. "I guess you can walk there if you want. Must be nice."

She was chattering, she realized. Took a deep breath and started again. "Do you live here alone?" She pulled off her boots and set them in the entryway. "And see, I'm remembering."

"Good on ya, remembering. And yes to both. I can walk to the beach, and I live alone. Used to have flatties, but I'm on my own now. That's why I need you to keep me company. Keep me from being too lonesome."

"You look pretty," Koti went on as he gestured her toward the lounge. "I always like the colors you wear. They brighten the place up."

"You look good too," she told him, eyeing his black sweater and jeans. "Handsome. But I'm nervous. Your house is too fancy. And this feels too much like a date."

"Hope so," he agreed. "That it's a date. Not that you're nervous. How can I help you relax? Other than the obvious."

"Let's eat," she decided. "That should help."

He laughed. "Should make you feel at home, anyway. I got Indian. Come into the kitchen."

The TV was on in there, she saw. He'd been watching the pregame analysis. As they sat over their meal, the program went to a commercial break.

"Wow. You in stereo." She felt better now that she'd found something to tease him about. "Turn it up."

He groaned, but complied as the body wash commercial continued, with its slow-motion footage of Koti in the shower.

"Who's this ad supposed to appeal to?" she asked him as the camera lingered on his tattooed arm, reaching up now to lather his broad chest. "Are women buying this stuff? How many straight men are getting a charge out of this?"

"Dunno. Just hope you are."

"I've got the real thing." She smiled across at him. "Much better in 3-D."

"Glad you think so." His own smile started slowly, grew warmer. "Be glad to give you a private demonstration of that advert later tonight. Though you're the one who'll be getting the soaping."

She shifted in her chair, cleared her throat. "We still have a game to watch. So I'm going to ask you why you take off your clothes in every ad. You're at least sleeveless, every time. That's not true of the other guys."

"Been making a study, have you?"

"Pretty obvious. So why is that?"

He shrugged. "Reckon my physique is what I have to offer. What the public wants to see. So it's what the sponsors are willing to pay for."

"Doesn't that bother you?"

"Nah. Been that way a long time. We all have our talents. I'm lucky mine's something that's made me popular, helped me earn a crust as well."

She frowned. "That's not your talent. Those are your looks. And all the training you've done, which hasn't hurt at all. If you weren't so good at rugby, you'd be a male model or something. Just another handsome guy on a billboard. And nobody would know who you were."

"I don't like the modeling much, tell you the truth," he admitted. "Always pushing at me, tweaking things. Fixing my hair. No Maori man likes people up in his space like that. Makes me jumpy."

She raised her eyebrows. "I thought you liked people being up in your space. Isn't that what we've been talking about?"

"When they're invited. And you're definitely invited." He looked across at her, saw her looking back at him. Felt the certainty growing. "I want you up in my space. But most of all, I want to be in your space."

He got up, came around to the other side of the table. Stood looking down at her for a minute. Then reached for her, lifted her out of her seat. "Come up here."

His strong hands went under her, pulled her off her feet. Her legs wrapped around him as he pulled her closer. It was as good as he'd imagined, holding her tightly against him that way. Better. He lowered his mouth to hers, took it in a kiss. Felt her mouth opening under his, kissing him back, her hands going around his shoulders, pulling herself into him with an urgency and heat that had him burning.

Her hands went to his hair, wrapped themselves in it as she pulled his mouth to hers. They kissed like that for long minutes, lips and tongues chasing, exploring. Like it was the first time. Like that was all there was.

"Koti," she breathed, pulling back at last. "Your game. It must be on."

He laughed a bit unevenly. "You must be joking." He walked her, still wrapped around him, into the lounge. Laid her down on one of the black leather couches and came down over her. Put a hand on the side of her face and kissed her again, loving the way she looked underneath him.

"Told myself I was going to take my time," he told her, pulling back at last and coming up on one elbow. He ran his hand down her sweater, over her breast, her waist, down her leg in the brown tights. Down all of her, then back up again, slowly, looking into her eyes. "If I ever got this chance. I promised you I'd tease you all night. It's going to be so hard to wait. But I'm going to do it."

She reached for him, her hands finding the hem of his sweater and shirt, diving underneath them, up his sides. Ran them greedily over the smooth skin covering hard muscle there. "Not necessary," she assured him breathlessly. "I need to see you. I need to touch you. And to feel you inside me. I need that most of all. I don't think I can wait much longer."

He smiled slowly, lifted her own sweater delicately, uncovering a bare inch of skin. Ran his thumb lightly over that inch, then just a little bit upward, stroking her skin under the wool. Watched her shift under him, saw her eyes darken, her tongue come out to lick her lips. "That's the way it's going to be, though. Slow. Till you burn. Till you scream."

"Oh, God," she moaned. "I'm already burning."

He came down over her again. Kissed her beautiful mouth once more, pulled her small tongue into his own mouth. Moved to her throat, stretched out so invitingly beneath him.

"You make me feel like a vampire," he whispered. "Want to bite you."

She moaned as he suited the action to the words. He kissed her, bit her, licked her there. She pushed herself against him, squirming as his mouth found each sensitive area. Her hands moved under his shirt, grabbing him now, running down his sides and back up again. Over his back.

"Take this off," she gasped, pulling at his clothes.

"No." He pulled her hands down, pinned them with one of his own above her head. "Not yet. You're going to be naked for a long, long time tonight before I take anything off."

He liked her this way, he decided. He'd keep hold of her for a bit longer. Until he was done playing with her. Or until he had her boneless under him, all the way to the point where she'd stopped thinking. Where she didn't want to move anymore.

"I like this jersey," he told her, his free hand pulling it up a bit farther. "And I like what's under it. I like that so much. You have the most beautiful skin. First time I saw you, I wanted to touch it. Been wanting to do it every day since." He watched his hand moving slowly over that smooth surface, up her body, around her side, saw her eyes drift slowly closed as he reached her breast.

"Open your eyes, Kate. I want you to see me. Watch me do this."

Reluctantly, she forced them open. He inched the sweater up farther, pulled it above her breasts. Looked down at her, her hands still stretched overhead, her eyes staring into his own.

"Very nice," he told her. "So pretty. I think you were planning to show this to me tonight." He ran a hand under the edge of the delicate bronze-colored lace. Moved it over her, watched her gasp as his thumb found the hardening nipple. He trapped it between his fingers, heard the gasp turn to a moan, and smiled.

"You like that, do you? Good to know. I'll do it some more." He played with her then, more long minutes going by as he listened to her, watched her responding to him. At last, he flicked the fastening between her breasts, peeled the bra away. Lifted her upper body to pull it off her, together with the orange sweater.

"I liked that," he told her as he settled her back down again. "But I think I like it even better now that I've taken it off. Because it's time for me to kiss you here. And that's another thing I've been wanting to do for a long time."

He moved down the couch, kissed her mouth again, her throat, nibbled at the sensitive spots under her ears, over her collarbones. His hand moved to cover her breast again, tease the nipple, until his mouth moved down to join it.

Kate arched as his mouth finally found her nipple. Jerked against him and cried out as he bit down gently. "Too slow," she moaned. "Please, Koti. Please. I need you. I'm dying."

"You've made me wait this long. Your turn to wait now. Till I say it's time. You don't get to choose tonight. It's all for me."

She should feel threatened, she knew. He was controlling her with his words, his mouth, his talented hands. But somehow, it didn't feel that way. She knew if she objected, he'd let her go. She didn't want him to let her go, though. She was melting, dissolving. All she wanted was for him to go on.

She lost track of time as he stayed there. She wasn't even trying to touch him anymore. She didn't think she could move anyway. Her world had narrowed to the sensations he produced as his hands and mouth continued to work. When he finally reached for the zipper of her skirt, she moaned with relief, moved to help him.

"No," he told her, pushing her hands out of the way. "I'll undress you. My job now." He dropped her skirt into the pile of clothes on the floor, looked down at her dressed only in her tights.

"That's a good look on you," he decided. "Should make you walk around a bit, show it to me. I'm betting, though, that your panties match the bra. And if that's true, I need to see them."

Slowly, he peeled down the tights. His hands moved down her thighs, down her calves along with the brown microfiber, stroking all the way. When the tights had joined the rest of her clothes, he moved his hands back to her thighs.

"You're so beautiful. So smooth and strong." He ran his thumbs up her inner thighs, moving her legs gently apart. "I've been watching what those legs can do all these weeks. But what I want most is something that hasn't happened yet.

Seeing them, feeling them wrapped around me, while I come inside you."

She shivered, pushed up into his hands. "Do that, then. Please, Koti. Do it now. I'll do whatever you want. But don't make me wait any more."

He smiled. "You're going to have to wait a bit more for that, though. Because we're just getting to the good part, aren't we? Be a shame to hurry now." He kept his thumbs stroking, stroking, over her inner thighs. Closer and closer as he watched her. Mouth open, panting now. Eyes closing again.

"Open your eyes, Kate," he told her. "I want you watching me."

She dragged them open as his hands settled over her at last, that thumb still moving. She cried out at the sensation, as strong now as an electric shock.

"Very nice," he said approvingly. "Very wet. And beautiful little panties." He moved his hand again to watch her respond. She shifted under him again, moaned, lifted her hips toward him.

"You're noisy," he told her. "That's good. It's going to be too easy to make you scream, though. I'm going to have to slow down, make this last."

"Please," she begged. "Please. I need more. Touch me. Please, Koti." She moved against his hand, urging him.

He wasn't sure how much longer he could hold out. He was excited almost past bearing. Once he had her panties off, he wasn't going to be able to wait. He'd have to delay that as long as possible, he decided. Because he needed to watch her come first. Noisily. Messily. Out of control with wanting it. With wanting him.

He reached under the lace. Before he did anything else, he had to feel her. Feel where he was going to go, later. He sighed as his fingers slid inside her. Oh, that was good. Warm and wet and tight. It was going to feel so good in there. As good as he'd ever imagined. She was going to be all his tonight. Any way he wanted her.

They didn't hear the ringing at first. Wrapped up in sensation, drowning in each other's eyes, they could hear nothing but the blood pounding in their heads, her cries as he touched her so slowly. But the musical tinkle gradually intruded on their consciousness as it rang four times, five. Stopped, then started again.

"Don't answer it," he groaned.

"I have to." She struggled to sit up. "Almost the only person it could be is Hannah. She's alone. I have to."

He swore. Got up and went to the entry hall, found her purse, brought it back to her. She sat up, pushed the hair out of her eyes. Scrabbled through the bag until she found the phone, then brought it out and glanced at it.

"Hannah," she told him. Took a deep breath and answered. "Hi. Everything OK? Watching the game?"

"Kate." She stiffened in alarm at the strain in Hannah's voice. "I'm so glad you answered. Can you come over? I've been having these contractions. I thought they were just Braxton-Hicks, the practice ones, but now I'm not sure. Could you come?"

"Oh. Oh my gosh. Of course I can. It'll take me a while to get there, though. Shouldn't you call your midwife?"

"I already did. I'm waiting for her to call back now. But I'd like somebody here. Just in case."

"I'm starting right now, and I'll be there as fast as I can. Call me while I'm on the way and tell me what's happening, all right? And Hannah. If you get worried, *at all,* call the ambulance, all right?"

"I don't think it'll happen that fast, even if it is happening," Hannah said. "But please, do come be with me."

"On my way," Kate promised. "Call me back once you hear from the midwife."

She hung up, reached for her clothes from the floor, began to pull on her tights. "Hannah thinks she might be having the baby. I need to go right now."

"I'll drive you," Koti said immediately. "If you need to take her to hospital, or even to talk to her on the way over there, that'll be better. That way you can look after her."

He got up, grabbed his mobile off the table and shoved it into a pocket that suddenly had room again. Found both their jackets and tossed hers across. "Soon as you're ready."

Chapter 16

"Sorry about that," Kate said as Koti piloted the car quickly but carefully onto the motorway and toward the Harbour Bridge into the City. "Not quite the ending you'd envisioned."

"They say babies have the worst timing," he agreed. "I'd say this takes the biscuit, though. Never mind. We have time. This is what's important now."

When Kate's cell phone rang again, she snatched at it. "What's happening?" she asked Hannah abruptly.

"The midwife just called me back. She wants me to come into the hospital and get checked."

"Have you called Drew?" Kate pressed. "Or somebody on the team?"

"I'm going to do that now," Hannah said. "I wasn't sure it was anything. And I hate to worry him when he's so far away. But if I'm going to the hospital, I need to call him, I think."

"You sure do," Kate said firmly. "It's his worry too. He needs to know as soon as he can." She saw Koti nod in agreement. "Hang up and call."

"Another contraction," Hannah said in a strained voice. "Get here soon."

Kate heard the line go dead. She set the phone down, looked at Koti. "Are you up for going to the hospital? I have a feeling there's going to be a baby tonight."

"Course I am. It's going to take Drew some time to get back here, though," he frowned. "No late-night flights from Christchurch. How about you? You ready to be a birth coach?"

Kate swallowed. "I guess I have no choice, do I? If that's what Hannah needs."

"Isn't it early, though?" Koti asked. "Do you know how far gone she is?"

"A few weeks early, for sure. I'm not sure how bad that is. But I *am* sure that's what she's worrying about right now."

When they pulled into the driveway outside the big house, Koti joined her in leaping from the car and hurrying up the steps. Hannah had thought to leave the door unlocked for them, and Kate pushed through it with relief, calling for her friend.

"Still here." Hannah came into the hall and stood leaning against the wall. "Koti. You're here too?"

"Just the driver," he told her. "Are you all right?"

Hannah nodded, but Kate could see the strain in her face. "They're closer together now. Stronger, too. I think we need to leave right now."

"I'm glad you came," she told Koti. "You probably know the way. Auckland City Hospital."

"I'll get you there. No worries." Koti helped her gently down the stairs and into the car, while Kate got in behind him, where she could see and touch Hannah in the passenger seat.

"Drive fast," she told Koti, as she saw Hannah stiffen with a contraction. She might not know much about childbirth, but it was hard to mistake Hannah's audible breaths and the way she held her abdomen.

"No worries," he said again, grimly this time. "On our way."

"Were you able to reach Drew?" Kate asked Hannah with concern, once she felt the hand that had been gripping hers relaxing again.

"No. All I could do was leave a message for the trainer. They were playing again by the time I called, and he didn't answer. Is the game over yet?" she asked Koti.

He glanced at the dashboard clock. "Not quite. Another ten minutes or so. You'll hear from him soon, though."

"Why don't you give me your phone, so I can answer it?" Kate suggested.

Hannah fumbled it out of her purse, then handed it back. She lay back against the car seat for a few minutes, then stiffened again and reached for Kate's hand.

"Should we be timing these?" Koti asked when it was over. "They seem pretty close together."

"I'm not sure it matters." Hannah laughed a little, but Kate could feel the tension and fear in the hand still gripping hers. "I think it's pretty clear this baby is on the way."

"It's going to be all right," Kate assured her. "We're almost there. Aren't we?" she implored Koti.

He smiled at Hannah, his voice calm and encouraging. "Sweet as. Another few minutes, and you'll be the most exciting thing to happen to Auckland City Hospital all year. Birthplace of another All Black, eh. He's a boy, right?"

Hannah smiled back at him, tears close to the surface. "He is. I hope he's all right. That he isn't too little," she said, a sob escaping her.

"He's all right," Koti told her with certainty. "Can't wait, that's all. Wants to meet his mum."

Hannah sobbed again, and Kate pressed her hand. Then dropped it hurriedly to fumble for Hannah's phone, ringing at last.

"Hannah's phone," she answered.

"Who's this? What's happened?" She heard Drew's voice, sharp with worry.

"It's Kate. And Hannah's all right," she said quickly. "But the baby's coming early. We're on our way to the hospital now. Almost there."

"Let me talk to her," he commanded.

"We're at the emergency entrance," Kate told him as Koti pulled in. "I'm going to call you back on this number in a few minutes, OK? I'll call you back," she repeated as she disconnected and hopped out of the car.

"Give it to me," Koti said. "I'll ring him, soon as I park the car. You need to help Hannah now. I'll find you. Go on."

Kate nodded and handed him the phone. *Let me do this right,* she prayed as she hurried beside the orderly pushing Hannah through to the maternity ward. She wished she'd watched a movie, at least. She was so unprepared.

Hannah was quickly settled into a birthing suite and changed into a hospital gown. Within minutes, her midwife appeared, her face and manner calmly reassuring.

"Baby decided to make an early appearance, did he?" she asked Hannah, pulling up a stool to examine her. "Let's have a look."

"Early and fast. Six centimeters already," she told her, after an examination that was clearly uncomfortable. "Where's Dad?" she asked Kate.

"Christchurch. Playing," Kate told her. "He'll be trying to get back now. But I'm not sure that's going to happen in time."

"Not likely," the midwife agreed. "We'll have a present for him when he turns up, eh," she told Hannah.

"What about the baby? Is he going to be all right?" Hannah asked desperately. "It's too soon."

"Barely preterm," the midwife reassured her. "He'll be 37 weeks in a few days. We've got the fetal monitor on you, and his heart rate's normal. He'll be a bit small, need to be watched more closely. But he should be just fine. Unfortunately, you're too far into labor for us to offer you much pain medication. We don't like to give narcotics too close to the birth. Especially with a young baby like this. You're going to have to manage this one naturally, I'm afraid."

"I can do it," Hannah told her with conviction. "I don't want anything that's going to increase the risk, even a little bit."

The midwife left, promising to return in a few minutes. Kate was grateful for the competent, professional nurse who remained. She knew she was out of her depth here. All she could do was hold Hannah's hand and reassure her. She hoped it was enough.

Another nurse appeared at the door, a little wide-eyed. "I have Koti James waiting out here. He's got Dad on the phone. But we can't let you use the mobile in here, I'm afraid. Only in the waiting room."

"Have him come in," Kate decided. "He can tell her what Drew said, anyway. And then he can call Drew back."

When Koti appeared, putting his head around the door cautiously and then stepping inside at Kate's invitation, she updated him quickly on the midwife's report.

"How's Drew getting back?" she asked. "What's the plan?"

"They're getting a plane sorted now." Koti moved around where Hannah could see him and gently picked up her other hand. "He'll be with you soon as he can manage it. And you know he can manage a fair bit. Said to tell you," he cleared his throat, "tell you he loves you. That the baby will be fine. And to remind you to trust him when he says that. Because he's always right."

Hannah smiled tremulously. "Thanks," she said, squeezing his hand. "Would you go call him back? Tell him I'm all right, now I've heard from him. Tell him I have you and Kate here to help me."

"And Koti," she said as he nodded and turned to leave. "Please tell him to be careful getting here. No risks, OK?"

"I'll tell him," he promised. "No risks."

When Kate looked back later, she could hardly believe she had made it through the next couple hours. She marveled at Hannah's strength as she labored through the increasingly strong contractions, asking for frequent updates on the baby's condition.

"I just want him to be born," she told Kate desperately between contractions. "So he can be here, and safe, and looked after."

The midwife returned as promised, and Hannah seemed to relax a little at her confident assurances. Koti came in and out at regular intervals. When Hannah heard that a flight had finally been arranged to get Drew home, some of the tension seemed to leave her.

"Tell him I'm fine," she told Koti every time, even though Kate wouldn't have described it that way. She didn't think Hannah could be any more relieved than she was herself when it was finally time to begin pushing. Ten minutes later, though, she was wishing she was anywhere else. She'd known that having a baby wasn't easy, of course. But hearing the restrained Hannah cry out in pain made her want to run from the room. She gritted her teeth and went back to encouraging and reassuring her friend.

At last, when it seemed to her that Hannah's fragile body couldn't take any more, the baby's head appeared, with the rest of him following in quick succession. The midwife caught him with deft hands, and soon the welcome sound of a newborn's cry filled the room.

"Here's your son, Mum," the midwife told Hannah, placing the baby gently on Hannah's abdomen. "We'll warm him up with you while we cut the cord. A beautiful boy."

Hannah's trembling hands went down to hold him as she looked at the little body. "Oh," she breathed. "He's here. Look, Kate. He's here."

"He sure is," Kate said, beaming with relief and joy. "You did it. You did such a good job."

"We're going to have to take him from you for a bit now," the midwife told Hannah after the baby had been weighed, measured, and checked by the waiting pediatrician. "He's a wee bit small. We want to make sure he's kept warm, keep an eye on him."

"Is he all right?" Hannah asked in alarm. "Is something wrong?"

"Nothing's wrong," the midwife reassured her again. "A healthy boy. Just a bit thin, like all babies born at this age. He's full-grown in length—56 centimeters. 22 inches," she went on as she saw Hannah trying to calculate. "But only six pounds. He hasn't had time to put any fat on yet, which means you'll need to be more careful about keeping him warm. We'll keep him in the neonatal unit for now to observe him. Just a precaution, Hannah."

Hannah looked desperate as the nurse gently put the baby into the Lucite bassinette and prepared to wheel him away.

"Kate," she urged. "Please, ask Koti to watch him. Watch him until Drew gets here. Please. And to come back and tell me. I need to know he's OK."

Kate nodded. For the first time that evening, she left Hannah alone, and went to find Koti.

He jumped up from where he was sitting, hands clasped and head bowed, in the waiting room. "What? Is it all right?"

"It's perfect," Kate answered, lightheaded with relief. "Better call Drew and tell him that he's on his way to see his son. But Hannah wants you to go to the neonatal unit. They've taken him there to monitor him. Can you stand outside and watch him? And come tell her he's all right, from time to time?"

"She's been working so hard," she said with a break in her voice. "And she's been so worried that something would be wrong. Now they've taken him away, and she's frantic to know how he is."

"No worries. I'll call Drew, then I'll be there straight away," he promised.

Drew picked up on the first ring. "Koti? What's happening?"

Koti smiled. "You've got a son, mate. Doing well too, from what I hear."

Drew exhaled. "And Hannah? How's she?"

"Good as gold," Koti reassured him. "Where are you?"

"Taxiing," Drew said grimly. "Took bloody ages to get a plane sorted. We're taking off now, though. Be there in a couple hours. They're both all right? You're sure?"

"Good as gold," Koti said again. "They've taken the baby to the nursery, keep an eye on him, from what I understand. Hannah asked me to watch him. I'm going to do that now."

"Don't leave them," Drew commanded. "Stay with them till I'm there."

"No worries," Koti told him. "I'm here till you are. Kate too."

"We're taking off now. Tell Hannah I love her."

He disconnected, and Koti absently put the phone back into his pocket. Walked out to find the nursery. To watch over Drew's family until he could do it himself.

He was still there two hours later, leaning against the corridor wall, when he saw Drew headed down the corridor towards him. Usually so self-possessed, the other man looked rumpled and grubby, his hair on end as if he'd been pulling his hands through it. Koti could see that he'd thrown his warmups on over his uniform and gone straight to the airport. Worst of all, he still had staples closing a long wound in his forehead. He hadn't even taken the time to have them removed and the cut stitched after the game.

Koti stood up as Drew came to a stop in front of him. He watched the new father turn to search for his baby through the glass wall of the nursery. Heard his breath catch as he saw his son in the bassinette labeled "Callahan—Boy." Sleeping peacefully, swaddled snugly in a blanket, his tiny head covered by a blue cap, the baby showed no sign of all the drama that had attended his birth.

"He's all right?" Drew asked Koti.

"No worries, mate," Koti assured him. "They've been checking on him. It means Hannah hasn't been able to see him, though. That's been hard on her."

"Where is she?" Drew asked urgently. "Show me."

Koti walked him down the hall to the room where Hannah had been transferred. Stood back as Drew entered the room. Kate was curled up in a chair by the bed, but jumped up on Drew's arrival.

Drew didn't hesitate. He went straight to his wife and pulled her gently into his arms. And the reserved Hannah, whom Koti had never seen at a disadvantage before that evening, burst into tears and threw her own arms around her husband.

"I'm sorry," she sobbed. "I shouldn't have made you go. I'm so glad you're here. We have a baby. Did you see him?"

As Drew held her and murmured words of love and encouragement, Kate edged around the two of them and joined Koti in the doorway.

"I'd say that's our cue to leave," she muttered.

"Too right." Koti sighed in relief. "Should we say goodbye?"

"I don't think they'd even hear us," Kate smiled tiredly. "Let's go."

Chapter 17

They paused a minute outside the nursery to take a final look.

"He's so tiny," Kate marveled. "But let me tell you, having him was an effort. A really big effort. I didn't realize. When she was in the middle of it, I thought, no thanks. This is too hard."

"But when he was born . . ." she sighed. "I suspect Hannah thinks it was worth it."

Koti took her hand and squeezed it. "Reckon they both do. It may not have been what they were expecting, but it turned out well. Thank God. You were awesome. Bet you didn't know you could do that."

"I thought I'd been terrified before," she admitted. "But this was something else. I'm glad I was there. I'm glad you were, too. You were so good. So calm. But I've never been more scared in my life."

"Me too," he told her fervently. "Calm. That's a laugh. I've never felt so helpless."

They looked at each other and started to laugh. The long night of strain, the joy of knowing everything was all right at last, were finally released.

"Drew's poor face, though," Kate managed at last. "He looked like Frankenstein. Those staples. I can just hear Hannah fretting over him."

"In a hospital, isn't he," Koti grinned. "Somehow, I think he'll be able to find someone to stitch him up."

"And me," he remembered. "Coming into the room where a woman's having a baby. Trying not to look. Never felt so out of place in my life."

"I thought you were wonderful." Kate reached out impulsively to hug him, so grateful to be there with him, all the drama and tension of the past hours so happily concluded.

His arms went around her too. Back where they belonged. He pulled her to her toes and settled his mouth over hers. Reached a hand behind her head to hold her there, used the other arm to pull her more tightly against his body.

Kate felt herself melting into him. Reached up to his shoulders again and kissed him back with all the passion he'd aroused in her earlier. Her mind might have been on other things, but her body seemed to remember exactly where they'd left off.

The sound of a throat clearing nearby brought Koti back to himself. He opened his eyes to the sight of a nurse holding a stack of files and frowning at him.

"May want to take that outside," she suggested dryly. "Come back in nine months or so, the rate you're going."

"Sorry," he told her with a grin. "Carried away." He grabbed Kate's hand, looked around for the elevator.

"Over here," she told him, pulling him towards it and pressing the *Down* button.

As the doors closed, he pulled her into his arms again. They were still kissing, breathing hard, when the doors opened. Broke apart to hurry through the lobby to the carpark. Ran to his car together, holding hands.

As he slid into the driver's seat, he reached for her. No more slow burn, it was all heat now. He reached a hand under her sweater, palmed a breast as he pulled her towards him. He couldn't get enough of her mouth, her neck.

"I can't wait anymore," he warned her on a gasp as he kissed her. "It's going to have to be fast."

"Oh, yes," she breathed into his mouth. "Please."

He nodded, wrenched himself away, turned the car on. Kept one hand on her leg as he drove in silence, with as much intensity as he'd felt earlier, during the drive to the hospital. This felt just as urgent, his body compelling him forward. He fought the urge to speed. It was only a twenty-minute drive this time of night, he told himself desperately. He could wait that long. They were almost on the bridge now, anyway. He couldn't stop.

At last, he was pulling the car into his driveway and turning off the engine. They jumped out together, ran to the house. Koti unlocked the door, slammed it shut behind him, desperately glad to have her at last where he needed her. Her feet left the ground as he kissed her, lowered her to the rug in the center of the entryway, came down over her.

No finesse now. He pulled her sweater over her head, unhooked her bra and tossed it away. The rest of her clothing followed in quick succession, until she was naked beneath him. She yanked at his shirt and sweater, watched him pull them over his head, kick off his shoes. He wrenched off his jeans and underwear until he was finally, gloriously naked on his knees before her.

"Tell me you have a condom here," she begged. "Because I need you right now. Please, Koti. No more teasing. I need you now."

He reached in the jeans pocket, pulled out the packet. "Three of them," he told her as he ripped it open. "We're going to need them all."

She shuddered as he came down over her. His skin against hers was warm and smooth, his body solid over her. He rolled to an elbow, reached out to touch her, his fingers moving inside her as they had earlier, feeling the heat there. His thumb was stroking again, and she jerked against him.

"Please." She pulled at him. "Please. Now. I need this so much."

"I need to see you first," he gasped. "Promised myself." He moved down her body. Put his hands behind her knees and pushed them up as she moaned.

"Too much?" he asked. "All right?"

"Oh, God," she breathed. "Yes. No. Please. Now."

He settled over her, set his mouth to her.

She did burn. And she screamed. And begged him to do it again. Over and over, she convulsed around him. Finally, he couldn't stand it any longer. Moved up her body. Wrapped his arms around her knees to open her to him. One last bit of control as he eased inside, feeling her stretch to receive him. It was so tight, so warm.

"Wait," he gasped. Held himself rigid over her until he felt the sensation receding a bit, had himself back from the brink. And began to move. Trying not to go too fast. Not to be too much for her.

Kate was someplace past thinking. Everything was sensation. His arms holding her legs. The length of him coming into her, again and again. She needed more, though. She was on the brink again, and she needed more to get there. "Please. More," she gasped. "Harder."

He swore. Pulled almost out of her. Waited there until her eyes opened.

"Please," she begged him again. "Koti, please."

This was where he needed her. Pupils dilated, focused only on her pleasure, needing him, open to him. Out of control. Slowly, slowly, he slid back inside as she keened a welcome. Out again, the pause as she begged him, then back into her. He saw her excitement build, felt her writhe underneath him. Power surged through him. Finally, when she was crying out with it, he began to move faster, give her more. Harder and faster now, her cries matching his strokes. He felt her around him as she began to come at last, the spasms gripping him, pushing him higher. Lost himself in her pleasure and his own as he emptied into her with a triumphant shout.

He collapsed on her, rolled quickly to his side so he wouldn't crush her. Let go of her legs, felt them sliding down his own. He pulled her trembling body more tightly to him, realizing for the first time that they were on his entryway floor, that she'd been cushioned only by an area rug.

"Are you all right? Bruised?" he asked, running his hand down her body. "Sorry. Didn't even let you have a couch to lie on. I was lucky to make it this far."

"No," she assured him. "I don't think so. Bruised, I mean. I can't tell, actually." She gave a shaky laugh. "Ask me tomorrow."

"Come up to bed," he urged her, sitting up and pulling her with him. Climbed the stairs with her in silence, slid between the sheets of his wide bed.

"Nothing smart to say, eh." He brushed her hair from her face and kissed her.

"I can't. Worn out. Stunned."

He kissed her gently again. "No wonder. How many times can you do that?"

"Do what?" she asked, without opening her eyes.

"Kate. Most women can't come over and over like that. Didn't you know that?"

Her eyes flew open. "No. Too much work?"

He laughed and ran his hand down her slender body for the pleasure of feeling her skin, felt her shudder again under his touch. "Nah. Best surprise party I've ever had."

"Good," she sighed with relief. "I should go home, though. I'm exhausted."

"Not going to stay?" He frowned at her.

"I need to sleep. And I need a shower. I don't even have a toothbrush. I'm sure you're as tired as I am. We both need to go to bed."

"I have a shower, though. A bed, too. I even have an extra toothbrush, I think. And I want you here when I wake up in the morning. We're not done."

"It *is* morning," she pointed out. "And I don't know if I can take any more."

"You can take it," he promised. "I'll make sure you want to. And it's too late to be driving home. Come on. Let's have a shower."

"Sure you need to go home?" he asked again, twelve hours later.

"I'm so sure," she groaned, bending over to pull on her boots in the entryway. "Because I'm so sore. I need to rest."

"Your fault," she told him crossly when he laughed. "Not everyone's a conditioned athlete."

"Maybe if you didn't have that special superpower, you wouldn't have had to work so hard."

"I thought you said you liked it. Now you're complaining about it?"

"Not me," he assured her fervently. "I'm a fan."

"By the way." He cleared his throat. "If I did anything, if I do anything that's too much, you need to tell me."

"Everything you do is too much," she told him, reaching up to run a hand over his smoothly shaved cheek. "You just about killed me."

He smiled. "If I do anything you don't like, then," he clarified. "You can say. There's so much more I want to do to you. And I'm not going to be stopping to ask permission. But I won't hurt you. And I'll listen, if you tell me no."

"I know you will. Thanks for making me feel safe with you. Though you're scaring me a little now. You've already done so much. I'm wondering what's going to happen to me next."

"That's the way I want it. Stay a bit longer and I'll show you," he suggested, pulling her against him and lifting her off her feet so he could kiss her the way he wanted to.

She leaned back in his arms, smiled into his eyes. "Hmm. So tempting. But I have to get home. I'll see you Wednesday morning, if you want to swim." She wriggled her way out of his arms, gave him one last kiss, grabbed her bag, and was out of the house without more discussion.

Koti felt oddly disconcerted as he watched her go. Could it be that she didn't want it as much as he did? No, he decided. She couldn't have been any more enthusiastic. He was used to being the one who got up and left, that was all.

Wednesday, he reminded himself. Suddenly, that seemed a long way away.

With a sigh, Kate opened the door at last to the apartment she'd left more than twenty-four hours earlier. If she'd ever had a more eventful day, she couldn't remember it now. She badly needed some time to herself to try to sort it all out. Reflexively, she pulled her phone out of her purse to charge it, and realized it had been turned off since her time at the hospital. When she turned it on again, she was horrified to see she'd missed two texts from Hannah.

How could she have forgotten? She hadn't given a thought to Hannah or the baby since Koti had kissed her in front of the nursery window. She sighed with relief as she read the latest message.

Baby doing well. Thanks for everything. Text me back.

What would Hannah think of her long silence? Kate thought guiltily as she typed her message. She hoped her friend had been too preoccupied to notice or care.

Hannah's first concern when they finally spoke, though, was for Kate. "I'm so glad to hear from you. I was concerned when I couldn't reach you, and Drew couldn't get in touch with Koti. But I guess you must both have been exhausted."

"Oh. Right. Uh . . ." Kate began, her tired mind stumbling in the effort to come up with an excuse.

"Uh-oh," Hannah realized. "Why *was* he with you, last night? Why did he just happen to be available to drive you, the minute I called?"

"Aren't you supposed to be wrapped up in your baby, not thinking about me?" Kate protested. "How is he? How are you? And Drew? I sure hope he got his face stitched up, or he's likely to be inflicting permanent psychological damage on that poor baby. And what's his name, anyway? I can't keep calling him "the baby."

Hannah laughed, happy to be distracted. "We're both being released tomorrow morning. And Jack Clifton Callahan is wonderful, thank you very much. We've decided he's the most beautiful baby in the world. Objectively speaking, of course. He's with me now, thank goodness, though they're still checking on him. Sleeping and eating and being fussed over by Drew's mum. All the good baby things. I'm being waited on too. I don't even get to change my own baby. All I'm doing is feeding him, eating, and sleeping myself."

"That's good. You just keep doing that. I'm so glad you thought to let me know everyone was all right."

"Thanks to the two of you," Hannah said, serious now. "I can't tell you how much we appreciate your help. I don't know what I would have done if you hadn't been there. Both of you."

"It was a privilege," Kate told her. She found she meant it. As terrifying as the experience had been, sharing the birth with Hannah had been something she would never forget. "And I'm sure Koti feels the same way."

"Speaking of which," Hannah went on, "be careful, OK? He has a kind heart, I know. We both saw that last night. But he's a major player. I don't want you to get hurt."

"Don't worry. We're just good friends," Kate assured her. "Well, no, that's not true. I'm not exactly sure what we are now. But he's good company." *And how,* she thought to herself.

"Well, if you're sure," Hannah answered dubiously. Kate heard the rumble of Drew's voice in the background. "Drew says thanks as well. And that I'm supposed to hang up and rest. Talk to you soon."

"When you're home, and up for a baby visit, let me know," Kate said. "I can't wait."

Chapter 18

"Kate." She heard the voice dimly, and brought her attention back with a jerk from the spreadsheet she was studying. She hadn't been able to settle to her work with her usual concentration that morning. Only after lunch, and a stern internal lecture, had she regained the focus that was now being interrupted.

She turned reluctantly to see the bouquet that the deliveryman was carrying in her direction, to the eager interest of her officemates. He set it down on her desk with a friendly "Cheers," and took himself off again. Kate reached for the envelope and opened it, aware of the eyes on her. She found herself flushing at the message on the card.

Everything I hoped. See you Wednesday. Koti

"Oooo, new boyfriend?" Brenda had come to stand next to the desk, and Kate's hand instinctively closed over the card.

"Lovely," the other woman continued approvingly, studying the bouquet of calla lilies and roses in vibrant shades of yellow and orange. "He has some imagination, anyway. No naff red roses."

"Who is he?" Heather asked from her seat two desks over. "Can't have been going on too long. Or you're a damn sight more discreet than the rest of us."

Kate joined in the laughter around her, tucked the card firmly into her purse. "Sorry. Keeping this one to myself for now," she said lightly. "Too good to share." She positioned the vase in the corner of her desk, smiled at Brenda, and turned back to her computer.

It was no use, though. The numbers she stared at meant nothing to her. Thank goodness it was Monday, and Koti wasn't on the premises. She found herself torn between pleasure at his thoughtfulness and distress at being exposed to her coworkers' curiosity.

At last, she gave in to her impulse and ducked out of the office. She found a quiet spot in the lobby and called him.

"Thanks for the flowers," she began. "They're beautiful."

"Did you like them? I worried a bit, after I sent them. Because of what you told me. I didn't want to bring up any bad memories."

She was touched. "Not the same thing. Not at all."

"That was your color, I thought," he said. "Same as the jersey you were wearing the other night. I looked at that jersey long enough to remember it."

"I loved them," she assured him again, struck by the effort he had taken. On the other hand, he probably sent flowers to every woman he slept with, she realized with a sudden pang. Maybe she shouldn't assign too much importance to the gesture.

"But, Koti," she went on firmly. "I had to grab that card so nobody would see it. I'd rather keep this quiet. Don't come visit me in the office anymore, OK? I'm afraid it'll be obvious, if you do."

"Why is it a secret?" She could imagine his frown at the other end of the line. "Not doing anything wrong, are we. Nobody's cheating on anyone here."

Kate hesitated. She hadn't realized until she saw the flowers how uncomfortable she was with making the change in their relationship public. But she knew why. Koti had more than his fair share of romantic history, all of which was public knowledge in the Blues office. She didn't want to be envied and questioned. Or dismissed as another woman on his list, she thought with a shudder.

"I'm not ready to be public about this," she finally told him. "Let's face it, we don't even know if it'll last more than a few weeks. We don't know what we're doing yet, and I'd rather not share till we do."

"Not hard to suss out," he objected. "We're dating. Nothing spectacular about that."

"Except that there's too much spectacular about you," she pointed out. "Most of which is well known to everyone here, believe me. So please, keep it quiet for now, OK? At least out of the office. I have to work here."

"You'll find that Auckland's a small town," he warned her. "Hard to keep a secret here."

"Good thing everyone already knows we're friends, then," she told him firmly. "Because that's my story, and I'm sticking to it."

Kate was shoving the towel into her swim bag when the knock came at her door Wednesday morning.

"Who is it?" she called cautiously.

"Koti," she heard.

She opened the door in surprise. "What are you doing here? I'm not late to meet you, am I? I was just leaving."

He stepped inside, shut the door. Leaned against it and pulled her into his arms. "I thought about it. Swimming. And then I thought about what I really wanted to do this morning. No contest."

A smile spread slowly over her face as she pulled his head down for a kiss. "Well, I could skip one day, I guess. If you promise to work me out."

He lifted her, felt her legs coming up to wrap around him. "Oh, I'm going to work you out. Bedroom's this way, eh."

"Not big enough for me to do my best work," he commented as he dropped her onto the bed in the tiny room. "But I'll make shift with it for now."

She came up onto her knees beside him. "Oh, no. I don't think so. I think I'm in charge now. You're in my flat, and it's my turn. Because I haven't had nearly enough of a chance to play with you."

He smiled, rolled to his back, pulled her on top of him. "Is that right? I reckon we could work with that for a bit, then. I'll do my best to be your sex toy."

"That's right." She moved to straddle him, dressed only in her swimsuit. "You're wearing way too many clothes, though. I'm going to have to take care of that right now."

She pulled off the hoodie and T-shirt, then reached down for his shorts. "No underwear, huh. Somebody was planning ahead."

"Always," he gasped as she ran her hands over him. "Condom in my shorts pocket too."

"Good to know," she agreed solemnly. "I don't think we'll need that for a little while, though. Seems to me I have some torturing to do first. You have a debt to pay in that department, don't you think?"

He reached for the straps of her suit, pulled it to her waist. Sat up to help her out of it. Sighed as he reached up to cup her breasts, slide his hands down her body as she settled back over him. "I do. And you're welcome to collect. I'll try to endure it."

"You do that," she told him with a satisfied smile. "You just try. You can start by stretching your arms over your head. Just like you made me do. I'm not tall enough to hold them there, so I'm going to have to rely on your sportsmanship."

"You do have sportsmanship, don't you?" she taunted as he slowly complied. She lay over him, moved up to kiss the Maori tattoo. Started at his forearm, kissing the bands of muscle there, then worked her way to his bicep, around to the smooth skin below. Finally reached his shoulder, covering it with kisses. Her hands moved over his chest, found the flat nipples and teased them until he groaned and shifted beneath her.

"I'll do my best," he got out. "Can't promise."

"Oh, I don't think that's nearly good enough." She was lying over him now, loving the feeling of him underneath her. She kissed his mouth lingeringly, then moved down to his throat, his neck, bit and licked at him there. Took her time with him. Finally wriggled down a little lower, put both palms flat on his chest. Ran them over him slowly, covered his skin with kisses.

She raised her head to look up at him. "I've decided I need a promise here, before I go any further. A promise to hold still for me. To do what I say."

"Promise," he ground out between gritted teeth as she kissed her way down his body, her hands moving over the muscles of his abdomen, his thighs. "For a while. Then it's going to be my turn."

"I'm counting on that," she agreed. "Meanwhile, you can lie still and feel this. Make your own plans, though. Be my guest. If you think better under torture than I do, that is."

He barely heard her. The closer she got, the more he needed to pull his arms down. Hold her head. Show her where to go, what to do.

She didn't need his help, he thought dazedly as time went on. She was doing fine on her own. She was doing too much on her own. He was burning. And soon he was going to be past help. His arms came down of their own volition. And then he did hold her head. Held her against him and groaned until he couldn't stand it anymore.

"That's enough," he gasped, pulling her up to him. "Playtime's over."

He rolled so she was beneath him. Took her mouth, tasted himself on her. Let his hands move over her body at last. "You've had your fun. My turn now. And you're going to be sorry you teased me."

"Oh, yeah?" She smiled up at him. "What are you going to do to me?"

"Haven't quite decided yet. Know where I'm going to start, though." He slid down her body, kissing and stroking. She was so wet already. She'd been excited by what she'd done, having him under her control, had she? He'd have to do something about that.

She'd thought it had felt good, pleasing him, feeling him beneath her. But that was nothing to the way he was making her burn now. His hands and mouth moved over her, nothing slow or subtle this time. Driving her up and over, again and again.

"Koti. Stop," she gasped. "Slow down. Too much."

He came up to join her. "I don't think so. Seems to me we've hardly started. Why don't you find that condom and put it on me? Because I've decided what happens next."

She did as he asked. Exclaimed with surprise when he picked her up and set her down on the floor.

"Thought I was going to keep you in bed this morning," he told her as he arranged her the way he wanted. "But you changed my mind. After what you did to me, I need you on your hands and knees."

"This is so nasty, though," she moaned, her body tingling with the aftershocks, the anticipation of what was coming.

"Very nasty," he agreed from behind her. "And just what I need from you today."

"This is nice," he told her, rubbing his hand over her bottom. "Looking at me like this. Showing me what a bad girl you are."

He gave her a spank that had her jerking back in surprise, crying out. He swatted twice more, a little harder now, then ran his hand over her, rubbed the sting away. Then rubbed a little more, just because it was so smooth, so pretty.

"Sorry, baby. Couldn't resist. And," he groaned as he eased himself inside, "I didn't want to. It felt so good."

She moaned as he moved inside her. "It felt good to me too," she got out. "But that's so bad of me. You're so bad for me."

"That's right," he told her as he began to move faster, harder. He heard her beginning to pant. Pulled her hips back hard with one hand, reached with the other to touch her, rub her where she needed him. "I'm bad for you. And that's good, because you're a bad, bad girl yourself. That's why you needed that. And why you need this."

He smiled as he felt the effect he was having on her. Began to move even faster, to drive into her. Over and over, listening to her, looking at her head lowered beneath him, her hair hanging down over her face.

He felt the contractions around him, felt them pulling him upward. And then he wasn't smiling any more. He felt himself being gripped by her, taken up with her, up to the knife-edge of sensation, shouting his own release aloud.

Afterwards, he lifted her back onto the bed. Moved to kiss her, stroke her, soothe her where she still trembled against him. "All right?"

She shook her head, eyes closed. "You should ask me while you're doing that to me. Because while it's happening, I don't feel all right. It's so intense, I can't stand it. But now . . ." She sighed and opened her eyes. "Somehow, now, I feel great. Embarrassed, but great."

"Why should you be embarrassed?" he frowned down at her. "Nothing to be embarrassed about. We're just playing. Nothing wrong with that."

"I didn't know I was so . . . so kinky," she admitted, a blush rising from her chest to her cheeks. "That I'd enjoy that. Being . . . you know."

"Being smacked?" He smiled against her hair. "I knew I'd enjoy smacking you, though. Been thinking about doing that to you for a while now." He pulled her more tightly against him. "We don't have to put a label on what we do. I'm not going to hurt you. I just want to enjoy you too. And you have to admit, it felt better than swimming."

"So much better," she sighed. Then realized what he had said. "Oh, no. What time is it?" She craned her neck to look at the alarm clock. "I can still make it. But I need to get ready."

He got up obligingly, began to pull on his discarded clothes.

"I'll walk you out to your car," she told him. "Just give me a second to put something on."

"Here." He pulled the hoodie over her head. "There you are. Dressed."

She looked down at the oversized garment, reaching nearly to her knees, and laughed. "Covered, anyway."

He reached for her hand and pulled her out the door as she grabbed her keys. "You don't have to lock up for this, surely," he protested as she used the key in the deadbolt.

She shrugged. "Habit. Caution."

When they reached his car, he wrapped her in his arms and looked down at her. "Thanks for changing your plans for me. Best swim date I've ever had."

She looked up at him with a smile. "It worked for me too. As you may have noticed."

"I'm still not allowed to come see you in the office, eh," he frowned. "How about coming to dinner with me tonight?"

"Sorry. Gym date with Brenda. If I break it, and she finds out why . . ." She shook her head. "Publicist, remember? Gossip, more like. How about tomorrow?" At his nod, she added, "Over here, though. More discreet. Text me, OK? I'll even let you pick me up at home this time."

"Good of you," he agreed. "As your flat is well and truly tainted by my presence now." He bent down to kiss her again.

"Sorry, dear," Kate heard. She stepped back, startled, to see the elderly lady gesturing to the newspaper slot in the wall next to where they stood.

She pulled Koti aside in confusion. "Oh, hi, Mrs. Ferguson. Ummm . . . yeah. Um, this is Koti James."

"I can see that, dear. Morning, Koti. I'm Kate's landlady, Janet Ferguson. It's nice to meet you. I haven't seen you playing recently, have I?"

"No, ma'am. Bit of a hiatus while the test matches are going on. We'll be starting up again Saturday week."

"Well, best of luck to you then. Mr. Ferguson and I will be looking out for you." She smiled again at the pair of them and turned back to the house, newspaper in hand.

Kate rested her head against Koti's chest and groaned. "Oh, man. Now I'm not just the neighborhood Yank. I'm the *slutty* neighborhood Yank."

"Sorry," she heard again from behind her. Two adolescent schoolgirls this time, digging exercise books and pens from their backpacks in excitement. "Can we get your autograph?"

"Oh, for . . ." Kate began.

"It's all right," Koti assured her. He signed quickly, but shook his head when one of the girls pulled out her mobile to take a photo.

"Sorry, not a good time," he told them firmly as Kate glared.

The girls looked from him to her in disappointment. Koti turned his back to them and Kate saw them walking away, glancing back at the two of them with avid curiosity. She was uncomfortably aware of how she looked, wearing only his oversized sweater. Wrapped around him too, she remembered.

"Yeh, staying over here'll work," Koti told her with a grin. "Discreet."

"They might know you, but they don't know me," she pointed out. "Except Mrs. Ferguson, of course. Oh, man. Especially when I'm dressed like this. I might as well have a sign around my neck. "Just Had Sex with Koti James!""

"I like that look on you. Messy. Naked under this thing, eh. Sweet as." He ran his hand down her back, bent to kiss her again. "If you had more time, I'd be taking you back upstairs and showing you exactly how much I like it. But I can see it may not be the image you're aiming for. You may want to avoid wearing my clothes in the office."

"Thanks for the tip. I'll do that. Now you really do need to go, or I'm going to be late." She pulled his head down and kissed him hard. "Have some more ideas before tomorrow night, OK? Much as I hate to admit it, that was pretty good."

He laughed aloud as he got into the car. "I'll work on it," he promised. "Hard against the wall next time, I reckon." He laughed again at her shocked expression and pulled away, the grin still on his face.

Chapter 19

"Nice," he said approvingly when she opened the door to him the next evening in a close-fitting dress of jade green. "I always appreciate your short skirts. I like the shoes too."

"They make me taller. I need all the advantage I can get with you."

"Nah. I told you, you terrify me," he assured her, finally leaning down for the kiss he wanted.

"Sure you want to go to dinner?" he asked when they came up for air. "Maybe you'd rather fix me something later."

"Nice try. But no. I didn't get dressed up for nothing. Show me the town, big boy. We'll build some anticipation here."

He laughed. "What do you think I've been doing since yesterday? Just teasing, though. You look too pretty. I can see you need to go out."

"So how'd things go today?" she asked him when they were settled into a cozy Italian restaurant in Takapuna. "Must be different with the whole team together again. More intense."

"Yeh. It's better, having the All Black boys back. Not as intense as it will be, though, because of the bye this week. Which means we'll have some time to spend together. We can go out on Saturday night like normal people."

"I was hoping I could get you to go surfing with me again," she said. "I'd like to keep practicing. I know I still need lots of coaching, and it might be my last chance for a while to get that from you. Brendan was telling me today that things would be heating up after this week. Because it looks like you guys are going to be playing in the quarterfinals, at least."

"Brendan?" He looked at her with a frown. "Brendan who?"

"Brendan McKenzie. The prop. Why, is there more than one Brendan on the team?"

"Why was he talking to you? When was this?"

She put down her fork and stared at him. "He stopped into the office for something today and came over for a chat," she said slowly. "Don't tell me you have a problem with that. He's a funny guy. I enjoy talking to him. I work in the Blues office, Koti. I do see the guys from time to time, you know. Do you want an incident report every time?"

"Did he ask you out?" he persisted.

"No. If he had, I would have said no. I haven't taken up a new career as a rugby groupie, much as it appeals to me, if that's what you're worried about."

He ignored the sarcasm. "Time to make this public. I'm not comfortable with all this secrecy."

"You don't get to decide that," she told him firmly. "I'm fully capable of dealing with any mild interest I might excite. For heaven's sake, Koti. I'm not some blonde bombshell. And as you've pointed out many times, I don't exactly have a come-hither personality. What are you worried about?"

"I know those boys," he countered. "I want them to know that you belong to me. And that I hold onto what's mine."

He saw her stiffen, realized what he had said. "Hang on. I didn't mean that. Not exactly."

"Oh yes, you did," she told him, eyes flashing with the danger signals he recognized by now. "And I'm not putting up with that. You can take that attitude and go straight to hell."

She started to say something else, thought better of it. Threw down her napkin and got up with a jerk, grabbing her purse and jacket and rushing from the restaurant.

Koti swore. Paid the bill as quickly as he could and went to the doorway, looking up and down the street for her. She'd be walking home, he decided. She couldn't go very fast, though. Not in those heels.

Sure enough, within a block he had caught sight of the furious little figure marching along the footpath, outrage evident in every step. He increased his pace to catch up with her. Moved to overtake her, then stood in front of her to block her way.

"Don't run away from me. If you have something to say, say it."

She stopped, glaring up at him. "I'm too mad at you right now. I'll just blow up. I need to cool down first. Figure out what I want to say."

"Go ahead. Yell. I can take it. Give it back too, come to that. If you cross the line, I'll tell you."

"Then here we go. I told you this before, but apparently you didn't listen. I'm telling you again now, and you'd damn well better hear me this time, because I am deadly serious. I do not like possessiveness. What we do in the bedroom is one thing. But you don't own me!"

"Never said I owned you," he protested.

"I think you just said exactly that. And that's unacceptable. What are you worried about, anyway? Why would I want to make my life any more complicated than it already is? To get more sex? I can hardly handle what I'm getting now. I'm not interested in dating anyone else. But that doesn't give you the right to try to control me. You don't get to tell me what to do or who to talk to."

"You don't like possessiveness, eh," he shot back. "How about those girls yesterday? You didn't seem too happy about that."

"Because I was half-naked at the time, and kissing you! They were interrupting us. Anyone would be upset."

"What about that Aussie girl at the caves, then? A bit hard to miss those looks you were giving her."

"Yeah, right," she scoffed. "She was hanging all over you. Wrapping herself around you like a boa constrictor. Of course I'm going to get annoyed if some girl built like that is shoving it in your face. It's not like I can offer that."

"I like what you have. Thought I'd made that clear by now. You didn't see me give her any encouragement, did you?"

"No," she admitted. "And if some guy is feeling me up the way she was doing to you, I give you permission to be upset too. But that wasn't the case here, and you know it. Quit trying to twist this around."

"Be upset? Yeh, I'd be upset. Reckon he'd be upset too, after I did him over. How am I twisting anything?"

"You can't be this clueless," she began. Then stopped as she heard her name being called.

"Kate?" she heard again, and turned at the voice. With dismay, she saw Hemi and Reka approaching along the footpath.

"This town is too small," she muttered. "Great. Perfect timing for our big reveal."

The other couple stopped in front of them, Reka looking from one to the other in unveiled curiosity. "How ya goin'?" she asked them. "Thought you didn't like this fella, Kate. Looks like that's changed."

"Not at all," Kate answered with a scowl. "I was just telling him what I thought of him, in fact."

"We're having a fight," Koti said with a rueful grin. "No worries. Goes with the territory."

"And I'm winning," Kate pointed out. "Because he was a jerk."

Reka shared a look with Hemi. "Ah. The penny's just dropped. Didn't realize the two of you were an item. You never tell me anything," she complained to her husband.

"Huh. We're not. Not any more," Kate said. "Not unless he apologizes."

Hemi looked at Koti sympathetically. "In the dogbox, eh. Trust me, mate. Apologize. May as well accept it. You're wrong."

"You don't even know what it's all about," Koti protested.

"Don't have to. I've been married a long time now."

Reka nudged him. "Oi. Because you *are* wrong, almost all the time. That's why you have to apologize so much."

"See what I mean?" Hemi appealed. "Accept it, and you'll be a happier man."

"Yeh, he will. Just like you are," Reka told her husband. "Because you're still married to me. And married men are happier. Studies show that. They're happier, and they live longer."

"Sure about that? Or does it just seem longer?" Hemi laughed.

He put a big arm around his protesting wife, gave her a squeeze. "Lucky to have you. Lucky you put up with me. I know that. Let me take you on to dinner, show you I mean it. Leave these two to work it out, eh."

Reka reached out and gave Kate a hug. "Don't let him off the hook," she counseled. "It's good for him."

"You're a good boy, Koti," she told him. "But you need someone who isn't dazzled by you. Keep you from getting above yourself. I've always thought so."

"No worries," he grinned back. "Kate's got that sewn up."

"Well, that was embarrassing," Kate sighed as Hemi and Reka continued up the street.

"I'd say your secret's out," Koti said. "At least with the team. Which makes this argument pointless."

"Nice try. Still waiting for my apology." She crossed her arms, the toe of one high heel tapping.

"What am I apologizing for again? I've forgotten by now. Better remind me. Make sure I don't do it again."

"Very funny. You're apologizing for being a possessive jerk. Which you know very well."

He stepped towards her. Gently pried loose her hands and held them in his own. "I'm sorry I fancy you so much that I can't stand the thought of other fellas hanging around. Because you're making my life dead uncomfortable just now."

"That's it? That's your big apology?"

"Yeh. That's it."

"Right," he sighed as she continued to scowl. "I'm sorry I made you do your block again. And I promise, I don't think of you as my property. I know you're your own person. And that you have the right to talk to anyone you like. But it's never going to make me happy to think about somebody chatting you up. Can't help it. That's how it is."

"Well," she conceded, "I'm not exactly thrilled when I see girls throwing themselves at you either. And I have a lot more to annoy me that way than you do. I guess we're going to have to agree to trust each other. And that means no more jealous fits in restaurants. If it bothers you, keep it to yourself." She glared at him again.

He held up his hands in surrender. "Agreed. Do my best, anyway. Can we go home now? Let me find a way to make it up to you. I'll make it special, I promise. Satisfaction guaranteed."

She laughed reluctantly. "I've figured that much out. And I'm not sure I can take anything more special. We hardly had anything to eat, though. What about dinner? Should we try to get something else?"

"I'll make you a sandwich. Come on."

"You're an expensive date," he complained later, coming back into his bedroom wearing only a pair of sweatpants, a pair of hastily assembled sandwiches on a plate. "I have to provide tea, even after I took you out. You know, some women would be offering to cook for me right now."

"Guess you'd better date one of them, then," she said cheerfully, pulling herself up against the pillows.

"Not quite ready to chuck it in," he conceded. "Even if I do have to make the sammies."

She smiled happily and took a bite. "You're good for certain things yourself, despite your many character flaws."

"Geez, thanks. Glad to know I have something to offer you."

"It came as kind of a surprise, tell you the truth," she mused. "I always comforted myself with the idea that you were probably lousy in bed. Every time you got me worked up, I'd think, never mind, the fantasy is bound to be a lot better than the reality. I figured I was sure to be disappointed, so it was just as well."

"What?" he asked, outraged. "Why would you think that?"

She shrugged. "I figured that anybody who'd had that many women so eager to be with him would never have had to do much work or care about what his partner needed. I thought you'd be selfish."

"I am selfish, though," he objected. "I do exactly what I want. Haven't you noticed? Doesn't mean I'm . . . what was it? Lousy at it? Cheers for that, by the way."

"I already told you I was wrong," she pointed out. "And sorry, but someone who just gave me that much pleasure can't be called selfish. Not in bed, anyway."

"That's what feels good to me, though. Seeing you so excited. Hearing you. Knowing I'm doing all that to you. That's what I want. Makes me feel powerful, if you want to know the truth."

She turned her head to look at him. "This is why I can never decide if you have too high an opinion of yourself, or if you don't give yourself enough credit. Taking pleasure in somebody else's pleasure is the opposite of selfish. Even if you do it for your own reasons. Which are valid, by the way."

She set down her half-eaten sandwich and moved closer. Reached up to kiss his cheek, ran her hand down his chest. "Because you are powerful, when you're doing that to me. You make me so crazy I can't think. Can't talk. You make me want you so much."

"And this would be the upside," he told her, moving the plate aside so he could pull her into his arms. "For all that temper. I'll take the fiery bits, when you show them to me here."

Chapter 20

Koti swore as they neared his house late Saturday afternoon after an all-day outing to the west coast, only to see a car parked in the driveway.

"Were you expecting somebody?" Kate asked as he pulled into a spot on the street instead.

"Nah. But I'm not too surprised. That'll be my sisters. That's Grace's car. Bet it's more than just her, though."

"Oh." Kate felt a pang of uncertainty. "Well, why don't you drop me off at home, then? That way you can have a visit."

"Oh, no. Strength in numbers. Come on." He hopped out and began untying their surfboards from the roof rack.

"I'm not sure this is a good idea," she said nervously as they walked toward the house. "I'm a mess right now. And not ready to meet your family in any case."

"Thought you didn't back away from a challenge anymore," he pointed out. "And my sisters can be a challenge, trust me."

"You're really helping here. Thanks a lot." Kate wished she'd at least taken the time to put on makeup after she'd changed out of her wetsuit. She tugged her sweater into place over her jeans and took a deep breath as Koti opened the door.

"Oi! Who's here?" he called as they stepped inside and found themselves enveloped by a delicious smell of roasting meat.

"Koti!" A tall, beaming woman came out of the kitchen, wiping her hands on a dishtowel. "Lovely to see you, darling."

"Hope!" she called. "Koti's home."

Koti returned his sister's hug and kiss, then pulled Kate forward as another woman entered the room.

"These are my sisters. Grace," he indicated the maternal-looking woman who had greeted them. "And this is Hope," he added as he hugged and kissed the other woman, a statuesque beauty with Koti's bronzed complexion and luxuriant black hair, pulled back like her sister's into the knot Kate was beginning to recognize as the preferred Maori style.

"This is Kate," he told the women, grasping her hand firmly in his own. "We've been surfing, so we need to get cleaned up before we can chat. Didn't know you were coming."

"Poor you," Hope said sympathetically to Kate. "Having us sprung on you like this."

"We did text you, Koti," she said reproachfully. "Didn't you see?"

"Surfing. Like I said. Where are the kids?"

"Back home, with the boys," Grace told him happily. "We decided this morning to come up for the weekend, do some shopping. It was an impulse, eh. We've had a good day, been in all the shops. Bought them out, more like. I'm glad you weren't away, though. We checked the fixtures first, so we knew you weren't playing."

"So you decided you'd just descend on me. For the weekend, I take it," he grumbled.

"Of course we did," she confirmed. "Because you will've missed us. And you haven't visited Mum in three weeks. It's clearly time for your family to check on you, make sure your head's still on straight. But go on, now. Take this poor girl upstairs and let her have a bath. She looks half frozen. We've got tea started already. It'll be ready by the time you're done."

"Go on and get warmed up," she urged Kate again, making shooing motions at both of them. "Then you can come down and have a glass of wine, let us get to know you."

Kate followed Koti upstairs in stunned silence, then sat down on the bed with a thump. "Whew."

"Told you. Good job Joy isn't here. You only have to deal with two of the three."

"Your sisters are named Hope, Grace, and Joy?" she asked in disbelief. "They're pretty names," she went on hurriedly. "It's just a little overwhelming, hearing those names all together like that."

He laughed. "Not as overwhelming as meeting the three of them together. Be glad Joy couldn't come. She's the most talkative."

"Wow. I'll take your word for it. Are they all older than you, or younger?"

"You're joking, right? All older. I'm the baby. Can't you tell? Hope's the youngest and quietest. Grace is the oldest. And the bossiest."

"I'm getting the picture. And your house is their house, I take it. I'll bet they all have keys, too."

"Too right. Can't exactly say I don't have room, can I?"

"Nope. The price of success. And of family."

"All right, then," she decided, getting up off the bed. "If I'm going to appear before this tribunal, I need to get cleaned up. I wish I had something nicer to wear, though."

"What are you doing?" she asked in alarm as he stepped into the shower with her a few minutes later. "Your sisters are downstairs."

"Yeh, they are," he agreed, pulling her into his arms. "Which makes this our chance, doesn't it? You can be loud here, too," he encouraged her as he poured body wash into one palm and began to run his soapy hands over her skin. He smiled as he saw her neck arch, heard the low thrum begin in her throat. "Bonus for both of us."

"And I promised hard against the wall, I seem to remember," he added at last, lifting her under the spray so the water poured onto her. "Haven't delivered on that yet, have I. No time like the present."

When they finally rejoined the others in the kitchen, Kate devoutly hoped Koti's sisters had missed the implications of their long shower. Her legs still felt rubbery, and she turned red at the thought of what they'd just done, twelve feet overhead. She found Grace checking the oven while Hope prepared a salad at the large center island.

"I can tell you're both feeling better, now that you're warmed up," Hope smiled approvingly. Kate blushed again, feeling like a schoolchild caught in some misdemeanor.

"We are." Koti grinned at them, pulled Kate up against him. "Much better. Hungry, too. What are you making for us?"

"Leg of lamb, roasted vegies, and salad," Grace announced, pulling the pan from the oven. "Pour the wine, Koti. We bought some quite nice Pinot Noir. Over on the bench there."

"What can I do?" Kate asked.

"Nothing. Just sit down and have a chat while we finish up here," Hope instructed.

"How often do you two get up to Auckland?" Kate asked when Koti's sisters had served the delicious meal and everyone was contentedly tucking in. "Do you always do your shopping here?"

Grace laughed. "Really just an excuse to get away from the kids for a bit. And to keep an eye on our little brother, of course." She looked across at him fondly.

"How many kids do you have?" Kate wondered.

"I have three, Hope has two," Grace answered. "Their dads are coping now. It's good for them. Mine are ten, seven, and five, and Hope's are five and two. We need a break from time to time."

"So you have five nieces and nephews," Kate told Koti. "Wow. I didn't realize."

"Seven," Hope corrected. "Joy has two as well. How about you, Kate? How many nieces and nephews do you have?"

She laughed. "I'm way outgunned here. None. I'm an only child. Even my parents are back in California. I'm afraid you'd find my family life awfully tame in comparison to yours."

"Yeh. Because that'd be a nightmare," Koti said with a straight face. "All that peace and quiet at the holidays."

"Oh, you love it," Grace told him. "You know you do. Everybody's favorite uncle, aren't you. You're so good with the kids. Time for you to have some of your own."

"You must live close to each other, I'm guessing," Kate put in hurriedly. "Is that near where you grew up?"

"We all live in Hamilton," Hope said. "All three of us. Close to each other, and to our mum and family in Cambridge as well. We tried to convince Koti to play for the Chiefs again, when he came back." She looked at him reproachfully. "But he went to Auckland instead."

"Wonder why," he muttered, taking a sip of wine.

"At least he's not playing for the Highlanders," Grace said. "He's close enough for us to visit, anyway. Make sure he stays out of trouble."

"I'm beginning to see why you're so attractive to women," Kate told him. "You've had lots of practice being appealing."

"Not that I got to see that at first," she explained to his sisters. "I hate to tell you this, but your brother did not make a good first impression on me."

"On *you*?" he spluttered. "I thought you were two sammies short of a picnic, myself."

"'Mad as a meat axe' were, I believe, the words used," Kate agreed.

"That was later, though. You started by warning me off the beach. I couldn't stand you. Well, I always liked the way you looked," he amended. "Just not too fond of that stroppy side at the time."

His sisters traded glances. "You seem to be getting along well enough now, though," Hope ventured. "Looks like you got it sorted. How did you meet? Sounds like it was memorable."

"I work for the Blues," Kate told her. "Koti was one of the first players I met, in fact."

"And I've been trying to keep her from meeting the others ever since," he said.

"Another sensitive subject," Kate pointed out. "Not to mention yet another failure of the famous Koti James charm offensive."

"That's unusual," Grace said. "It doesn't let him down much. Three older sisters and a mum, eh. He's had women fetching and carrying for him since he was born. Knows how to make them feel happy to do it, too."

"You don't have to tell Kate that," Koti complained. "She doesn't need any more ammunition. Think I'd better keep her from getting any more background information, in fact. Why don't you two go watch telly or something. We'll do the washing up."

"My house, remember?" he reminded them when they objected. "Much as you like to forget it. Go on, now."

He herded his sisters into the lounge and closed the kitchen door in relief. "Sorry," he told Kate. "You don't actually have to help me if you don't want to. But I needed a break."

"They're crazy about you, though," Kate objected as she began to put away the leftovers. "You obviously have a loving family. And it sure looks to me like you're the pet."

"Too loving, I sometimes think," he muttered, rinsing plates and putting them into the dishwasher. "They're missing some boundaries. Think I'm still their baby brother."

"And on that note, why don't you take me home after we finish this?" she suggested. "Despite what you're saying, I'm sure you'd like some time with them. And I'm not that comfortable staying with you while they're here."

"Why? Because they'll be shocked that you're sleeping with me? We can always rumple the sheets in the fourth bedroom so you can pretend you spent the night there," he teased. "Not that they'd believe it. But I'd rather you stayed. As you can see, I need the support."

"Right. Because they're so hard on you," she scoffed. "They adore you."

He grimaced. "Having you here will help remind me I'm not eight anymore. Growing up in that house full of women, all mothering me."

"Where was your dad?" she asked hesitantly. "If you don't mind my asking."

"Took a hike," he said shortly. "When I was eight, like I said. And since even Hope is four years older than I am . . . A bit hard to feel like a man with my sisters kissing me on top of the head for years. Can't tell you how relieved I was when I finally grew taller than all of them and they couldn't reach it."

She laughed, but was touched all the same. "You haven't heard from your dad since then?"

"Oh, I've heard from him. As soon as I made a bit of money, started being written up by the journos, he was on to that. Never contacted my mum or my sisters, of course. Just me."

"I take it you didn't follow up with him."

"Shit, no. Told him to fuck off," he glared. "Sorry. Language. Makes me ropeable to think about it, that's all. After he left my mum to raise the four of us by herself. He sent money. Had to do that. But that was all. Reckon he decided he was entitled to more fun than he was having, and we were in the way of that. My mum didn't have that choice."

"Sounds like she's a strong woman."

"She is. Strong and proud. My sisters too. They're all good mums to their own kids. Married pretty good blokes, too. I know I have a good family, and I love them. Just wish they'd see I'm grown up now. Which is why I'd like you to stay tonight. Help remind me I'm a big boy," he said with a grin, shaking off the serious subject.

He good-naturedly put up with his sisters' reminiscences of his boyhood during the rest of the evening, but it was with obvious relief that he finally ascended the stairs to his bedroom with Kate.

"Koti, no," she hissed in shock when he reached for her under the covers, his clever hands moving to pull her nightgown over her head. "We can't do this now. Grace is right next door. I'd die of embarrassment tomorrow. Plus, we already did it, remember?"

"That's right. And now we're going to do it again. You'll have to be quiet this time, though, won't you? Like a little mouse. Think you can do that?" He kissed her neck. Reached the spot under her ear he knew she loved, bit her there.

"No," she moaned as his teeth closed over her skin again. "So you need to stop."

"Hmmm. You are a noisy girl. I've noticed that. I've got an idea, though. Every time you forget, I'll stop what I'm doing. Wait till you can be quiet before I start up again. Give you some incentive to behave."

"Don't make a sound, now," he reminded her as his hand moved to stroke her. "Or I'll stop." He bent his head to her breast, bit down.

Hand and mouth stopped as she moaned. "You aren't even trying. Concentrate."

"Koti, wait. No," she protested as he began to move again.

"No?" he asked, looking up. Moved his hand again.

"Oh, no," she moaned. "Don't stop. Please."

"Going to try harder?" he asked her sternly. "Because so far, you aren't impressing me."

"Oh," she sighed. "Yes. I promise. Please. I'll try."

Fifteen minutes later, he looked up reproachfully. "You have no self-control. All this stopping and starting. What am I going to do with you?"

"We need to stop," she gasped, her body shuddering. "I can't do this. You're killing me."

He smiled. "Just a bit longer. Try harder. You need a bit more discipline, that's all. And I reckon I'm the man to give it to you."

In the end, she couldn't help herself. As she began to cry out, she felt his hand close tightly over her mouth. The effect, after the exquisite torture of the preceding minutes, was too much, and she lost herself in wave after wave of the most intense sensation of her life.

"That's it. I can't take any more," she moaned as he finally came up to join her.

"Oh, I think you can," he assured her. "Never mind. I know how to keep you quiet now. Come on, baby. Open up for me."

With a sob, she did as he asked. And found herself lost again. Her eyes opened in shock as he began to talk softly in her ear, telling her what he was doing, all the things he wanted to do. She began to spiral again, taking him up with her. When they finally went over the top together, his hand was covering her mouth again as he pressed his own face into the pillow, muffling his shout of triumph.

She lay against the pillows, spent and stunned. "You are one nasty man," she said at last. "I can't believe you said those things to me."

"Reckoned it was time to see how you liked it. I'm no expert, mind, but I'd say you liked it a lot. I think you like my hand over your mouth, too. You're a pretty bad girl yourself."

"And if you still feel eight years old after all that, you must've been some precocious child," she told him severely.

"Mmmm. I think I can stand up to my sisters now," he agreed, leaning over to kiss her. "All I'll need to do is look at you, imagine what we just did, and I'll feel like a man again."

"Great. Every time you look at me tomorrow, I'm going to turn red."

"Yeh. That'll be fun too."

Chapter 21

"We'd better be off soon," Grace said reluctantly the next morning, standing to clear the table of the bacon and egg breakfast she had cooked for all of them. "I have prep to do for tomorrow."

"What kind of prep is that?" Kate asked curiously.

"Didn't Koti tell you?" Grace asked in surprise. "We're teachers. All of us. Joy, Hope and myself, and Mum too. Our boy here's the only one who escaped." She bent to kiss the top of his head as he rolled his eyes at Kate and she stifled a laugh. "His talents lay in other directions, didn't they."

"I'll bet he did well in school too, though," Kate objected. "Didn't you?" she asked Koti.

"Pretty well," he acknowledged. "Went to Uni. But I was playing rugby as well, and it got too hard to do both. Only did a couple of years."

"It seems to me he has plenty of talents," Kate said to Grace. "But something else came up that was a better choice for him at the time."

Grace looked from one to the other of them in surprise, a plate in each hand.

"Good on ya, Kate," Hope chimed in. "We're not used to thinking of him that way. But I wouldn't care to have one of my students pigeonholed like that, come to think of it."

"I do it too," Kate admitted. "Koti called me on it once. Remember?" she asked him. "It used to take me by surprise when he'd say something insightful. Sometimes it's not so easy to be pretty. People tend to underestimate your brains, I think."

"Oi," he complained. "Sitting right here, aren't I. And I'm not pretty."

The three women looked at each other and laughed. "Sorry," Kate told him with a grin. "But your public disagrees with you. We could call you gorgeous. Would that be better?"

"No," he scowled. "Talk about something else."

"Let's talk about getting back to the kids," Hope decided, ever the peacemaker. "Thanks for letting us descend on you, love," she told her brother, leaning over to kiss his cheek. "And for giving us the chance to meet Kate."

She stood and told her sister, "Bet we can leave the washing-up for these two. If I know Doug, there'll be heaps of that to do at home. May as well save my energy."

"I see Hope knows how to get things done," Kate told Koti as they turned back into the house after waving goodbye to the sisters fifteen minutes later. "All so diplomatically, too. Wish I could be more like that."

"Never happen," he said. "No worries, though. You have the direct approach mastered."

"Then I will directly tell you that I need to get home too. I have a lot to do before the week starts up again."

"Me too. Hemi's agreed to watch game film with me today."

"You asked him," she realized with pleasure.

"Yeh," he shrugged. "Reckon it can't hurt. Get some pointers about where I could improve my form. I talked to Drew as well. He's giving me some extra help at practice."

"That can't have been easy," she said. "It must have taken some guts."

"It did," he admitted. "But Drew made it easier. Thanked me for my help with the baby, said he owed me. So I was able to slip that in there."

"Guess I'll see the effects next weekend. You'll have to tell me what to watch for. What you're going to do differently. Not that I'll be able to tell if you do it. Maybe the announcers will pick up on it, though. That way I can pretend I noticed."

"We're in Canberra for that," he reminded her. "Which means I'll be gone from Thursday morning, on through to Sunday afternoon."

"I'm glad we had this weekend, then. Surfing and . . . and everything. I'm doing better, don't you think? At surfing, I mean. Must be my coach."

"That, and the pit bull in you. You don't pike out, I have to say."

"Anything worth having is worth working for," she agreed. "That's what my dad would say. That and, 'Anything worth doing is worth doing right.' That last one is pretty much the accountant's motto."

"Remind me never to play board games with your family. Your Scrabble evenings must be a nightmare."

"It's true," she laughed. "How'd you know?"

"Wild guess. But here's my question. Why not bring some things over tomorrow after work, stay with me till I leave? We have some serious catching up to do here."

"Don't you think it's early days for me to be putting my clothes in your closet? Going a little fast, aren't we?"

"If it gets to be too much and you need your own space, you can always go home for a night," he pointed out. "Or start another fight, make me toss you out."

"Comforting. But I guess we can try it. I have to warn you, though. I'm not much more of a cook than you are. I don't want you to get your hopes up and think you're getting some kind of domestic goddess. I'm not like your sisters. I can eat it. I just can't make it."

"Thought you were Italian," he sighed. "Oh, well. Can't be helped. We'll have to work together, I reckon. If we have an epic fail, there's always takeaway."

"All right, then. You're in charge of groceries, since you're off tomorrow. Buy what you can make, and you'll probably stay within my capabilities too."

"Well, this didn't work out too badly," she told him on Wednesday night, as he polished off his plate of pasta topped with the sausage and pepper sauce they had prepared together. "We even made an edible dinner every night. Who knew?"

"It's been good," he agreed. "And now you'll get a break from me, do what you like. Recover," he said with a sly smile.

"Which probably means reading," she admitted with a smile of her own. "Or for some real excitement, watching a movie on TV. Maybe I'll try surfing on my own on Saturday, at one of the easier spots. You have a pretty good idea what my frenetic social schedule is like. I'll try to make time in there to watch your game, though. Maybe I'll see if Hannah wants company for that, Saturday night. I'd like to see that baby again."

"And speaking of schedules," she went on, "why don't I drop you off at the airport tomorrow morning? That way I can drive straight in to work afterwards."

"Thanks. If you don't mind picking me up on Sunday afternoon too. I used to get a lift from Hemi, but his car's chocka now, three bubs in the back seat."

"Kind of public, don't you think?" she objected. "With the whole team there?"

"Why? Can't a friend give another friend a lift? I'll want to see you anyway. Plus, that way you can come home with me straight away, save me a booty call," he added with a grin.

"Oh, that's just charming. How can I refuse, when you ask so nicely?"

"I'm sure you could find a way. But I'd rather you didn't. Come on, Kate. Meet me. I'll make it worth your while, I promise."

"Oh, all right," she grumbled. "I guess I'll want to see you too, by then."

Kate pulled into a space in front of the international terminal and hastened inside. Traffic had been heavy. She hoped Koti wasn't through Customs already, and waiting for her. She was relieved when she entered the arrivals lobby and spotted Hannah and Reka in the crowd. The team couldn't have arrived yet.

"Kate," Reka said with pleasure. "You and Koti worked things out then, I'm thinking."

"We did. We had a fight," Kate told Hannah. "Which of course Hemi and Reka managed to witness."

"If you're going to have it in the footpath in the center of Takapuna, someone's bound to see," Reka pointed out.

"Doesn't matter where you have it, I'd say," Hannah smiled, shifting the sleeping baby in her arms. "It's like living in a fishbowl, sometimes."

"I haven't met your kids before," Kate said to Reka. "They look like they keep you pretty busy."

"Why, just because they're jumping about like monsters? Wonder why you'd think that. Ariana and Jamie," she announced, indicating the two dark, curly-haired children playing a hand-slapping game next to her. "And this is Luke in the pushchair."

The two-year-old in the stroller looked up at Kate with big, solemn brown eyes. "Hello," Kate told him with equal seriousness, giving his little hand a shake. He giggled and looked away bashfully.

"I can see why you wouldn't have room in your car for anyone else," Kate said.

"Heaps of room. We have a people mover," Reka answered. "Hemi claims he can feel his testosterone draining away every time he gets in."

"A minivan," Hannah explained.

"Oh." Reka caught on, seeing the surprise in Kate's face. "Koti told you he needed a lift home, did he? That boy has more angles than a geometry text."

Kate laughed ruefully. "I should be flattered, I guess. But you're right. It can be hard to stay one step ahead of him."

"Somehow, I think you'll manage, if anyone can," Reka told her with a satisfied smile. "Here they are, though," she broke off, as the figures in their blue warmup jackets began to appear in the entryway, duffels slung over their shoulders, to a scattering of applause and cheers from the crowd.

Hannah and Reka made no attempt to rush forward. "Wait a bit," Reka counseled Kate. "They'll find us in a minute."

Kate watched with surprise as a small crowd converged around the players. Drew and Koti, she saw, attracted the most autograph-seekers, though the other players came in for their share as well.

"This is mild," Hannah told her. "There are always a few diehard fans, though, who know the schedule and make the trip. Especially on a Sunday like this. It's much worse for the All Blacks."

"I didn't realize Koti was quite so popular," Kate said absently. "Not just the girls, either."

"Heaps of those," Reka laughed, as the phone cameras clicked and Koti signed his name to the papers thrust in his path. "But the boys admire his skills as well. The kids love him."

Kate's breath caught a little in spite of herself as Koti's eyes finally met hers, the flashing smile spreading over his face. She was dimly aware that Drew and Hemi had joined their families, but her attention was all for the man approaching her, dropping his duffel to pull her into his arms.

"Very friendly kiss," she said as he put her down. "Oh, well. What the hell." She reached up to pull his head down again. "I missed you."

"And by the way," she added, pulling back at last and doing her best to scowl at him. "Nice try, but Reka's just told me she has plenty of room in her car."

"Is that a fact," he said. "Must have been misinformed. Or maybe I just wanted to see my girl sooner."

Kate turned to hide the foolish grin on her face, and saw Drew taking Jack from Hannah. She was touched at the sight of the baby, still so small, being held against his father's broad chest.

Drew looked up and caught her eye. "Grown since I left, eh," he said with a proud smile.

"I can't believe how much bigger he is," she agreed. "I came over last night to watch the game, and I was impressed. He must have been doing some good eating."

"Takes after me, not his mum," Drew said. "Probably for the best."

"I wanted to tell you two, while I had the chance," Kate went on. "If you need a date night or something, now that he's grown a bit and is doing so well, I'd be happy to come over and babysit. I think I know the ropes now."

Drew looked at Hannah, brows raised.

She nodded. "If it were just for an hour or two. It'd be hard to leave him, but if it were Kate, and we stayed in St. Heliers, and we had our mobiles . . ."

"And a Nannycam, I reckon," Drew said. "Or we could stay in range of the baby monitor. Have a picnic out on the deck."

Koti laughed. "My sister Hope says that the cord stays attached after they're born. Just invisible. Seems to me it stays that way for a long time. Stretches itself thinner and thinner over the years, till it's a thread. The bond's still there. But the mum can let go, a bit at a time."

Hannah looked at him in amazement.

"I know," Kate told her. "Isn't he full of surprises? He has seven nieces and nephews. That explains part of it."

"Well, since you're an expert," Hannah said with a smile, "you're welcome to come over too, if we get Kate to babysit. Maybe next Monday night, since you boys will have the day off."

"Thanks," Koti said. "As that's my date night as well."

"Babysitting on your date. That'll be pretty special," Hannah commiserated.

"I was there when this little fella was born, wasn't I. Reckon I should get to know him. And I don't trust Kate to know what to do."

"I do too," Kate objected. "Just feed him and change him. Easy."

Koti and Hannah looked at each other and laughed. "I'd better come along," he decided. "Just in case."

Chapter 22

"We need something that goes with fish." Kate stood undecided in the produce aisle of the Takapuna New World the following Sunday. "Potatoes or rice? Which would you prefer? I went to the Market this morning and bought fresh John Dory. That Maori guy in the fish stall can fillet a fish faster than anyone I've ever seen. I wouldn't want to get in a knife fight with him."

"I don't fancy fish tonight," Koti objected. "I was thinking about a steak."

"Unfortunately, though, fish doesn't keep. And I'm excited about trying something new, in our ongoing attempt to become competent in the kitchen. I even got advice on how to cook it, and I'm looking forward to seeing how it turns out."

He grunted in response, his expression glum. With a shove and a sigh, she moved the trolley to one side of the aisle and turned to face him.

"Look, Koti. If you didn't want to go shopping with me today, why didn't you tell me so? I could have done my own and left you alone. There's no reason for us even to have dinner together if you'd rather be by yourself. Because you seem pretty tired. Pretty grumpy too, if you want to know the truth. My attempts to cheer you up aren't working, and I can't read your mind. So you'd better tell me what's going on here. Is it the game last night, or is it something to do with me?"

"If you have a think about it for a minute, you may be able to come up with the reason," he told her with a scowl. "In case you didn't notice, my form was rubbish last night, and we lost the game. Hard to win when the team's off pace anyway, and you're a man down. Because some wally made a bad tackle and was sinbinned."

"You mean when you were sent off, nobody replaced you?"

"No," he said sarcastically. "Nobody replaced me. Do you even listen to the commentary? Ten minutes with fourteen men on the field. That's a bloody long time. Asking your teammates to make up the difference. Which they couldn't. Maybe you noticed that."

"All right. I get it. Watch how you talk to me, though. I understand that you're upset. But being rude to me isn't going to help. It's just going to make me walk out on you again. Fair warning. You're about ten seconds away."

"Sorry," he muttered. "I'm shocking company. Should have stayed home, you're right. But I'm wondering why I'm even trying to do this. Supposed to be more aggressive with the tackling. All I did was tackle too high and get sinbinned for it."

"Is that all you did, though?" she objected. "I realize I don't entirely know what I'm looking at. But it seems to me you've been tackling more. Passing the ball more instead of just running with it, too. Making better decisions. All those things you've been working on. So you made a mistake. Why can't you admit that to the guys and keep working at it? Were you expecting to be perfect as soon as you started trying? And it's not like it's knocked you out of the playoffs, is it? You're still in the quarterfinals next week, right?"

"Right," he said reluctantly. "The Stormers, in Capetown. A longer trip than if we'd won, which'll make it tougher."

"And does one mistake by one player—or one good play by one player—win or lose the game anyway?" Kate continued. "You said the whole team wasn't playing as well as usual. Was yours the only mistake? It seemed like I saw a lot of missed kicks in there too."

"Nah," he admitted. "We were a bit off pace last night, like I said."

"So it wasn't just you. And we've established that it wasn't the end of the world. Just one mistake. All right, then. Our ice cream is melting. What do you want to do here? Want me to drop you off at home after this? Or should I come over so we can cook that nasty, fresh-caught fish that you aren't in the mood for? What's going to make you feel better?"

He perked up a bit. "Well, if you really want to make me feel better, I can think of a few things we could try."

"You're kidding." She stared at him. "As grouchy as you've been? How can you possibly be interested?"

"Is this a trick question? Or do you really not know the answer to that?"

"So you want me to come over. Got it." She began to push the trolley again.

"Oh, no. It's going to take more than that," he decided, his mood improving by the second as he took the trolley from her. "It's going to have to be something pretty special."

She looked at him suspiciously. "Just how special?"

He glanced around. "Manuka honey," he decided, pulling it off the shelf. "Medicinal, eh. Let's see how it works."

"What exactly are we talking about here?" she demanded.

"I would've thought it was obvious. But I know how you like me to tell you exactly what I want. What I'm planning to do."

He leaned over and murmured in her ear. "I'm going to make you lie still. Then I'm going to spread it on you. Going to take some extra time with my favorite bits. And then I'm going to lick it all off. Very, very slowly. Because I need to hear you scream again."

He felt her body swaying towards him. "Hmph. I don't like Manuka honey, though." Her attempt at unconcern was falling a little short, but he could tell she was giving it her best effort. "What about me?"

"Reckon you'll have to choose something of your own, then, if you want to participate in this exercise," he said, a slow grin spreading over his face. "Looks like this is going to be my lucky night after all."

"Here." He grabbed a bottle of maple syrup and tossed it in the trolley. "American. Just for you."

"That's Canadian," she objected.

"Close enough. Let's go."

"Oh. That's so cold. And sticky." She jumped as he carefully poured the first drops of the amber liquid onto one nipple.

"I'm very thorough, though," he promised, as he spread the honey lovingly with his fingers. "I think I can promise not to leave any of it on you. Or in you. If I miss any, you can tell me. And I'll start over."

"See if this is any warmer," he suggested as he bent to take her nipple into his mouth. She felt his tongue and teeth scrape over her and arched towards him with a moan.

"Break," she gasped, long minutes later. "I'm melting here. And you aren't giving me a chance to play. Where's my maple syrup?"

"Hmmm. There are a lot of calories in this," she taunted him as she used her hands to smear his body with the dark stuff. She painted his chest first, worked on him there, then moved down to outline the perfect definition of his abdomen. Looked up at him, her mouth curving into a mischievous smile as her hands finally moved lower, and she spread the liquid carefully over him.

"Maybe I've changed my mind about licking all this off you," she mused, her small hands still busy. "About taking my time so I don't miss any spots. Especially down here. You wouldn't want me to get fat. You've been good enough to mention your concern."

He groaned. "You can go on a diet tomorrow. Come on, baby. Lick it off me now."

"Be sure you get it all," he moaned as his hands fisted in her hair. "Oh, my God. I think I'm dying."

"Mmm. Missed a spot up here," she told him at last, moving up his body, sliding over him as she went, the honey that still clung to her mingling with the syrup to create a sweet, sticky mess that added its own friction.

"Best part," he groaned as she slowly sank onto him and began to move. His eyes locked onto hers as he reached for her, began to touch her, watched her arch her back and gasp in response. "Watching you come. Feeling it all around me. Come on, now. Show me."

"That's it. That's so good," he crooned as she gave in to the pleasure. "You're so beautiful. Do it again, baby. Show me what you can do."

"Koti. Stop," she gasped at last. "I can't, any more."

He rolled her to her back, bent his head to kiss her. "But you do it so well. I could watch that again and again. Or I could just do this. Because it feels so good inside you."

He began to move again, slowly at first. Watched her respond to him and increased the tempo. Harder and faster, giving her more, pushing her higher again until, finally, she began to cry out. This time, as she went over the top, he rode with her, through a peak that seemed to last forever, and down the other side.

"That was at once the most ridiculous and the most exciting thing I've ever done," she decided as they washed each other clean in the shower. "Not to mention creating a whole lot of laundry."

"You didn't seem to think it was so ridiculous while we were doing it," he pointed out, addressing a particularly sticky patch with a diligence that had her leaning against the wall of the shower with a moan. "Face it. You're a bad, bad girl. You just don't know it yet. Baby steps."

"If that was a baby step, don't tell me what the next one is," she told him, doing a little soaping of her own. "I'm not sure my heart can take it."

"Thought I'd already mentioned a few things from time to time. Things we haven't done yet."

"You weren't serious about that. Were you?" she asked doubtfully. "This is getting awfully kinky."

He smiled. "You're such a baby. We haven't done anything kinky yet. We're just getting started." He bent to kiss her as the water beat down on them. "Haven't even tied you down yet, have I," he murmured in her ear.

She stepped back, eyes wide. "You wouldn't do that, would you?"

"Oh yeh, I would. Only if you want to play. But I'm thinking you will. We'll save that for a special occasion, though. After a fight, I'm thinking, when we're both still heated up. And when we have hours to spend. Because once I have you like that, I'm going to want to keep you there for a while."

He ran soapy hands over her, felt her lean into him in response. "Just now, though," he decided, lifting her into his arms, pulling her legs around his waist, "I'm hungry, and I need my tea. So I reckon we'll go back to an old favorite. Hard against the wall. That works pretty well for me too."

"Just don't tell my mother what I'm letting you do to me," she moaned, wrapping herself more tightly around him.

"No worries. Nobody's business but ours what we do. I won't tell your mum, and you won't tell mine."

Chapter 23

"What do we do?" Kate wailed along with the baby. Their babysitting job had started off so well. She'd managed to change Jack without too much trouble, and he'd taken his bottle like a champ. So what was he crying about now? She was beginning to panic.

"What does he want? Is he sick? How could he have got sick so fast? They haven't even been gone an hour. Should I call Hannah?"

The baby in her arms took the opportunity to cry even louder. "Oh no," Kate moaned. "I said her name. I didn't realize that would upset him more."

Koti laughed. "Give him to me. The more upset you get, the more you wind him up. Come on," he coaxed. "Let me have him."

He laid little Jack down carefully on the oversized couch next to Kate and pulled off the crumpled receiving blanket that had twisted around him.

"They like to be wrapped up tight," he explained. "Comforting. Like being inside mum, eh."

Kate watched as he swaddled the baby, tucking the final corner in with a practiced hand. "How do you know?"

"Do you imagine any of my sisters would've missed the opportunity to lecture me on baby care?" He lifted Jack, already slightly less hysterical, and settled him snugly against one broad shoulder.

"Probably not," she said. "He's still crying, though."

"Not for long," Koti told her confidently. He stood up and began to walk, one firm hand cradling the little figure while the other supported his head.

"How many times are you going to do that?" she asked as he made his fourth or fifth circuit of the lounge, dining room, and kitchen.

"Till he stops crying, of course. Lucky this is a big house. This gets a lot more boring when you can only take ten steps in each direction."

Gradually, the baby quieted, his wails dying down to hiccupping sobs and then silence. "Not asleep yet," Koti decided. "I'm not risking it." He sat down next to Kate, still holding Jack firmly against him. "Let his parents worry about good sleep habits. I'm going to hold him for now."

Kate lay back and fanned herself with her shirt. "I'm exhausted. Whatever babysitters get paid, it isn't enough."

"Good thing you have me along, then," he said smugly.

"All right, I admit it. I'd have been completely panicked without you. I just never expected you to be good at this."

"And that would be . . . why?"

"Because you're a . . ." She stopped. Shrugged. "You know."

"Go on. You can say it. I'm a *man*. Who can't possibly know anything about childcare."

"There I go again, tripped up by my preconceptions," she admitted. "I never thought of babysitting with a guy, though. No, that's not true," she corrected herself. "I thought of it once." She started to laugh, remembering.

"Oh, good. A bedtime story. Tell me," he commanded.

"All right. But it doesn't show me in a very good light, I'm afraid. I was in high school. I used to babysit for this couple. Believe it or not, I do know how to babysit. I just didn't realize that little tiny babies were so much harder. Anyway, they had a little girl. She was maybe two, and they'd go out once she was in bed. So it was the easiest job ever. I never had to do anything, just hang out there, read or whatever, till they came home. And then one night, my boyfriend asked if he could come over."

"And I know," she continued, "that's Rule Number One for teenage babysitters. No boyfriends. But what can I say? I did it anyway. So he came over, and we're sitting on the couch. Not making out or anything. Just talking. And all of a sudden, we see the headlights in the driveway."

She put her hands over her face in chagrin and laughed. "The one time—the *only* time—these people ever came home during the evening. And it had to be that night. My boyfriend took off like a rabbit out the back door. I could hear him crashing over the fence while the parents were coming in the front door. I'm such a lousy liar, I know they could see it all over my face—in case they missed all that noise. He must have fallen over a garbage can or something. I was mortified. I felt like they'd caught me drinking all the liquor and having sex."

She sighed. "I can't remember why it was that they came back. Forgot something. Something like that. All I can tell you is, they never asked me to babysit again."

He laughed. "And that's your life of crime, eh. I knew you were a bad girl. Never realized you were that depraved."

"It's true," she admitted. "I've always been ridiculously straight and narrow. I'm an accountant, for heaven's sake. I never even colored outside the lines. Heck, I *drew* the lines. With a ruler. And now you know why. The one time I was daring and tried being bad, fate lowered the boom on me. I'm also the only person I've ever heard of to get *both* a ticket for jaywalking, and for riding my bicycle at night without a light."

"It's true," she insisted again at his hastily muffled shout of laughter. "I'm a career criminal. I got caught every single time."

"If Hannah and Drew had known that," he agreed, "they would've had second thoughts. Good thing you had somebody responsible along."

"And this bub's asleep," he added, lifting the relaxed little form carefully and getting up to put him back into his bassinet.

"Whew. This whole baby thing is a lot harder than I realized. Having him." Kate shuddered, remembering. "And then taking care of him."

"Somehow, though, most people seem to survive it," he pointed out. "And even have more. Just takes some getting used to, I reckon."

"I'd say, easy for you to say," she told him. "But as you seem to know a lot more about it than I do, I suspect it'd be wiser to keep my mouth shut. And since we can't pass the time by making out, according to the Babysitting Rule Book, why don't you tell me about your own shady past? Somehow I'm guessing you have more lurid tales to tell than I do."

"Not as much as you may think. Because of the footy. But yeh, I nicked a few lollies from the dairy as a kid. Drank too much, later. Hooned around with my mates."

"What does that mean?" she frowned. "Hooned? Doesn't sound good."

"You don't have that word? Just means, driving around too fast. Your radio on too loud. Being a general pain in the neighborhood. Course, in my neighborhood, someone was bound to tell my mum. Which was probably the point. Rebelling, trying to be the bad boy and not everyone's sweet baby," he grimaced. "But when I realized I could have a real career, I started getting a bit smarter. You could say rugby kept me out of major trouble. Plus you're tired, of course, by the time you're done training for the day."

"That's not a very interesting story, though," she complained.

"All right. I'll tell you something that'll make you happier," he decided. "My closest call. When I was 20 or so, still at Uni, I was out with friends, at the bars in Hamilton. And I had the car, which wasn't usual. I wasn't intending to drink much, obviously. Ended up getting stonkered, of course. Woke up the next morning hungover as hell, with no recollection of how I'd got home. The car was there, no damage. The friends too. Scared me shitless, though. Lucky not to've been brought in on a drink-driving charge. Or had an accident, killed somebody. I was never that stupid again. Lucky for me, because a sportsman in New Zealand lives under a microscope. As you may have noticed."

"I sure have. In the U.S., professional athletes are almost expected to behave badly. That doesn't seem to be the case here."

"Nah. Doesn't mean they don't get on the turps sometimes, make right wallies of themselves. But the public don't like it. Don't forget it, either. Do something like that and they'll still be talking about it years later. There'll be an article about your recent lack of form, and they're bringing up the old story again. As an example of your general lack of character. With everyone and their aunt ready to comment, take their chance to sink the boot in as well, thanks to the wonders of the Internet."

"Do you notice something about all this, though?" she asked. "Here we are, two people who have pretty much followed the rules. And a lot of that, whatever this says about us, is because we've always figured we'd be caught if we didn't, and pay the price. Well, in your case. In mine, obviously, I *knew* I'd be caught. And yet some people can do *everything* wrong—break so many laws, create so much havoc. And basically get away with it. What's wrong with this picture?"

"You're talking about that Paul now."

"Yeah. He did his best to ruin my life. And there was nothing I could do about it. He walked away scot-free. I used to be nicer, actually. You might've liked me better if you'd met me a year ago. Because now I'm not nearly as interested in being polite if someone's behaving badly. I'm sticking up for myself from here on out. Not going to be a victim anymore, an easy target like that."

"Good on ya, far as I'm concerned. And who said I didn't like you?" he demanded. "In case you haven't noticed, I'm sitting on this couch with you on my day off, babysitting for the Skipper. Why d'you think I'm doing that? Believe me, I can think of loads more interesting ways to spend my time. Some of which I'm counting on trying out with you later, by the way, so you'd better be prepared."

"But you're always complaining about my temper. You can't tell me you like it when I'm walking out on you in restaurants, or yelling at you for being a jerk."

"Or jumping out of my car," he reminded her. "Don't forget that. That was pretty surprising. *Like* might be the wrong word. I reckon you're interesting, though. Challenging. I was raised around Maori women, remember? They don't hesitate to speak their minds. You may have had occasion to notice that recently."

She laughed. "I confess I have. Very good point."

"Courage is important to Maori, in women as well as men. The courage to speak and to act. Not many shrinking violets amongst Maori women. In fact, the most famous Maori love story is all about courage, a woman's courage."

"Tell me. I'll bet it's more uplifting than my babysitting story. This might be almost as good as hearing another song."

"It is a song, though. The song I sang you, *Pokarekare Ana*, remember? The love song of Hinemoa and Tutanekai. It's one reason you hear that song everyplace, because the story's so well known. If you really want to hear it, I'll tell it to you."

"Hinemoa was the high-born daughter of a chief," he began as Kate settled in to listen. "She lived in a village on the shores of Lake Rotorua. You've heard of Rotorua?"

She nodded. "Where all the hot springs are."

"That's it. A beautiful lake as well, with an island in the middle of it called Mokoia. Four kilometers from Owhata, Hinemoa's village. A long way."

"Almost two and a half miles," she agreed. "Big lake."

"Yeh. Well, Tutanekai lived in his own village, on that island. The two of them met during ceremonial visits between their villages, and they fell in love. But Hinemoa's family wouldn't agree to a marriage, because Tutanekai's birth wasn't as good as hers. Course, that didn't stop them being in love. At night, Tutanekai would sit on his verandah and play his flute for Hinemoa. The sound would carry across the water, and she'd know he was playing for her, calling to her."

"It carried two and a half miles?" she asked dubiously.

He glared at her. "It's a love story. Just listen."

"Her relatives suspected that the two of them were still in love, even after they'd forbidden it, and they were afraid she would try to make her way to him," he went on. "So at night, they'd pull the waka—the canoes—high up on the beach, to keep her from crossing the water. But one night, as she heard the sound of Tutanekai's flute across the water, Hinemoa couldn't wait any longer, and she came up with a plan. She tied gourds to her body to help her float. Then she swam all the way to Mokoia, with the voice of the flute guiding her. No wetsuits then, of course. You'd never have made it. She was naked, and when she reached the island after hours of effort, she was exhausted and cold, so she lowered herself into a hot pool at the water's edge to warm up. To hide and wait."

"After a bit, she heard someone approaching. She made her voice deep, so she sounded like a man. Called out and asked who was there. She found it was Tutanekai's servant, come to fill a calabash with water for his master. From her hiding place, she grabbed the calabash from him when he dipped it into the water, and smashed it on the rocks. The servant ran back to Tutanekai and told him what had happened, but Tutanekai was so dispirited, he couldn't be bothered with the story, and brushed him off. But after the servant went back to the spring with another calabash and the same thing happened, Tutanekai decided he had to take action. He took his club and went down to find the man who had insulted him so badly, and to kill him."

"Of course," Kate agreed. "Because obviously, the penalty for breaking your calabash would be death."

"Nah. The penalty for insulting a warrior like that would be death," he corrected her. "Anyway. As I was saying before you interrupted me, he went down to the pool and called for the man to come out and fight. Reached down into the water and grabbed an arm to pull him out. When he did, of course, he saw it was Hinemoa. He wrapped her in his cloak and took her up to his house. In the morning, his family found her there. And in the face of their love and devotion—and because the deed was done, though they tend to leave that out of the story—both families agreed to their marriage."

"You can see Tutanekai's flute for yourself, still, in the Rotorua Museum," he finished. "And the descendants of Hinemoa and Tutanekai still live around Lake Rotorua today."

"Like Romeo and Juliet," Kate said. "But with a happy ending. What a good story."

"And a true story," he pointed out. "Next time you hear *Pokarekare Ana,* you'll know what it means. That it's the love song of Tutanekai, calling to Hinemoa across the water. Telling her how much he loves her, asking her to come to him."

He sang the chorus softly.

"E hine e
Hoki mai ra
Ka mate ahau
I te aroha e."

"It means, "Oh girl, return to me, else I will die of my love for you."

"So romantic," she sighed.

He smiled. "Maori are nothing if not romantic. Loving, talking, and fighting, those are our best skills. And women did some of the fighting too, in the old days. Bet you didn't know that. It wasn't very long ago, either. Only about 150 years. Sometimes I think it's still in the genetic memory."

"Course, in spite of the fact that you're dead fierce, and courageous with it, you'd have been a miserable failure as a Maori," he went on musingly. "Too small and skinny. Not able to swim across any cold lakes. Not even good eating."

"Well, *that's* disgusting. And I was told I wasn't supposed to make any cannibalism jokes. That it was a sensitive subject."

"It's not too nice," he agreed seriously. "But it did happen. No point trying to deny it. These days, New Zealand likes to embrace the Maori traditions. Partly because it's so good for tourism. But sometimes that can mean whitewashing the past. It's a warrior culture, and there are loads of practices that went along with that, things that people would like to forget now. Cannibalism. Slavery. You can't just show off your moko and your hei toki and pretend the rest of it didn't exist."

"In other words, OK for you to make that joke, but I'd better steer clear," she decided.

"Afraid you're right." He turned at the sound of Jack beginning to cry. "And he's off again. Why don't you go warm the bottle this time. I'll check his nappy."

"He can't need to eat again, though," Kate objected. "I thought they ate every four hours. Something like that."

He laughed as he bent to pick up the baby. "You really are hopeless. They eat when they want to. And because he was little, he needs more feeding up. Ask Hannah when she gets back. She'll tell you she spends most of the day feeding him, I'll bet."

Kate couldn't help being relieved when Drew and Hannah returned fifteen minutes later to the sight of Koti giving a bottle to a clean and contented baby. She was glad they were back. She was even happier that she hadn't had to do this alone. Somehow, she didn't think the picture greeting them would have been nearly so peaceful.

Hannah barely acknowledged them, just went straight to Koti and took the baby from his arms.

"I need to feed him," she told Kate once she had Jack safely back. "Come with me and tell me how things went."

"Fidgeted all the way home," Drew smiled as Hannah bore the baby off to their bedroom. "I'd say that was the limit. It was good to get out for a bit, though, just the two of us. Cheers for that."

"No worries," Koti assured him.

"How'd you go?" Drew asked.

"I had to use some of my baby-wrangling skills. Carrying the ball, eh. He had a bad moment there, but we got him settled again."

"Hope this makes Hannah feel better about leaving him for a bit from time to time," Drew said. "I reckon the first time's the hardest. And those first few weeks, we had to wake him up, make sure he ate. Turns out they can be too sleepy when they're born early like that. That's made her hover a bit more."

"But," he cleared his throat. "I wanted to talk to you about something else, now that I have the chance. Seems ungrateful of me, after everything you've done. The night he was born, and tonight. But Hannah's worried about Kate."

Koti frowned. "What? I haven't done anything to hurt Kate. I wouldn't."

"That's the point. Your love life isn't my business, I know. But you have a bit of a reputation. Kate isn't a party girl. And she's been through a rough time. Be honest with her. Don't let her think it means something if it doesn't."

"I don't know what it means yet," Koti objected. "Haven't had time to find out."

Drew nodded. "Fair enough. Like I said, not really my business. Except that I feel a bit responsible for her, since we helped her get settled here. And I don't like to see Hannah unhappy."

Which, Koti knew, was the bottom line. He looked at the other man pityingly. The most powerful sportsman in New Zealand, reduced to putty in his wife's hands. It was a bit pathetic, really.

He stood with relief to greet Kate, coming down the stairs again. "Everything sorted?"

She nodded. "Time to go. Thanks for letting me babysit him, Drew. He's such a sweetie. But I have to tell you in all honesty, Koti did most of the work. Turns out he knows a lot more about newborns than I do."

Drew looked at Koti with speculation. "Got a soft side, have you?"

"That's what I've been trying to tell you," Koti said, a hint of challenge in his eyes. "I'm not such a bad bloke. Kind to children and small animals."

"Sometimes even to women," Kate agreed, taking him by the arm. "Goodnight, Drew."

Drew leaned down to kiss her cheek. "Thanks for the help tonight. You too, mate," he told Koti. "See you tomorrow. Heaps of work to do."

Chapter 24

"Kate. You're in. Come talk to me." Kate arrived at the office the next morning to find Brenda with that day's *New Zealand Herald* spread out on her desk. "What do you know about this?"

Kate looked over the other woman's shoulder. "What?"

Brenda pointed to the tiny item in the paper's gossip column.

> Who was the petite brunette doing a bit of shopping—and having words, we hear—with Koti James in the Takapuna New World on Sunday? Details, please!

Kate shrugged, attempting to sound casual. "Huh," was all she could manage.

Corinne joined them. "I heard something myself," she said with a sidelong look at Kate. "Brendan told me you picked Koti up at the airport last weekend, Kate. Said he was pretty, ah, friendly about it, too."

Kate flushed. "Well, I told you we were friends," she faltered. "And, well . . ." she capitulated, "Yeah. More than that now."

"What?" she protested, as the women traded glances. "You were the ones who told me to go for it, have an adventure. Now you've decided to hate me after all?"

"Nah," Brenda sighed. "Just have to be a bit jealous. Give me a moment with my disappointed heart here."

Kate settled herself at her desk with a sigh of her own. Pulled out her mobile phone and texted Koti.

Secrets out oh dear.

She wasn't completely surprised to see him sauntering into the office that afternoon, hoodie and 100-watt grin in place. She plopped her elbows on her desk, rested her chin in her hands, and watched his progress across the room.

"Nice performance," she complimented him when he finally came to a stop. "Very casual."

He laughed. "Just popped by for a chat on my way home."

"Yeah, right. Give it up. I'm on to you."

"Are you planning to cook dinner with me tonight?" he asked. "We didn't say, last night."

"And you had to ask me that in person, huh? But yeah. I'd like that. Come over and we can fix that steak you wanted so badly. And I can help you prepare for the quarterfinals. Give you the right mental attitude."

"Yeh. That's it. Help me prepare. I'll look forward to that. I have a few training ideas in mind."

Kate knew she had a goofy grin on her own face that was evident to everyone in the office, but she couldn't help it.

"Walk me out," he coaxed, and she didn't find it the least bit difficult to agree.

"I shouldn't be kissing you in the carpark," she protested weakly as she did just that. "It's very unprofessional."

"Very," he agreed. "No doubt you'll be struck off the register, or whatever it is they do to accountants."

"Yeah," she decided, reaching up to hold his face in her hands and pull it down for another kiss. "But what a way to go."

"Brilliant. You're wearing the sheep pajamas," he complained as she opened the door to him that evening.

"What?" She looked down at herself. "I went to the gym after work and got wet and cold on the way home. These are comfy. And you're not exactly dressed up yourself." She eyed his sweats critically.

"I'm the boy, though. I don't have to be pretty."

"Too bad for you that I didn't get the memo," she agreed. "Are we still making dinner, or did you want to go out and look for a more glamorous girlfriend? Dena's still out there somewhere. You can bet she's dressed the way you like."

"Reckon I'll make do with you," he sighed as they moved into her tiny kitchen. "I can always take them off later."

"Good plan. Because I'm actually wearing really nice underwear. Want to see?" she teased, pulling down one side of her pajama bottoms to show him a ribbon-trimmed pair of green panties. "They have a little bow in front too. But I'm saving that."

"I'm staying, then," he decided. "Besides," he added practically, "I'm starved."

"It does sound good." She pulled the steaks out of the refrigerator as he turned the fire on under the grill pan. "Just let me shut down here." She began to clear files from the tiny kitchen table.

"What were you working on?" He glanced from the stove to the spreadsheet still open on her laptop. "Putting in some overtime?"

"Nope. Just my household budget, going through my weekly expenses. I like to keep current with it."

"You have a spreadsheet for that?" he asked in surprise. "You track everything?"

"Why? Don't you? How do you handle your finances?"

He laughed. "Not that closely, I'm afraid. I have an accountant for the important stuff, of course. Otherwise, I don't stress about it much."

"I have an accountant too. Me," she pointed out as she shut down the computer and moved it out of the way. "And here among the little people where I live, it's all important stuff. Besides, I like staying on top of it. Of what's going in and out. It's satisfying."

"Mmm." He reached out to pull her into his arms. "I know you like to stay on top of what's going in and out. And I'll do my best to make sure it's satisfying."

"What are you, fifteen?" She attempted to scowl at him even as he lifted her for a kiss. "That's really juvenile." She gasped as his lips moved over her throat and over the sensitive spot beneath her jawline, before his mouth finally settled over hers.

"Immature," he agreed, reaching a hand under an innocent sheep to feel the soft skin beneath. "Go on, now. Tell me what else is wrong with me. Meanwhile I'll be down here, looking for that bow."

"I thought you were hungry," she protested.

"Starved," he told her. "See what you can do about that." Then concentrated on kissing her.

A sudden piercing shriek had them jumping apart from each other. "Shit." Koti lunged for the grill pan, swore again as he burned his fingers. Grabbed for a tea towel and pulled the smoking pan of meat off the burner, wrenching the knob to the *off* position.

Kate flew to the kitchen window as the smoke alarm continued its insistent shrieking. "Why is it still so bad?" she wailed, grabbing the tea towel from him and trying to fan the smoke out the open window. "You turned it off."

Koti opened the oven. One look, and he was reaching for the tea towel again. "Could be this," he told her as he set a roasting pan full of charred shapes on the stovetop and turned off the oven.

"Oh, no." She dropped into a kitchen chair and clutched her head in her hands. "My vegetables. I was so proud of myself. I started them early and everything, so they'd be ready."

He started to laugh. "We're rubbish at cooking. Time to face it. This must be that epic fail."

She looked at the blackened mess and had to laugh herself. "Well, we've established that you don't want me for my date wardrobe or my culinary skills, anyway. I guess the only thing left is sex. We still need dinner, though."

"We do," he agreed. "And then sex. What d'you reckon? Thai takeaway?"

"Sounds good to me. Let somebody cook who knows how. I'll call, and you can go pick it up."

"Why do I have to pick it up?" he complained. "Why aren't you coming with me?"

"Because I have to clean up this mess," she pointed out. "Want to trade?"

"Nah. Now that you put it that way."

"Huh. I thought so."

"So," he said when they were settled at the table at last with their perfectly prepared Thai food. "You actually like what you do. Accounting."

She looked at him in surprise. "Of course I do. Why do you think I chose it?"

"Dunno," he shrugged. I thought maybe your dad did it or something. Can't imagine why anyone would choose that. Isn't it a bit boring?"

"Nope. I like it. The analytical part, solving problems. Figuring things out. It can be almost like a mystery, sometimes. Numbers are a lot easier to work with than people, anyway. Numbers make sense."

"I can see that."

She leaned against the wall and lifted her legs across his lap, snuggling down to get more comfortable. "What do you think you'd be doing if you weren't playing rugby right now? Not modeling, I'm guessing."

"I don't think I'd ever have chosen that," he said, closing his hand over a slender ankle. "You'll laugh, though."

"Why would I laugh?" she objected. "What? You wanted to be a firefighter?"

"Oh. Wow." She sat up straighter. "You would've totally been on one of those firefighter calendars. The hose over the shoulder, the suspenders against the bare chest . . . I can see it now. What a lost opportunity."

"Be quiet," he scowled. "I thought you wanted to hear this."

"I did. I do," she said, chastened. "Go on. I'm being serious now. Not imagining you as Mr. January. Hardly at all."

"No, really," she urged as he shot her another glare. "Tell me."

"I was thinking I'd work with kids," he muttered. "That's all."

"Really? Like coaching?"

"Nah." He shook his head. "I thought I'd be a teacher. I was working on a History degree, when I was at Uni. Was thinking I might teach that, in high school."

"Wow. You're right, that is a surprise. I don't know why it should be, though. You know a lot about it. I've always been impressed."

"Really?" He looked cheered.

"Sure I have. And you don't just know facts. You think about what it all means. So I can completely see you doing that. You're good with kids, too. At least I've heard you are. I've only actually seen you with babies. But I can vouch for that much."

"I like kids," he confirmed. "I always enjoy the visits we do to the schools. Talking to the kids, playing a little footy with them. And we need more Maori teachers. Especially men. Role models and that."

"All the girls would fall in love with you, though," she mused. "If it were high school. Unless you got fat and bald, I suppose."

He laughed, oddly relieved that she hadn't dismissed the idea as ridiculous. "Maybe they wouldn't bunk off school, then. As long as I wasn't fat and bald, that is."

"One thing's for sure, your sisters would be thrilled. Although to make them really happy," she teased, "you'd have to teach in Hamilton. And live next door."

He groaned. "Let's not take this to extremes."

Chapter 25

"I have to say," Kate sighed a week later, "this is the upside of you being gone so much. Getting to say hello again."

"You said it so nicely, too." Koti pulled her up against him. "That was almost as good as the win. But we should make a plan, you're right. It's been a bit of a struggle, having to fit in our fights between games. Why don't you ask for a couple days off once the season's over? We could go somewhere. Do some surfing, maybe."

"Sounds good to me," she said. "I feel like I've hardly been anywhere. I come to live in scenic New Zealand, and all I see is my office, the beach, and a bunch of rugby games. None of which I'm complaining about, actually. Could be worse. But I'd like to go someplace. When would it be?"

"I'd like to say, in two weeks, after the final. Course, that may change if we get knocked out in the semis next week."

"I thought you were favored to win that," she protested. "Everyone says you're playing better than the Highlanders."

He laughed. "That's why you actually have to play the game, though. The papers make it sound like it'll be a doddle, but it's never that easy. It comes down to injuries, preparation, attitude, your form on the night. Making it through the knockout rounds is always a hard slog. We'll be ready. Pity the Highlanders will be as well. We'll see who comes out on top next week."

"Well, whichever week it is, I'll check about getting the days. Although my other boyfriend's going to be disappointed," she sighed. "To miss his regular Saturday-night date."

He grinned. "I didn't think you could really be watching the games. You're so shockingly uninformed."

"Because the rules make my eyes glaze over," she admitted. "Besides, I shouldn't tell you this. It's not good for you. But I mostly just watch you."

Which was difficult enough to do the next weekend. "Ouch," she winced when she opened the door to him on Monday evening. "That looks so painful." She reached out with gentle fingers to touch the area around his bruised cheekbone, the fresh stitching showing black against the livid skin. "I saw it happen last night, but I didn't realize it was so bad."

"Nah. No worries. Just a momentary disagreement with Josiah Mapu's knee in the ruck."

"He kneed you in the head?" she asked with outrage. "I didn't realize that's what had happened. I thought that was illegal."

"If it's deliberate. Which I don't think it was. The ref didn't either, which is always a pity. A yellow card might've made it an easier win, eh. But he's not a bad bloke, Mapu. And we got the win. That's what counts. That we'll be off to Brisbane for the final."

"Are you going to be well enough to play, though? You seem like you're limping too."

"Just some bruising. I'll be fit as a buck rat again by Saturday night, no worries."

"I don't see how you guys can do this, play week after week, when you get so banged up every time," she objected. "It's really too much."

"It always feels like hard yakka around this point," he agreed. "But you have to consider the alternative. We could've lost last night. Then we wouldn't have had to play any more Super matches till next season. You can bet that the Highlanders would be happy to trade places with us just now. I had three weeks of rest a couple months ago, remember?

And I didn't enjoy it a bit. The definition of "rest" is, what you'll have heaps of after you lose."

She was reading in bed Friday night when her phone rang. Seeing his name on the screen, she picked it up with pleasure.

"Hi, you. I was just thinking about you. Are you in the hotel? How are you boys doing? How'd practice go today?"

"Yeh, at the hotel, and pretty good to both the other questions," he answered with a smile in his voice. "Captain's Run today, the day before the match. That's always a short one, Drew making sure everyone knows what he's meant to do on the night. Wish we were playing at Eden Park tomorrow, though. The Reds crowd is always hostile."

"It sounds like it might be getting tough now. The night before a big game like this, with no more practice to work out the jitters."

"I am a bit nervy now I'm in the room, nothing else to think about," he admitted. "That's why I wanted to talk to you. I need you to relax me."

"Well, sure. I'd be glad to, if I can," she answered doubtfully. "I'm not sure what to say that's relaxing, though."

"You could start by telling me what you're wearing," he suggested.

"What? I don't care how nervous you are, I am not having some kind of weird phone sex chat with you. Especially not if your roommate could walk in at any time. He'd better not be there now."

"No worries. He's off to the flicks with some of the other boys. Here I am, all alone. Lonesome, too. Missing you. Come on, now," he coaxed. "Tell me what you're wearing."

"All right. Just for you, I'll tell you. Because unfortunately, I'm wearing your favorites. I could make something up, I guess, but my imagination isn't as good as yours."

"Not the sheep pajamas," he groaned.

She laughed. "Afraid so. What are you going to do about that?"

"You'll just have to take them off, then. Let me concentrate on what's under there. You can start by unbuttoning the top."

"You have to tell me you're doing it," he informed her into the silence. "I can't see you. I need some help, imagining."

"OK," she said in resignation. "This is weird. I'm embarrassed. But I'm taking it off now."

"You need to go more slowly. I've got a long evening ahead of me. Need to stretch this out if you're going to distract me. Take off the bottoms, now. Slowly. Slide them down those gorgeous legs. And imagine it's me doing it. How I'd be touching you on the way. How my hands would feel, sliding down your thighs."

"Oh, God. You already have me going," she sighed. "I don't know how you do that. They're coming off now. I'm dropping them on the floor."

He closed his eyes. Lay back against the pillows and felt better than he had all day. "What are you wearing now? Anything?"

"You're going to like this better. Much, much better. I'm wearing that white undershirt with the little straps, and the matching panties. The ones with the pink ribbon woven through at the top. And the little pink rose in the middle."

He groaned. "I love those. This is going to be so good. We're going to go so slowly. Right, then. You can start by running your hand over that ribbon. The shirt first. And reach underneath while you're doing it, just a bit. Not too far, now."

"Doing that now," she told him. "Touching the ribbon. Reaching underneath."

"Not too far," he reminded her sternly. "You need to wait till I tell you you're allowed to."

He heard the hitch in her breath as she obeyed. "OK," she sighed. "I won't. Not till you say."

"You're listening so well. Now the undies. Same thing. Just the ribbon, and under the ribbon. Nothing else. Not yet."

"Doing that too. Really slowly. Oh, Koti. It feels so good."

"That's good, baby. You're doing so well. Now take your hand and slide it under that shirt. So slowly. Over your belly, then your ribs. Over all that gorgeous skin. Till you're touching yourself. Running your hand over your breasts. Doing what I'd be doing to you, if I were there. And while you're doing it, I want you to think about my hand being there. My hand sliding over you. Touching you."

"You have to tell me you're doing it," he said into the silence, hearing only her breath. "That's required."

"Oh," she breathed. "I'm doing it."

He smiled again as he listened to her, pictured her. "Time to pull that shirt up," he decided. "Slowly, remember. Pull it up so it's under your arms first. And slide your hand over yourself. I want you to imagine my mouth on you. And that I'm biting you. Because you know what that does to you."

Her breath was coming faster now. "I wish you were here, doing that to me. But it feels good anyway. It feels so good."

"I know it does, baby. Now pay attention, because you're going to have to concentrate. Listen to me. I want you to pull that shirt right off you. You'll have to put down the phone, because you're going to need two hands for that. And while you're doing it, you need to think about how slowly I'd be pulling it off if I were there. Where I'd be kissing you while I did it. And how you'd be arching up against me, asking me to touch you, starting to beg me. And when you've done all that, when you've taken your shirt off, you'll be lying there with just those little white panties on, won't you? And then I want you to pick up the phone again. So I can tell you what you're going to do next."

He listened to the whisper of fabric, then heard her pick up the phone again. "I did it, Koti. I'm not sure I can do the rest of this, though. It feels so good. But I feel so . . . so naughty doing this with you listening. And saying those things to me."

"That's because you are naughty, though. Haven't I told you that? You're a bad, bad girl. I already know that, remember? All you have to do is listen to me, and do what I say. Just like you'd do if I were there. It's only you and me here. You're showing me how beautiful you are, that's all. Making me feel how much I want you, everything I want to do to you. The way you always do, every time I'm with you."

"All right," she sighed. "I'll do it for you. I don't think I can stop anyway. You're making me so crazy."

He exhaled in relief. "You're doing so well. You're so gorgeous, baby. I love to tease you so much. But this next part is a bit hard, so you're going to have to listen really closely to what I'm telling you. I want you to reach down to those little panties and touch yourself. Only on the outside, though. No reaching underneath. Not yet. And tell me when you're doing it. All you have to say is, 'I'm doing it, Koti.'"

"I'm doing it," she said softly.

"That's good. That's so good. Keep doing that. And imagine it's my hand there on you. That I'm reaching down to touch you, feel you there. And that you're opening up for me."

"Now comes the part I like best," he went on as he listened to her breathing, the sighs that were escaping her now. "You get to take that hand and slip it inside. Going to have to spread your legs a bit more to do that, aren't you? Just like you do when I'm touching you. And think about how I'd be doing that. How I'd be holding your legs, moving them apart so I could see you. How I'd be touching you, kissing you."

"Oh," she sighed, as her excitement mounted. "This is so bad of me."

"That's right, baby. It's so bad. You're a bad, bad girl. I know exactly what to do with bad girls, though. And I'm going to tell you all about it. You just listen. Keep touching yourself while I tell you. Because I'm going to make you crazy."

Her heart was beating so hard, she thought he must be able to hear it. Part of her still felt embarrassed, as if someone really were watching her perform. The rest of her, though, was almost unbearably excited as he continued to tell her what he wanted to do to her. What he'd be doing to her tonight, if he were there. What he was going to do the next time they were together.

She stopped answering him as her focus narrowed to his voice, her body, the feelings he was arousing in her. She felt the shift as she began to climb, her breath coming faster. Hearing it, he answered with a final suggestion that made her gasp and sent her spiraling over the top, crying out her release.

When her breath had returned at last, she told him with a sigh, "I keep thinking I've done the nastiest possible thing with you now. And I keep being wrong."

"Too right. Because I have so much more to do with you. So many things I need to do to you. Like I've been telling you."

"That's it, though. I keep thinking you're just talking. I guess you've shown me."

"Oh, I don't think so. Think I still need to show you. Starting in a couple days. And when you're watching tomorrow, if I score a try, I'll let you know. That I'm thinking about you. And that you helped me relax and get right tonight."

"I'll watch for that," she told him. "I'm going to sleep now, though. Because you relaxed me, too. And because if I think about this any more, I'm either going to get excited again, or horribly embarrassed. I don't even know which."

He laughed gently. "Don't be embarrassed. You're beautiful, and you make me want you so much. Can't wait to show you how much. But go to sleep now. Good night, baby."

"Good night," she told him with a smile. Pressed the *End* button and fell asleep with the phone still cradled in her hand.

Chapter 26

"I'm so nervous," she confided to Hannah the following evening. "How do you stand this?"

"It never gets that much easier, to tell you the truth. It helps to have somebody to watch with. Jack's pretty good company, but his conversation leaves a little to be desired. Thanks for coming over to hang out with us."

"On the other hand," Kate mused as the pregame commentary drew to a close, "I also feel like I'm fourteen years old, watching the boy band I have a crush on."

Hannah laughed. "I know what you mean there, too. Don't enjoy being a WAG, huh?"

"Nope. Very weird."

"Same here, especially at first. I think the answer to that is that you have to separate the persona from the person. I'm married to the person who comes home after all this, win or lose. Who's doing his job like anyone else, however visible it is."

"Yeah, but a wife doesn't normally watch her husband doing his job, does he?" Kate pointed out. "That part *is* odd. Like if you were married to a surgeon and you watched all his operations."

"Well, maybe a little bit more enjoyable than that," Hannah smiled. "You have to admit, it's fun to watch them play, though it can be scary too. And it's not like I have to critique Drew's performance. He gets plenty of that. He sure doesn't need it from me. I wouldn't know anyway, even though I watch him the whole game. He always looks good to me."

They watched in relative quiet for a while. Hannah was surprisingly knowledgeable, able to explain strategy and penalties that still baffled Kate.

"How do you know so much?" Kate asked at last.

"You must have figured out what rugby players do during their time off," Hannah said. "I've watched a fair amount of this game on TV by now, with expert analysis provided."

The score shifted back and forth during the first half, neither side holding a clear advantage. To Kate's inexpert eye, both teams seemed to be playing well. Their strong defensive efforts meant that the score stood at only eight to seven at the half, each side having scored only a single try.

Hannah got up as Jack began to cry.

"What a good rugby baby," she crooned as she lifted him out of his bassinet. "Crying at halftime."

"You'll have to tell Drew about that," Kate agreed. "That must have taken some serious training."

Hannah was still feeding the baby as the Reds began the second half by kicking off to the Blues. Immediately, the visiting team began to move the ball down the field. Kate's heart filled with pride as she saw Koti flicking one of his seemingly casual offloads to the player next to him, and heard the commentators remark on the beautiful pass. She held her breath as he continued to run, receiving the ball again and dodging two tacklers. Jumped to her feet as he dove across the try line to score.

"Try!" she shouted, doing an extra little dance out of sheer exuberance. Felt the grin stretching across her face as she saw Koti leap easily to his feet, to be surrounded by his teammates. Watched with disbelief as he turned to the camera and crossed his hands over his heart. Her own heart melted at the gesture.

"James is playing out of his skin tonight," she heard one of the commentators remark as the team trotted back into position.

"He looked a bit ropey at times in the early weeks, but he's back to full pace now," agreed the other. "That phase was a thing of beauty."

"What was that little performance about, there?" Hannah asked with interest. "Do you know? I'm guessing you might."

Kate blushed. "I might. Something he said, last night."

"Hmm. I thought that might've been meant for you. I'll admit, I wasn't sure about this when I first found out about it. But it seems to be working out for you."

Kate sat down again, still smiling. "It is, so far. It's added quite a bit of excitement to my stay in New Zealand, I have to say."

"I'm glad," Hannah said sincerely. "I've wanted so much for you to be happy. You were so fragile when you got here. I hated to see you like that."

"It didn't start out as my best year. But it's turning out to be a fairly good one after all."

When the Blues finally sealed the win with a penalty kick after the eighty-minute clock had run down, with the referee blowing the whistle on a final score of twenty-three to sixteen, both women hugged each other with a sigh of relief.

"Phew." Kate sat back on the couch with a thump. "I'd have had my aerobic workout for today even without the surfing this morning. I'm exhausted."

"Do you want to stay over?" Hannah asked. "You're welcome."

"No. I'll get on home now. But thanks for sharing." Kate gave Hannah a final hug, then moved to the door to find her shoes. It was true, she realized. She was exhausted. But so proud of Koti, she could burst.

This time, the crowd at the airport was much larger, the wait for the team that much longer. Kate felt another surge of pride at the sight of Koti surrounded by eager autograph-seekers, his spectacular performance the night before ensuring a hero's welcome.

"You were just great last night," she told him as he put her down after an enthusiastic greeting of his own. "I had to do my Happy Dance after your try, it was so good. I know you're not allowed to celebrate much on the field. It's lucky there are no rules for me. I'd have been sinbinned for sure."

"I'd've liked to have seen that. Did you see what I did for you?"

"I did. That was pretty special too."

"Had to do something, didn't I. Considering your help relaxing me, and how well it worked. I may have to get you to do that every time."

"Hah. In your dreams, big boy. That was a one-time deal. I'm embarrassed even thinking about it. I don't know how I let you talk me into these things."

He smiled. "Reckon I could talk you into it again, too. Because I know what you're really like, don't I."

"I thought of what we should do, on our holiday," he told her as they walked to her car. "I realized it when we were flying back across the Ditch, and coming back to the rain. It's fine in Queensland this week. Warm, too. A good spot for a winter holiday, since we'll only have a few days. What do you think of going to the Gold Coast to do our surfing? You haven't been to Aussie yet, have you?"

"I haven't. I haven't been much of anywhere. Is it very different from here?"

He laughed. "You'll see for yourself. You can tell me what you think."

"Well," he told her on Tuesday evening when she turned up for their cooking date, "what d'ya reckon? I've been selected for the ABs squad these next couple months, for the Rugby Championship."

"Koti! That's wonderful!" she exclaimed, throwing her arms around him. "Congratulations. All that hard work paid off. You must be thrilled."

"Not entirely. Not starting, at least not straight away," he told her with disappointment. "I'll be on the bench for the first game, at any rate."

"I'm sorry to hear that, but still, what an accomplishment. Good for you."

"Only thing is, it means practice starts up again next week, and I'll be traveling more. Farther away too, some of the time. South Africa and Aussie of course, but Argentina as well. First game is two weeks from Saturday. Good thing we have that holiday planned."

"Guess I'd better call my other boyfriend, then. Start setting up those Saturday night dates."

"Not such a wonderful thing, is it? You wonder why anyone would want to date a footballer."

"I don't want to date a footballer, though," she said. "I want to date you. Because you make me laugh. And you make me crazy. Just not on the weekends."

"Not to mention my cooking skills."

"Oh yeah. You're a real master chef. Witness the hamburgers on the menu tonight."

"So what's the first game?" she asked when they were eating. "We burned these a bit, by the way."

"You shouldn't kiss me while we're cooking. Sydney. Oz again."

"They're going to revoke your citizenship soon," she told him. "If you keep spending so much time over there."

"It's so built up. All these tall buildings, and everything. So glitzy." Kate craned her neck to look around as they made their way down the Gold Coast Highway to Broadbeach. "This isn't at all what I thought Australia would be like. Isn't it supposed to have red dirt? And I thought it would be more like a New Zealand beach area. Quiet and remote, you know."

"And that there'd be kangaroos as well, hopping down the streets, I reckon."

"I'll admit I'm disappointed about the kangaroos. I'm guessing I'm not going to see any koalas on this trip either."

"Not here, anyway. Loads of kangaroos and koalas in Queensland, together with just about everything else, but not on the Gold Coast. This is all about the surfing and the beach."

"Wow," she breathed when they walked into their 40th-floor hotel room a half hour later. "You didn't tell me it would be this fancy."

"We both deserve a proper holiday. I know I do. And it doesn't seem to me that you've had much of that either. You can't have been very relaxed when you first arrived."

"Not exactly. Just the opposite, in fact. But why does our hotel room have a kitchen?"

"Most motel rooms in Aussie and En Zed have kitchens. Haven't you noticed?"

"I've never actually stayed in a motel in New Zealand. And I've never stayed anyplace like this in my life. This kitchen alone is fancier than anyplace I've ever lived. This doesn't mean we have to cook, does it?" she asked in sudden alarm.

"Nah. I don't think we'd better risk it. Don't want to set off their smoke detectors."

"Wow. Look out here!" She stepped through a wall of windows beyond the lounge. "Come see this. There's a huge balcony. And look at the view of the ocean. This is amazing."

"Aussie beaches aren't too bad," he agreed, joining her in looking at the sweeping vista, the beach curving for miles in each direction. "Wait till you feel the sand. I have to admit, Aussie sand is choice."

"And this is all a bit like taking Cinderella to the ball," he complained as she continued to explore the suite. "When you've finished with your tour, and comparing this to your own lowly hovel, maybe you'd like to come over here and give me a kiss."

"Sorry." She reached up for him. "This is very, very cool. I don't even need to go anyplace else. I'd be happy just to stay right here."

He smiled down at her. "Oh, I think I can guarantee that we'll be spending some time here. But you may want to venture outdoors as well, since we've come all this way."

"You were right, this is a great place to surf," Kate told him as they rested on their boards beyond the break on Sunday morning. "The waves, the beach, everything. Gorgeous. It helps that the water's so much warmer too."

"Thought that would suit you. And it means I can keep you out here with me longer."

"Everybody must stay at the beach all the time in Australia, if it's always this nice."

"Have to, don't they. Queensland gets bloody hot in the summer. Humid, too. That's when we feel lucky to live in En Zed. Although the surfing is good. As long as the sharks and jellies don't get you."

"Jellyfish," he explained, seeing her blank look. "Everything in Australia is trying to kill you, haven't you heard? Half of the ten deadliest snakes in the world live in Queensland. And then there are the poisonous spiders and the jellyfish. Not to mention the crocs and the great white sharks. Another point in favor of New Zealand. Very benign place, En Zed."

"But they're right next to each other. How come all the scary things didn't come on over?"

He laughed. "Didn't you notice that the plane ride took hours? They're close in comparison to all that water in every direction, but it's still 1500 kilometers."

"Oh. Duh." She laughed at herself. "Sorry. I know this is the baby beach, though, by the way. I figured that out. You can go on over and do the tough stuff, if you want to push yourself. With all these people around, it's not like I'd be out here on my own."

"This is my holiday, though. I pushed myself enough last week. I'd rather be with you today."

"Aww. Thanks. But watching you surf is almost as much fun as doing it myself. I love seeing what you can do."

It was true, she reflected as she watched him catch a wave and ride it effortlessly to the beach. Watching him do anything athletic was a treat. But she was still falling off her own board half the time in the more challenging conditions. She needed all the coaching she could get.

"Ready to go for lunch?" he asked at last.

She nodded gratefully and made her way to shore. Stumbled with fatigue as she got to the shallow water and rose to her feet.

Koti reached to take her board from her, tucked it under his other arm. "You should have told me you were getting tired. We could've stopped any time."

"I didn't realize it myself till I got out," she admitted as they walked toward the showers. "I need a rest, that's all. You're so fit, you forget how much work this is for us civilians."

He reached out to help her pull her wetsuit off her shoulders under the beachfront shower. "At least I can help you with this now. And you know how much I like that."

She smiled up at him, shivered in the cold spray. "I do. Here, I'll unzip you too. It's like unwrapping a birthday present, watching you come out of that package."

He laughed. "Funny, that's how I feel about it too."

"Do Australian women have to be so good-looking, though?" she complained, scowling at a trio of young women who had stopped along the beachfront path to watch them, and who were obviously enjoying the sight of Koti emerging from his wetsuit as much as she was. "You should have warned me."

Koti glanced across at his interested audience and smiled. "Aussie girls are bloody fit, you're right. Stop glaring at them like that. You're going to turn them to stone. I thought you didn't approve of possessiveness."

"They look at you like you're some kind of treat, and they've just remembered they skipped lunch. I wish so many of them weren't tall and blonde. They're starting to give me an inferiority complex."

"Oh, I don't know. Not sure tall and blonde is my favorite any more. You may have noticed that I've developed some new tastes lately. I'll have to wait till after lunch to show you, though. I need to build up my strength if I'm going to keep up with you."

Chapter 27

"This is very cool, I have to say." Kate sat, legs outstretched, against the head of the big bed, looking across to the expanse of blue water beyond. "I should go sit on the balcony and enjoy it while I have the chance. But this is pretty comfortable too."

"Plus you might put on more clothes, which would mean I wouldn't get to see my favorite undies. I think I like those even more now. All I have to do is look at that little pink rose and I'm well and truly on my way."

"And you're more excited about a hotel room than anyone I've ever known," he added, scooting across to rest his head in her lap. "Not many luxury holidays in your past, I take it."

"No." She shook her head absently and began to massage his scalp, enjoying the feel of his wavy hair under her fingers. "How about you? I can't imagine that your mom was able to afford any vacations like this. Not with four kids."

"Nah," he agreed. "Holiday parks for us. Sweet as, though. We'd go to the Bay of Plenty or the Coromandel, every summer holidays. Somewhere on the beach. Get a cabin with bunks. We were squashed in there, but it was fun. Loads of other kids to play footy or cricket with, swim, fish, whatever. I'd meet up with the other boys and run all day."

"Sounds better than my family vacations," she said. "A kitchen and flush toilets, I take it."

"Communal. Nothing special, but you're right. And what, you grew up in a shed? Or a refugee camp?"

"Nope. Vacationed in a tent, though. Every single year. About as far from this as you can imagine. My dad's idea of a good time was to camp out for a week and fish for trout. I'm

225

not very fond of camping to this day. Dirt. Mosquitoes. Outhouses," she finished with a shudder.

"Outhouses?"

"Outdoor toilets. Privies. You know, no flush."

"Ah," he smiled. "Long drops."

"You're kidding. That's disgusting. Just about as disgusting as the actual thing."

"So can you fish?" he asked interestedly. "If I'd known you were keen, we could've gone to Taupo. Major trout fishing around there."

"No thanks," she told him firmly. "I fished for a while, with my parents. Then when I was eight or nine, my dad said I was old enough to kill my own fish, and clean it. That was the end of my fishing career right there."

"What, do you think the meat in the shops grew on a tree? Somebody had to kill that animal."

"Of course I know it didn't," she answered crossly. "That doesn't mean I want to be the one to bash the cow over the head and butcher it."

"Steer," he corrected.

"Whatever."

"Weren't you lonely, then, with no brothers and sisters?" he asked after a bit. "I can't imagine it, a holiday on my own like that. Even if I hadn't had all those sisters, I have so many cousins, I've never been alone that way."

"No. I only have a few cousins, myself. And they're far away. But I suppose I didn't know any better. There were benefits, too. I'm good at keeping myself company. Which has come in handy, being over here by myself. Some of my weekends have been a little bit like a camping trip, come to think of it. Better bathrooms, but just as much reading. But I'm also good at making friends. No alternative, with no siblings to play with."

"Oh, I've noticed that. Your astonishing talent for friendship. Must be your easygoing nature."

"Hey. Your first female friend, remember? I'd say that's a major accomplishment."

"It is. Especially as men don't really have female friends." She looked down at him and frowned. "Of course they do. That was the whole point, remember?"

"I remember. And I'm sorry to disappoint you. But no man—no straight man—is friends with a woman he isn't interested in hooking up with. Or at least wouldn't mind."

"That's not true," she objected. "Look at us. You didn't even like me."

"Doesn't matter. That didn't mean I didn't fancy you. That I wasn't thinking about it. Just like every other male friend you've ever had."

"I'm choosing not to believe that," she decided. "Because that would be so awkward. Maybe you're just oversexed, have you thought of that?"

He laughed. "Probably true. But I'm still right."

"Anyway," he sighed, settling himself in more comfortably, "sounds like your family wasn't much more flash than mine."

"Hah. Not hardly. My dad works for the post office, and my mom works in an insurance office. There you go. They have a house. It's paid off, too," she told him proudly. "But they're still frugal. That's probably where my accountant tendencies come from. You can bet there were no gorgeous suites on the ocean when I was growing up. And it's not like I've been able to afford them since then, either. I draw the line at camping, as you may have noticed. But I've never done anything close to this. You must be used to it by now, though."

"Yeh. Still quite nice, though. All the travel gets a bit wearing, tell you the truth. It helps to have a comfortable spot to go back to at night, even if it isn't home."

"It seems to me that you have a much different life, at home or on the road, than the one you knew growing up," she suggested. "Unlike me."

"True. It's a bit disorienting, actually. Out of the usual order of things, isn't it. Normally, you start out skint, don't you. Struggling to pay the bills on your pitiful wage when you're young. Then you work up over the years, maybe get a mortgage. Hoping to be comfortable when you're older. In this business, though, it's all backwards. You're just a young fella, and suddenly you can buy a flash car, even a house. Especially if you can do the adverts as well. It's easy to forget you're in a career that'll only last ten, twelve years, if you're lucky. That's one thing I like about being here. In New Zealand, I mean, not Oz. Close to my family and my mates. The money's not nearly as good. But everybody's quick to remind you of your roots. To tell you you're not as special as you may think."

"But I am pretty special, all the same." He sat up and pulled her off the bed. "Because I booked you in for a massage at the spa downstairs. I thought it would feel good after all that surfing. And it's about time to go."

"Wow," she told him that evening, stepping out of the shower to find him buttoning his shirt in front of the mirror. "You look way too handsome. I don't think I should risk taking you out in public."

"What?" He looked down at his self-striped charcoal shirt and black slacks, both cut close to his body in the European style so popular Down Under. "Nothing flash about these."

"No?" She reached up to kiss his cheek. "It must be how you look in them, then. If we're going someplace nice, and you're going to look that spectacular, you need to give me some privacy so I can work on getting beautiful myself. Because it's going to take a serious effort for me to match that."

"How long do you need? Our booking's for eight."

"I'll be on time," she assured him.

"Right, then," he decided. "I'll meet you in the lobby, when you're ready."

"Bloody hell."

Koti looked up from checking his messages at the exclamation from the man next to him. He stood, hardly knowing what he was doing, and watched Kate walk across the lobby towards them. He'd always loved the way she looked, but he'd never seen her like this. Her shiny hair was tousled around her face in a careless style that managed to look both elegant and sexy. A bronze-colored dress in some kind of rich, shiny material ended well above the knee, its tiny straps clinging to her shoulders. Her legs in their high heels looked endless in the short skirt, and her golden skin glowed in the reflection of the rich color.

As she caught sight of him, her brilliant smile spread across her face, and his heart gave a funny little twist. Her outsized life force, the amount of energy that somehow managed to emanate from such a small body, always took him by surprise. But tonight she seemed to make the very air around her vibrate.

She came to a stop in front of him, that blazing smile still lighting up her face. He took her hand, bent down to kiss her cheek. "You're gorgeous. You made my heart stop when I saw you."

He was aware of male heads turning to watch her as they made their way across the elegant lobby, his hand still wrapped firmly around hers, the marble floor echoing the tap of her heels. She didn't want to know when he was feeling possessive. Right, then. He wouldn't tell her. But he wasn't going to let go of her tonight either.

"This is great," Kate told him when they were seated in the intimate little restaurant, looking out on the parade of visiting humanity, all out to sample Broadbeach's vibrant nightlife. "I know I tease a lot. But I want you to know something. Even though it's only been a few days, this is the best vacation—holiday—I've ever had. And not just because it's been way beyond my pay grade. Everything about it has been wonderful. So . . ." She shrugged and smiled. "So, thanks."

"I should be thanking you, though," he said. "You're the one who's made it special. Having you all to myself. That's been the treat." He reached out and took her hand across the table. "Thanks for coming with me. Wish we could stay longer. Be nice to run away together for a bit, wouldn't it?"

"It would," she agreed. "But we both have to get back to work. And you have something important to go back to, don't forget. You've earned this break first, though. And you deserve it. You should be so proud of yourself, Koti. At everything you've accomplished these past months."

"So should you. You've done more than I ever could. After everything you've been through, you've built a whole new life for yourself. I've never known anyone braver."

"I had some help, though," she pointed out, squeezing his hand in gratitude. "First Hannah and Drew. And then you. I would have survived without you. I might even have been able to enjoy my life again. But never this much. Never like this, the way it's been."

"Oh, shoot." She reached for her napkin. "I'm going to cry now. I told you, it's dangerous for me when you're this wonderful. I lose all my defenses."

"You don't need your defenses tonight," he promised. "Because tonight is just for us."

Chapter 28

"Do you realize," Koti asked the next morning during the short drive to the tiny Gold Coast Airport, "that we've been together almost five days now without an argument?"

"A record," Kate agreed. "You're going to get bored. Unless you count that little skirmish over my driving back there."

He scowled. "Still don't see why you insisted. I'm used to driving on the left, after all. And I've been here before. You haven't."

"Yup. You're taking your life in your hands right now. You might want to leap out while you're still in one piece. See if you can hitchhike the rest of the way."

"I need to practice, Koti," she went on seriously. "It's a little scary to drive in a new country like this, even if I'm used to staying on the left now. And that's how I know I need to do it. When you've been a victim, when that fear's been running your life, it's hard to get out of that mindset. It's so easy to give in to it, even when it's over. And before you know it, you're limiting what you do, bit by bit. First you won't drive at night. Then you don't want to go anyplace new. You end up putting yourself into smaller and smaller boxes. Until you're afraid to leave the house."

"You don't seem to have done that, though," he objected.

"I sure wanted to. When I came here, I was a wreck. Scared of my own shadow. Don't you remember how it was when I saw you on the beach those first couple times? When I'd find you standing over me? You terrified me. It took professional help to get to this point, to know what I need to do. Which basically boils down to, if something's hard, I need to do it. Because it'll be easier the next time. And I'm expanding my boundaries instead of constricting them."

He looked at her, fresh understanding and respect dawning. "I didn't know that. Or that you were scared of me. You don't seem scared of me now."

"Yeah. Well. It didn't seem like a good idea to actually scream and run, you know. Though I came pretty close. And now . . ." She stopped to think about it. "Kind of amazing that I'm not, isn't it? As big and bad as you can be at times. But I do feel safe with you."

"Glad to hear that. Because you are. As big and bad as I am." He gave her his best wicked grin. "Pity you didn't tell me all this back at the hotel, though. Instead of grabbing the keys and announcing, 'My turn to drive.'"

She laughed. "I guess my diplomacy skills aren't quite as good as my self-knowledge. Thanks for giving me the chance to explain myself."

He nodded. "And now I need to share. I need to go see my mum when we get back. She texted me this morning. Wants me to come for Sunday tea, now that the season's over."

"All right," she said agreeably. "I can take the bus from the airport. That's no problem. Because otherwise, you'll be tacking on a lot of extra driving."

"I thought you might want to come with me," he suggested. "My sisters will be there, with their families of course. You've met two of them already. That should lessen the shock and pain."

Kate frowned. "That'd be weird, though, wouldn't it? Taking me to dinner at your mom's house?"

"No, why?" he objected. "Give me company on the drive, too. I won't stay over. Just a few hours. It'll be good fun. You'll get to meet the kids and all."

"I hope it's all right that I drive this time," he said sarcastically, pulling the keys from his pocket as they walked through the Auckland Airport carpark. "Seeing as it's my car, and we're going to my mum's house. The location of which, I'll point out here, you do not know."

Two hours later, they pulled up in front of a modest house in a middle-class neighborhood, with a crowd of children playing outside.

"Koti, love." The older woman hurried from the house and reached to engulf her son in a hug. "Did you have an injury you didn't tell me about? Or hurt yourself surfing?"

"Nah, Mum," he replied, confused. "Why?"

"Just wondered why you weren't driving," she said. Then turned to Kate with a warm smile. "But I'm being rude. Introduce me, darling."

"Mum, this is Kate Lamonica. Kate, my mum, Amiria James."

Amiria reached for Kate's hand, gave her a kiss on the cheek. "Haere mai, Kate. I'm glad you're here. And that you drove, if Koti's hurt himself."

He sighed. "I'm not injured, Mum. And it's a long story. Something to do with overcoming fear. And being hard for me to resist, I reckon. Kate and I had an argument, and I lost. Again. That's why she drove. But I'm fine."

"Thank goodness. I can't help worrying. Oh, and call me Amiria, please, Kate. I'm so glad you can join us for tea. I've heard all about you from Grace and Hope, of course, but what a treat to get to meet you myself. Come into the house, now."

"She's just adorable, isn't she?" she told her son with delight as she ushered them inside, pulling Kate to her and giving her a squeeze.

"Careful, Mum. You're in dangerous waters there, using the *a*-word. You're meant to think she's formidable. Imagine Maggie Thatcher."

Amiria laughed and winked at Kate. "He loves to tease. But I don't care, you are adorable, and I don't mind saying so."

Kate smiled back. "You're allowed to say so. Thank you. And thanks for letting me crash your family party."

"Uncle Koti!"

He laughed as a little girl came barreling into him. He picked her up and planted a big kiss on her cheek. "This is Ruby," he told Kate. "One of Grace's."

"Come play with us," Ruby pleaded. She was echoed by the rest of the crowd of children who had run up to join them, and were now enthusiastically tugging him away.

"We've been waiting for you for *ages,*" put in an older boy. "I'm a flanker on my new team, Uncle Koti, did you know that? I got the Tackle Man trophy last week, too. Come on, and I'll show you what I've learnt."

"Keep your shirt on. Be there in a bit," he promised. "Are you OK if I leave you?" he asked Kate. "My presence is required, as you can see."

"It's tough being so popular," she commiserated. "Go ahead. You've been sitting for a long time anyway. You need to run around as much as they do, I'll bet."

Amiria laughed. "She knows you too well, I can see that. You go on, Koti. Plenty of us here to entertain Kate."

She wasn't kidding, Kate saw as they entered the house. She'd known Koti had a big family. Still, she wasn't prepared for the impact of his three sisters and their husbands, plus the younger children, filling the lounge to overflowing with chat and laughter. They were all so big, too. She felt ridiculously undersized, like Gulliver in the land of the giants.

Hope and Grace exclaimed at the sight of her, jumping up to embrace and kiss her, and introducing her to the third sister, Joy. They pulled her down on the couch with them, and Kate found her unaccustomed shyness disappearing as she became engrossed in the lively conversation.

Koti came back into the room, bringing five happy, chattering children with him, while his mother and sisters were starting to put the meal on the table.

"Wash hands, everyone." Amiria pushed them in the direction of the bathroom. "You too, Koti. You're filthy."

"Nana, guess what? We all jumped on Uncle Koti," giggled Ruby. "We tackled him and he fell down."

"He only fell down because he wanted to," her ten-year-old brother informed her loftily. "He's too strong for kids to tackle hm."

"Don't know about that," Koti said, clapping the boy on the shoulder. "Seems to me you're getting a fair set of muscles yourself. I'll be having to watch myself soon."

The boy glowed with pleasure, and Kate heard him begin to tell his uncle about his own rugby season as the two went off to clean up.

"I'm never going to remember everyone's name," Kate apologized when they were sitting down to dinner. "There are too many kids."

"Going to be even more, too," Joy said. "Did Mum tell you, Koti? Both Hope and I've fallen pregnant again, can you believe it?"

"Getting pretty far out ahead of you, bro," her husband Jonah told him

"Somebody has to be the fun uncle, though," Koti protested. "Reckon that's my job."

"Seems like you may be getting closer, anyway," Joy said with a sly glance at Kate.

"Joy." Her mother shot her a quelling glance.

"Sorry," Joy said, chastened. "Not appropriate."

"It's lovely to have you with the family for tea again, Koti," his mother went on smoothly. "I do worry about what you're eating. Hope and Grace said there wasn't much in your fridge, last time they were up."

"I'm doing better with that, though," he said. "Kate and I have been practicing. Cooking," he added hastily, seeing Jonah smother a laugh.

"You're teaching him to cook?" Grace looked at Kate with approval. "We've never managed that."

Kate laughed. "Believe me, I'm not doing any teaching. We've been learning together, by trial and error. A fair amount of error. We've only had to throw out the whole dinner once, though. And that was a while ago, huh, Koti? I'd say we're making progress. We hardly even burn anything anymore."

"I want to learn to do lamb next," Koti told his mother. "We may be ready to expand our horizons that far. Can we ring you this week, have you talk us through it?"

"Of course, love."

"Getting domesticated, eh," Doug said to Koti with a grin. "Watch yourself, bro. That's a slippery slope."

"One of us has to be," Koti answered. "And Kate's a dead loss."

"Hey. No worse than you," she protested.

"Like I said. A dead loss. As bad as me," he admitted.

"You boys can watch the kids," Amiria commanded once everyone had finished eating. She got up from the table and began to clear. "We'll do the washing up. It'll give us a chance to have a chat."

Kate wondered how much more chatty these women could get. She soon found out, as their affectionate teasing and laughter filled the warm kitchen.

"You've been in En Zed six months now, I hear," Amiria said to Kate as they worked together to fill the dishwasher. "What do you think of it so far? Have you had a chance to get around much, see a bit of the country?"

"Sadly, no. I've mostly been working. I haven't had any vacations—holidays, I mean—except this one we just went on. I'm clear on the fact that Australia is very different from New Zealand now, anyway, so I won't make any embarrassing comparisons."

"Probably a good idea," Hope smiled. "We do tend to resent that."

"Got it," Kate assured her. "And I have managed to have a few adventures here. Koti's taught me to surf, which was quite a challenge—for both of us. He also took me Waitomo for one of those blackwater rafting trips. That was probably my favorite thing I've done."

"You're brave," Hope said with admiration. "I've never done that. I don't mind the caves, just don't want to do all that dropping down and climbing up. Weren't you scared?"

"A little," Kate admitted. "But it was amazing all the same. Looking back at it, the best part was being down there in the dark with the glowworms, and hearing Koti sing. The Maori songs—the couple of them I've heard, anyway—are so beautiful, even though I don't understand the words. And he sings so well. I've always wished I could do that."

"You must sing, though, with your own family," Amiria protested.

"Not unless you count 'Happy Birthday,' or the occasional Christmas carol. The only time I've sung recently was in a karaoke bar. And that was almost a disaster."

"That just means you need to practice more," Grace said firmly. "Would you like to learn a song yourself?"

"What, now? I really can't sing, though. Not on my own. I'm not just saying that."

Grace laughed. "You won't have to sing alone. That's the idea. We all sing it together. We'll teach you *Tutira mai nga iwi,*" she decided. "That's one every Maori knows. You'll be able to impress people then, when you can join in. It's easy as to learn, too."

Without giving Kate a chance to protest, she began singing a line at a time, encouraging Kate to practice each after her. The tune was catchy and simple, and Kate found to her surprise that Grace had been right. Even though she didn't know what the words meant, they were easy to pick up.

"Time to put it all together," Grace announced, as the lesson concluded along with the washing-up.

"Oi!" she clapped her hands as they reentered the lounge. "Get the rest of the kids. We're going to have a sing with Kate, here. *Tutira mai nga iwi.*"

They all really did sing, Kate found with pleasure, as men, women, and children joined in with joyful abandon, slapping thighs or tables in time to the beat as they sang.

"HI AUE HEI !!!" Kate shouted out the final chant with the rest, then dissolved with them into laughter and applause. "What does it mean, anyway?" she asked. "This one isn't sad, I can tell that."

"It's about unity," Joy told her. "It says, 'Line up, all of us together. Think as one, act as one. Love each other, learn together. All of us together.' That's the *'tatou, tatou, e'* you kept singing—all of us together."

"Ah. Kind of a Maori pride thing," Kate nodded.

"That's it," Joy agreed.

"I guess you guys don't need a karaoke bar to find the courage to sing," Kate mused.

"Nah," Grace's husband Tane grinned. "No alcohol or background music required. We grow up singing and just keep on. If you're not careful, you'll be here all night singing, now that you've got us started."

"Talking of that," Koti rose from his seat, "we'd better be on our way. It's gone six-thirty, and Kate has to work tomorrow. See you, Mum." He leaned down to give her a warm hug and kiss. "I'll come again as soon as I can."

Chapter 29

The entire family came out to wave them away as they left. Kate settled back into her seat with a contented sigh.

"No fight over the car keys this time, anyway," Koti said with relief. "That was dead embarrassing, turning up like that."

"I'm glad I don't have to drive back, to tell you the truth," she said. "I'm so full, I feel like a python that's eaten a goat. I'm going to lie back here and focus on digesting. I can see where your sisters got their cooking ability. Your mom might even succeed in talking us through the lamb thing."

"Now you know why I don't live in Hamilton. If I did, I'd lose all my endorsements straight away. Nobody'd want me to take my shirt off."

She reached over and put a palm on his flat abdomen. "Still feels pretty good to me. Guess we got you away in time. And by the way, it's a wonder you aren't even more spoiled than you are. Because I've never seen anyone so doted on in my life. I always wondered how those mothers could swear their darling boys couldn't possibly have murdered anyone, when they were caught with five bodies buried in the basement. Now I know."

"What, because I'm a serial killer? Nice," he objected.

"No. Just that if you were, they'd still think the sun rose and set on you. They don't exactly hold your feet to the fire, do they?"

"And is that bad?" he frowned across at her.

"That's what I've been trying to decide," she admitted.

"Well, don't hold back. I should have known I'd get your opinion."

"Do you really not want me to tell you what I think? Because I can keep it to myself, if you don't want to hear it."

"Nah," he decided. "Better tell me, now you've brought it up. I don't have to agree with you."

"No, you don't. OK. You have a whole lot of unconditional love. Not just from your mom, but from your sisters too. And that's great. Pretty unusual, too. But you also get all that unconditional approval. And *that* I'm not so sure about."

"What does that mean?"

"Did you hear that, back there? If the All Black selectors hadn't chosen you this time, there'd have been something wrong with them. It could never have been for any other reason—say, that you hadn't worked hard enough, or somebody else was better. Because you're perfect as you are, no improvement needed."

"You obviously did deserve to be selected," she went on hastily at his frown. "I'm not saying you didn't. You did work hard, and you are the best. I know that. And you *are* pretty great, in my unbiased opinion. But frankly, I'm surprised by that. That you turned out as well as you did, and have got as far as you have, with all that invitation to complacency at home. Somebody must have been pushing you, somewhere. So who was it?"

"Wish you weren't so smart," he grumbled. "My coach, in high school. And my Uncle Nepia. The one who gave me my pendant. My mum's brother. They both made me keep working. Told me when I wasn't trying hard enough. And in case you haven't noticed, I'm still getting it from the senior players and the coaches."

She nodded, satisfied. "I knew there had to be somebody. But it sounds to me like you mostly got that for rugby. Not so much for life. Good thing your mother and sisters are so decent, that you had their example to make you the good guy you are. Because otherwise you might have been unbearable. So entitled. Which I'd guess has been an issue anyway, in the past at least."

"And what does *that* mean? That I think I'm entitled to have whatever I want, just because I want it?"

"Well, yeah. What, am I the first one who's ever said that?"

"The first one to say it that bluntly, anyway."

"You don't think you've had a bit of a free pass? That you get away with more because of how you look, not to mention all that flashy talent? Because women, especially, think you're charming and wonderful, even when you're behaving badly?"

"I don't behave that badly, though," he protested. "Tell me when I haven't behaved well with you."

"Not much," she admitted. "Well, except at the beginning. But I suspect that's because I don't let you get away with it."

"So why are we having this conversation?" he demanded. "If you've put me in my place. None of that shocking unconditional approval."

"I thought it was interesting, that's all. It's the accountant in me again. I have to analyze everything. Maybe I overdo it, sometimes."

"Ya think?" he asked sarcastically.

"OK," she said penitently. "I went too far. Sorry. Let me back up. I liked your mother and your sisters very much. They're warm and kind and funny, too. They made me feel at home, and that matters, when you're as far away from your real home as I am. And I've repaid them by criticizing them to you for being too loving. Next time I'll write all this in my diary, instead of telling you. How's that?"

He sighed. "Nah. I have to admit, it's interesting, getting an outside opinion. You're honest, at any rate."

She laughed. "I am that, I'm afraid. But let's change the subject. Tell me about your—your iwi, right? Your tribe. Were your ancestors from this area too?"

"Yeh. This whole area is the Waikato district. After the river we're driving beside now. You've heard of that."

"I have. That much I know."

"And that's my hapu as well. My subtribe. The Waikato. But the iwi is a larger group. The Waikato are part of the

Tainui iwi. Which comes from the Tainui waka, part of the Great Fleet."

"The group of canoes that came to New Zealand in the beginning."

He nodded again. "That's the story. That the eight great travelling waka came from Hawaiiki, the homeland, six hundred years ago, and landed in the Bay of Plenty. Then they spread out, each waka sailing to a separate area to settle. The Tainui ended up on the west coast. Sailed up the Waikato. And over time, the different hapu, the subtribes, developed out of that larger iwi. The Waikato were the group that settled inland here, close to the river."

"But there's more than the iwi and the hapu," Kate said. "The word I always see in the paper is whanau. They're always talking about somebody's whanau being at the hospital, or somebody being farewelled by his whanau at a funeral. It's got me confused. It's your family, I know, but it seems like it goes beyond that."

"It's your extended family. Which extends a long way, all the way out to second, third cousins. Anyone connected to us. It doesn't have to be a blood tie. A Maori can have hundreds of cousins, all part of our whanau, and all important to us. We know who they are, because we grow up knowing our whakapapa, our genealogy, at least to some extent."

"I'm beginning to see why being an only child is so foreign to you," she said. "I have to tell you, just that group back there was pretty overwhelming to me. I can't even imagine what you're talking about."

He laughed. "You should see us at the marae, then. The meeting house. All the kids running around, the aunties and uncles. One thing a Maori never has is a shortage of family. Family and the land, that's what matters most."

"'*Whatungarongaro te tanga toi tu whenua,*'" he quoted. "'As man disappears from sight, the land remains.' Not in the Pakeha sense, that we own it. But that we live in it, are part of it. That it's part of us. That's why every iwi has a spiritual connection to a specific mountain and body of water."

"And let me guess. Your body of water is the Waikato."
"You're listening," he said approvingly. "That's right."

"Waikato-taniwha-rau.
He piko, he taniwha.
He piko, he taniwha.
Waikato of a hundred taniwha.
At every bend a taniwha."

"The taniwha are powerful spirits. Monsters, sometimes. But you can use the word for a chief, too. The taniwha of the Waikato are supposed to be powerful chiefs, guardians of the tribe. The river is part of our mana, our spiritual power. Because when you're Tangata Whenua—a person of the land, Maori, your connection to the land is as important as your ancestry, your connection to your people. We don't see ourselves as standing alone in the world, or separate from it, the way Pakeha do. Each of us is—you could say a strand in the web. As well as our bond to the land, we're bound to those who have gone before, our ancestors. To our whanau, all our family ties here as well. And we know that those who come after us will be bound to us in the same way."

"And that still matters even now, those traditional values?" she asked. "I have to say, that surprises me. That it seems so central to your life."

"It's pretty deep-seated, that you're Maori. Even if we aren't fluent in te reo, we know the songs and legends, the proverbs. And because family's so important, we grow up surrounded by those values and beliefs, and they become part of us."

"Part of New Zealand too, some of them at least," Kate observed. "That's not exactly the record indigenous people have had in other countries. I wonder why that is."

"Because we didn't lose, that's why. Different story. The founding document of New Zealand isn't a constitution. It's the Treaty of Waitangi. A treaty between equals, not the Maori chiefs submitting to the Crown."

"I've heard of the Treaty, of course," she said. "And that it was still enforced. But I didn't realize that part of it."

"Maori are pretty hard to defeat. We got loads of practice, didn't we, all the tribes fighting each other over hundreds of years. We've always been good at going to war. Not to mention that everyone spoke the same language. That was massive, that the tribes could communicate and work together. And you know, even after the Treaty in 1840, there was still resistance, right here. The Waikato campaign of the Land Wars, the Maori fighting against land confiscation. The last bit of the railroad to be put in was through here, because there wasn't a final peace—or any Pakeha allowed to settle here, either—until the 1860s."

"But anyway. That's why te reo is one of the two official languages of Aotearoa, and why Maoritanga is as integrated as it is into the culture. Because we didn't lose, back then. And we've kept ourselves from losing ever since. There are still issues, of course. Maori are still poorer overall, less educated, don't live as long. And all the social issues that go along with that. But we're not on the margins either."

"Isn't it a problem, though," she asked him hesitantly, "when you have that kind of cultural connection, to date someone who isn't Maori? Everyone was so welcoming to me today. Are they actually upset, though, and not showing it? Your mother, especially. At least I'm not blonde. But not exactly Maori either."

"You've got a Maori heart, though. A warrior's heart. And like I said, kinship ties aren't just blood. I'm not pure Maori either, and neither are my mum and dad. Around two-thirds of Maori kids born these days are mixed, in fact. There's been so much intermarriage over the years. Not just with Pakeha, but with the Islanders as well. I have some Samoan in me, on my mum's side. Which is good. Made me bigger. And a good quarter or more Pakeha. Reason I don't have a Maori surname."

"Why is that? All the intermarriage? Seems unusual, for such a proud culture."

"Why d'you think? In case you haven't noticed, we're good-looking."

She laughed. "You've got me there. No argument."

"And speaking of being good-looking," he went on. "There's a banquet and awards ceremony next Saturday for the NZRFU. Want to go with me, let me show everyone what a gorgeous girlfriend I have?"

"What's the . . . the whatever you said?"

"En Zed Rugby Football Union. The awards for the season. It's a major. And I'd like to take you with me."

She was already shaking her head. "It'll be in the papers, then, right? With pictures, I'll bet. Sorry. I'd like to go, but I can't."

"Whyever not? Thought we weren't keeping this a secret anymore. And you can't be worried about how you'll look. If you wear that dress you wore last night, I promise, you'll be beautiful."

"Thanks. But I can't take the risk of my name—not to mention my picture—showing up in the paper. I've worked too hard to stay hidden to risk that now."

"What, you're worried Paul will see it? How likely is that, at this point? And anyway, I'm here, aren't I. Even if he sees a photo and flies all the way over here, unlikely as that seems, he's not going to attack you with me around."

"Yes, but you won't be around, will you? You can't protect me if you're in Argentina. You aren't with me all the time anyway, even when you're here. And he's a stalker, Koti. That means he watches and waits for his opportunity. And it also means he's obsessed. I've been gone more than six months now. A long time. And a couple months ago, remember, he was still looking for me. I'm not going to draw a big red arrow on a map and show him where to find me."

"Right," he sighed. "I'll go by myself. It'll be boring, though. If you change your mind, let me know."

She looked across at him with a puzzled frown. "You wouldn't really want me to put myself at risk, would you? Just so you're not bored at some banquet?"

"Nah," he grumbled. "Course I wouldn't. If you really think there's still a risk, of course you should stay home. But I don't want some secret girlfriend that I can't take out."

"You don't want me?" she asked, startled. "If I can't go out with you?"

"Didn't say that," he sighed. "Sorry. It's hard for me to believe there's still any danger, though. Not after all this time. I think you might be overreacting, don't you?"

"You sound like everybody else. I thought you understood better than that. The average stalker does this for almost two years, Koti. This guy isn't normal, and you can't judge him by normal standards. He wanted to kill me, and he still does. I know it. I can feel it. And I want to stay alive. Even if you have to go to dinner by yourself."

"Sorry," he said again. "You're right, it's hard to imagine. Wanted you with me, that's all. Wanted to show you off."

"I'd like to have seen you too," she assured him. "You'll just have to come over afterwards and show me how gorgeous you look all dressed up. Plus for that booty call."

He laughed reluctantly. "There is that. Reckon I'll make it an early night. Dress code, though. No sheep pajamas."

"I'll see what I can do. I'll surprise you, how's that?"

"Anticipation," he agreed. "My favorite thing."

Chapter 30

Koti shifted restlessly on the bench. He'd known he wouldn't be starting the game, of course. But he'd hoped for more than fifteen minutes of playing time against the Wallabies in this first test match. This wasn't the kind of progress he'd thought he was making. The kind he needed to make, if he were going to justify staying here.

He thought back with dissatisfaction to the conversation he'd had with his agent a few days earlier.

"I've heard from Leicester and Northampton, both asking about you for next season," Bruce had told him. "As well as Perpignan, that I mentioned earlier. A French team would likely offer you more, but any of those teams would pay well. Are you interested?"

"Don't think so," Koti answered. "I'm well suited here just now. But don't tell them no yet, either," he decided. "I need to see how I go, these next weeks."

"Don't wait too long," Bruce cautioned. "Your form's been good lately, especially your performance in the final. The further out we get from that, the less negotiating power it gives us."

"I know that," Koti told him irritably. "But I need time to think it over."

Now, watching the All Blacks put the finishing touches on a convincing win over the Wallabies, he wondered again. Was he wasting his time here? So he had his game jersey. How much was that worth, if he were going to play this little? Wouldn't he be looking at it, next year or ten years from now, and thinking, 15 minutes on the paddock, 65 on the bench?

He hadn't been happy in England before. But the money was good. And being here, if he weren't selected next season—how was that going to feel? He'd made it onto the squad. But was it enough to make up for what he was giving up?

It was true, he had ties here. Ties he'd miss if he left. Would a few years away really matter so much, though, in the long run? Maybe he was being stupid, turning his back on this opportunity. He could look into it more, at least. That didn't mean he had to do anything about it.

"Find out what they're offering," he told Bruce on Monday. "We should know, at any rate. I haven't made any decisions yet. But I'm thinking about it."

"What's wrong?" Kate asked him that evening. "You're not usually this quiet. You haven't even given me a hard time about overcooking the kumara."

"Dunno," he shrugged. "Tired, maybe. Jet lag."

"Jet lag," she said flatly. "Right. It's a three-hour flight, Koti. And I've never seen you like this. So come on. Tell me. It's the playing time thing, isn't it. Being on the bench."

"Yeh," he admitted. "Can't seem to get a look in."

"That's not really true, though, is it? You did play. It seemed to me you did a good job, too. What does the coach say?"

Koti shrugged. "Still on the squad, for this next game in Jo-burg. And also still not starting. Much of a muchness, isn't it." He opened his mouth to tell her about his conversation with Bruce. Then shut it again.

"What?" Kate asked. "What is it?"

"Nothing. Just thinking."

How could he talk this over with her? She wouldn't understand how frustrating he was finding his lack of progress. Wouldn't understand how he could think about leaving again. And she'd want to know what it meant for the two of them. His mind shied away from the thought. Time enough to think about that. He didn't even know that he was leaving yet. No point upsetting her with something that might never happen. He'd leave it, for now.

"Kate. I'm glad I caught you before you left for work," Hannah told her the next Wednesday. "Because I've had a great idea. Do you want to come to Wellington with me on Friday night? It's going to be my first-ever trip with Jack. After South Africa last week, and with Buenos Aires coming up so soon, I figured I'd get brave and take him. This is the one trip I'm sure we could do. Even if he cries the whole time, it's only an hour. If you came, we could hang out together on Saturday before the game, and I could show you the city. What do you think? Doesn't it sound fun?"

"It does," Kate said cautiously. "But I'm not sure it'd be a good idea for me to go. There's something weird going on."

"Weird how?" Hannah asked with concern. "With Koti, do you mean?"

"Yeah. He's been . . . I don't know. Kind of distant. I noticed it when they got back from Australia, but I figured he was just tired. And upset about not getting to play more," Kate admitted. "And since there were only a couple days there before they had to leave for Johannesburg, I couldn't really judge. But since he's been back from South Africa . . . he's just different. He still seems to want to spend time with me. But when we do, it's not quite the same. It's hard to put my finger on it, but it's there."

"Have you asked him about it?"

"Are you kidding? This is me we're talking about. Of course I have. But I'm not getting much in response. Nothing that satisfies me. I know everything isn't about me. He could be upset about something else. But if he were, I think he'd tell me about it."

"It's sure seemed like you two have been getting close lately," Hannah agreed. "Are you afraid it *is* you? That he's cooling off?"

"Yeah. I am." It hurt to admit it, but it was a relief too. She'd been dancing around the idea for the past week, not wanting to confront it directly. It was time, though.

"I don't understand it," she said slowly. "Things were really good in Australia. He took me to meet his family, too. No, that's not quite true. He was going to dinner at his family's and he took me along."

"That isn't casual," Hannah said. "That does mean something, whether he set it up in advance or not. Have you had a fight since then?"

"No. Everything was great, like I said. At least it seemed like it to me. But since the Championship started, there's been this distance. Like he's slipping away from me. I don't know, maybe he met somebody he liked better in Australia," Kate tried to joke.

"I doubt that," Hannah said seriously. "But it could be he got a little scared, felt like you were going too fast, and he's pulling back now. He might not even realize that's what he's doing."

"You could be right. If that's the case, my going down to Wellington doesn't feel like a good idea. I'm not going to chase around after him if he's not interested any more. I'd force the issue, but I've tried already, without any result. It seems best for me just to back off right now. If he's feeling pressured, I'll take the pressure off. We've only known each other for seven months. It's not like I need a commitment."

"And if we're going to break up," Kate forced herself to say, "well, I'll deal with that if it happens. Better now than later. And I have a feeling something *is* going to happen, pretty soon. This is either going to get better, or it's going to get a whole lot worse."

Her heart sank as she said it. She knew it was logical. But it hurt to say it out loud. She'd been confused at first by Koti's retreat, then angry. Now, though, she needed to know, one way or the other. "If it's still like this next week," she decided, "maybe I *will* force the issue. I can't keep walking on eggshells."

"I think that's a good idea," Hannah told her firmly. "If the guy can't see what a prize you are, he doesn't deserve you anyway. You can do better."

"Oh, Hannah," Kate said with a shaky laugh. "I don't think I can. But thank you. You're such a good friend."

"Did you see the ABs game Saturday night?" Brenda asked over Monday lunch in the building's cafe.

"Mmm-hmm," Kate nodded as she finished a bite of sandwich. "Pretty good one, I thought. Argentina plays with a lot of passion, don't they? Some of those guys are awfully handsome, too. They might even have been worth a trip to Wellington to check out in person, don't you think?"

"Yeh. Pity Argentina's so far away. That's too much of a long-distance romance, even for me," Brenda complained. "They need to select a few more good-looking boys for the Wallabies squad. Every time I have a look at those fellas, I wish I hadn't. Pity. I could commute to Australia."

"Pity about Koti, too," she continued in a more serious tone. "I'm guessing that was a bit of a stunner. Unless you two have other plans."

Kate put down her sandwich, her mouth going dry. "What?" she asked. "What was a stunner?"

Brenda faltered. "The long-distance thing, I mean. With England."

"You don't know," she realized, seeing the stricken look on Kate's face. "I've put my foot in it. I heard it, so I thought it couldn't be news to you."

Kate found herself drifting off, as if her head were floating somewhere above her body. She forced herself to focus, to ask the question. "You need to tell me now, Brenda. What is it you've heard? What is it I don't know?"

"Could be it's just a rumor," Brenda hastened to say. "But I heard that Koti had been talking to a couple English teams. That he was planning a move back there for next season."

"Where did you hear this?" Maybe it was a mistake, Kate thought, while the sudden chill, the prickling anxiety she felt running up her arms, told her otherwise. She crossed her arms to warm herself, protect herself against the blow she knew was coming.

"Publicists' grapevine," Brenda told her, real pity in her eyes. "They're talking, over there. I don't think he's signed anything, or I'd have heard. But there's been contact. And not just on the teams' side."

"And this has been going on for a while," Kate said flatly.

"Afraid so. Couple of weeks, anyway."

Kate nodded. "Excuse me. I have to get back to work now."

She walked blindly out of the café and straight to the ladies' room. Locked the stall door, hung her purse carefully on a hook and stood, hands braced against the wall, trying to force her mind out of its stunned disbelief. To think the situation through clearly.

If it were true—if Koti were talking to overseas teams, and had been for a while—he'd had plenty of time to tell her. How many evenings had they spent together over the past weeks? How many times had she asked him what was on his mind? Yet he'd never even hinted at it. She knew he'd been frustrated with his limited playing time, but he'd never mentioned this option. Why was that?

Not because she wouldn't have been interested. That was clear. No, it was because he was having a good time with her. And he didn't want his good time cut short. The way he'd have known it would be, if he'd told her what he was planning.

She'd thought she meant something to him. That they were going somewhere. Well, he was going somewhere, all right. The only problem was, she wasn't going there with him.

Her heart twisted with pain at the thought of him leaving her. No, she corrected herself. Of her leaving him. Because she wasn't going to hang around and wait for the end. She was going to have it out with him. If it were true, then the sooner it was done, the sooner they broke it off, the sooner she could move on.

A tiny voice of hope whispered that perhaps it was all a mistake. She'd let that little voice whisper. But somehow, she knew it wasn't going to turn out that way.

She had a sudden vision of herself, as if she were looking down from above. Pitiful. Locked into a bathroom stall, propped against the wall for support, close to tears. Trembling with shock and disappointment, because her world had shifted. She straightened up. Took her purse off the hook and opened the stall. Washed her face and hands, letting the warm water run over her chilled fingers until they lost some of their tension. Gripped the counter and looked at herself in the mirror.

"Time to cowboy up," she said aloud to her dry-eyed reflection. "Put on your big girl panties and cope." Picked up her purse and marched back into the office to finish her day.

"Hi, baby." Koti gave her his usual cheeky grin as he stepped into her tiny flat that evening. "Miss me?"

He leaned down for a kiss, but Kate hastily took a step back, avoiding him. She reached around behind him and slammed the door shut.

"Come in," she told him, unsmiling. "We need to talk."

His smile faded. "What's wrong? Did something happen?"

Kate walked into the middle of the lounge, then turned around to face him, arms folded. "I heard some interesting news today. News that surprised me."

Koti began to look a bit hunted. "Oh, bugger. What did you hear?"

"That you were talking to English teams. That you were planning on a move back there. Sooner rather than later, I'm guessing. What do you think? A month? Two?"

"Nothing's signed yet. But yeh, there've been some conversations."

She nodded, the final door of hope slamming shut. "Over quite a few weeks, I gather. When were you planning on letting me know about all this?"

He put his palms out in front of him. "Hang on. Before you go off. I didn't want to upset you when all I was doing was talking. I reckoned I'd tell you when there was something to tell."

"No." She shook her head and stared him down. "That isn't it. You didn't tell me because you didn't want to upset your nice little arrangement. Your little friend who was always available for sex. Or a laugh, or some sympathy if you'd had a bad day. You figured you'd string me along as long as you could. Who knows, maybe you were planning to get somebody else to tell me. I could even read it in the paper, how about that? Then I might just have slunk away. You'd have had all the fun, and none of this unpleasant emotion from me."

He flushed with anger. "What's wrong with me waiting? So what if I'm leaving? You've never made any secret of the fact that you're only here for a year or two yourself. And I've never got hysterical about that."

"Exactly," she pounced. "I've never made any secret of it. Normally, and I'm telling you this because you seem to be ignorant of it, when you date someone, you aren't putting an expiration date on it. You're seeing where the relationship is going. You're open to the possibility that it might grow. And then, guess what, maybe you'd stick with it. Change your other plans to do that. But if there's no future because you're leaving in a month, that's not a relationship at all. That's recreation."

"I didn't want to hurt you, though," he protested.

"Yeah, right," she scoffed. "Because it doesn't hurt at all to have you betray me. To let me go along like this, knowing how I feel about you. Knowing you're going to dump me as soon as it suits you. As soon as you don't need me anymore."

"Hang on. I've never made any promises to you."

She stared at him. "Wow. That's pretty cold. But you're right, of course. You didn't promise me anything but a good time. And I had plenty of warning signs, didn't I? Even

Hannah told me you were a player, and not to get involved with you."

"That's nice, isn't it?" she continued as she saw the shock on his face. "That's what your dream girl thinks of you. Then there was Dena."

"Dena? What does she have to do with it?"

"She thought she had a relationship with you too, remember? I was so smug at the time. I even thought it was funny, heaven help me. Because I can see now, you never bothered to tell her she didn't. God forbid you'd have to say something she didn't want to hear, lose your Mr. Charm title. Instead, you just let them find out the hard way. Then you can walk away. No strings, no scars. You're like Teflon. Nothing sticks. And it's their problem for thinking there was more to it than there really was. They're not just left alone. They're ridiculous too. Because you never promised them anything."

She stopped, feeling deflated. After all, it was herself she was talking about. *She* was alone. *She* was ridiculous. Because she had wanted him too much. Had imagined something that had never really been there at all.

"You can't help making women fall in love with you, I guess," she went on more slowly. "And you caught me at a vulnerable time. I knew better, and I did it anyway. Well, poor me. I made a mistake. I thought there was more to you, more to us, than there really is. I was wrong." She shook her head. "But never mind that you've let me down. You've let yourself down too. That hurts almost as much. I thought this was your dream. Now, because you've had a setback or two, because it's going to take some hard work and you might not succeed, you're just going to run away, and avoid all that? Wow, you really take the easy road, don't you?"

"How do you know so much about what I want, or what's right for me?" he shot back. "It's a perfectly rational decision to go overseas, where I can make more money. I'm marketable just now. I may only have another five or six years to play football. This is my chance to get myself right for the future. I'd be a fool not to take it."

"It would be perfectly rational if it was what you wanted to do," she agreed. "But it isn't. You've told me so. That you want to live here, in your own country, near your family. And that you want to be an All Black. What happened to all that? Your dream?"

"I've tried it though, haven't I? I've been trying all year. And I've had bugger all playing time. You've seen that. Why beat my head against the wall if I can't make my dream come true?"

"What if you can, though? A couple months ago, you weren't selected at all. You worked on that. And now you're on the team. So you're not starting yet. You're still playing. It seems to me you've made a lot of progress. You played almost forty minutes the other night. Why would you give up just when it looks like you might achieve your goal? It's as if you don't believe, deep down, that you have what it takes to succeed at this. At something that would be a stretch for you."

"You're better than this, Koti." She looked up at him searchingly, hoping against hope that she could reach him. That she could make him see what she saw in him. "You can ask more of yourself. You have it inside you, and you can do it."

"You seem to be an expert at who I am, what I should do," he said angrily. "But I don't believe it. That isn't what's bothering you so much. It's that I'd be leaving you."

"No. You're wrong," she told him levelly, her heart sinking. It was hopeless, then. "Because if that's how you really feel, I don't think I want you anymore. Set aside how you're selling yourself short, how you won't let yourself push to see whether you can make it to the top, because you're scared you might fail. Even if I wanted a man like that, a man who won't put himself to the test, I sure wouldn't want one who deceived me like this. Who doesn't have the guts to be honest about his plans. And, let's not forget, who's planning to walk out on me."

"That's what this is really about. That I'm not committing to you."

"Oh, yeah," she flashed back. "Sucks to be me. I'll have to cancel my subscription to *Brides* magazine now. Get over yourself. I just told you, you've shown me who you really are. And I don't want it."

"And that's what you think of me. That's how you see me."

"That's it. Now if you don't mind, I'd like you out of my house. Because I'm done with this. I'm done with you."

She forced herself not to slam the door after him. Leaned her head against it and succumbed at last to the tears she had held off all day. Cried until her eyes swelled and her nose ran, sobbed until her chest hurt. Walked to the bathroom, looked in the mirror at the mess she'd made of herself, and cried some more to see it.

Because despite everything she had said, despite all the weaknesses she had catalogued for him, she still loved him. She wanted to be with him, support him, share her life with him. But he didn't love her. Had never loved her. She'd lost him, but she'd never had him at all.

Chapter 31

Koti heard the door shut behind him. He still couldn't believe it had happened. He'd been in such a good mood, looking forward to seeing her, telling her about the game. Cooking dinner together. Spending the night with her. And now here he was, on the other side of the door. Shut out.

He drove home on autopilot, then sat staring at his house. It looked too big and empty, and he couldn't stomach the idea of spending the evening in it alone. He didn't want to go out, either. He got out of the car at last and turned toward the beach. The tide was almost out. He could walk around the point now. All the way to North Head, if it came to that.

An hour later he had done just that, and was standing on the windy summit, looking out through the darkness to the water below. A nearly full moon cast a path of light across the sea. Pity life didn't offer a lit roadway like that. With a clear sign at the end that you'd chosen the right course.

He hadn't handled the conversation well, he knew. His own fault. What was he going to do without her, these next weeks? It was all going to be pretty dull. She'd had time to cool off now, though. Maybe he could explain, apologize. It had worked before, after all. He pulled out his mobile to give it a go.

She picked up, to his relief. But she didn't bother with a greeting.

"I don't think it's a good idea for us to talk anymore," she told him. "We're done."

"Kate. Don't ring off. Let me say something. I'm sorry. You caught me off guard. And then I lost my temper. Didn't say what I should have. I'd like to say it now."

"All right. I'm listening," she said warily.

He took a deep breath and began, choosing his words carefully this time. "I didn't tell you I was thinking about leaving. That was wrong. I kept thinking I would, soon. But I wasn't sure what it would mean, for us. And I knew you'd be upset. So I put it off. But I wasn't stringing you along. Not deliberately."

"I guess that's nice to hear. But it doesn't change much, does it? You're not telling me anything new here."

"Yes, I am," he insisted. "I'm saying we don't have to break up. Why can't we go on as we are for now? Who knows how we'll feel, a couple of months down the road? This is good, isn't it? And I want to be with you, baby."

"First of all, you aren't allowed to call me that anymore. That's over. Because that isn't going to work. I'm supposed to hang on, hoping you'll fall in love with me. That you'll want to be with me the way I want to be with you. I'm not going to do that, Koti. You want a girlfriend. You want someone to hang out with and have sex with. That's fine. Go get her. It'd probably be decent of you to tell her it's a short-term assignment, but that's not really my problem anymore."

"I don't want some random girl, though," he objected. "I want you."

"Well, you can't have me," she said sadly. "I'll admit, I wish you could. Because this feels awful. But it was your choice. If it makes you feel any better, I'm pretty sure my heart's broken. I don't think yours is. I suspect you'll get over this a lot faster than I will. But I need to cut it off now."

Silence. She'd rung off, he realized. He swore aloud. Shoved the mobile back into his pocket and started the long walk back to Takapuna.

Kate dragged herself into work the next morning after a near-sleepless night. The depth of her pain had come as a surprise when she'd lain awake at four o'clock this morning examining it. How had she become so attached to him? It must have been the circumstances. She'd relied so much on his friendship during these past months. At first because she hadn't had anyone else. And then because it had been so much fun. Losing him had left a hole she couldn't see how to fill.

She was grateful once again that so much of her job was solitary. No meetings today, thank goodness. Just a stack of work that she could lose herself in. She might not be as productive as usual, but it beat having the same thoughts circling around and around in her head, useless and pointless.

"Kate. Wanna go for lunch?" She looked up to see Corinne, Brenda, and Heather standing next to her desk.

"No, thanks. I don't really feel like talking today. I'll take my lunch later. You go ahead."

She intercepted the glance they exchanged. They were feeling sorry for her. That was fairly hard to miss.

"And all of you know about this now, don't you? Who else knows?" she asked Brenda with resignation.

The other woman looked chagrined. "I'm a publicist," she apologized. "That's what I do. Publicize. Sorry."

Kate looked around. Several other heads were turned her way as well, clearly interested in the conversation. She'd get this over once and for all, she decided. The pitying looks and curious stares were going to be too hard to take, unless she confronted them directly.

She stood to her full height. "I've just decided to do a little publicity of my own."

Brenda's eyes widened in alarm. "Are you sure that's a good idea?"

"Doesn't matter. I'm doing it anyway." Kate raised her voice to address the roomful of office workers. "Hey, everyone! Listen up. I have an announcement." She picked up her ruler and banged it sharply against the desk.

Once she was sure everyone's attention was focused on her, she began. "I'm guessing all of you know I've been dating Koti James for a while now. So you can hear the news here first. It's over. If anyone wants the job, there's a vacancy.

Just temporary, but you'll have a good time. Don't expect anything more, and you won't be disappointed."

She forced herself to stop. "That's all," she finished lamely, and sat down with a thump. She was embarrassed, but oddly relieved as well.

"Bloody hell," Corinne breathed. "That's a first."

"Go have your lunch," Kate told them. "I'm lousy company today."

The others nodded and wandered off, casting a look back at Kate as she sat at her desk and tried to focus on her work again. An unusual number of other staff had left their desks too, she saw. No doubt to discuss her interesting revelation.

Bethany, the office manager, was the next to make an appearance in her field of vision. "Let's go into the conference room and have a chat," the older woman said firmly.

Kate followed her straight back, feeling very much as if she'd been summoned to the principal's office. Something that had never actually happened to her. Well, wasn't this fascinating? She was having all sorts of new experiences this year. Maybe she'd get to experience being fired now as well. In her current mood, that seemed like the next inevitable boulder to come crashing down on her.

"Well." Bethany looked at her seriously once they were both seated. "That was interesting."

"And unprofessional," Kate agreed. "On the other hand, one quick burst of speculation, and it's over. Instead of people whispering about it all week."

"There is that," Bethany admitted. "But it still wasn't appropriate. I understand that you're going through a rough patch just now, but I'm going to have to ask you to leave your personal life at home."

"Of course," Kate answered with relief. She wasn't going to be fired after all, then. Not today. At least one aspect of her life wasn't falling to pieces. "It won't happen again, I promise."

"It hasn't before. That's why I'm letting this one go. Put your head down, keep doing good work, and you'll get through this. You may want to talk to someone outside as well, get some help."

"I don't think it'll come to that. I picked the wrong guy, that's all. But thanks."

"Be careful what you wish for, eh," Bethany said with a small smile.

"Exactly," Kate agreed with a humorless laugh of her own. "Maybe that's a lesson learned for everyone. It sure has been for me."

"We're taking you out with us, Friday night," Brenda told her the next day. "We've decided you need some distraction. Maybe some rebound sex as well."

"I don't know," Kate said dubiously. "That's a big no on the rebound sex. It's pretty much the last thing on my mind. I'm not sure I'm up for much social time right now, either."

"Which is why you need us," Corinne insisted. "You don't have to talk, just listen."

"And drink," Brenda added helpfully. "Come on. If you don't, I'm going to think you're still upset with me for spreading the news."

"I am upset with you, though," Kate scowled at her. "Sort of. Or maybe I'm just upset, period."

"All right," she capitulated after a moment's thought. "I might as well. Better than sitting at home feeling sorry for myself. I'm not drinking so much this time, though. Last time I went out with the three of you, the bus ride home across the bridge was a nightmare. I spent the whole trip praying I wouldn't get sick."

She thought with a pang of that night, and the morning that had followed. Of Koti joking with her about it, letting her sleep, buying her breakfast to settle her stomach. That wouldn't be happening this time. And that was enough reason to go out, right there. If she couldn't enjoy herself, she could at least maintain some semblance of a social life.

Because she had a lot of time to fill, and she didn't want to spend all of it alone.

She might not want rebound sex, Kate decided on Friday morning as she looked through her closet. But a little male attention wouldn't hurt. Her pride had suffered a serious blow. No matter how much she tried to tell herself otherwise, part of her still whispered that if she'd been more beautiful, more glamorous, Koti wouldn't have let her go so easily. Well, she'd make sure she looked her best tonight. Maybe nobody would put her on a poster, but she'd bet she could make a few heads turn herself if she put her mind to it.

"You've made the papers today," Brenda told her, handing her a copy as soon as Kate entered the office. "I wanted to let you know straight away, and that I didn't do it. They must have got the info from somebody else. Probably somebody here."

Caught . . . and free again

We hear that **Koti James** has just had a very public split from his latest, Blues officeworker **Kate Lamonica**. The two had been spotted together for months, looking very cosy indeed. The good times came to an end, it seems, with a row in the Blues office. Good news for his many fans: the popular centre is on the market once again.

"Damn," Kate breathed, her heart sinking. "They didn't even get the story right. I didn't think of this when I made my announcement. Just what I've been trying to avoid. This'll be on the Internet now."

"Afraid so," Brenda sympathized. "Though I suspect it would've made the papers eventually in any case. But En Zed's a long way from California. Hard for me to believe that anyone's going to make the trip all the way out here after all this time, no matter how mad he is."

"You don't know him, though," Kate told her. "He's capable of just about anything. And I know he's still looking for me. But it's a tiny item. And I can't be the only Kate Lamonica in the world."

"Too right," Brenda said encouragingly. "He's not likely even to see it."

Kate hoped that was true. But she was afraid to count on it. She'd finally begun, these past weeks, to feel like a normal person again. One who didn't have to check every exit, scan every face, be on the alert in every situation. And a lot of the reason for that had been Koti. When he'd been with her, she'd been able to relax. But that wasn't the case anymore.

"I'll be careful," she decided. "That's all I can do now. And I'll hope and pray that he's finally lost interest. That he's gone from my life."

Koti sat on the bench in the locker room, stuffing his gear back into his duffel after another disappointing training session. During the past few days, he'd tried to put the confrontation with Kate out of his mind. Still, he'd found himself just that bit off pace, his offloads lacking their usual crispness, his performance in the drills slower and less precise.

Maybe it was the lack of sleep. Or the suddenness of the change. He hadn't adjusted yet, that was all. He'd picked up his mobile a dozen times, his fingers hovering over the speed-dial button. Then set it down again. There was no point, was there? He needed to put this behind him. Focus on what mattered.

"You've been a dead loss this week, haven't you."

He looked up, startled, to see Drew frowning down at him.

"Sorry," Koti muttered. He thought about making an excuse, or explaining. Didn't know how to begin.

Drew sighed and sat down on the bench beside him. "Whether you go overseas to play isn't my affair. Everyone has to make that decision for himself. But you need to focus on getting right for these games. For yourself, and for the team. You've been working on your form. Everyone's seen it. It's why you were selected, this round. But you need to be consistent, every day. No matter what's happening in your life. And I have a pretty fair idea what that is. Heard about what happened with Kate. Not exactly a secret now, is it."

Koti winced. He'd heard about the announcement Kate had made in the office, of course. More than one person had been kind enough to mention it.

"Hannah tells me Kate's pretty broken up about it," Drew went on. "I can see you are too. Don't want to sink the boot in, but I asked you to be honest. Not to let her think it meant something if it didn't. Seems to me you could've told her about your plans. It had to be hard for her to find out that way. You stuffed up, mate."

Koti shifted uncomfortably. "I meant to explain. Tried to, after she found out. But you know how she is. She went off, before we could work it out. And she won't listen now. In any case, I need to focus on my career just now, do what's best for my future. I can't let my feelings about a woman get in the way of that. There are more important things in life, eh."

Drew looked at him with pity. "Nah, mate. There aren't." He shook his head in resigned disappointment and stood up. "You've shown some discipline these past months. Do what you need to do to get focused. See you back at the hotel."

Koti came to a dead stop in the middle of the Queen Street sidewalk. With an hour to go before the team's 10:30 curfew, he and his roommate had decided to take in a bit of the milder nightlife available before returning to the hotel. Now, though, he stood rooted to the pavement. Colin walked ahead a few steps, then circled back, realizing Koti was no longer with him.

"What's up?" he asked. Then turned to look in the direction of Koti's gaze. "Checking out the talent?"

Koti didn't hear him. He stood and waited until the four women stopped in front of them, Kate's chin going up in the defiant posture he'd seen so many times. She was wearing that bronze dress she'd bought for their trip to Oz, with her highest heels. A thin wrap sweater in a metallic fabric was tied at her side, making her waist look impossibly small. She'd fixed some kind of shiny pins in her hair tonight, pulling one glossy brunette wing back from her face. She looked good, as good as he'd ever seen her. And she was out on the town. Four days after she'd given him the push, and she was out again.

"How ya goin', Koti," Brenda said at last as he stood mute. "Fancy meeting you here."

"Yeh," he said absently. Then tore his eyes from Kate as he felt Colin's nudge in his side. "Yeh," he said again. "Brenda. And sorry, can't remember," he apologized to the other two women.

"Heather and Corinne," Brenda reminded him. "And you know Kate, of course," she prompted.

"Kate." He looked at her again.

The chin went a little higher. "Koti. How are you."

The elbow in the ribs again. "Sorry. My roomie, Colin Thompson."

"Good to meet you." Colin flashed a grin at the four of them, with a lingering look for Kate. "Are you off somewhere special, or can we join you, buy you a drink?"

"Oh, I think that'd be a bad idea," Brenda said firmly. "Kate's been out of circulation for too long. She needs to meet some new people tonight."

"I'm new," Colin protested.

"Not new enough," Brenda told him. "Too much old baggage hanging round you. And we need to get on. See you boys."

Colin and Koti stood aside to let the women pass, then watched them make their way up the street.

"Want to explain that?" Colin asked as he and Koti moved on. "Bit of history there?"

"Yeh, a bit," Koti admitted.

"Well, if it's over, maybe you wouldn't mind giving me her number. I like those tiny girls. And she's choice as, eh."

"What?" he protested as Koti swung around to glare at him. "You don't want her anymore. Although if you don't mind my saying, you're a bloody fool. She didn't seem too keen on you either. Thought you had a better technique than that. What'd you do, dump her by text?"

"Never said I didn't want her anymore, did I?" Koti demanded. "Or that I dumped her. And I'm not sharing. Rack off."

"Oh. I get it. *She* dumped *you*." Colin laughed. "Sorry, mate. Just have to enjoy the thought of that. Bet it hasn't happened much. She did look stroppy. What'd you do? Cheat?"

"No, I didn't cheat," Koti growled. "Cut the rough, willya. Are we going to get a fizz? Thought that was the plan."

Colin looked at him more sympathetically. "You do have it bad. Reckon we'd better have that fizz back at the hotel bar. Not sure you're fit for much else just now. Could get yourself into trouble."

The bar was crowded with players enjoying a final bit of relaxation before the game the next evening. A fair few young women had joined them as well, Koti saw. He sat at a table, nursing his soft drink as he absently watched Colin chatting up an attractive blonde. Kate wouldn't be hooking up with anyone, he told himself. Surely she wouldn't do that, not so soon. She was after some distraction, that was all. He was uneasy all the same. She'd looked too pretty. And angry enough with him to do just about anything.

"Hullo, darling." He turned at a familiar hand on his shoulder, pulled back to allow Dena to slide in next to him. "Thought I might see you here tonight. Congratulations on being selected again."

He answered politely, still abstracted, as she pressed closer. "I just heard something else interesting," she purred. "That you'd been dating someone, but that you were single again now. Was it that girl I saw you with at Mac's?"

"Yeh," he said reluctantly. "That was the one."

"Mmm. Not surprised, I have to say," she said judiciously, running one finger around her wine glass, then reaching her hand up to stroke her collarbone and push her heavy auburn curls over her shoulder.

Koti watched the show with detached interest but little enthusiasm. He couldn't remember now why he'd once found her so attractive. Her performance was seductive, but so practiced. Nothing spontaneous about Dena. She'd never leave any aspect of her appearance—or her presentation of it—to chance. You'd never catch Dena in sheep pajamas.

"I hate to be bitchy," she went on, looking at him under her lashes, "but she didn't seem like your type. And I should know what that is. We had some good times together, didn't we?"

"We did," he agreed. "But that's a while ago now, Dena."

She pouted, then reached up to rearrange his hair, her hand lingering on the side of his face. "But what have you been doing in the meantime? You've missed out on a fair bit, I'd say. That girl—what's her name?"

"Kate," he told her reluctantly.

"That's right. Kate," she said with distaste. "I never could figure out what she had that would interest you. I'm not surprised you got tired of her. I mean, she was so little. Skinny, too. And I know how you like something to hold on to." She pressed a breast against his side. "Hardly even pretty, I thought."

He stood up abruptly. "Reckon my taste changed. Need to go, anyway."

"Never mind." Colin slid into the chair Koti had vacated. "He's a bit preoccupied just now. But I'm not. I'm single and available, too. And happy you're here."

Koti used the keycard to open his door, then sank down on the hotel bed. He had to put this out of his head. Kate was moving on, it was clear. He needed to do the same.

He shifted restlessly. He didn't want to be here alone. He wanted to talk to somebody. Call somebody. He reached for the telephone, then dropped his hand again. Because the person he wanted to talk to was Kate.

Chapter 32

"Oi, cuz," Hemi said with surprise, joining Koti in the Blues' carpark Monday afternoon. "What are you doing here?"

"Oh. Uh . . ." Koti cast about for a reason. "Just come to collect something."

"Odd I didn't see you inside, then," Hemi said. "Since I was just in there, signing some paperwork myself."

"Whoa, boy." He put out a hand to explore the large dent in the rear bumper of the sporty car. "What happened here? Bit of a ding, eh."

Koti shrugged. "Pulled out in the New World carpark. I was a bit distracted, bashed somebody else who was pulling out at the same time."

Hemi nodded. "I noticed you've been distracted. Better get that sorted, unless you plan to stay on the bench for the next game."

Koti thought about arguing, but he knew the other man was right. Hemi went on to offer a suggestion, but Koti had stopped listening. He'd spotted Kate leaving the building, heading for her little car. This was his chance. "Hang on a tick," he said absently, leaving Hemi in mid-sentence.

"Kate." She'd been fishing through her bag for her keys, but whirled at the sound of his voice.

"Koti," she said cautiously. "What do you want? I need to leave."

This wasn't starting out right. "I need to talk to you, though. Can't we work this out? D'you want to go for dinner?"

"I'm not sure what there is to talk about. What's changed?"

"Just that I don't see why we can't be friends anymore, at least. I know I stuffed up. That it was a shock. And I'm sorry I hurt you. But you hurt me too. And I miss you. I want to be with you."

He saw the flash of temper in her eyes, heard the indrawn breath. Then she was lashing out at him. "You can't always get what you want, though, haven't you heard that? Not even you, special as you are. I never believed you were really this selfish, underneath. I thought you'd just been able to get away with it for too long. Hadn't had to think about anybody but yourself."

"What do you mean, I can't always get what I want?" His own temper was flaring now. "I know that. That's the point. That's why I'm leaving. Because I don't have what I want."

"And whose fault is that?" she challenged him. "Not everything's going to be handed to you, whether you deserve it or not. That isn't the way life works."

"And as for me." She put back her head and looked up at him squarely. "I fell in love with you. I'm not going to beat myself up for that anymore. I couldn't help it. And you don't love me back. That's too bad for me, but you couldn't help it either. We're not in the same place. I understand that now. But you need to understand this. I'm not some puppet that you can use and then set aside when you're done. I deserve more than that. And I'm not stupid. I'm not going to walk right back into that heartache. I don't have the time to waste on you anymore, Koti. You can't give me what I need. So I'm going to go on and live my life. And eventually, I'm going to find a grown-up man who wants a grown-up woman to love him. And is ready to love her back."

He stepped back, feeling as if he'd been slapped. "If that's how you feel, reckon you're right, then. I can find somebody else too. I don't need you, do I."

He saw the tears come to her eyes before she dove back into her purse again, pulled out her keys, fumbled with the car door. She slammed it shut behind her and pulled out of her space with a series of jerky movements. Then she was gone.

Koti stalked back toward Hemi, his face thunderous. "Did you see that?" he spluttered. "She won't even talk to me. Buggered if I know what she wants. I've done everything she asked, all along. And now she doesn't even want to be friends. Just talks a load of rubbish."

"Is that how you feel about her?" Hemi asked. "That why you're throwing a wobbly? Because you want to be friends, and she doesn't?"

"Course it is," Koti flung back. "She's mad. Keeps changing her mind. How can a man cope with that?"

"Reckon you just get another friend, then," Hemi shrugged. "Or not. You have enough mates already, from what I've seen. Why do you need her? What does it matter anyway? Going off to play for the Poms, I heard."

"Nothing's signed yet," Koti muttered. "I don't want to lose her, that's all."

"Why not?" Hemi pressed. "What's so special about her? No shortage of girls around. They'd be more than happy to be your friend, if that's all you're offering."

"Not like her," Koti admitted. "She gives me so much agro. But I miss her. I want to see her, talk things over. Just be with her," he finished lamely.

"But you don't love her, eh."

Koti shrugged. "Lately, I thought we were taking things further. But now we've gone in the opposite direction. And I can't fix it."

"Huh. It changed, did it. When was that? When she found out you were leaving her?"

"Yeh. But I'm not gone yet. Am I supposed to tell her I'll be with her forever? What's wrong with having a girlfriend, as long as it lasts?"

Hemi shook his head. "Waste of time talking to you." He turned to walk away.

"Wait," Koti called. "You have something to say, tell me."

Hemi turned back. "Right, then. But you aren't going to like it. You weren't selected for the ABs, last series. So you've been working on your skills, got on the squad this time. Good on ya. But at the same time, you start talking to overseas teams. Because you're still looking for the easy way out. Not willing to bust a gut for it, show the selectors you'll do whatever it takes."

"And now there's this girl," he went on. "She loves you. Anyone can see that. And you aren't even man enough to think about what that feels like for her. Rip her heart out, won't you, if she lets herself love you the way she wants to, and then you're off to England without her. All you care about is whether she's there for you when you're randy, or want to whinge to her about something. What are ya," he spat in disgust.

Koti took a step towards him, hands raised, flushing angrily at the insult. Hemi stood his ground and stared him down, his steady gaze hard on Koti until the younger man dropped his eyes.

"Yeh, you can take a swing at me," Hemi continued, his voice even. "We can have a stoush in the carpark. You may even win. Doesn't matter. Because I'm going to tell you anyway. Time to decide if you're a boy or a man. You want the good things, you need to harden up and earn them. You were born with the talent. You've got the strength and speed. The looks and the charm, too. You can run away, make your dollar, be the glamour boy. Have all the girls you want. But you'll never have mana. Because the best things, the important things, aren't that easy to get. You want that girl, you want the ABs, you're going to have to get stuck in, make the sacrifices to get them. Otherwise, good riddance, for her and for the team."

"*Kaua e mate wheke. Me mate ururoa,*" he finished. "Have a think about that. Your choice." Then he really did walk away, leaving Koti standing alone in the middle of the carpark, flushed and angry.

I don't have the time to waste on you anymore. You can't give me what I need.

You'll never have mana.

The words resonated in Koti's head as he got into his car, slammed the door. He drove mindlessly onto the motorway, headed towards Takapuna and home. And found himself, without realizing he'd done it, driving straight past his exit.

An hour north, the rain started. The winter night closed around the car, the wipers doing their best to keep the windscreen clear as the wind and rain intensified. He thought about listening to music, but it seemed like too much trouble. He was tired now, the difficult drive in the rainy dark, all the emotion of the past week catching up with him. As he passed Kaitaia, he knew he should stop, try to find a room at this final outpost. But still he pressed on, drove the final hundred kilometers toward the northern tip of the island, and Cape Reinga. That was his destination. It was where he needed to be.

It was after ten by the time he pulled into the deserted carpark and dragged himself stiffly out of the car. The rain had stopped, though the wind still blew. The night was mild for the time of year, this far north. Still, he shivered in his warmup jacket as he stood looking out through the dark, north to the sea.

He walked slowly to the edge of the cliffs. Stood facing into the fierce wind from the north, listened to the crashing of waves below, where the Tasman Sea met the Pacific. Te Rerenga Wairua, the Leaping Place of the Sprits. Here, after burial, the legend said that the spirit of a Maori left this world. Traveled up the country to this spot, the Hill of Farewell. Leaped over the cliff to the ancient pohutukawa tree that sat on the very tip of the Cape, slid down a root to the sea below. Came up for a last brief glimpse of its home when it reached Manawatawhi, largest of the Three Kings Islands. Last

Breath, where the spirit paused for its final farewell before joining its ancestors beyond.

You'll never have mana.

Standing in the wind, listening to the pounding of the surf against the rocks, he thought at last about what Hemi had said. Seeing the contempt on the face of a man he had looked up to, had longed to emulate, had been almost worse than the cutting words. If he left New Zealand, he left all this. Left his whanau, his home, his birthright. He fit here in a way he couldn't anyplace else. His spirit had never felt at ease during the years he'd spent in England. And that wasn't going to change. It was only going to be worse, now.

Because he wanted to be an All Black. It had been his childhood dream, and the desire burned more strongly than ever to reach that pinnacle. He suddenly longed with a ferocity past bearing to wear the black jersey, see the silver fern on his chest. He couldn't give up that dream. If he had to change, he would change. Would do whatever he had to do.

And what about Kate? What about letting her go? He had pushed the thought aside when he'd first considered the overseas offers. It had felt wrong even then, but he'd told himself the pain would be temporary. He'd finally realized, this past week, how much it would hurt. How much it was already hurting.

When had she become so important to him? He wasn't sure. It had crept up on him slowly. All he knew was that now, he couldn't contemplate a life that didn't include her too. That could be even more challenging than the road to the All Blacks, he knew. Somehow, though, he was going to find a way to do it.

He felt the power of this most tapu place surrounding him as he made his resolutions. He could do this. And he was going to do it.

Kaua e mate wheke. Me mate ururoa.

Don't die like an octopus. Die like a hammerhead shark.

Hemi was right. He wasn't going to give up without a struggle. If he failed, if he fell, he'd know he'd gone down fighting, the way a warrior should. With all his strength and courage, all the way to the end.

He turned, filled with a certainty and resolve he had never experienced, and made his way back to his car. It was a long drive back to the first motel along the road south. He was going to get a few hours' sleep. Then he was driving back to practice. And starting over.

Chapter 33

Kate opened her eyes. Another day. Wednesday, she realized. A swim day. She lay in bed a while longer, than decided that she'd better get up and start it. She was late. But the water was cold, and she didn't feel like swimming anyway. She'd make herself do it, but she'd keep it short. Without enthusiasm, she made her tea and toast. Pulled on her suit, then a long sweater and shorts over it. Grabbed the bag with her wetsuit and towel, picked up her keys, and turned to the door.

One moment she was pushing the door open. In the next, he was barreling into her, propelling her backward, driving her into the wall. Stunned by the impact of her head against the hard surface, she was barely aware of falling to the ground. Of something falling on top of her, her hair being pulled viciously. She cried out at the pain, until her head was slammed into the floor. Once, twice.

She looked up, dizzy with the impact and the pain. Gasped with fear as she saw Paul straddling her, one hand still wrapped in her hair. Crazy eyes. He was saying something. She concentrated. What was he saying? What was happening?

"You've been fucking somebody else all this time, haven't you? Haven't you?"

"*Haven't you?*" he screamed. She flinched at the noise, struggled to free herself from his hold. The hand in her hair tightened, and she cried out.

"He's not going to have you. I'll kill you. I'll kill you first." He was panting now, his face red, eyes staring.

Then his hands were around her neck. Pressing. Squeezing. The pain filled her, and the panic. It was her dream. No breath. She couldn't get any breath. She had to breathe. She pulled her arms up desperately. Clutched at his hands, tried to wrench them loose. Nothing.

"How does that feel? Does that hurt? That's how you've hurt me. This is what you've done to me. This is what you've made me do."

The pain and the fear were roaring in her head now, a relentless tide closing in on her, drowning her. She had to get away. Had to breathe. Frantically, she shoved her hands into his face, clawing at him in her panic. Only realized she was still holding her keys when he reared back, grabbing his eye.

Run. The voice in her head was screaming it. She rolled to her feet, leaped for the open door. Was almost there when she felt the hand close on her arm, spin her around.

He was crying now, shouting in rage and pain. "Bitch! You fucking bitch! I'm going to kill you!"

He swung her around hard, and she hit the wall again. She felt something snap as her arm twisted behind her, cried out at the impact and the sudden sharp jolt of pain. She was dropping to the floor again now, taking the standing lamp with her in a crash, his body pushing her down. Down on her face this time. His knee in her back, shoving her into the floor. She was smothering, her nose and mouth pressed into the deep pile of the carpet by his hand on her head as he continued to rage behind her.

His hands went around her throat again. She was pinned beneath him. Couldn't move her head. Couldn't resist. She was dimly aware of him shouting as the pain, the blackness closed in again. And then . . . nothing.

Koti paced back and forth on the beach. Kate always swam on Wednesday. Even this past week, he'd seen her in the water. So why wasn't she here? Had she seen him waiting and turned away? No, he'd have spotted her, he was sure of it.

His uneasiness grew as the minutes passed. Was she sick? Or just unhappy? If something was wrong, he needed to be there. And if there was nothing wrong, he needed to talk to her. To try to persuade her that he had changed, convince her to take him back. He couldn't wait any longer.

His decision made, he got in the car. The sense that something wasn't right continued to nag at him. He found himself speeding, forced himself to slow down to the limit. Nothing was wrong. She was taking a break, that was all. He should focus on how to talk his way in the door. That was going to be the hardest part.

He saw with relief that her car was still parked on the street outside the house. She hadn't gone anywhere, then. He'd be able to talk to her this morning. To take the first step toward getting her back.

But as he walked around the corner of the house and looked up the outdoor stairway to her flat, he saw that her door was standing open. He frowned. Kate was always careful. Even if she were taking out her rubbish, she'd have taken her keys, locked the door behind her. He'd teased her about it, but he knew the caution stemmed from her experience with Paul, and was a habit she hadn't found easy to break.

He hesitated, looking around for her, that sense of unease growing stronger. Heard a crash from the flat above, Kate's voice crying out. He wasn't even aware that he was running as he leapt up the stairs and pounded through the door. Saw her there, lying face down on the carpet. The man over her, pinning her down, his hands around her throat.

A bellow of pure rage exploded from him as he reached down and grabbed the other man by the back of his shirt, pulled him off Kate with one swift movement and yanked him to his feet. Koti landed two quick shots to the ribs that doubled him over, followed them with an uppercut that lifted the smaller man off his feet and sent him crashing senseless to the floor.

Kate was still face-down on the ground, not moving. He couldn't risk the bastard coming to, attacking her again. Koti quickly pulled off his hoodie and T-shirt, rolled the other man over and tied his hands behind his back as best he could with the shirt. That would have to do for now.

He turned back to Kate, his breath coming short with fear. Crouched next to her and turned her over gently. Was she breathing? He couldn't tell. He reached for her wrist, then saw the sickening angle of her arm. Swallowed his fear again and moved to her other side to feel for a pulse. Sick with relief, he detected the faint but rapid beat. She was alive, then. He'd been in time. He dropped to sit next to her. Put his head into his hands, elbows propped on his knees, and took a few deep breaths. Then pulled out his mobile and dialed 111 with shaking fingers.

Kate opened her eyes to find Koti beside her. She looked up at him in confusion. What had happened? Why was she on the floor, and why was Koti here? Her throat burned, her neck hurt, and her arm . . . what was wrong with it? She tried to move it, to see what had happened, and cried out with the pain.

"Don't move," Koti urged her. "Lie still. Help's coming."

"What . . ." Kate croaked, her voice raspy and weak. "What?"

"I reckon that was Paul," Koti told her, stroking her hair back from her bruised face as he sat shirtless on the floor next to her, holding her good hand in his. "And that he found you."

Kate's eyes widened. As the memory returned, a wave of fear and anxiety overwhelmed her. "Where is he?" she asked urgently. "He'll kill you."

"Nah. He's out for the count. He's not going anywhere, either. He's not going to be able to hurt you again."

"Did you kill him?"

He shook his head. "Knocked him out, that's all."

She closed her eyes again. "Shame."

"I could kill him now, if you like," he suggested. "Before the police get here."

She smiled faintly. "No. Stay with me." Swallowed painfully. "Hurts."

"I know, baby. Help's coming. They'll get you sorted. Hang on, now."

She felt the dizziness return, and with it another flood of anxiety. "Don't leave me. Don't leave me with him," she whispered urgently, the pain strong again now. "Stay with me."

"No worries. I'm here with you. I'm staying with you."

Where were the police? Koti wondered despairingly. He looked across to check on Paul. The other man was stirring at last. Koti didn't like leaving his feet free. But to tie him up better, or to hit him again, which was what he really wanted to do, he'd have to leave Kate.

He looked up with relief at the sound of sirens. The ambulances arrived first, followed quickly by the police. Two officers, taking a quick look around and then approaching him, the only uninjured party.

"What's happened?" one demanded.

Koti explained as briefly as he could, watching anxiously as Kate was loaded onto a gurney.

"Reckon you've broken some ribs here," one of the paramedics remarked, kneeling over Paul. "He's coming round, though."

"Pity," Koti muttered. "Should have hit him harder."

"Look, mate," he told the officer. "You can ask me anything else you like, but it's going to have to be in hospital, because I'm going with her."

"Fair enough," the man agreed. "We'll need to question her as well. We'll send a policewoman along for that, make it easier."

Kate made a sound of distress. "Stay with me," she begged Koti. "Don't leave."

"I'm here," he promised. "I'm with you."

When they got to hospital, though, he found that the police had other ideas. While Kate was hastily bundled off, he found himself in a room with a different officer, in plain clothes this time, who insisted on taking him through the events of the morning once again.

"You went to her flat. And why was that?" The other man's expression was impassive, his cold gaze steady.

"I told the other fella," Koti said restlessly. "She always swims on Wednesdays. I was going to meet her, but she didn't turn up."

"Going to swim, were you?" the detective asked.

"Nah. I wanted to talk to her."

"About what?"

"We had some things to straighten out," Koti told him. What did this matter?

"Because you'd had a fight," the other man suggested.

"Yeh. We'd had a fight. As everyone knows, now."

"So you went to her flat. And there was someone else there with her."

"Yeh. Like I said." Koti was impatient now. What was all this about? "I heard her scream, saw the door open. Ran in and found this mongrel on top of her, choking her."

"Or maybe not," the detective mused. "Maybe you got there and found her with someone else. That'd make any man see red. What did you do then?"

Koti stared at him. "What? What are you saying? That *I* strangled her?"

"You were upset. She'd broken it off with you. And you found her with another man. Bound to be a shock. And you reacted. You hit him. Then you went after her. You didn't mean to choke her, maybe. Just to shake her."

"This is bollocks." Koti stood up. "We're done here. I've told you what I saw, and what I did. Ask her what happened. She'll tell you the same."

"We'll do that," the detective told him unsmilingly. "I'll ask you to stay in the waiting room while we do, though. And not to leave the building."

"No worries," Koti told him with disgust. "I'm not going anywhere."

Hours later, he was still sitting in the waiting room, staring at the floor. He reminded himself for the hundredth time that Kate had been conscious and talking when he'd been separated from her. That had to be a good sign. But nobody had been willing or able to tell him how she was since. When he saw the detective approaching again at last, he jumped up, trying to read the other man's expression.

"We've got it sorted," the detective told him, still without a smile. "You're free to go."

Koti stared at him in disbelief. "I'm not going anywhere, except to see Kate. I thought I'd made that clear. And I want to do that now. Where is she? How is she?"

Relief made him momentarily weak as he finally entered her room and caught sight of her. Very much alive, doing her best to get out of bed, thwarted by a beleaguered nurse. And crying.

He dropped into the chair next to the bed and took her hand. "Shhh, love. Shhh, now. It's all right. Everything's going to be all right."

Kate turned to him, crying even harder now. "You're here. I thought they'd arrested you. They asked me all these questions. They thought you did it. I was so scared."

"Nah." He reached for a tissue and gently wiped her tears away. "Here I am. They asked me too. Fair wound me up. Checking, I reckon. Our stories will have matched, though, and it must've been straightforward enough once they knew that. Good as gold."

"Paul's here, though." She clutched his hand more tightly, her still-raspy voice rising in panic. "Here in the hospital. They brought him here. They told me so. I don't know where."

"Doesn't matter," he told her firmly, pushing his own rage aside for the moment. She needed him now. "Because I'm here too, aren't I. And I'm not going to leave you."

"Promise me," she begged. "I'm so scared."

"Bloody hell." He kicked his shoes off and climbed onto the bed with her. Looked up at the nurse challengingly as he put an arm carefully around Kate and held her to him.

"No argument from me," the nurse assured him as she saw Kate's agitation dying down under the influence of Koti's soothing voice and touch. "I'd say you're good medicine. Ring for me if you need me."

Kate was calmer at last, resting against Koti, when the sound of hurrying footsteps in the corridor heralded the appearance of Hannah and Drew.

"Oh, sweetie." Hannah rushed across the room to her. "I'm so sorry. We came as quickly as we could, after I got Koti's message. What happened? Oh, your poor face."

Koti made the description as brief as possible, not wanting to upset Kate by dwelling on the details.

"How horrible," Hannah said in distress. "Oh, Koti. I'm so glad you were there."

He nodded. "And now you two are here to stay with her, I need to ring Kate's parents, let them know what's happening." He gave Kate a gentle kiss and eased off the bed. Looked at Drew, jerked his head toward the door. The other man nodded in understanding and followed him down the passage, out of earshot of the room, where Koti stopped and turned to him.

"Didn't want to say this in front of Kate. But I wanted to ask you to keep an eye on her. She's got concussion, and a broken arm of course, but that's not the issue, why they're keeping her here. It's her throat. It's pretty damaged, hard for them to tell how much. If she seems to have any trouble breathing, complains of any swelling in her throat, ring for the nurse straight away."

Drew nodded. "I'll tell Hannah too."

"The other thing. That mongrel's here too. In hospital. They say he's under a police guard. But how careful are they going to be? He's not that big, doesn't look dangerous. But I saw him, and he was berko. On her, trying to kill her. He'd try again, if he got the chance. He nearly did already." Koti leaned back against the wall, scrubbed his hands over his thighs in agitation at the memory. "If I'd got there a minute later... I thought she was gone. Thought I was too late."

"That's the point, though, isn't it," Drew told him steadily. "You weren't too late."

"My fault, though," Koti went on wretchedly. "My fault that he knew where she was, that that piece was in the paper, and online for him to find. That has to be how he tracked her down. And my fault that she was home alone this morning."

"But she wasn't alone," Drew pointed out. "I still don't understand why you were there, but you were." He reached out and grasped Koti's shoulder with a steadying hand. "You saved her, mate. It's over now."

"Worst morning of my life," Koti said. "That moment. And then waiting, not knowing. Reckon I know how you felt now, trying to get back the night Jack was born, not knowing what you'd find when you got here."

"It's true, we're in the same club now. And nobody's queuing up for membership," Drew agreed. "But I'll return the favor you did me. I'll look out for her. He'd have to go through me first."

"One last thing," Koti told him. "I'm not going to be flying to Argentina tonight. I'll ring Pete as well, of course. But I wanted to tell you. Sorry if I'm letting the team down, but I'm not leaving till her parents are here with her. Till she's out of danger, and that bastard is locked up."

Drew nodded. "Course you're not. I'm not sure how it happened, but it sounds like you've got your priorities sorted at last. Go on now, make your calls. Take your time. Hannah and I will look after Kate while you're gone."

"And, mate," he added. "Get some breakfast. You look shattered."

Koti laughed shakily. "Too right. Think a coffee'll help?"

"Can't hurt."

Koti was relieved to see Kate looking calmer and more settled when he returned to the room. "I rang your parents," he told her. "They'll be on a plane as soon as they can manage it. And I bought you a toothbrush. I know how important dental hygiene is to you."

Hannah smiled, then got up and kissed Kate goodbye. "We'll be going, then, since you're obviously in good hands. I'll call you tomorrow, once you're home again."

"Take care of her, Koti." Hannah gave him a hug as well. "I'm so thankful you were there."

Drew reached out to shake Koti's hand, laid his hand again on the other man's shoulder. "Well done, mate. See you next week." He began to move toward the door, then turned and added with a smile, "And by the way. Those new priorities had better include your workouts, soon as Kate's on her feet again. We need you back training with us."

"I'm so tired. I just want to sleep," Kate said, once she felt Koti settled firmly against her side again. "But I need to know why you were there. I don't understand any of this. I'm supposed to tell you to go away. But I want you here with me."

He squeezed her hand. "And I want to be here. I want to be with you. That's what I came to tell you this morning. I waited for you at the beach, and when you didn't come, I knew something was wrong. So I went to find you."

"Lucky for me you did, I know. That was really close."

"Too close," he agreed. "But it's over now."

"Is it? He'll go to prison this time, I hope. But they aren't going to keep him there forever. What about when he gets out?"

"He'll be PNG, that's what. Deported back to the States, Persona Non Grata. He'll never get into En Zed again, I can promise you that."

"But I won't be here," she protested. "So how does that help me?"

"I hope you will, though. Here, or wherever I am. That's what I came to tell you. I know I've been the world's biggest drongo. It's taken me all this time to realize how I feel about you. But I know now. And I'm not going anywhere, not without talking it over with you first and making a plan. I'll be giving it heaps from here on, you can count on that. On the paddock, and with you. So I need to ask you, are you willing to try again? To give me another chance?"

She looked up at him searchingly. "Yes," she told him at last. "I am. Because I've missed you so much. I didn't know how much you meant to me either, not until you were gone. Is that really what you came back to tell me?"

"It was." Relief overwhelmed him as he held her close. "Oh. And to give you this." He fumbled in his pocket, brought out a small bag made of woven flax. "I bought it for you yesterday, after practice. Had to go to three shops to find the one I wanted."

"You have to open it for me, though," she told him. "Not enough hands."

He opened the little bag carefully, drew out a bone pendant formed into a twining design, inlaid paua shell gleaming along one curving edge.

"It's beautiful," she breathed. "What does it mean?"

"Depends what level you're talking about. It's an infinity symbol. It means that no matter how far away from each other we may be, the bond between us is still there. That our paths will come together again. So you can look at it while I'm gone and know that I'm thinking about you. That I'll always come back to you. And there's a koru here too, see? This curving bit. That's for new beginnings, starting over, remember? Which seemed right."

"And on the other level," he told her seriously, "it means, '*E ipo, e iti noa ana, na te aroha.*'" He smoothed back her hair, touched her cheek gently with the back of his hand. "'My darling, though my present is small, my love goes with it.' I reckon this won't be the last thing I give you. But I thought we could start with this."

"It's beautiful," she told him again, the tears falling now. "I don't seem to know what else to say. And I keep crying. I'm sorry."

"Can you put it on me now?" she asked as she wiped the tears away. "I want to wear it."

He lifted the pendant on its black cord gently over her head, settled it carefully around her bruised neck.

"How does it look?" she asked.

"Beautiful. Right."

"But oh, Koti," she remembered. "Hannah helped me clean up a little. And I saw how I looked. How can you even look at me? I look so . . ."

"Battered," he agreed, leaning over to give her a gentle kiss on the forehead. "Yeh. You do. Every time I look at you, I wish I'd hit that bastard a few more times. Give it a week, though, and you'll be as gorgeous as ever. But it doesn't matter anyway. Because I'm not in love with your pretty face. Not even with your pretty body. I'm in love with the person you are. With your warrior's heart and the spirit that shines from you every time you smile. With the way you give everything you have to everything you do. I'm in love with the beautiful person you are, inside and out. All the way through."

"Oh. That's . . . oh. Really?"

He nodded, squeezed her hand. "Totally and completely."

She felt the tears welling, spilling over. Sniffed. "Kleenex, please."

He smiled and handed her a tissue from the box, watched as she blew her nose and blotted her wet eyes.

"Well," she told him, a huge, foolish smile spreading over her face despite her throbbing head. "Well, ditto."

He stared at her. "*Ditto?* That's it? That's the best you can do? I don't think so. I need to hear it too. Then you can go to sleep."

"All right." She looked at him tenderly. She'd almost lost everything today. Her life should have been over. But instead, she'd gained something precious. Something she had thought was lost forever. Her heart swelled as she spoke.

"All right, then. I can't talk the way you can. But I'll tell you. I don't love you for your pretty face. Not even for your pretty body." She smiled again as he grimaced, then looked into his eyes and spoke from her overflowing heart. "I'm in love with you, too. Completely and totally in love with the beautiful person you are, inside and out. With every last wonderful bit of you."

Epilogue

Kate was deep into the zone, all her attention focused on the fiscal report she was preparing, when she gradually became aware that the usually bustling office had become silent. She glanced up from her computer, turned towards the doorway. And stared.

There was Koti, walking through the room with his loping stride. He wasn't looking around him, though, or greeting the other women with his usual cheeky grin. He was staring straight at her.

That wasn't what was so different, though. It was the hoodie.

Pink. *Bright* pink. With—she squinted. Why was it sparkling? Were those *sequins?*

He kept walking, never breaking eye contact with her, no smile on his face. Came to a stop at last in front of her desk. Looked down at her where she sat, frozen.

"Why?" she finally asked.

"Came to tell you I lost," he told her.

"You lost. What? The bet? I thought we both lost, months ago."

"Nah. You won. Because I can't be friends with you anymore. Or lovers either. I need more. And I have something to offer now. Starting for the All Blacks, for the November tests in Europe. I got one thing I've gone after. Time to go after the other one. Harden up and ask for it."

"Oh, Koti," she said, standing up and putting her hands on his pink forearms, looking up into his eyes. "You always had something to offer. Don't you know that?"

"What does that mean? What kind of answer is that?" he asked, beginning to look worried.

"I don't know. What's the question? And why are you wearing a pink sweatshirt to ask it?" She began to laugh even as she felt the tears threatening to spill.

"Because I want you to know that I'm putting myself on the line. Win or lose. No shame. That I'm yours, and I always will be. I love you, and I want to live my life with you. I want to have kids with you, watch them grow up. I want to get old with you. I want to die with you holding my hand."

"So." He took a deep breath. "What I'm asking is, will you stay here with me? Will you marry me?"

"Yes," she said simply, the tears falling in earnest now. "Of course I will. Because I love you too. Because you're wonderful."

He put his arms around her, lifted her off her feet. Bent down to kiss her. Kate wrapped her arms around his shoulders, felt the sequins on the ridiculous pink sweatshirt under her hands. And kissed him back as the room erupted in applause.

When he finally put her down, his voice wasn't quite steady. "That's what I was hoping. Wasn't sure, though. Figured I'd get under your defenses."

"But Koti," she told him, grabbing a handful of pink to wipe her eyes. "I've lost too, don't you realize? I just said you were wonderful, in the middle of the office. And I kissed you. I'm afraid we've both lost. What a pair."

"Reckon we've both won, though," he said, laughing a little with relief and joy as he continued to hold her against him. "You'd better shut down, because I'm taking you out of here. We're going ring shopping. I didn't dare buy it first."

"That's good, because I want to choose it with you. I just have one condition."

"Oh no," he groaned. "I can see I'm going to have to put out another poster to afford this. Or pose in my undies."

"Nope. This one's free," she assured him. She pushed him into her chair. Reached down and grabbed the pink sweatshirt by the hem, then pulled it over his head, shoving it into her wastebasket.

"It's almost summer," she told him. "And I'm not going anywhere with you in this disgusting thing. We're going to walk down the street, and everyone can look all they want at you. And I'll glare right back at them. Because you're mine now."

"Too right," he grinned. "From now on, I'll have you there to protect my virtue."

"From now on," she agreed tenderly, "you will."

A Kiwi Glossary

A few notes about Maori pronunciation:
- The accent is normally on the first syllable.
- All vowels are pronounced separately.
- All vowels except u have a short vowel sound.
- "wh" is pronounced "f."
- "ng" is pronounced as in "singer," not as in "anger."

ABs: All Blacks
across the Ditch: in Australia (across the Tasman Sea). Or, if you're in Australia, in New Zealand!
advert: commercial
agro: aggravation
air con: air conditioning
All Blacks: National rugby team. Members are selected for every series from amongst the five NZ Super 15 teams. The All Blacks play similarly selected teams from other nations.
Aotearoa: New Zealand (the other official name, meaning "The Land of the Long White Cloud" in Maori)
arvo, this arvo: afternoon
Aussie, Oz: Australia. (An Australian is also an Aussie. Pronounced "Ozzie.")
bach: holiday home (pronounced like "bachelor")
backs: rugby players who aren't in the scrum and do more running, kicking, and ball-carrying—though all players do all jobs and play both offense and defense. Backs tend to be faster and leaner than forwards.
bangers and mash: sausages and potatoes
barrack for: cheer for

bench: counter (kitchen bench)
berko: berserk
bikkies: cookies
bit of a dag: a comedian, a funny guy
bits and bobs: stuff ("be sure you get all your bits and bobs")
blood bin: players leaving field for injury
Blues: Auckland's Super 15 team
bollocks: rubbish, nonsense
boofhead: fool, jerk
booking: reservation
boots and all: full tilt, no holding back
bot, the bot: flu, a bug
Boxing Day: December 26—a holiday
brekkie: breakfast
brilliant: fantastic
bub: baby, small child
buggered: messed up, exhausted
bull's roar: close. "They never came within a bull's roar of winning."
bust a gut: do your utmost, make a supreme effort
Cake Tin: Wellington's rugby stadium (not the official name, but it looks exactly like a springform pan)
cardie: a cardigan sweater
chat up: flirt with
chilly bin: ice chest
chocolate bits: chocolate chips
choice: fantastic
chokka: full
Chrissy: Christmas
chuck out: throw away
chuffed: pleased
collywobbles: nervous tummy, upset stomach
come a greaser: take a bad fall
costume, cossie: swimsuit (female only)
cot: crib (for a baby)
crook: ill

cuddle: hug (give a cuddle)
cuppa: a cup of tea (the universal remedy)
CV: resumé
cyclone : hurricane (Southern Hemisphere)
dairy: corner shop (not just for milk!)
dead: very; e.g., "dead sexy."
dill: fool
do your block: lose your temper
dob in: turn in; report to authorities. Frowned upon.
doddle: easy. "That'll be a doddle."
dodgy: suspect, low-quality
dogbox: The doghouse—in trouble
Domain: a good-sized park; often the "official" park of the town.
dressing gown: bathrobe
drongo: fool (Australian, but used sometimes in NZ as well)
drop your gear: take off your clothes
duvet: comforter
earbashing: talking-to, one-sided chat
electric jug: electric teakettle to heat water. Every Kiwi kitchen has one.
En Zed: Pronunciation of NZ. ("Z" is pronounced "Zed.")
ensuite: master bath (a bath in the bedroom).
eye fillet: premium steak (filet mignon)
fair go: a fair chance. Kiwi ideology: everyone deserves a fair go.
fair wound me up: Got me very upset
fantail: small, friendly native bird
farewelled, he'll be farewelled: funeral; he'll have his funeral.
feed, have a feed: meal
first-five, first five-eighths: rugby back—does most of the big kicking jobs and is the main director of the backs. Also called the No. 10.
fixtures: playing schedule
fizz, fizzie: soft drink
fizzing: fired up
flaked out: tired

flash: fancy
flat to the boards: at top speed
flat white: most popular NZ coffee. An espresso with milk but no foam.
flattie: roommate
flicks: movies
flying fox: zipline
footpath: sidewalk
footy, football: rugby
forwards: rugby players who make up the scrum and do the most physical battling for position. Tend to be bigger and more heavily muscled than backs.
fossick about: hunt around for something
front up: face the music, show your mettle
garden: yard
get on the piss: get drunk
get stuck in: commit to
give way: yield
giving him stick, give him some stick about it: teasing, needling
glowworms: larvae of a fly found only in NZ. They shine a light to attract insects. Found in caves or other dark, moist places.
go crook, be crook: go wrong, be ill
go on the turps: get drunk
gobsmacked: astounded
good hiding: beating ("They gave us a good hiding in Dunedin.")
grotty: grungy, badly done up
ground floor: what we call the first floor. The "first floor" is one floor up.
gumboots, gummies: knee-high rubber boots. It rains a lot in New Zealand.
gutted: thoroughly upset
Haast's Eagle: (extinct). Huge native NZ eagle. Ate moa.
haere mai: Maori greeting

haka: ceremonial Maori challenge—done before every All Blacks game
hang on a tick: wait a minute
hard yakka: hard work (from Australian)
harden up: toughen up. Standard NZ (male) response to (male) complaints: "Harden the f*** up!"
have a bit on: I have placed a bet on [whatever]. Sports gambling and prostitution are both legal in New Zealand.
have a go: try
Have a nosy for…: look around for
head: principal (headmaster)
head down: or head down, bum up. Put your head down. Work hard.
heaps: lots. "Give it heaps."
hei toki: pendant (Maori)
holiday: vacation
hooker: rugby position (forward)
hooning around: driving fast, wannabe tough-guy behavior (typically young men)
I'll see you right: I'll help you out
in form: performing well (athletically)
it's not on: It's not all right
iwi: tribe (Maori)
jabs: immunizations, shots
jersey: a rugby shirt, or a pullover sweater
journo: journalist
jumper: a heavy pullover sweater
ka pai: going smoothly (Maori).
kapa haka: school singing group (Maori songs/performances. Any student can join, not just Maori.)
karanga: Maori song of welcome (done by a woman)
keeping his/your head down: working hard
kia ora: welcome (Maori, but used commonly)
kilojoules: like calories--measure of food energy
kindy: kindergarten (this is 3- and 4-year-olds)
kit, get your kit off: clothes, take off your clothes

Kiwi: New Zealander OR the bird. If the person, it's capitalized. Not the fruit.
kiwifruit: the fruit. (never called simply a "kiwi.")
knackered: exhausted
knockout rounds: playoff rounds (quarterfinals, semifinals, final)
koru: ubiquitous spiral Maori symbol of new beginnings, hope
kumara: Maori sweet potato.
ladder: standings (rugby)
littlies: young kids
lock: rugby position (forward)
lollies: candy
lolly: candy or money
lounge: living room
mad as a meat axe: crazy
maintenance: child support
major: "a major." A big deal, a big event
mana: prestige, earned respect, spiritual power
Maori: native people of NZ—though even they arrived relatively recently from elsewhere in Polynesia
marae: Maori meeting house
Marmite: Savory Kiwi yeast-based spread for toast. An acquired taste.
mate: friend
metal road: gravel road
Milo: coffee substitute; hot drink mix
mind: take care of, babysit
moa: (extinct) Any of several species of huge flightless NZ birds. All eaten by the Maori before Europeans arrived.
moko: Maori tattoo
motorway: freeway
muesli: like granola, but unbaked
munted: broken
naff: stupid, unsuitable. "Did you get any naff Chrissy pressies this year?"
nappy: diaper

new caps: new All Blacks—those named to the side for the first time
New World: One of the two major NZ supermarket chains
nibbles: snacks
nick, in good nick: doing well
niggle, niggly: small injury, ache or soreness
no worries: no problem. The Kiwi mantra.
No. 8: rugby position. A forward
not very flash: not feeling well
nutted out: worked out
OE: Overseas Experience—young people taking a year or two overseas, before or after University.
offload: pass (rugby)
oldies: older people. (or for the elderly, "wrinklies!")
on the front foot: Having the advantage. Vs. on the back foot—at a disadvantage. From rugby.
Op Shop: charity shop, secondhand shop
out on the razzle: out drinking too much, getting crazy
paddock: field (often used for rugby—"out on the paddock")
Pakeha: European-ancestry people (as opposed to Polynesians)
Panadol: over-the-counter painkiller
partner: romantic partner, married or not
paua, paua shell: NZ abalone
pavement: sidewalk (generally on wider city streets)
penny dropped: light dawned (figured it out)
people mover: minivan
perve: stare sexually
phone's engaged: phone's busy
piece of piss: easy
pike out: give up, wimp out
piss awful: very bad
piss up: drinking (noun) a piss-up
pissed: drunk
play up: act up
playing out of his skin: playing very well
PMT: PMS

Pom, Pommie: English person.
pop: pop over, pop back, pop into the oven, pop out, pop in
possie: position (rugby)
postie: mail carrier
poumanu: greenstone (jade)
pressie: present
puckaroo: broken (from Maori)
pudding: dessert
pull your head in: calm down, quit being rowdy
Pumas: Argentina's national rugby team
pushchair: baby stroller
put your hand up: volunteer
put your head down: work hard
rapt: thrilled
rattle your dags: hurry up. From the sound that dried excrement on a sheep's backside makes, when the sheep is running!
rellies: relatives
riding the pine: sitting on the bench (as a substitute in a match)
Rippa: junior rugby
root: have sex (you DON'T root for a team!)
ropeable: very angry
ropey: off, damaged ("a bit ropey")
rort: ripoff
rough as guts: uncouth
rubbish bin: garbage can
rugby boots: rugby shoes with spikes (sprigs)
Rugby Championship: Contest played each year in the Southern Hemisphere by the national teams of NZ, Australia, South Africa, and Argentina
Rugby World Cup, RWC: World championship, played every four years amongst the top 20 teams in the world
rugged up: dressed warmly
ruru: native owl
Safa: South Africa. Abbreviation only used in NZ.
sammie: sandwich

second-five, second five-eights: rugby back
selectors: team of 3 (the head coach is one) who choose players for the All Blacks squad, for every series
serviette: napkin
shattered: exhausted
sheds: locker room (rugby)
she'll be right: See "no worries." Everything will work out. The other Kiwi mantra.
shift house: move (house)
shonky: shady (person). "a bit shonky"
shout, your shout, my shout, shout somebody a coffee: buy a round, treat somebody
sickie, throw a sickie: call in sick
sin bin: players sitting out 15-minute penalty in rugby
sink the boot in: kick you when you're down
skint: broke (poor)
skipper: (team) captain. Also called "the Skip."
bunk off: duck out, skip (bunk off school)
smack: spank. Smacking kids is illegal in NZ.
smoko: coffee break
sorted: taken care of
spa, spa pool: hot tub
speedo: Not the swimsuit! Speedometer. (the swimsuit is called a budgie smuggler—a budgie is a parakeet, LOL.)
spew: vomit
spit the dummy: have a tantrum. (A dummy is a pacifier)
sportsman: athlete
sporty: liking sports
spot on: absolutely correct. "That's spot on. You're spot on."
Springboks, Boks: South African national rugby team
squiz: look. "I was just having a squiz round." "Giz a squiz."
stickybeak: nosy person, busybody
stonkered: drunk—a bit stonkered—or exhausted
stoush: bar fight, fight
straightaway: right away
strength of it: the truth, the facts. "What's the strength of that?" = "What's the true story on that?"

stroppy: prickly, taking offense easily
stuffed up: messed up
Super 15: Top rugby competition: five teams each from NZ, Australia, South Africa
supporter: fan (Do NOT say "root for." "To root" is to have (rude) sex!)
suss out: figure out
sweet: dessert
sweet as: great. (also: choice as, angry as, lame as . . . Meaning "very" whatever. "Mum was angry as that we ate up all the pudding before tea with Nana.")
takahe: ground-dwelling native bird. Like a giant parrot.
takeaway: takeout (food)
tall poppy: arrogant person who puts himself forward or sets himself above others. It is every Kiwi's duty to cut down tall poppies, a job they undertake enthusiastically.
Tangata Whenua: Maori (people of the land)
tapu: sacred (Maori)
Te Papa: the National Museum, in Wellington
tea: dinner (casual meal at home)
tea towel: dishtowel
test match: international rugby match (e.g., an All Blacks game)
throw a wobbly: have a tantrum
tick off: cross off (tick off a list)
ticker: heart. "The boys showed a lot of ticker out there today."
togs: swimsuit (male or female)
torch: flashlight
touch wood: knock on wood (for luck)
track: trail
trainers: athletic shoes
tramping: hiking
transtasman: Australia/New Zealand (the Bledisloe Cup is a transtasman rivalry)
trolley: shopping cart
tucker: food

tui: Native bird
turn to custard: go south, deteriorate
turps, go on the turps: get drunk
Uni: University—or school uniform
up the duff: pregnant. A bit vulgar (like "knocked up")
ute: pickup or SUV
vet: check out
waiata: Maori song
waka: canoe (Maori)
Wallabies: Australian national rugby team
Warrant of Fitness: certificate of a car's fitness to drive
Weet-Bix: ubiquitous breakfast cereal
whaddarya?: I am dubious about your masculinity (meaning "Whaddarya . . . pussy?")
whakapapa: genealogy (Maori). A critical concept.
whanau: family (Maori). Big whanau: extended family. Small whanau: nuclear family.
wheelie bin: rubbish bin (garbage can) with wheels.
whinge: whine. Contemptuous! Kiwis dislike whingeing. Harden up!
White Ribbon: campaign against domestic violence
wind up: upset (perhaps purposefully). "Their comments were bound to wind him up."
wing: rugby position (back)
Yank: American. Not pejorative.
yellow card: A penalty for dangerous play that sends a player off for 15 minutes t the sin bin. The team plays with 14 men during that time.
yonks: ages. "It's been going on for yonks."

About the Author

Rosalind James is the author of four books in the *Escape to New Zealand* series. Rosalind is a former marketing executive who has lived all over the United States and in a number of other countries, traveling with her civil engineer husband. Most recently, she spent several years in Australia and New Zealand, where she fell in love with the people, the landscape, and the culture of both countries.

Visit **www.rosalindjames.com** to listen to the songs from the book, follow the characters on their travels, watch funny and fascinating New Zealand videos, and learn about what's new!

Special thanks to Dean Morier, Ph.D., Professor of Psychology, Mills College, Oakland, CA, for his assistance with stalker psychology.

Cover design by Robin Ludwig Design Inc., http://www.gobookcoverdesign.com/

Printed in Great Britain
by Amazon.co.uk, Ltd.,
Marston Gate.